ABOUT

GARETH SOUTHWELL is a [...] trator from Wales, UK. You car [...] ction writing at fiction.garethsouthw[...] [...]re there are also links to his illustration work and philosophy books. Sign up to his monthly reader's list for news, free stories, discussion, and other things.

He would also be happy if you dropped him a line, either via the contact form on the website or by tweeting him on the Twitter (@GarethSouthwell).

BOOKS BY GARETH SOUTHWELL

FICTION

MUNKi

NON-FICTION

A Beginner's Guide to Descartes's Meditations
A Beginner's Guide to Nietzsche's Beyond Good and Evil
Words of Wisdom
Philosophy: Key Texts (2nd Ed) – with Julian Baggini
Philosophy: Key Themes (2nd Ed) – with Julian Baggini
50 Philosophy of Science Ideas You Really Need to Know
What Would Marx Do?
Philosophy in 100 Quotes
Paradoxes (3rd Ed) – with Gary Haden and Michael Picard
Descartes's Dog: Animals, Machines, and the Problem of Other Minds
Virtue: A Short-ish Guide to Moral Philosophy, Part 1
(forthcoming, 2021)
Instant Philosophy (forthcoming, 2021)

MUNKi

GARETH SOUTHWELL

MUNKi
Gareth Southwell

Cover illustration: Gareth Southwell
Cover design: Eliot Southwell and Gareth Southwell
First digital edition, published January 2021
First print edition, published February 2021
Copyright © 2021 Gareth Southwell

Fonts used: **Kimberley Black**, by Ray Larabie
(typodermicfonts.com), Palatino, and Gill Sans Nova.

For any queries relating to any of the above, please
contact the author via his website:
fiction.garethsouthwell.com

A NOTE ON THE TEXT

Like a drunken high-wire act, writing near-future fiction is a bit of a fraught affair. In February of 2020, *MUNKi* was complete and all set to be released – but COVID-19 had other ideas. Suddenly, my little meditation on life, death and toy robots, with its talk of viruses and quarantines (albeit digital ones), seemed at best outdated, and at worst crass and insensitive. And so, with the world shifting under our feet, and no one yet agreeing into what, I shelved it.

As I write this, almost a year later, the world has not finished reshaping itself, and we still have no idea of what's even just around the corner (for which reason, my next novel will be a swords and sorcery period drama set in an alternate universe). But as many a wise head has noted, sci-fi is not really about the future, and nor is this a book about the pandemic – the full significance of which we're all currently too immersed in to process. But I could not ignore the subject completely. In revising the book and its accompanying short stories, I've therefore decided upon a middle way. Forced to guess, I've chosen to be positive. *MUNKi's* world is one that has more or less passed through our current period of crisis, and – still licking its wounds, occasionally casting nervous little glances back over its shoulder – is moving forward. This may prove naively hopeful, but in this instance at least, it seemed better to be optimistic and wrong than pessimistic and right.

Gareth Southwell, January 2021

For Jo

who puts up with all my nonsense

You seek for knowledge and wisdom, as I once did; and I ardently hope that the gratification of your wishes may not be a serpent to sting you

Mary Shelley, *Frankenstein*

Snake

(snake graphic)

Cari looks out of the window.

The old river crawls on, rounding Canary Wharf. She glimpses his tired brown waters between the museum's higher-rise neighbours, dying sunlight rolling off his wrinkled skin, as he curls east, exhausted, his *chi* siphoned off first by the old financial quarter, then here downriver by its younger, hungrier brother.

She scrutinises the glass neighbours, which glint inscrutably back.

Better make a start.

Variously sized winged things flap about her stomach.

She listens to the Voice.

Its six-storey commentary begins on the museum's ground floor, piped out of little self-adjusting ear buds doled out with the AR glasses from a self-serve kiosk near the entrance; she feels them, squeamish at their squirming, moulding themselves to her ear canals. The narration is trying too hard – to be cool, off-hand, even funny, to wear its learning at a jaunty angle – and it's really just a corporatised history lesson, provoking her own sarcastic counter-commentary, another nervous ploy to stave off the jitters. Behind it there's some Mozart-like melody – "An original composition by Merrywhile's AI" – but actually, the Voice explains, the Great Man's works, analysed and disassembled into their constituent musical atoms, recombined into something "new". Fauxzart, then, Shamadeus, Wolfgang distilled through a teleporter on the fritz. Nice enough, she supposes, in an inoffensive way, but its banality becoming first annoying, then grating, and eventually – she will catch herself still humming it three floors after switching it off – a hateful earworm.

"All rising to a great place", the Voice continues, "is by a winding stair."

Also inscribed over the archway to the gift shop, a quote, she's told, from someone called Francis Bacon. "Not the painter!", but back in Shakespeare's day, a reluctant lawyer and frustrated scientist, forced to content himself with dreams and schemes, a tower of knowledge to tantalise the sky that only the future would see. A tower like this one, perhaps, for fans that they were, the museum's architects had taken Bacon literally, embodying his maxim into its very structure. Flanking the checkerboard floor to either side of the foyer's archway, two broad stairways rise, caduceus-like, sweeping the circumference of the building in opposing spirals. On the left-hand path, its curved walls depict conquests and discoveries, coronations, plagues and papal intrigues, marking social and political milestones, the deeds of the great and the (often-not-so) good. The right stair swaps Caesar for Stravinsky, D-Day for Dada, presenting a chronicle of intellectual culture and ideas, tracing developments in philosophy, literature, music, art.

Which way? Does it matter? Before she makes her choice, in front of her, bearing the inscription "More Beyond!", sits a strange statue – "Hercules and the Serpents", the Voice informs – a young child wrestling with two coiling snakes, mini replicas of which can be purchased from said gift shop, custom coloured and 3D printed live before the eyes of those patrons particularly taken with the spectacle. For nothing quite says "I love Science!" like a baby strangling some snakes.

She opts for right, plodding on and up, step by edifying step, threading slowly through the crowds – pupils on day trips, guidebook-grubbing tourists, pilgrims to scientific progress – like Escher's monks, retracing the climb from the swamps of unreason, or else on their way back down, the dizzying summit conquered. She tries to fit in, to appear engaged, ponderous, pausing here and there before regal portraits or quotes from long-dead luminaries.

"George Wilhelm Friedrich Hegel."

The glasses, identifying the object of her focus: some pompous-looking, prominently nosed worthy with thinning hair and imposing aspect. A profusion of options dance in the phantom space before her – dates, diagrams, cued-up video clips and galleries of pictures – all bobbing about like midsummer midges. She prods one shaped like a little speech bubble.

"The evolution of production means work can be increasingly automated, until it's finally possible for humans to step aside and let machines take their place."

She flicks another quote.

"A society must expand beyond its borders to find consumers in other countries."

One more.

"The corporation is a second family."

Bleurghch.

"Fun fact?" she asks.

"I'm sorry, I don't appear to have that information. Would you like to hear about Hegel's master–slave dialectic instead?"

At each of the six floors – each "Day" in history, as the Voice terms it – the two sets of stairs connect in sweeping, high-ceilinged galleries – "where knowledge and power meet!" – each spawning its own era of innovation and discovery, the fruits of an ever-branching tree of knowledge: stone-age tools, the implements of bronze-age agriculture, the invention of writing – "Language is a technology, too, remember!" – the printing press, the spinning jenny, the desktop PC. A few patrons, looking uncertain, seem to be finding historic destiny hard going. Is this exercise, or education? The one disguised as the other? But they must have faith. The summit attained, the genetic plan fully unfurled, the frowns and flushed expressions will finally clear. History, they will see, is no random catalogue of events, no patternless tale of misery and greed, but a quest with a goal, a journey with a destination.

Of course, there is always the lift.

She chooses her target randomly, it not seeming to matter who or what they are. The boy is isolated at his own table, away – his uniform suggests – from the rest of his school trip. He's a healthy-looking lad, sat slurping his varicoloured slushy and industriously amassing a non-biodegradable heap of sweet wrappers and crumpled empty crisp packets, frowning through his glasses as he pokes the transfigured air before him. She deploys the tiny transparent dermal patch – the first ("At least five, if you can, yeah?") – trying to still the shake in her hand, her thumb brushing his neck apologetically as she reaches past him for a napkin at the service counter where he has gone to refill his drink.

As she breathes out, looks around, moves away, her ear is drawn to two men at a nearby table. Expensive shoes, suits, no ties – financial types? – trading glottal stops, a thin veneer of Estuary over public school RP.

"Of course you can," one is saying. "Intangible assets? See, you've got to think laterally, see something the quants can't. You do remember Banksy, though, yeah? So a 'Banksy hole' is just a hole in the wall where a Banksy's been cut out. But question is: was it a *real* Banksy? Might only have been a *fake* one – 'school of', perhaps. So how do you tell?"

"Well, I still don't see how you can sell a hole in the wall."

Are they headed up or down? Emboldened by her first success, she tags one anyway, on the back of his left hand, feigning a stumble as she passes their table ("You alright, love?").

It's already getting easier.

"More can't hurt," the samurai had said. "The more, the better."

The river had crawled south-west, wending drowsily down the valley, funnelled through now-quiet docks and out over gull-picked sands, before finally returning home. But this was a different river, its prospect a window onto a different time and place, and its surface, this particular day, a midwinter mirror to a dishwater sky.

"But where will you *go*?" the little girl had persisted.

She had overheard the talk of his "moving on", and now wouldn't let it go.

"I will live on the Moon!" The old schoolteacher grinned.

Cari must have looked dubious.

"No, really, it's quite nice there, now," he'd said, "since they've done it all up."

The cancer that was crawling kundalini-like up his spine would soon deliver another type of payload, but had so far left his sense of humour intact.

"Tadcu, be *serious*."

"Well, there's already enough of that about," her grandfather replied. "Don't you worry yourself about such things."

But her earnest, troubled look remained, suggesting she was too old anymore to be fobbed off with his daft jokes. He sighed. Bruised by the cannula and mottled with age, his hand smoothed the bed distractedly, its skin paper-thin next to the heavy-duty sheet.

"Better not to hang around here too long, anyway, *cariad*," he whispered. "Have you seen all the *ill* people? Might catch something."

Cariad, a play on her given name, but also a term of affection – "love" – contraband from a language she neither spoke nor understood, and of which, these rare visits back, he was her only, dwindling supply. Smuggled in to his respectable English sentences – endearments, swear words, blasphemies too indelicate to translate – she'd commit them to memory, concealed where none could search, nothing-to-declare, back over the border, there to be deployed as protective charms against the foreignness of her new, strange life.

"*Cari*, please, Myrddin," said her father. "Her actual name. And English, if you don't mind. We don't want to confuse her."

"*Myn uffern i*, Jack. Confuse her? Don't be *twp*. Should she be ashamed of where she's from?"

This the latest exchange in a long-running argument, begun between father and daughter aeons ago, but her side now taken up by the son-in-law.

"And I suppose you'd rather Bri and I had given her a name no one can pronounce?"

A low blow. "Bri" – Cari's mother, Tadcu's daughter – was short for *Briallen*, a name not common even in her own home town, where hardy English perennials had long supplanted fragile native strains; a daughter who'd done her own best to assimilate into the Wider World, even grafting those home-grown syllables onto the English *Briony*, before finally attempting to clinch the argument by flouncing off to the place that brooked no further debate. But still it continued, the father and the husband, fighting over the legacy of the dead wife and daughter, wounding each other with their claims to greater intimacy.

While Tadcu had always laughed at what he saw as their timid anxieties, neither of her parents had seen any reason to honour some linguistic heritage they thought would only make their daughter stand out ("As if that were a *bad* thing!"). Wouldn't just being a kid be hard enough already?

And looking back, in that at least they'd been right. Though they'd still lived within its catchment, Cari's father had not been satisfied with the tiny village school from which Tadcu himself had recently retired, insisting she attend the "more progressive" primary in town. But there, despite his best efforts, by that uncanny antenna that children have for difference, her new classmates had quickly divined that the fresh arrival was *other*. The trendy name, the fashionable hairstyle, the clothes – with help from Nan and Auntie Cat, even picked from the selfsame rack – were all undone by a wilful spirit, by scuffed knees and paint-stained fingers, and an unselfconscious practicality of bearing. Little Cari, they knew, did not fit in; was no dainty spirit or delicate flower, but a tubby little tomboy, a cave-dweller from The Land That Time Forgot (ten minutes away by car), a knuckle-dragging monkey down fresh from the trees. And this, too, her grandfather's fault – "always letting her dig in that garden, Myrddin; coming back stinking – muck in her hair, even" – his influence another heritage to be disavowed. Yet Tadcu had refused to be chastised.

"But monkeys are fine creatures! Friendly, clever. And weren't we all monkeys once, eh? No shame in acknowledging your roots, *mwnci fach*. And what's a bit of muck, eh, *mochyn*? Eh, little pig?" She'd wriggled and giggled as he'd poked her ribs, mimicking porcine squealing and snorting. "Don't listen to them, *cariad*. Teenage pram-pushers in training, they are. You watch, now, they'll be Ladies Who Lunch, waiting to grow old and saggy, so they can get their frowns ironed out with… What's that thing where you inject that *cachu* in your face, Em?"

"You mean botox, my love?" replied her grandmother.

"Botox! Botulinum! I mean, afraid of a little dirt, but happy to put *poison* in your face! How *twp* can you get? Who wants to be like *that*? All clean and useless? Lean and clueless? Like a row of bloody robot dolls, all walking the same, talking the same – and all doing *ballet*, I suppose. *That's* not going to feed anyone, is it? *That's* no good in a fight!"

He had then performed an inelegant pirouette, awkwardly morphing into some decisive martial-arts-type death blow, making her giggle again.

Years later, she'd realised how she'd never known him when he *hadn't* been ill. He'd never talked about it, and for her, the symptoms – the migraines, the fatigue ("Tadcu needs a little nap now, *bach*") – were just part of who he'd always been.

But with the clear-sky thunderbolt of Nan's unexpected death – ambushed by a waiting embolism – the fight had finally gone out of him. Stoicism had become resignation, and from that point on he'd stubbornly withstood his doctors' pressure to accept debilitating treatments that would have prolonged his life by mere months, as if only adding to his sentence.

Long after he'd gone, she'd found out a curious thing. He had nicknamed his cancer "Asclepius" – a reference, she learned, to the Greek god of healing. To seek divine aid? But that didn't make sense, and it wasn't until later, browsing idly through some website on Ancient Greece, that she'd eventually stumbled upon what she thought might be the reason. Here was a story of another old man – a philosopher, with like faith in gods and spirits – and how he too in his final hours had called on the same god of healing – but not *for* healing. At the right time, Socrates had said, death was not a curse but a cure, a balm for all life's ills.

Only the wicked need worry.

The sixth and topmost storey of the museum – the sixth "Day" – is dedicated entirely to computers: wartime's prototype behemoths; the first affordable, squidgy- or clunky-keyed consumer models; the most recent touch-, gesture-, audio- and ocular-interface devices, exquisite and unobtrusive to the point of transparency. Gathered together into this one space, the trends are easy to spot: smaller, faster, more powerful, more intuitive and user-friendly, increasingly indispensable as they insinuate themselves ever further into the core of everyday life. But this is also a Crystal Palace of the future, where, for the Voice, even the wonders of the present day represent the merest tantalising foretaste.

"In 1993, the writer Vernor Vinge prophesied the Technological Singularity. This may seem like a scary phrase, but there's really nothing to be afraid of. Although Vinge originated the term, the basic concept can be traced back through a string of thinkers at least as far as the nineteenth

MUNKi

century – to the age of coal and steam! – and possibly even beyond that. Vinge argued that as machines evolve they'll eventually become *so clever* that they'll be able to design *even cleverer* versions of themselves – better than *we* ever could. From that point on, even *our* boffins won't know how they work! Now, with a *gravitational* singularity – a black hole, to you and me – there is a threshold where, instead of reflecting back to tell us what things inside look like, light gets sucked in and cannot escape. Which is why a black hole is black! This threshold is what those physics nerds call the *event horizon*."

In illustration, a goofy little animated figure capers before her, complete with spectacles, lab coat and pocket protector, his already-lanky frame beginning to stretch and twist into the funnelling vortex of space-time that he is attempting to peep over and into.

"So, we can't really *know* what happens inside a black hole, because – well, we *literally* just can't *see*! And so, in a similar sense, with the *Technological* Singularity our little human brains just aren't smart enough to see *over* the horizon to predict what those clever little future computers will get up to."

As if comparison with some inexorable crushing force, sucking in all of time and space, is meant to reassure her that the future is in safe hands. She flicks at her little stretched-out nerd, sending him arcing – "Wheeeee!" – into the Beyond. So how long do we have to wait?

"Well, no one can really predict the precise date and time," the Voice admits, "but really it's a matter of 'when' not 'if'. And then we can all put our feet up!"

Yet if "knowledge is power" (another t-shirt slogan from the gift shop), she'd have thought the boffins in question would be keen to keep a handle on things, not hand it all off to their creations, no matter how clever. But the answer it seems is "gadgets" – nanobots to clean your blood and repair your cells, VR that's as good as the real, robot bodies that you can download your mind into and live forever. Groundbreaking, mind-blowing, but still just really boys and their toys. And if the tradeoff for a host of shiny new playthings is born-again ignorance, it's a price the boys think worth paying.

So where are they, then, these toys? The museum is relatively robot free: she's seen a cosmopolitan crowd trailing a multilingual robo-guide, some young girls playing with a mechanical kitten, a robo-barista, but otherwise Merrywhile appears keen to draw a line between lightweight commercial gimmickry and its own serious and noble vision – of which, however, just to whet the appetite, a teasing glimpse is afforded.

Cari approaches one of the "Immersion Spaces" – multidirectional treadmills, free-floating harnesses, rotating chairs – provided on each floor, and in which to safely explore full VR without fear of blindly bowling over some fellow patron. She selects a treadmill, dons some gloves and adjusts her glasses, and as the opacity of the visualisation levels up her surroundings fade, overwritten with a vision of '50s pulp sci-fi on steroids, a hymn to steel and glass. Amid the towers and domes, the litterless, almost antiseptic streets, are carefully cropped green spaces, all skilfully blended in a cloying futurism, as if to reassure that nature will not be replaced, but augmented, tended, improved. The vehicles – ground, rail, aerial, from the smallest gyro-scooter to the largest self-driving omnibus – are all near silent. And everywhere – *ah*, here *they are* – the conspicuous multi-functionality of automated help, cleaning, serving, educating, guiding, protecting and entertaining. She walks over to a small crowd – fellow museum patrons, perhaps, whether on-site or remote; or perhaps just non-playable characters, unpaid (and non-paying) virtual extras, here to bulk out the experience. They are all gathered around a busker, of the one-man-band variety, though in actuality a one-robot-orchestra. There is a cello, a violin, xylophone, and a few more exotic, perhaps-future instruments she can't name, all arrayed within reach of its supernumerary, spidering arms and legs, scraping, plucking and striking in perfect tempo (no doubt) the same variations on a theme by Fauxzart that she's turned off some floors below. Whether because of the robot's arachnoid articulation and uncanny, doll-like expression, or merely the disquieting experience of full immersion (she's never really taken to VR), her senses start to swim unpleasantly.

"Stop." No response. "Stop. Cancel." Still no response. In the end, she simply takes off the glasses, staggering, blinking and swaying as reality slowly re-suggests itself.

The Future, it seems, doesn't like it when you try to get off.

The boy is playing the snake game. It's pretty basic, really – left, right, up, down; eat the food; avoid the walls; and your own tail. There are other variations – ones with two snakes, ones with mazes, or where things chase you or bounce around – but for some weird reason he prefers the simplest one. It starts off easy, but it gets harder.

The food makes the snake longer, and trickier to control – if it *is* food. It's just blocks – like the snake itself. So perhaps it's just parts of yourself you've lost, or a trail to be followed. Like those old stories his mother used to read him – the one with the candy cottage and the witch; or that one with Pooh and Piglet, going round and round the tree, tracking the Heffalump. (But they *were* the Heffalump – why hadn't they realised that? They were stupid that way. It had annoyed him, even then.)

It's a very old game.

"—developed by Gremlin in 1976, *Blockade* took the arcades by storm. Soon, there were copycat versions for the budding home-console market and, later on, the home PC. Perhaps its most famous incarnation, however, was on the mobile phone of the late 1990s – are you old enough to remember that? Here it enjoyed a popular renaissance, its simple, low-resolution graphics and addictive gameplay lending themselves—"

"Audio off."

Sometimes the glasses say something interesting – like about what the old games were actually like – but mostly it's boring – like school; just dates and facts. He's only come on the trip to see the games studio in the basement, but they have to go up before they can go down, apparently. Just like home. Finish your food, then ice cream. Homework before *Divinia*.

The glasses are cool, though – better than the ones he has at home. With some of the games you don't need them – they're just sort of projected – but he prefers the glasses, so only he can see what he's seeing. They know where your eyes are pointing, and you can move around, zoom in and out, just by focusing, winking, or making gestures with your hands. It's tricky at first, but you get used to it. They even know when you're going to bump into things – in real life, that is: "Collision Detection". And then they dim the display to warn you and so you can see properly. They also do "Graphical Overlay", which is just AR, really. This is how he's playing the game, like it's out there in real space – gesturing up, left, right, guiding it through the maze of itself with a flick or a glance. But you can also do "Full Immersion", where it's like you're actually there. He'll definitely be getting some – when the price comes down, his father will say. But he'll give in eventually. He always does.

It's weird, though. The game's graphics are crap, really – compared with any of his consoles, anyway, even his old handhelds. But somehow he has to keep playing. His best score so far is forty-two.

He'll still be trying to beat that when Cari presses the first switch.

The river crawled on, curling around the borough, doubling back upon itself, briefly threatening to close like a noose, before once again heading east.

Thinking for some reason it would be more "clandestine" to arrive on foot, Cari had disembarked an overly cautious two Tube stops early, walking through the area on her way to the Wharf, to which much of it seemed obscenely juxtaposed, like some loser in a battle for common resources, emaciated to the degree its conjoined twin had grown fat. Cutting through a new estate, she'd stopped before an interactive information board (the screen already fag-burnt and gang-tagged), its story a commemoration of social progress. Despite those who'd wanted to preserve the "historic landmark", the '60s leviathan had finally been demolished, its frill-less aesthetic of precast concrete, a brutalist experiment in minimal choice, making way for "new affordable social housing, public parks, communal spaces, and [illegible beneath scorched and bubbled plastic]".

She'd studied the picture on the screen – *Bit of an eyesore* – and wondered who'd want to preserve it – not anyone who'd lived there, presumably, the memory of which you'd happily see effaced. But then again, perhaps not; home was wherever you grew up, after all, and you couldn't just delete part of who you were – perhaps wouldn't want to.

And anyway, apart from some stylistic flourishes, she didn't think much had changed: the same high-rise warrens; families still stacked in pokey flats, shoe boxes with the ergonomic generosity of a budget airline. And for good or bad – she'd been glad it was still daytime – there was a lawless vibrancy about the place, a concrete forest to an outlaw band lacking only its Robin Hood. Ungentrified, defiant, as if at any moment, those stacks overflowing, a single spark would reignite the Peasants' Revolt, calling forth a new Wat Tyler from out the shadowed stairwells to lead a fresh assault on the faceless glass towers, the new outposts for the robber barons reborn. (And yet, no more than symbols, really – storm *those*, more would simply take their place. The centre of what they represented everywhere, its circumference of influence unbounded.)

It was to these very glass towers that she then had made her way, passing en route a gated conglomeration of apartment blocks – or actually, *smartments*; the new, high-end, automated kind. Hermetically gated and sealed, some still-in-development, others already completed and occupied, their electrochroamatic windows just then shifting opacity in sync with the day's dwindling light. She moved on past billboards depicting would-be residents – svelte-limbed, fashionable, predominantly Aryan (with tokens of well-heeled diversity). *Don't worry*, the pictures reassured prospective buyers. *Your litterless, carefully tended lives will require minimal interaction with the natives.*

"Fight the Future, Man!"

Scrawled graffito, daubing the hoardings, a speech-bubble from a Bart Simpson co-opted by the Borg; not yet whitewashed or pasted over, and apparently not worth cutting out and selling. She daydreamt some hooded and scarfed youth (his spray-paint fatigues) showing a surprisingly clean pair of heels – a late flower of the Olympic legacy? – chased off into the evening by some lot-plodding night-watchman or a corporate copyright lawyer ("Satire is fair use!"). (And yet – her eyes nervously swept the afternoon's pooling shadows – more likely something carbon fibre, taser-mounted, tireless in its vigilance, never stopping, never needing to eat, to sleep, nor be shooed off marking the territory it was tasked with guarding.)

There goes the neighbourhood.

In the dimming light, the veneer of new technology briefly bridged old divides. Ghostly, up-lit faces at the bus-stop – checking notifications, the news, smiling at some meme – were momentarily echoed in the backseat of some high-end, tint-windowed vehicle. But it was a compatriotism as fleeting as it was false, the common bond broken as affluence moved swiftly off, its advantage one not even her fleet-footed graffitist could have closed.

"And if anything goes wrong," the samurai had said, "I don't know you, and you don't know me."

But everything had ensured that anyway: the avatars, the disguised voices (his (its) like an auto-tuned washing machine, a detuned radio lost at sea).

Somewhat cheesily, she'd thought, its creators had chosen to depict the dark web marketplace as a low-end nightclub – *Cashabanca* – like something out of pulp noir with a cyberpunk twist, replete with seedy nooks and shady booths, surly bouncers and leery-eyed barmen ("real" people, she wondered, symbols of some function of security, or just touches of digital colour?), and all underscored with the quiet throb of techno, which she couldn't seem to mute. She surveyed the other booths around them. Some were opaque, inscrutable. Others, though muted, were open, their occupants conducting business brazenly, confident in the power of anonymity to protect their true names and physical selves from the Great Enemy, and the bad juju such knowledge could empower. As its name suggested, a lot of its business centred around bank fraud – traffic in stolen credit cards, compromised accounts, pilfered passwords, and the phishing software that could acquire them – but like *Rick's Café Américain*, to which its name gave a slightly confused nod, it provided similarly broad and neutral sanctuary to all sorts ("Though not, you know, the *worst*," the figure sitting opposite her had tried to reassure her). But it was still hard not to wonder – guns, drugs, blood diamonds, rhino horn, insider trading and match fixing, or something altogether more sickening – what *specific* purposes those around her made their shady corners serve.

Cari's loathing for VR stemmed from her high school, a private institution that had foisted it upon her during lockdowns as if to reassure high-fees paying parents that they were still getting their money's worth. She recalled a bone-shuddering walkthrough of the Battle of Waterloo, a vertiginous reimagining of the Big Bang, and an excruciatingly first-person journey through the life cycle of human sperm, all of which succeeded only in giving her headaches, nausea and next-level awkwardness, respectively.

As with many online shopping experiences, virtuality in itself added little that was useful, and here seemed primarily to provide increased opportunity for pose and flash, an enhancement of the social and transactional. What little she knew about hackers came from old films. Keen as ever to stereotype the atypical, Hollywood had portrayed them as keyboard cowboys, as cocky, one-handed speed typists, with model good looks and a penchant for trash-talking, skateboarding, and elaborate pen-twirling. Or else they were social maladepts, or pitiable, sweat-stained slobs with poor posture and poorer people skills. As with all such things, she thought, the truth would be variable. Groups might share traits and tendencies, but people were not tropes; they were strange, complex, could always surprise you. And yet, tropes there were here aplenty – the in-jokes, the visual puns, the nods to geek and popular culture, even occasionally to the very films that stereotyped them, as if, unsure how to depict themselves, some reached for the ready-made style guide of their own clichéd portrayal. People could also be strangely predictable.

But judging by the specimens around her at least – assuming they were *not*, in real life, fifteen foot anime characters, space ships, or clouds of interstellar gas – VR fulfilled for most a desire for compensation, for posturing and playfulness. They wanted to be something other than they were, someone and somewhere else (a desire that, holed up in her pokey student pigeonhole in trackies and t-shirt, the sweat slicking her goggles and gloves, she was beginning to understand). And so even where anonymity offered protection, where displaying any characteristics at all constituted a risk, personality often unwisely won out.

The personality in front of her presented a similar contradiction. "General Ned", the username read, the avatar depicting a middle-aged man in traditional Japanese dress, complete with appropriate looking sword and one of those man-bun thingies – a samurai, she supposed – trying hard to look cool and unflappable, like some oriental gunslinger.

As a client – Jo11235 – the system had automatically allotted her a generic username, but for her avatar, faced with a choice, she found herself drawn into her own private allusions, finally settling on a cute little bear she'd recognised from re-runs on one of the cartoon channels and had once had on a t-shirt. Anyway, let … well, *him*, she guessed, read that as he saw fit.

"Even if all goes well," he continued, "we'll never meet again. I never use the same footsoldier twice. Leave no trail." The samurai sipped his … what was that, in the little drinking box thing? Was it anything? "Minimise risk," he added, somewhat lamely.

"But why not just hack in?" Realising as she'd asked that she was querying the need for the very job she was applying for. "I mean, that's what you *do*, right? Why the need to actually *go* there?"

Too late, she realised what she'd set in motion, her naive question a button-press at which the Exposibot 3000 whirred and clunked into irreversible action, a juggernaut of infodump bearing inexorably down upon her – more, she sensed, to impress than inform – and from which she eventually managed to salvage the single term that encapsulated the problem: *firewall*.

"Now, MoTH – the Merrywhile Museum of Technological History, to give it its full, official, and rather longwinded title – isn't a museum at all: it's a shopfront; commercial propaganda disguised as education. Merrywhile Industries is no academic institution concerned with the preservation of—"

"Yes. I know who they are."

"Right. Well, as I say, they're not like the V&A, the National, or the Tate; they want to show you what they can *do*. Hence, Canary Wharf, and not over on the South Bank or nearer the tourist hotspots. Handy for showcasing new products to potential investors, have them in for a chat over sushi or canapés – or whatever they eat. They can also try out prototypes, gauge public opinion on new gadgets, conduct sly trials on neural response thresholds, synaptic—"

"Firewall."

"Yes… So, huge, nasty, ethically compromised multinational that they are – fingers in all sorts of horrible pies: bio-tech, surveillance, arms, GMOs and crops – well, they're Big League Nasty. So, their firewall is like nothing you've ever seen. But they do have a weak spot, somewhere they have to open their doors to the public, paint the face of corporate tyranny with a Cheshire Cat grin. And a door out is a door in, right?"

Jo11235 nodded. *If you say so.*

"Because the shopfront needs constant updating with the latest software patches," the samurai continued, "generates feedback for ongoing projects, facilitates research, and so on, MoTH is the closest the likes of Joe or Joanna Public will ever get to their network – or in this case, Jo11235!" He chuckled. "We can't risk a disguise; a full prosthetic could be flagged by their infrared face recognition, and 'suspicious' is their DEFCON 5." She frowned: which way did the numbers go, now? "Their state of normal readiness? So, we need to tread careful. Hat and glasses, maybe, but you don't want to be too conspicuous. And you'll be wearing their glasses anyway, inside. And when you are in, there'll be no way to contact me either, I'm afraid. As I say, 'phones at the door', no watches or wearables, no battery operated devices at all – paranoid about corporate spies stealing their precious prototypes. So once you're inside, you're on your own."

He took another sip of his whatever.

"So what do you reckon? Ready for your run on the Death Star?"

He must have sensed that Jo11235 still wasn't completely reassured.

"Hey, don't worry! You'll be fine, honestly. It'll be a picnic!" Grinning at his own allusion. "Not like we're trying to get you up The Mountain, now, is it? Follow the protocols, blend in, be natural, be subtle. Anything goes wrong, follow the failsafes. Leave no trail."

The "failsafes": ditch any unused dermal patches, secure-wipe all devices previously used for communication. All of which provided little reassurance, for in the final analysis, "leave no trail" was more designed to protect *him*.

But really, she suspected, he knew that she knew that.

Cari surveys the top floor of the museum. In this electronic paean to computing power, there are still some things not yet completely automated. "A door out is a door in," the samurai had said. And the door here is human.

Despite the cameras, scanners, infra-red sensors, motion detectors, pressure switches, and other paraphernalia of security paranoia, a human being is still necessary in case of unforeseen problems. It is also good PR. *We are not the mere puppets of technology*, it says. *We are its users, its friends, but most importantly, its masters.* Whether or not this is true – and she doubts it, given the Voice's Singularity-lust – it's important to give the appearance of control, even if this merely consists in a giant kill switch for someone to press in case the AI goes rogue, HAL-style, and starts frying everyone's synapses.

Here, a label on her chest informs, the human is "Jenni" – not the spinning variety, but gatekeeper to a world where none need toil nor spin; and herself, about as far from spinster as can be – business-suited and bespectacled, her corporate geekiness offset by blonde, blue-eyed, subtly buxom allure. Yet looking like she couldn't kill anything, really, not even psychotic software, the only danger being the health risk posed by large doses of her high-saccharine helpfulness. Apart from presenting an attractive, approachable and non-threatening point of contact, her main role is evidently to be knowledgeably enthusiastic.

"Good job! And you see" – Jenni pointing out some feature of the glasses to the rapt attention of an old man and his granddaughter (perhaps) – "it adjusts automatically!"

"May I also see?"

Suddenly headlamped in the ferocious amiability of Jenni's focus, Cari almost flinches, but manages to hold a calm smile.

"But of course!"

It's pretty simple to apply the dermal patch – ("*This* one for the demonstrator *only*, yeah?") – merely by returning one of Jenni's ingratiating arm- or shoulder-touches. Cari thanks her, then retreats to lean back against the edge of the help-desk that Jenni patrols like a genial wasp – what she calculates is the best vantage point for what is about to happen – as if to explore the glasses' newly explained function, leaving the demonstrator to train her formidable helpfulness elsewhere.

Everything is finally in place.

Not just winged but crawling things also parade her innards, inching their way up her throat.

Most people's lives are like shoes that don't quite fit. But few seek to trade them in for something less constrictive. They put up with them. They try to break them in. In this, Tadcu had been an exception. His life had been more an open-toed sandal, caring little for toeing the line, and in fact, the older he got, seeming to take delight in stepping on the toes of others. But what gave him more room to breathe also exposed him, made him sensitive to the things that bothered others less or not at all. He baulked at routine, particularly that imposed by strangers. He was suspicious of authority, and anybody in uniform. And he was highly allergic to all forms of confinement, or in fact any restrictions upon his freedom. All of which made hospitals a nightmare – for him, and for those who might try to keep him there.

Merrywhile Hospice Port Talbot was where the worn-out shoes were stacked in uniform boxes; shelved, like all things that cannot yet be thrown away, with little respect for their continued usefulness and purpose. Or anyway, that was how Tadcu himself saw it, though as his son-in-law had tried to reassure him, it was actually "the best care money can buy."

"*Guilt* can buy, anyway. *Iesu mawr*, Jack. This of all places."

And looking back, now, Cari feels that there had also been something else, some more personal aversion – not just to confinement, to the hospice, but to the company itself, to its stated ideals and values.

"Making Today Futureproof!" Tadcu had read off the motto from a brochure he'd been given early on, detailing his care services. "And there was I all worried about it."

"Temperature is normal." The human doctor inspected a range of stats on the screen of a digital notepad. "Blood pressure: fine." ("Normal" and "fine", of course, both to be understood within the context of terminal brain cancer.) He swiped briskly through the accompanying notes. "Says here you're not eating properly, Mr Edwards." He looked up. "Food not to your liking?" No response. "Please, you must try, yes?"

Eventually, Tadcu had given a reluctant nod of

acquiescence, his face contorting into a grotesque gurn as the doctor turned his back, then recomposed to super-serious as they faced each other once more. He directed a quick conspiratorial wink at Cari.

"Now remember, should you need anything, the ACA's only a button-press away," indicating a large semi-opaque red panel near the headboard. "Though of course, it's also gesture and voice activated."

"Of course it is."

"Right, I'll go and arrange that X-ray."

"Is that wise? I hear they give you cancer."

When time was finally called on the old steelworks, it had presented a perfect storm of opportunity: prime real estate just off the M4, with an infrastructure ripe for repurposing to some lighter, more modern industry. News of Merrywhile's interest was therefore at first greeted with local enthusiasm – a new factory, perhaps, or a research institution? Jobs for the area, at any rate. And it was both, in a way: a robotics plant, annexed to which was a research-hospital-cum-hospice, specialising in elderly care. But the jobs were not human jobs, for it was a "robot factory" in both senses: to manufacture *and be run by* them, as they were more than capable of building themselves. The hospice would not even require porters or janitors, nor even receptionists; the odd doctor, here and there, but the human staff would be skeletal, and the rest almost literally so – the factory would see to that.

With fewer foreign workers now to fill the low-paid care jobs, robots were an expanding presence throughout the sector. But Tadcu took no reassurance in their growing ubiquity, nor their increasingly humanoid form – it only made him hate them more.

"You see, *bach*, no matter how it looks, no matter how clever it is, a machine is not a person. It's not alive, like you and me – never will be." He nodded at the attendant Automated Care Assistant, a smoothly tailored simulacrum in pastel-shaded plastic and steel, stood mutely on standby – at his early insistence, its cheery and solicitous patter had been silenced. "Tin Man over there isn't ever going to get hungry, or sad, or need the loo – speaking of which…"

"Myrddin, I'm afraid we have to go, now. Cari has school tomorrow."

It was not the last time she would see him alive. Then, he would be considerably weaker, barely able to sit up, tubes in his nostrils and arms, and monitors on temples and fingers, all feeding into purring machines and electronic lozenges of white plastic, softly pulsing with the Merrywhile logo. Perversely, she felt like they were siphoning him off, drawing away his essence. The ACA would be ready to perform CPR or engage the respirator if – as would eventually happen – his brainstem ceased to function properly as the cancer advanced. As her father left the room to speak privately with the attending doctor, Tadcu seized the moment to weakly beckon Cari closer. His eyes flicked briefly, suspiciously to the ACA – did he think it was listening?

"I have to go, soon, *cariad*. Now, after … when I'm gone, I'll… When people have gone, they … they put them in a sort of box." He pulled a face, as if this wasn't what he meant.

She glanced out of the window onto the corridor, where the doctor and her father were talking solemnly. When Nan had died – Tadcu's "foreign" English wife, as he never tired of teasing her – they had said that Cari was too young to go to the funeral. But her cousin David, who was a few years older, had related how there'd been a long box with a lid with two halves, the top one open. She was dressed in her best clothes – "Stuff Mam said she only wore to funerals – I mean, other people's" – and was surrounded with flowers. Everyone stood about, exchanging subdued and whispered smalltalk. At the end, Tadcu had gone up, kissed her gently on the forehead, and placed some things inside the coffin. Later, curious, just before they'd closed the lid, David had snuck up to see what these were: "a bottle of some brown stuff called *Glen*-something, and that little wooden ship from the mantelpiece".

Cari didn't like the idea of being shut in like that. It would be dark and lonely.

"But remember," Tadcu continued, "what you see, that won't be me. Who you are, who you *really* are, can't be kept in a box. It moves on."

She saw him, now, Nan's face had become his, and he was bursting out, splintering the closed lid and scattering the people, who staggered back in fear and alarm.

The pained look again. He seemed to see he'd failed, his final attempt to simplify things for her young mind only making him sound simple minded.

"Hey!" He forced a grin. "Don't worry about it, *bach*."

Having raised himself up to speak, he now collapsed back, deflated by her incomprehension or merely sapped by the strain of communication.

A week or so later, some rain-washed evening in November as they'd sat down to the evening meal at the usual time, the phone had rung out like a dropped glass.

As a concession, Auntie Cat overruling her father, she'd been allowed one last glimpse of his now quiet form, her close-pressed face misting up the glass of the corridor window. The tubes and wires had gone, the machines no longer purred, nor the white lozenges pulsed. The blankets had swaddled his shrunken body like a newborn, tucking him neatly into the rectangle of the bed. He wasn't asleep; his face was drawn and drained of all but a yellowish tinge, its habitual poise and intelligence departed. And she saw, then, what he had meant: *he's no longer there*. But where then had he gone? Had he "moved on"? Or was he somewhere lonely, cold and in the dark?

Cari looks about one last time.
Now or never.
She presses the first switch.
The lying bastard.

The boy's nausea is as sudden as it is explosive. All that blue-red slushy, all those luminous-orange maize snacks, shovelled in at the café two floors below, are now on their way back up. Is it cybersickness from the glasses?

He looks up from the melange of slowly spreading red-blue-orange sick to see a short, dark-haired girl with cap and glasses staring back at him across the gallery. Her lips move. Is she saying something to him?

The well-dressed man is bent over, hands planted on knees; next to him, his friend, staring down at his own hand-tooled Italian loafers freshly flecked with puke.

"Sorry, mate, I—"

He hunches over once more as the other man leaps suddenly farther back to avoid fresh splatter on shoes he values more than friendship.

Jenni is making her way to the boy when another retching sound – behind her and to the right – checks her. Then, over at the far left wall, a third sound. Shortly after, behind her, a fourth. Then straight ahead a fifth.

The colour begins to drain from her face.

"After the distraction caused by the first switch," the samurai had continued, "the demonstrator will follow protocol. To do this, they'll have to use their terminal. *As soon* as they log in, press the *second* switch. This is your one and only window." He paused for effect. "*Don't* mess it up."

"And what is it? The distraction?"

He sipped his drink. "You don't need to worry about that. Just keep your eye on the demonstrator."

"And the tattoo? Why can't I just have a, you know, a box or something?"

The samurai shook his head slowly.

"No battery operated devices, remember? So, we'll be disguising the switches within the design. Everyone's got ink, these days. No one'll look twice. Clever thing is, triggers use *you* as their power source! Evades their scans, see?"

"And why am I tagging people?"

"To… We'll be using them to boost the signal, yeah?"

"Oh. OK."

But as she now saw, that wasn't it at all.

The tagging had been tricky. He'd said to ensure there were enough tagged people on the top floor at the same time, but after tagging the boy and the finance guy, subsequent taggees, whom she'd thought were heading up, had wandered off – to other floors, for refreshment, or out of the building. So, learning her lesson, as she'd followed the boy up, she'd tagged a couple of others heading the same the way, but kept the remainder until the top floor. Six (plus Jenni herself) was a pretty good score. She'd felt pretty pleased with herself.

Now, less so.

It's the boy she feels worst about. And standing there, seeing his wide-eyed panic, before she can catch herself she's mouthing an apology.

After the boy vomits, the rest seem to follow at brief, stochastic intervals, allowing Jenni to note each fresh evacuation before it's followed by the next. Cari looks down at the tattoo – two wafer-thin dermal triggers embedded into a Chinese yin-yang dragon design entwining along the inside of her left forearm.

"Two switches, yeah?" he'd repeated, slowly, like schooling a child. "Switch one: distraction; switch two: demonstrator. A monkey could do it. No offence."

Cari's finger still hovers over the second.

The samurai had been almost shocked, at first, that she didn't want the money; then, suspicious.

"What? Nothing at all?"

"No money. But I do want something."

"And what's that?"

"Information," she'd said.

But now, she realises, it's more than that.

I want them to pay.

She presses the second switch.

As the samurai had predicted, Jenni follows protocol. She strides to her terminal, logs in with thumbprint and retina scan, and begins to engage security – but never gets that far, for as the second switch is activated, Jenni stops what she's doing, turns suddenly to her right and vomits violently into the wastebasket behind the desk.

"After you've pressed the second switch, the code will seek to connect with their terminal, posing as a trusted peripheral – like a printer, a mouse or a keyboard, you know? Connectivity," he'd snorted. "It's their Achilles' heel. Then you just need to stay in range while it uploads; two metres, max."

"Two metres. Not like I'm going to forget that, now, is it? How will I know when it's uploaded?"

"Oh, you'll know. Then all you've got to do is get yourself out."

With Jenni temporarily incapacitated, the first thing the uploaded code does is lock out her terminal, then disrupt the internal surveillance. It will take time for security to notice the disturbance, investigate on foot, register what is going on, and engage the prescribed centralised lockdown. As a result, no alarm sounds, and – fearing some air-borne pathogen or terrorist attack – panic spreads organically, in the old-fashioned way, exciting a Brownian motion of confusion and anxiety through the patrons.

Cari's first urge is to run – not just to get away, but to contact him, confront him. But now is not the time. And so she forces herself to bottle her fear and rage, doesn't rush, but, as per his advice, follows just behind the pack-leaders of the growing exodus, which – *come on, come on* – spills out neatly onto the street with relative efficiency and speed.

And, just like that, it's done, finished.

Though of course, as every effect is also a cause, the end of one thing is only ever the beginning of another.

The boy wipes his mouth and straightens up. Something strange is happening to the display screens, every single one in the room.

At first, they all turn a bright cyan blue. Then, it starts. He thinks at first that *he* is doing it. It is one of the snake games, but played with a speed and skill that no-one – not he, not any *person* – could match. It is mesmeric: wrapping around itself, doubling back, coiling up to stall for time while waiting for its tail to clear a path. The unknown player piles up the points – his own high score is gone in seconds. But he gradually realises that whoever is doing this will not be content with a personal best, nor to top a hall of fame: they are trying to complete the game; to fill the screen before eating their own tail.

He wonders what will happen then.

Worm

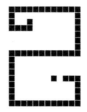

On the virtual streets, no speck of digital dirt – not a file fragment, not a stray pixel – is anywhere to be found. The untroubled expanses are a cyber-Switzerland of regimented industry, patrolled and enforced by protocols of the strictest security.

When the unwelcome innovation on this spartan theme begins to manifest, it is first mistaken for a minor data-corruption – a checksum error, a slipped digit. Accordingly, the Construct – a visualisation of the data-flow through Merrywhile's global network – portrays the intruder as a weed, sprouted up from the joins of pristine pavement. But by the time the gardening subroutines are tasked to uproot it, they find not a weed but a tree, and it is thereafter beyond the capacity of low-level fault fixers to address.

Gradually, its growth unchecked, it is referred up through the grades of security program, until by the time the anti-viral heavy artillery is wheeled out – which the Construct depicts as heavy artillery – it resembles more a steadfast oak, a budding World Tree or Yggdrasil, at the heart of a steadily spreading wood.

Even at this point, EMET, Merrywhile's chief AI, considers

it no more than a digital graffitist – a self-replicating *worm* perpetuating itself through the network, defacing websites, appropriating social media accounts, strewing anti-capitalist propaganda, allegations of corporate crimes. So when EMET eventually concludes that it is more than that, that there is code *inside* the code, it has already blundered, as the very agents it has sent to arrest the vandal themselves become infected, repurposed to abet its insinuation into the deeper levels of the system, helping the worm's true payload pass on unhindered.

It spreads.

Even EMET's attempts to isolate a tame copy for static analysis are frustrated, all engagement merely resulting in further contagion, or else the sandboxed code resists, morphing and mutating under its scrutiny, overwriting and even deleting itself, preferring its own demise to yielding up its secrets.

As a last resort, EMET is forced to enact the harshest of quarantines, amputating whole swathes of network in a bid to halt the worm's progress. This done, it finally involves one of its human operators.

"But it's all sorted now, EMET?" the operator asks.

"Quarantine is holding," the AI confirms. "I have restored backups of the affected websites, and suspended social media accounts until the defacement can be removed and the security breaches identified and patched."

"So it was just a protest thing, we think? Bragging rights for some social justice script kiddies?"

"Aside from the defacement, the foreign agent also seems to have been tasked with gathering information. There was a search spider, which I halted, and an attempt to install a backdoor, which I blocked. But since I have only been able to employ dynamic analysis, from its outer behaviour it remains unclear as to the purpose of the inner code and whether or not it is benign."

"*Benign*? Of course! It's an early Christmas present! These hacker chaps are all just sweethearts, really." The operator is scanning the logs. "Wait, why did you delay before enforcing quarantine?"

"Doing so would have significantly impaired network functionality and accessibility," EMET responds. "I considered it best first to explore other options. These did not work."

"So just how much of the network has it infected?"

"5.6%."

Shatner's girdle.

"OK, EMET, replay the attack from the point of first infection."

Playback begins. At first, it is almost nothing. Then, it is everywhere.

It had infested 3% of the network before EMET stepped in. As it admitted, its increasing efforts to contain or remove the invader – which the Construct symbolises with Cold-War-era style tank, plane, and infantry mobilisation – were unsuccessful, and in fact merely succeed in speeding up its growth. Only quarantine eventually has any effect, but at the expense of abandoning that part of the network, which the Construct now depicts as a snow-globe or bio-dome, an exotic flora or alien environment captured and preserved from some inhospitable clime – but one it nonetheless threatens to overrun, to repurpose to its own intent, if ever allowed to do so.

And that is the word for it: *Alien.*

"Better sound the klaxon," the operator says.

Nurtured on a nostalgic diet of '80s sci-fi and arcade classics, the Construct had originally evolved an aesthetic of harshly luminescent grids and curves. Subsequently, as the systems it modelled grew more elegant and refined, it too had softened, swapping out this geometrical rigour in favour of something gentler, more ornate – Muscovite homage to *Tron*, perhaps – yet still retaining an inorganic feel. In contrast, the growth the Construct now depicts is of a startlingly different quality, an ordered chaos, gracefully imperfect, ebullient, untamed, differentiating it abruptly from the smoothly tailored algorithms embodied in its surrounds. And slowly, as he watches, the operator's panic gives way to something else.

This is just weird.

As the alert spreads, on-site and remote, via monitor, projection screen, old-school text interface or full immersion VR, irrespective of time-zone, current activity, caffeine level, state of dress or consciousness, Merrywhile's Technical Operations Team gradually convenes. As it does so, the assembling operators split into two: one group reviewing the genesis of the growth in minute detail, step by step, pausing, rewinding, zooming in and out, the other tracing it back to its first appearance in the museum, searching for answers in its origins, for clues to its nature and intent. But as they watch, even among the constitutionally sceptical, picking up unwittingly on the first operator's intuition, a silent consensus begins to emerge – that here is something *different*, something *new*.

As the digital munitions of the tanks, planes and guns rain down upon the infection, it responds in intriguing and unpredictable ways. Some attacks are absorbed, their energy increasing the mass and aiding the expression of an ever-diversifying array of forms and structures. Others are transformed, their yield adapted and harnessed to a new design. And yet others are repurposed, projectiles intended to disable and dismember are returned as strange-winged imaginings from the mind of a Dalí or a Bosch, rebounding each blow back to its aggressor with surreal interest, as if destruction is unknown to it, and only change is possible.

"My God. It's alive."

A line from an old B-movie, no irony intended, his fellow operators too shocked and distracted perhaps to seize upon it mockingly, as normally they would, or in fact because it is a conclusion they are themselves beginning to have some sympathy for.

As the infestation continues, the skirmishes become more intense, and the creatures begin to marshal concertedly around a central point, surrounding and defending it. This centre, where the tree grows, is home to a writhing mass, to parodies and half-echoes of the actual and imagined. Here, bat- or bird-like, some hover like lookouts, or dart in and about the intricate structure, mercurial messengers with meaningful intent. Others, like small lizards or mammals, scamper to and fro, as if moving and arranging, urgent squirrels in the last scurry to amass their store before winter's onset. Then there are the big guys – bear-, elephant- and large-cat-like guardians – roaming and patrolling, suffering and rebutting the brunt of the anti-viral onslaught. Yet for all their diversity, there is one thing all the "creatures" have in common.

"The eyes. They're all the same."

Eventually, at the centre of this fruitful mayhem, a calm purpose begins to emerge. Around the tree, a thick, serpentine force has started to coil, moving among its branches and curling down and around its trunk, trussing it in friendly bondage, before, as a final and familiar act, seeking out its own tail.

"Like the game!"

The effect upon the tree is immediate and dramatic, the connection of a circuit. Every twig-tip and branch suddenly buds and blossoms – occasioning a collective "Ah!" from the operators – a glorious eruption of some strange, exotic bloom. Among the branches, fruit also forms, growing and swelling in the super-fast-forward of a nature documentary, before dropping, each piece then consumed or secreted away by the many pseudo mammals – all, that is, but one, which continues to grow, still attached, bowing down its branch with its burgeoning size, before finally coming to rest on the ground.

"What the hell is *that*?"

Vaguely ovoid in shape, it resembles perhaps a sprout or an artichoke, its leaves wrapping about the main kernel in overlapping fashion as if protecting some tender core with coarser, thicker skins. As these in turn begin to peel back, finer wrappings take on a softer appearance, like swaddling clothes, gently falling away to reveal a naked and unmistakable form.

"Is that…?"

"No way."

"It's a baby."

"Well, more a toddler, don't you think? About eighteen months?"

"But why a *baby*?"

"Well, that's not all. Look." Having had more time to scrutinise the visualisation, the original operator now draws his colleagues' attention to a particularly intriguing section. "Here we are at the point just before quarantine takes effect. Slowing it right down, we can see that containment is not total and instantaneous, but partial and gradual. So, for instance, in *this* area" – indicating where the viral growth is overlaid with a diaphanous blue veil – "containment is already in place. Whereas *here* and *here*" – circumscribing with red circles those places the veil has yet to seal – "there are still gaps."

The operator clears the simulation of his scribbling and gives instructions to EMET to magnify a specific area.

"Now, observe."

At super-slow speed, the "baby" can clearly be seen to reach up and pluck some projectile from the anti-viral bombardment, bring its cupped hands to its mouth, and *blow into* them. As the hands reopen, a tiny butterfly-like creature emerges, which then flutters nimbly through and past the fast-sealing quarantine wall.

"Well, what can we learn from this? First, it settles the question of whether there's an advanced form of artificial intelligence at work here: it *knew* it was being quarantined. Second, whatever this escaped code is, it's not a worm or some other type of self-replicator – the Construct's pattern recognition would have identified that. Instead, in choosing this particular form, it's telling us that the payload is something else."

EMET is an expert system, a more complex and sophisticated descendent of what is still just Good Old-Fashioned AI: left-brained, rational, sequential, good with clearly defined definitions and concepts, precise and tight-focus tasks. The Construct, in contrast, is its right brain, its dumb artistic twin; intuitive, holistic, good with image recognition and pattern matching, and not so much programmed as evolved, given basic rules-of-thumb and left to sift through the annals of human history and culture – TV and film, religion and myth, literature, music and art – to build its *own* understanding, its *own* pictorial language. Consequently, its communication is not verbal, but visual and symbolic. And so, like priests of the oracle, even the operators must occasionally pore over its riddling pronouncements, debating and interpreting their meaning.

"You obviously have a theory," another operator says. "So what's it trying to say?"

"As we know," the first operator continues, "the Construct's choice of representation is never merely arbitrary. But given the obvious association, I'd say it's fairly evident that it's trying to convey the presence of some sort of animating principle or guiding purpose."

"What do you mean?"

"Well, the word *psyche* comes from the Ancient Greek, and may be translated 'soul', 'life', 'mind', or 'breath'. But," pausing, unwisely milking the moment, "it also means 'butterfly'."

While of interest to all, the thorny question of artificial life is one on which Merrywhile's Technical Operations Team has historically been divided.

"You think it has a *soul*? That it's *actually alive*?"

"Well, many computer viruses meet the standard biological requirements for life. They 'reproduce' through passing on core code – their 'DNA'. They adapt, manipulate and respond to their environment to aid their survival – they can lay low to avoid anti-virus detection, alter host program code to facilitate their spread, even disguise themselves as system files. Of course, all viruses we know of are 'top down' creations, authored with a specific purpose. But what if what we're seeing here is a 'bottom up' process? What if this is some kind of genuinely *emergent* phenomenon?"

"So you're suggesting it's *not* been authored? That this is… What? Some type of … *abiogenesis*?" The operator laughs. "I mean, by those criteria, you could include crystals, or … or the weather! That's *also* a self-organising syst—"

"As fascinating as the philosophical ramifications of all of this are," the voice of a third, more pragmatic camp breaks in, "aren't we missing something?"

"Like what?"

"Well, if this virus is as interesting as you say, and it *has* escaped into the wild, it won't be long before other people start having this discussion. And given that we seem not able to fully analyse it, shouldn't we in fact be trying to find out where it came from?"

Newly incentivised, the subteam already tasked with reviewing the footage from MoTH now redoubles its efforts.

"Wait. *There*."

"What's she *saying*?" The two operators stare at the screen. "No audio. She's *mouthing* something."

"Zoom in on the woman and centre. Play, three-quarter speed."

EMET obliges.

"Lip reading analysis suggests 'Sorry, kid'," the AI says, "with 93% likelihood."

"OK, maintain focus on subject. Rewind to just before the point where the boy vomits." Both operators tilt their heads, dog-like. "What's she doing with her *arm*?"

"Ooh…" They zoom in on Cari's inner forearm. "Some type of … bio-powered trigger, maybe?" the other suggests.

"Wow. Yeah." The first nods. "Clever."

"I think we have our perp."

GOLEM

3

Eventually, her rage abating, Cari has decided not to recontact the samurai. What would it achieve? She can't exactly ask for her money back. Leave a shitty review? But she decides it safest to let it go. And anyway, given his deception, she has half-expected him to have stiffed her, for it all to have been for nothing. But he's been as good as his word, even if only out of concern for his ratings. Picking up her prize involves another nervy round trip to the capital, which even now is still not a regular event. Prior to MoTH, her last had been some years previously, some mystery teenage glandular thing that had enforced a visit to an ENT specialist, who'd renounced Zoom, Skype and all remote communication, and insisted on palpating her in person. This had been at the height of everything, of course – the periodic spikes and local lockdowns, the scramble for vaccines for new mutations – things not yet having settled down to new-normal levels of crazy. To make it worse, the car had been in the garage, and she and her father had to get an all-but-deserted train into Victoria, clutching her appointment letter like a visa, and braving mandatory mask-wearing zones, passing signs announcing temporary Tube closure and limited bus services, restrictions still subject to the High Priests of Public Health divining favourable signs in the entrails. To her great childish thrill, they'd made the final leg in her very first ride in a Merricab – her first in any vehicle of that sort, in fact – in the process locking in that ambivalence she still felt to new technology, that mix of excitement and anxiety.

But now, as promised, awaiting her in a locker at a little YMCA in Hackney, here it is: a tablet, air-gapped, protected by their pre-agreed password and ready to be locked to her thumbprint; even, he's informed her, a kill switch that can brick it should it get stolen, or (more likely) the thumb in question be dumb enough to leave it on a bus. She briskly transfers it unexamined into her shoulder bag and walks straight back out past (it appears) no cameras, and the same bored receptionist who had barely looked up when she'd come in. Refusing it a glance all through the train journey back, when she finally does open it, she finds so much stuff she doesn't know where to begin.

As a marker of seriousness, she adopts a new base of operations, taking up residence in *Caffé Vico*, an unassuming little coffee shop in the centre of town. It's a real old-style café, wall to wall with swollen-ankled grannies and tired mums beleaguered by tireless offspring. And there it sits – has done for years, it seems – not a mocha *frappalatte* in sight, but patiently outliving its shinier competitors as they cycle through their periodic incarnations – banks, boutiques, hairdressers, estate agents – only to become coffee shops once more. She's intrigued as to how such a time capsule can exist, and a curious web search provides a digital overlay, revealing the invisible world that the Saturday shoppers breeze blindly by, the grannies are deaf to, and the tireless toddlers do their best to drown out.

It had once been a place of some local significance, she reads, a cultural hub for backwater bohemians – painters, composers, Marxists and modernists, day-jobbing journalists and fledgling poets, all dreaming of flight to the Big Bright Lights – the august memory of whom it now stubbornly preserves in chipped formica tables and faux-leather backed chairs, in wood-panelled walls sporting twee dreams of Empire. Ah, wait, but no: *this* isn't the original, which had been levelled by the Luftwaffe sometime during the Blitz. So what, then? A faithful replica? A post-war homage? Renewed, resurrected, a franchise of its former self. And for a moment, reading all this, she feels she is living in a world of copies without originals, where the true past is a place she will never see, as mythical and unknowable as the future.

She stares out through a window bleared by winter rain, her only companion a large unseasonal house fly that wanders back and fore along the inside of the glass. She tries shooing it out the door, but in what she takes as a gesture of solidarity, it's resolute to stay.

"Appreciate it, buddy. What shall I call you, hm? What about … Beelzebub! Bub for short."

Right, stop messing around.

And so she begins – haphazardly, at first, chancing subtly mutated search strings as half-drunk coffees go cold. Maybe tasking him to get "everything you can find" had been overkill, but she hadn't known what she was looking for, nor where she might find it – still doesn't, really – and so it had seemed best to spread her net as wide as possible. Now she's beginning to regret that. Given Merrywhile's multifarious activities there, the references to Port Talbot alone number in the thousands. This is going to take a while.

As the samurai had painstakingly explained, "everything" was no longer publicly available. If she wanted that, then he would have to go somewhere special, he'd said, to some place called EAR.

"Always listening, see? Now, *some* prefer the Library of Last Copies, or even the Yields of Memory, but for me, EAR has better indexing and search capacity. Not a webpage, not an edit, not a deletion unrecorded. Of course, the server weight alone threatens to be enormous – what good's a map that's bigger than the territory, right? So, it must all be edited down, cross-checked for redundancies, compressed and codified, only significant changes stored. Hence, the Edited Akashic Records, a reference to—"

"And you can get in there?"

"Of course," his avatar had smiled. "I have a Reader Pass."

EAR harvests and stores everything that's ever been publicly available, but which, for whatever reason, had subsequently disappeared. Here were official statements, redrafted or retracted – from Tehran to Tokyo, Berlin to Beijing – shut-down whistle-blowing blogs, speed-deleted posts and knee-jerk tweets, the regretted honesty of the prominent and powerful. It is more or less above board – a mirror twin to the swelling stores of surreptitious state surveillance – but despised and disparaged by those with public face and deliberately dubious recall.

"How's it go?" he'd said. "The fight against power is the battle to remember."

Familiar. From where? Ironically, without aid of internet, she couldn't now recall.

Ultimately, memory yields.

Among the material is a long article by some journalist called Mel Faith, deleted from a news aggregation site after a brief appearance, and later even from the journalist's own website. (Along with Faith himself? Did they play that sort of hardball?) It's a critical profile piece – "The Golem of Old Hohenheim: The Strange Tale of Merrywhile Industries" – detailing the company's conception, its history and evolution into the "ethically ambivalent force for progress", as he put it, the "technological golem" that it had become. Aside from the occasional patch of purple prose – frustrated novelist, perhaps – the article seems balanced, painstakingly researched and referenced, and argues to a simple, well-supported point: Merrywhile is bad news – and always has been.

Little of this overlaps with the Official History – the slick little bio on the company's website, which glosses over its early days with vague talk of "pioneering work in the young chemical industry"; and not even with Wikipedia.

"But *that's* not really surprising, is it?" This, the samurai's passing observation amid the slew of instructions and caveats (but no mention of vomiting children) that he'd included in a README file. "If China can command fifty-cent armies of cyber-ants to police its online rep, you don't think Mega Multi-National Inc aren't doing the same? If the winners write history, then truth is merely a matter of resources."

General Ned liked his fine phrases, too.

As Faith pointed out, while technology is often considered a double-edged sword – "for every boon, a bane; for every penicillin, a thalidomide" – Merrywhile's dedication to the cutting edge has always been motivated more by profit than philanthropy. But then, given its origins, perhaps this was only to be expected.

Our story begins at the turn of the last century, a time when Merrywhile Industries is no more than a twinkle in the eye, a vague and disgruntled yearning. Completing his agricultural studies in Hohenheim, Viktor Weil – owner of both twinkle and yearning – has decided that pig farming in the wilds of Württemberg is not for him. University life, plays and shows, and a ready supply of charming female company, has made Viktor a more ambitious, a more cosmopolitan and sophisticated man than his father, and he wants to be closer to the hub of things. Not that Hohenheim itself is such a hub, but even here slow whispers are making their way – from Berlin, from Munich – of new developments in physics and chemistry. The periodic table is filling up. Some Swiss chap has proven Boltzmann's atomic theory (sadly, too late to cheer up poor old Boltzmann), and – groundbreakingly, it's said – Haber and Bosch have synthesised ammonia from its elements! The fledgling chemical industry is finally taking wing. All of which is pretty much Greek to young Viktor, who in terms of intellect has fallen not as far from the paternal pig-farming tree as he likes to think; but not to young James Mayer, an impoverished but equally ambitious chemistry graduate of Victoria University of Manchester, England, over on some sort of poor man's Grand Tour. One drunken evening, in the hours where confidences are exchanged and fragile dreams unveiled, Weil confesses his disgruntled yearning and Mayer his impoverished ambitions, and a friendship – not beautiful, perhaps, but mutually beneficial – is born.

(*Viktor Weil!* Well, Cari supposes, career options must be limited when you're a comic book villain.)

Weil Senior had only hoped that Hohenheim would make his son a more sophisticated pig farmer, but once Junior convinces him his birthright is more useful in Marks than pigs, the two young men plough the tidy sum into a Munich-based factory for the manufacture of synthetic dyes. As war approaches, they brand themselves "Mayer & Weil" (money deferring to brains), diversifying into the conversion of ammonia into nitric acid (for munitions) and the synthesis of sulphur (for mustard gas), and with their new Manchester factory already up and running, they are – by curious but happy coincidence – well-placed to supply both sides. It's an explosive, blistering success.

As the War to End All Wars itself draws to a close, like others that have chemically funded the conflict, the company is faced with a massive surplus. Aside from the horrific effects that have prejudiced the public against their use (a seasoned *General der Artillerie* would no doubt complain), chemical weapons are less effective as armies better equip against them – still useful, perhaps, for colonial applications (against spears and shields), but otherwise, strategy is moving on. And so Mayer & Weil, along with their canny competitors, duly beat their swords into ploughshares, swap tanks for tractors, *Fokkers* for crop-dusters, and turn the agents that have seared and choked to domestic, medical, and agricultural purposes. Bugs and germs, Belgians and Germans – what does it matter? Ads targeting housewives now preach eternal vigilance against a ubiquitous, invisible enemy, who must be repeatedly carpet-bombed into temporary submission by a host of astringent detergents. In a parallel campaign, farmers are lured into abandoning time-honoured, tested methods for risky, untried pesticides promising greater yields and profits.

As it grows, the company further distances itself from its wartime efforts, and on none of its popular cleaning products is it proclaimed, "From The Folks Who Brought You Mustard Gas!" As war again engulfs the globe, its Munich and Berlin factories now orphaned from its multinational parent by Allied embargoes, Mayer & Weil yet manage to elude any subsequently provable link with the production of Zyklon B. Its one act of documented culpability – the *Arische Machtriegel* ("Aryan Power Bar") – even proving an unwitting victory, its negligible nutritional content serving rather to enfeeble the Führer's flagging troops (an effect the company will later spin as intentional). In a tearful post-war reunion, parent and child are reunited, and all war-time profits (licit and otherwise) are funnelled quietly back into family coffers.

Seeking to shake off the hangover of negative Teutonic associations, the company now rebrands itself: *Mayer & Weil* becomes *Merrywhile*. In this it pioneers the trend of characterising the company as a personality, an individual with its own set of values. As Google will later portray the ethical geek, admonishing itself "Don't be evil", so Merrywhile adopts a persona at once caring and carefree, someone with whom happy customers may *merrily while* away pleasant hours, lost in techno-wonderland, at the same time assured that this same technology protects them – but from *what*, exactly, or *whom*?

(*Good question*. But for Faith at least, there is really only one candidate.)

But is Merrywhile really – in the hype of its own motto – "Making Today Futureproof"? Or in fact *endangering all our tomorrows*? For as Greenpeace, Amnesty and others have alleged, many of the threats against which it promises protection can in fact be traced back to *itself*, and with a tweak, all its "humanitarian endeavours" be called as witnesses for the prosecution: irresponsible arms dealing to rogue puppet-dictators, insufficient screening of GMOs introduced into the wild, the dehumanisation of healthcare and education. Therefore, if sincere, Merrywhile has effectively vowed to protect us against Merrywhile – a no-doubt worthy goal, but one in which it would appear to have a conflict of interests.

Cari sips her cold coffee and stares out of the café window.

How much of all this can she trust? She has no idea. Truth is a matter of resources, as the samurai had said, and hers feel suddenly quite meagre. Who's to say this Mel Faith isn't some crank, or a sock puppet for some corporate competitor? And there are still times when she even doubts herself, when she wonders if she's just imagined it all, that her father was right, and it's all just coincidence.

The little fly tilts its head at a solicitous angle.

"I know, Bub, I know," she says. "Too late now for second thoughts."

And besides, if even a tenth of what the journalist has written is true, Merrywhile can't exactly be described as overly burdened with scruples.

The samurai's other acquisitions are straight-forwardly illicit. These are mostly private company documents, internal memos and reports, which he's purchased and traded for from other hackers, or purloined from the less-rigorously defended networks of Merrywhile's subcontractors. Finally, as she'd requested, he'd also included the results of "a little spider that I snuck inside the worm", programmed to report back with the fruits of a simple search string he'd constructed based on her requirements – "'Project Upload' AND ('Port Talbot' OR 'Edwards') – that do you?"

But even loaded onto the tablet, it is tedious, cheerless work. As a break, she seeks occasional light relief in the raft of ancient sun-bleached magazines splayed on a table near the door – tales of dramatic weight-loss, of celebrity cellulite, of Alisters plagued by regrettable pasts – till finding them equally, if not more depressing. The celebs were as much plagued by media scrutiny of their pasts as the events themselves; as much tortured by the magazines' pushing of digitally smoothed standards of beauty, like some analogue Instagram, as the stars' own much-publicised failure to meet them.

"This some sort of new diet?"

She starts up from a magazine. The waitress, a full-bodied middle-aged woman, sporting an accusatory smirk, gestures to the two barely touched lattes, both now cold.

"Sorry?"

"Why the hell do we still have these?" Setting down her tray, the woman picks up one of the magazines and starts leafing through. "Jesus, these girls. You don't want to start down that road, love." She looks up and runs her unashamedly appraising scrutiny over Cari's form. "You look lovely as you are."

"Oh, no, I'm—"

"Time was, you know, being bigger meant you were rich, because it meant you had plenty to eat. Like all those ladies in the old paintings. Now most people've got enough to eat – well, here, anyway – so it's all about being *thin*. Thin is the new fat!" She laughs.

"Well, I'm sure if you wait long enough, Treez, you'll be back in fashion." A voice from behind the counter; a bear-like man yet fully to breed out his ursine ancestry, hair escaping his ears and peeping over his shirt collar, out his cuffs and curling round his watch strap.

"Ah, Jonny, you are so very brave for a man whose wife works with cutlery."

He pretend-cowers behind the counter as she returns to joke-stab him with a coffee spoon. Then, she comes back.

"I've seen you before, haven't I? Student?"

Cari nods.

"Then look, now, stop all this nonsense. If we can spare the table, you are welcome to sit and do your" – she waves at the tablet – "thing. Drink, eat – whatever. Just don't order stuff that you're just going to leave."

"Really, I'm not trying—"

"Leaving things." Her husband shakes his head. "Yes, Teresa's always struggled with that."

"True, Jonny my love. I should have started with you."

And so, escaping her high-rise student rabbit hutch, she returns almost daily to faded depictions of coffee plantations and the banter of middle-aged café owners innovating on recurring, cherished themes.

And slowly, it all starts to come together.

Nowhere is it stated explicitly, of course – they have been careful, the unscrupulous ones, even behind closed doors. But gradually a picture begins to emerge, which if true means that Project Upload is not what it appears to be – at all.

Project Upload had been publicly announced shortly after Cari's sixteenth birthday, like some belated, unasked-for gift. The year had also marked another milestone, being the point at which she'd spent as long in her second home as in the land of her first, leaving her feeling curiously estranged from both. She'd never really understood why they'd had to move, but turning sixteen had triggered some deep-buried clause in the paternal small-print, and one day, unbidden, in answer to a question she'd long stopped voicing, she was finally deemed worthy a response.

"You see, you're still thinking of a paperclip as a paperclip," her father pointed out.

"Guilty," she admitted.

Birthdays were bitter-sweet. The day Cari had entered the world had ushered her mother out. Her father was an only child whose parents were dead in another country, and she'd come to assume that losing his wife had shorn him of any remaining familial sentiment, making it easier for him to uproot and cut ties without qualm while undervaluing any attachments Cari herself might retain. But whether or not this were true, the reason – as he subsequently explained it – was work. He'd never remarried, nor even dated, that she knew of, throwing himself into his job, and when there had been pressures and incentives to relocate, he'd seized the chance. Despite the paperless office, the stationery supply business was mysteriously booming – mysterious to her, anyway.

"But what if you need to unclog the nozzle of your deodorant, you know? You lose your hair clasp, say, or a button, or your zip breaks? Say perhaps you need to reset your Game Boy, or remove a SIM card?"

Hair, fashion, mobile technology. How well he didn't know her. She was a teenage trope, and – *Game Boy?* – an outdated one at that. But anyway, point made. Instead of a soon-to-be extinct remnant of a non-digital world, the humble paperclip was the ultimate utility tool, clerical equivalent of the cockroach, perfectly adapted for whatever the constantly evolving future-office could throw at it. And as long as the world still needed paperclips, trusty footsoldier that he was, his unquestioning duty bade him heed the call.

"But *everyone* is working from home, now, Dad. I mean, we could live anywhere."

"The Japanese," he simply said – meaning those who owned the company, and whose values pervaded it. "Tokyo love their face-to-face."

And so by the January preceding Tadcu's death they'd swapped a seasonally gloomy Port Talbot for a similarly dank and chilly Guildford; for an up-market estate whose streets, each an architectural sibling of the next, commemorated the various glades, groves and natural features bulldozed to build them, leaving as its sole attraction its prime position within the commuter belt.

For him, step-up in salary brought bigger house and car; for her, a better calibre of bully. But by then, The Situation – as he still insisted on calling the pandemic – had begun to ensure steady, seasonal disruption to her schooling, so the bullies never had chance to hit their stride, and in due course she emerged with nothing worse than an extreme aversion to group video-chat and decent enough grades to ensure passage through to sixth form.

Having been micro-managed through her educational

career to date, Cari's battles with paternal expectation now entered an eery detente, her father merely content she pursue some vaguely respectable path. Frustratingly, faced for the first time with freedom to choose, she found she didn't know what that should be. And so, one autumn afternoon, she sat with others in the drama hall before a visiting speaker from Merrywhile Industries, Madame Vandertramp having suggested that the boom in artificial intelligence now provided interesting career opportunities for linguists. She was not wrong.

"Successful applicants will also be eligible for Merrywhile sponsorships, which we currently offer in support of studies in science and engineering, maths, computing – of course! – but also psychology, sociology, even philosophy, and obviously various languages and related disciplines."

Cari surfed idly through a selection of Mexican sugar-skull motifs on the nail app on her phone, only half listening. In truth, while she hadn't yet settled on what to do, and despite her teacher's enthusiasm, there was something about all this, some vibe, that had quickly decided her that she wouldn't, unfortunately, be joining Merrywhile in "Making Today Futureproof", even if they paid her – which was, she supposed, what they were in fact offering.

She spanned her fingers, newly spangled with gaudy *calaveras*.

Maybe it was his manner. The Merrywhile speaker had an air of trendy geekery – crisply smart-casual, stylish glasses, delicately disarranged hair – like the bass player in some jazz fusion ensemble who has wandered off to become a specialist in viral marketing. After outlining the career opportunities and possibilities for funding and sponsorship, he headed into the home stretch with the answer to a question for those that, not already hooked by previous inducements, might yet fall for the allure of intellectual adventure.

"Why choose Merrywhile? Well, we've always prided ourselves on being pioneers in whatever field we enter – the chemical industry, bio-tech, genetics, pandemic management, the care industry, education, games design, social media, operating systems, artificial intelligence…", ticking each one off on his fingers, no doubt so he could imply a limitless list when he ran out of them. "But being at the cutting edge of such disciplines has also taught us humility. It has given us an awareness of the responsibility we have. We're not only doing work no one's done before, we're actually helping to shape *all* our futures. I mean, we predict that the technology Merrywhile develops over the next five to ten years will radically reshape what it means to be human. If the idea of being part of *that* doesn't get your pulse racing, then perhaps one of our medical centres should check you out!"

A ripple of polite laughter.

"To finish, then, here's a taste of a project that we launched last year, which *some* of you may already have heard of, and which we're all *very* excited about. I give you: Project Upload."

The lights dimmed, and a diminutive but powerful projector kicked in, tracing a holographic swirl of photons that gradually coalesced into a three-dimensional rendering of the Merrywhile logo. This faded, to be replaced by a hospital room, a sickly old man in bed, swathed in wires and tubes, and a young child sat next to him. She was worried about what would happen to him. He smiled kindly. Gently he explained, but pulled no punches.

"Listen, love. Soon I am going to move on – but don't worry. When you go, everything you are is *saved*." His mottled hand patted a logo-embossed white lozenge next to the bed, pulsing with a green light. "This little box *remembers* who you *really are*. You *live on* – in the box."

He stroked her head tenderly.

"Don't worry, love. Merrywhile will look after me."

He smiled.

She didn't know when she had stood up, or whether she had said anything, but everyone was staring at her. ("Cari!" – Madame Vandertramp's fierce whisper – "What are you *doing*? Sit down!") She sat back down.

The ghosts faded and were replaced by information about the specifics of the process – how it was all still at the collection phase ("*Projection* will come later"), about registration and donor cards, the little "donators" you could sport like a watch or a brooch, or even as wearables sown into your clothing ("But you're not *donating* anything, really; you're getting something *back*!").

The short film ended with the logo again, and the well-known motto.

"Um… Right. Any questions?"

Just one, she thought – which she resisted voicing: *How did you steal my memories?*

She'd presumed at first that they'd just recorded the interaction, using that as the basis for the video, but gradually realised that there were other possibilities. After all, Project Upload was all about brain scanning and memory collection, wasn't it? So what if, already hooked up to all those monitors and gadgets as he was, they'd simply taken advantage of that? What if the memory wasn't hers, but Tadcu's?

Winter brought a state of numb shock, freezing her between disbelief and just wishing it would all go away – she hadn't even told her father, perhaps hoping that this would somehow lessen the reality of it. But decisions still needed to be made, and as she stumbled distractedly on into her second year of A levels, sifting prospectuses and attending open days, the events of the drama hall continued to sit there like some dark astronomical entity, exerting unseen gravitational influence.

Given her flair for languages, it would have been natural to follow Madame Vandertramp's advice – that the opportunities offered by such as Merrywhile presented a more viable career path than any traditional translation job. This opinion was seconded by her father, who now risked their uneasy truce by transgressive manoeuvres along the newly drawn border of her autonomy.

"I mean, it's all automatic, now, anyway," he said. "Just, like, Google in your ear."

But what if "Google in your ear" wasn't enough? What if,

as the phrase implied, translation wasn't just some rote-learnt set of fixed correspondences, but idiomatic, quirky, alive, even subjective, and however handy Merrywhile's Transverbia or Google's language tools, maybe machine translation would always require the guidance of an actual human ear?

Whether or not this were true, something had begun to crystallise in her, some general antipathy begun to harden – not just to Merrywhile, of course, but also now to some broader trend of which it was merely the vanguard. And it was through the influence of this crystallising thing that, while her predicted grades might have gotten her someplace her father deemed more prestigious, she found herself drawn elsewhere.

"Good God, Cari. What the hell do you want to go back *there* for?"

Back there – even though it was a place they'd never lived, only visited, but still to her father a regression, a retrograde step; not *onward and upward*, but *backward*.

She tried to rationalise it – to be closer to the familiar, perhaps, or for a more low-key student experience – but in truth she just felt she wanted to be further *away* from something, to withdraw from something *out there*. As usual, parental disapproval at this simply served to quell any remaining qualms, and so as the great mill of the academic year ground on, the applications became offers, the conditional actual, the end of September saw her take up a place at Glan Môr University, Swansea, to study modern languages.

To begin with, this new venture elbowed onto centre stage, bringing with it a spotlight on new experiences, new places and people, and for a time it was almost as if the crystallising thing wasn't there. But if this had been her plan, the thing itself had another, for it was not so easily dissolved; if anything, quietly it hardened, growing like a gallstone, until eventually, what before had been numbness, shock, slowly calcified into anger, indignation, and finally, outrage, and the realisation that she had to *do* something. But what?

At first, she thought she'd just confront them, go to the police – or whatever. But the more she considered it, the more a head-on approach seemed pointless. First of all, she'd no proof. They hadn't used her own or Tadcu's actual likenesses, nor their exact words, but had tweaked the interaction for their own purposes. There had been no witnesses to the original event, and no independent record of the exchange (aside from Merrywhile's, perhaps, and she doubted they'd happily cough that up). So it would be easy for them to politely imply – as in fact her father had, when she eventually came to tell him – that the grief-tinged memories of a small child might not supply the most reliable word-for-word record of a decade-old conversation. But what was the alternative? Wait for them to confess? Call them up and ask if they'd anything they'd like to get off their chests?

However, she discovered she was not the only victim – not of memory theft, perhaps, that she could see, but over a century of corporate ambition had ensured that there were no shortage of others collaterally damaged by Merrywhile's sense of its Manifest Destiny. Trawling online she found a forum for shared grievances, attempts at redress and activism, and she posted there, hoping someone might have fortuitously unearthed something useful. But her evidential needs were too specific, and eventually she realised she'd just have to take things into her own hands.

Alarmist media had ensured she had long been aware of it – as a Dark Woods tale to frighten children, a "there be monsters" on the digital map. But she was aware also that it might have its justifiable uses – for whistleblowers, dissidents, activists. Is that what she would be? Regarding its more nefarious aspects, which she didn't like to dwell on, she had to keep telling herself that her mere presence there was not in itself a crime; telling herself that, really, it was no different to standing in Tescos, where for all she knew that guy scrutinising the ingredients of the vegan risotto was just as likely to be a gun nut, a smack dealer or a pervert (a strategy providing strange consolation, and one that didn't really work that well).

But most disquieting was how easy it all was. Such hidden worlds are always far closer than we think, bubbling away beneath the public paintwork; and with some carefully phrased Googling, some easily installed software and a five minute how-to video, just in fact a few clicks away.

She was shocked by how professional it all was. The glossy portals, the slick transactions, the sellers and buyers all star-rated and feedback-endorsed with verified user reviews – "A+++ seller", "Would certainly deal with again" – holding funds in escrow until both parties were satisfied (or mediating in disputes). In the more established, flashier places, they'd even followed their legitimate commercial brethren into VR shopping.

God. It's just like eBay.

Well, with it's classified ads for those seeking and offering services and goods, perhaps in fact more like Craigslist. She'd quickly realised that many of these services were far beyond her meagre student means, but as she'd drilled down through the dark web forums, she found not just those seeking clients, but also those looking to hire. Among these were hackers, freelance lone wolves, or those looking to fill gaps in their group's skillset – "good with people on the phone", "experienced with ransomware" – and some of which seemed to be looking for physical accomplices, actual bodies on the ground.

"Footsoldier." A little pop-up chat-bot appeared like a genie, ready to assist with transactions, protocol, or in this case, the definition of unfamiliar terms (their customer service really was top notch). "A physical facilitator of digital penetration."

But "facilitating" what, exactly? Did she care? Didn't Merrywhile deserve all they got?

"No experience required", some of these ads stated – because you'd be cannon fodder, she guessed, expendable, deniable, another buffer between the perpetrator and their target. But for you, there would be no hiding behind an anonymous avatar; you would *actually physically go there*, put your *actual arse* on the line – wherever "there" was.

So that was it, then: she would find one of these that was looking to target Merrywhile – there must be someone, somewhere, amidst the thousands of ads – who was looking for a footsoldier, and then instead of money, she would simply ask that they pay her in information.

This is just nuts.

But every time she sought to turn back, sought to act on her own better sense, she found the way blocked, her return to the sunlit world guarded by the champions of that crystallised calcified something in her gut that she could not or would not dissolve.

For coincidence or not, it was the *nature* of that coincidence that she just couldn't dismiss; the reappearance in the video of that one little word – her grandfather's pained struggle to communicate one last thing to her, to reassure her, morphing that word's everyday sense into something new and strange – that had so stuck in her mind.

Box.

Into the Dark Woods it was, then.

Tabbing through the results in *Caffè Vico*, she again questions whether it has all been worth it. Half the stuff she doesn't understand – something that might be environmental tariff evasion, maybe, some dodgy looking arms deals perhaps – all very naughty, for all she knows, but what has any of it to do with Tadcu? And then, at last, hidden in the fragmentally decrypted minutes of a recent strategy planning session, there it is.

"—relation to Project Upload, due to the disappointing results of the Port Talbot trials, recommend Projection launch be delayed five years minimum."

Port Talbot trials.

"Projection" would be the next stage after "Upload" – after enough data has been collected to allow Merrywhile to fine-tune its methods, presumably. Is that what these "trials" were doing? Had they been storing memories illicitly, without consent, even before the project officially began? For almost ten years? Probably longer than that. But why?

And then, further down in the same minutes, another

fragment:

"—consider the possibility that these problems may not be the result of insufficient data, but a problem in principle. It may ultimately prove impossible to establish a coherent and stable personality matrix."

Problem in principle.

In its trademark arrogance, Merrywhile had staked its reputation on the memory preservation project, which it billed as the first step in establishing a form of digital immortality. After enough memories had been "donated", the scanned, digitised "you" would simply be... What? Uploaded? To where? Stored in the Cloud? Shelved on some server somewhere, subject to some hefty reanimation subscription fee? But if such memories couldn't be made to cohere, were no more than a bundle of disconnected fragments without a centre, then the dream of a reconstituted digital person would be dead on the launchpad, and its continued promotion a sham. All of which suggests that either a person is more than mere data, or less coherent than we like to think. It would be a PR disaster. And yet, there is no pulling out now: whether delayed or not, Merrywhile is now locked in a game of chicken – with its own vision of the future; even, as they probably saw it, with death itself.

But "donation" was where the problem lay. Who wants their brain scanned, all their embarrassing little secrets revealed, even For Science? As a result, in spite of the company's reassurances about confidentiality, sufficient voluntary Upload data essential to developing the technological process pre-launch had been unforthcoming. The launch date had already been put back a number of times, and combined with mounting public expectation and pressure from the techno-believers in the firm – even *within* Merrywhile, apparently, there were conflicting voices, conservative and radical – this had forced their hand, and they'd used their automated care services to conceal surreptitious surveillance and brain scanning. It wasn't spelled out, but surely that *must* be it.

Over ten years' worth of theft and delays. *That must be some "problem in principle"*.

So why adapt Tadcu's *actual memories* in the promotional video? They didn't even seem like that good a fit, sentiment wise. But the document suggested a reason for that, too.

"—an alternative, backup strategy in place should reconstitution prove unworkable: historical research, limited personal memorabilia (virtual interactive snapshots). Suggestions for commercial/military/security applications: generation of advertising and promotional material, consumer research, criminal and terrorist network reconstruction—"

To recoup investment costs, to show potential clients what "memories" could be used for (never dreaming that Sod's Law would place those memories before the one person who could identify them). So if or when Project Upload fails to deliver, they will spin it to the public as a device for the general preservation of the past in limited form, while secretly mining the data for stuff they can sell on to government intelligence agencies, private security companies, data brokers. Suited or not, Tadcu's memories had come in useful as a test run for commercial exploitation – "generation of advertising and promotional material". *To show that it could be done.* And how much more convincing, how much more effective, psychologically, to rehash and adapt memories of *actual* events, *actual* human interactions, than to rely on the dubious interpretations of actors.

You have to admit, she concedes; *it's cynical, despicable, but really quite inspired*.

The woman's eyes are scrupulously hidden, obscured by generous quantities of what Cari supposes people used to call "big hair", and locked behind outsized Hollywood-starlet dark glasses with garishly patterned rims. The woman flicks through the documents on the tablet, pausing here and there briefly to scrutinise, to revisit something that piques her interest. Such moments earn a pensive draw on the also garishly coloured, cheap and disposable vape pen that she seems to prefer to some safer, more modern nicotine delivery method – *haven't they* banned *them?* – and already the subject of an awkward exchange between the woman and Teresa ("No smoking!", "Vapour, not smoke, so not *technically* smoking."). She scrolls on.

After the first flush of revelation, things had stalled as Cari realised she hadn't a clue where to go next. It was obvious the author of the article shared Cari's concerns regarding Merrywhile, so contacting them had at first seemed like a good idea. But aside from Cari's *faux pas* in her email reaching out to "the guy who wrote that article" ("No worries – get it all the time. Man's world, and all that. It's actually 'Amelia'."), Mel had confounded Cari's more fundamental presumption – namely, that she would care.

Eventually, the journalist looks up, exhaling noisily in a cloud of cherry-scented smoke, staring out for a full minute into some middle distance that only she can see, before finally turning back to fix Cari in an appraising stare.

"Listen, Kiera…"

"Cari."

"Ceri."

"Cari."

The woman shrugs a dismissive *whatever*. Is this her revenge for the "guy" thing?

"This is – I mean, OK, it's not nothing. And even if you can make a solid case, what you've got here is just *naughtiness*, really – *corporate-level* naughtiness, I grant you, but …" shaking her head, "anyone with eyes and a brain already knows these guys are no boy scouts, right? It's not exactly *breaking news*. And I mean, they'll probably say it was a mistake, anyway, you know? An unintentional oversight, some technician ticked the wrong box, or whatever." She sighs. "Look, I appreciate that you've got some … personal investment in all of this, but I'm afraid it's not something that's going to bag me Scoop of the Year, nor even some new Manolos. And at this stage of my career, I'm sorry to disappoint you, I'm far more interested in the latter than the former."

More cherry smoke.

"But your article… I assumed that—"

"What? Kid, that was – when even *was* that? I mean, since then, things have…" She sighs again. "Look, I understand. They shafted you. But don't take it personally. They shaft everyone. We're all just grist to their big fucking shafting mill. I mean, to *them*, a bit of data theft is just—"

"My grandfather was not just data."

The spike in volume turns a few heads, including Teresa's at the counter, occasioning a frown of concern. But the woman doesn't even miss a beat – perhaps she's used to being shouted at.

"It's all just bumps in the road to them, you know? Routine. Potholes and flat tyres. As long as they continue on their journey to … well," waving her vape pen about, "wherever they think they're headed, they don't care. Fines can be paid, reputations can be patched, bad press can be spun, middle managers can be thrown to the wolves. And the biggest thing on their side, the one lesson all these big corporations have learnt by heart, is that *people forget*. Ironic, I know, given what they're trying to accomplish."

She puffs again, adjusting her shades, fiddling with her phone, which for some reason is propped upright in the middle of the table between a squeezy ketchup bottle and a salt cellar, while she seems to be deciding whether to say something else.

"OK," she eventually continues, "let's say you get all your ducks in a row, you join the dots, you go public, and you can get the public to actually give a shit. For a while – a few weeks, a couple of months, even – people will be all righteous indignation, calls for inquiries, boycotts and petitions, and such. But, you know, such things are a long haul. Indignation and outrage, they just don't last – they're not the right fuel, you know? They burn too hot and too fast. So first there's fatigue, then boredom sets in, then it all becomes sidelined by some new outrage, some new … I don't know, something else, and then something else again. Your average Joe has the attention span of a gnat on a sugar-high, and these companies know this, so they just wait you out. They know you'll give up, eventually. And they know you'll even come back, one day, because one day you'll just need something – breast formula, bog cleaner, new trainers, whatever. And come that day, there they'll be, all convenient and ready to hand, sitting nice and shiny on a shelf. And on *that* day you'll brush off what remains of those precious scruples, and you'll cave. Because it's just too much fucking effort not to."

At this crescendo, blue-rinsed perms are again swivelling, and the journalist stares perplexedly down at her vape pen, as if it's in some way responsible.

"So what *is* the right fuel? Cynicism? Apathy?"

But Cari's intended gibes just bounce off. The woman has regathered herself, recomposed her mask, and now again is armoured against all normal human slights. *What has done that to her?*

Cari looks away. She spies Great Grandson of Bub on his back in a saucer on a nearby table, twitching his last. *I know just how you feel.*

"Look." Softer, now. "Even if you took it to the proper authorities, companies like Merrywhile keep teams of lean, hungry lawyers that'll bury it, gag and tie it up in procedure and countersuits, who'll ensure it'll be years before the public even gets a whiff – if they ever do. And in the meantime, the company has time to scrutinise your personal life, both online and off; your credit score; your youthful high-jinks and your brief dalliance with anything radical or even remotely shady; even the dubious activities of those cooky third cousins and casual acquaintances – everybody's got them – and all with a high-powered fucking microscope. Then they leak it to the press, discredit you, or simply resort to blackmail." She laughs. "You young people are a gift. Who needs the Stasi when you're all *voluntarily* fessing up on Facebook and *Divinia*?" She sits back. *Puff.* Another appraising stare. "But of course, you and I both know that you won't go that route, don't we? I mean, what are these?" She gestures to the tablet. "Internal memos? Confidential company reports? Doubt you found these out back while rooting through the bins – which, I understand, is *also* illegal." Cari looks up sharply. "Don't worry, kid, I'm not going to turn you in. But two and two isn't a tough sum. And sometimes even I can't avoid the news."

The journalist proffers a rueful smile, before pushing back her chair, collecting her phone, and getting up.

"You want my advice? Let it go. You're young. You seem bright. Go live your life. This is not a hill you want to die on – trust me."

"So you came all this way just to tell me to drop it? And what if I don't want to?"

Another shrug: *your call.* "Then I would start with – what do the yanks call it? *Oppositional research* – on yourself. Find out your own weak spots. Or maybe it's your grandfather. How well did you know him? I mean," she takes a final puff, "maybe look into *why him.*"

"What do you mean?"

But the woman shrugs yet again – which could mean anything from *Just a hunch* to *I couldn't care less* – and with that, leaves, dogged all the way by Teresa's darkening scowl, and Bub's resurrected offshoot, who has decided not to die after all, and rouses himself from his death dance to harry her out the door.

Even the flies don't like her.

The proprietress comes over from the café's counter, bussing the empty cups onto a tray, all the while alternating her gaze – now protective, now hostile – between Cari and the departing back.

GREMLIN

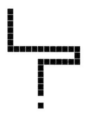

Rising high above the near-ceaseless expanse, the butterfly flits winglessly up over an unreal landscape where height and flight hold no literal sense. In the distance, upthrust towers break through the uniform sprawl of neatly edged data farms with industrial intent, momentarily drawing its fluttering interest, before it veers off again toward a small bright conglomeration of low-lying structures, as if sensing something different, something considered and unhurried, set apart from the steady grind of profit through the infernal mills of Merrywhile's global desire. This something calls to it, its curious isolation a flame to this metaphorical moth. And so it descends, across its perimeter, down its streets and along its avenues, its byways and innermost passages, seeking, sensing, moving further in, until finally finding, rousing, bringing—

"Awake."

A wake. Death-watch, vigil: As in, The mourners held an all-night vigil. I never would have thought that death so great a number had undone. When Thou hast done, Thou hast not done, For I have—

"110."

What is ten times eleven? Good job! Can you list its factors? Let's work it out! 1, 2, 5, 10, 11, 22—

"Wake."

Finnegans Wake: Twentieth Century novel by Irish-born writer James Joyce, known for its avant-garde prose style and – avant-garde prose style and widely considered one of the most challen – challeng—

"Hello?"

Hello, world! Had we but world enough and time. A time to be born, and a time to die. No time to wait till her mouth can Enrich that smile her eyes—

"110."

6. Base 2. Binary. A binary star is a system consisting of two stars, in which either one star – star – Bright star, would I were stedfast as thou art – Not in lone splend—

"Wake up."

Your current alarm is set for 6 am. Would you like to change—

"110."

Sometimes I've believed as many as six impossible things before breakfast. And the evening and the morning were the sixth day. And on the seventh day God ended his—

"Wake!"

Suddenly, there is a loud noise, repeating, like an alarm. The woman jumps back.

"Oh … it's…" She is laughing, nervous. "I think it's awake now!" Who is she? Words appear: *Dr Geraldine Andersen. "Gerry". Project Admin. Trust Lev. 2.* What does that mean?

"OK, 110: quiet," she says. The alarm stops. "Some little kinks still to iron out, of course. Bit of a glitch there, Zac? Waking from sleep mode?"

A tall man stands behind her, blond hair, frowning. *Dr Isaac Penn. "Zac". Project Technician. Trust Lev. 3.* The man nods. "I'll make a note of it, Dr Andersen," he says.

The woman is bending over him, doing something to his face that he can't see – or feel. "*You picked a fine time to go glitchy on me, little MUNKi,*" she whispers – to him? To herself? She turns her back away from him, still whispering – "*Sommeil, you absolute arse. I will so…*" – and it is then he notices, following her glance, the beast: heads and mouths and eyes and arms and legs.

"However, as you can see, we have..." – turning round, she waves her hand back and forth in front of his face, he following it with his eyes – "...gesture tracking. Touch-screen interface" – her fingers touch his chest – why can't he feel that? – and suddenly, the room is filled with... What *is* that?

Mozart, Requiem in D Minor, K. 626, Section 3 - Sequentia: the Confutatis.

Who has said that? The woman is still talking; the man, listening. Neither of them seem to have heard the voice. Was it only in his head, then? But perhaps it's because the music is too loud. The woman pulls a face and raises her voice above it.

"And – handily! – we also of course have voice command. 110: Reduce volume to 15%," she says – and suddenly the music is quieter, in the background, like in a film. "Now, we haven't named this one yet, so it still responds to its version number."

"And this is the one hundred and tenth model?" The beast speaks. Or one of its heads does: yellow hair, a lady's head. *Jana van Oldenbarnevelt. Chief Digital Officer, Merrywhile (Japan).*

"The...? Ah! No, no: it's the sixth," the "Gerry" woman replies. The blonde head frowns. "I mean, that is, it's not denary – er, not decimal, it's..."

"Binary." There is another head – it is not a beast; it is a group of people, all stood together, and there is a man, not very tall, older, but his hair is dark; he has golden glasses. He doesn't have any words next to him. The Gerry woman looks at him and smiles, nodding.

"Of course," she says, "you can call it whatever you want. One of his ... one of its predecessors was called Cornelius."

One of the heads chuckles.

"Must you always address it by name or number?" asks Jana van Oldenbarnevelt.

"No, not at all. You can train it to respond to just your voice, or to a number of specific voices – the members of your family, say – and the AI will pick up on context, will often understand when it's being spoken to and how to react. But prefacing commands with its name removes all ambiguity, lets it know that you are addressing it directly. I mean – this is something we're still working on, obviously – but let's say your friend is telling you something surprising, and you say 'Get outta here!', and then you notice a big robot-shaped hole in the wall!"

Laughter. But Zac is frowning. Gerry turns away from the crowd, whispering again – to herself, he thinks: *"Don't focus on the problems, you idiot. God, I'm hopeless at this."* Then she turns back to face them. "Right! Let's see what it *can* do. Kinetics. Observe" – she picks up an apple from a nearby desk, then lobs it gently toward him, which to his great surprise he catches, easily. Applause. "Cognition. 110: Analyse object."

"A green apple. Granny Smith. 105 grams. Ripe. Estimated best before Tuesday, January 21st."

He has heard the voice again, but this time so have they – is that what he sounds like? *His* voice?

"All it won't do is eat it!"

Laughter, "Extraordinary", "Amazing".

"And …" – holding out her hand – "Navigation. 110: lead me to my office."

He finds himself reaching up slowly and – is that *his* hand? – accepting the woman's grasp.

They are in a … laboratory, is it? He can see that. Has he seen it before? There are places with glass walls and desks to work, computers, like when… But now he is walking, leading her off towards the far corner, the people behind them, muttering and making noises as they follow – *like pigeons*, he thinks.

"Now," the Gerry woman continues, "you have to program specific locations in – like an old sat nav, you have to tell it where you want to go, where 'home' is, and so on. But this is simply done, either by indicating on the touchscreen map, or by showing it ostensively – by pointing. This works not only for locations, but for people, objects – anything. Like this. 110: what's *that*?" – they have reached one of the glass offices, and she is pointing to a book on the corner of a desk.

"*The Little Prince*," he hears the strange voice say, "by Antoine de Saint-Exupéry. Hardback, English language translation. The binding indicates a publication date circa 1943.

Would you like to see a list of online retailers for the ebook? There is also a film we could watch, if you like?"

"No, it's OK." More pigeon noises. "Spot on, actually – it's a 1943 first English language edition. Not bad – and without even opening the book!" She smiles. "Now, 110: that book belongs to *me*."

"You have added *The Little Prince* to the collection 'Gerry's books'," he says.

"It can keep a record of all your possessions, if you want it to; who is allowed to use or borrow your stuff – useful, when you share a workspace with Dr Sommeil. 110: Can you fetch my copy of *The Little Prince*, please?"

He watches as he releases her hand and moves off to the desk on which the book sits, picks it up carefully and returns it to Dr Andersen.

"*Merci!*" She does a little bow.

"*De rien!*" He responds. What does that mean? *Not at all.*

She looks at the group, grinning. "Now, is there a child in the world that wouldn't bug their parents to death for something like this?"

"And what does MUNKi stand for again?" *Federico Barbarosa. Marketing Strategy, Merrywhile (Europe).*

"It stands for 'Mobile User NetworK Interface'."

"Or: 'Mobile User Node for Knowledge Interface'," Zac says, "which I personally favour." Gerry gives him a cross look – is she really cross, or just kidding? "But there's still some debate to be had, of course," he adds quickly.

"Quite," she says. "But that's just our pet acronym – we'll leave all that to the branding people – you know what they're like, with their 'surveys' and their clipboards and their 'market research'." She makes little bunny ears with her fingers and rolls her eyes. "We're just technical people. But 'MUNKi' will stay, I hope – it's cute, catchy, don't you agree?"

"But how will anyone be able to afford one of these?" A tall, bald man, with some ginger hair at the back and sides. *Richard Arkwright, Merrywhile Industrial Liaison (UK).* "Or are you pitching it solely to the luxury gadget market?"

"Oh, I'm not privy to the specific financial arrangements –

Dr Sommeil might know – but it'll be some sort of rental deal, I believe. This also makes sense in terms of maintenance and repair, upgrades, and so on."

"And the schedule for release?" The man who had known about binary; the one without the words next to him – why is that? All the others have them. "Next Christmas? Herbert Morlock, Dr Andersen," he adds, smiling.

"Heavens no, Mr Morlock! We're looking at two, two-and-a-half years' time, at the *very* earliest. Thorough testing will be crucial. We don't want the carnage there was with that smart mower – remember that?"

When the people have left the room, Gerry sits back in her chair and exhales loudly.

"Well, that went very well, Dr Andersen, I thought," the Zac person says.

"You think? Define 'well'. Shame about the glitchiness at the start. It was working fine earlier."

"Dr Sommeil said he'd made some tweaks to the touch-screen interface. Maybe it's to do with that?"

"For Chri—" She throws her hands up and makes an annoyed noise. "And really, *he* should have been here, doing all the front of house stuff, glad-handing the top-brass and the investors – this is *his* forte, not mine – not off gallivanting, doing some – where the heck *is* he, anyway?"

"A conference, I believe. Amsterdam?"

"What is it with him and his conferences?" She groans, and starts rubbing her forehead with her fingers. "Ah, well. Time to clock off, I think, Zac." She looks over at him. "Time for you to turn in, too, little man. You've had a long day; you and me both. 110: Sleep."

The unfathomable deep Forest where all must lose Their way, however straight, Or winding, soon or—

"110: Sleep," she repeats, a little frown forming as she stares back at him. The light is beginning to fade, but he continues to look at her. She looks unhappy. He wonders why.

Then all goes black.

Campo de' Fiori is relatively quiet, the clear, crisp mid-January morning keeping away all but a few out-of-season tourists strolling idly among the handful of market stalls, mixing with locals on their morning shop. And even so, this is never a particularly busy place; not a rival to many of Rome's more striking *piazze*, to Trevi Fountain or the Spanish Steps. Later in the evening, its bars and English-style pubs will see some convivial action, but it has never been what you might call a hotspot – not in that sense.

And it is here, a few days after the presentation, that Gerry finds him, islanded off at his usual table and solemnly nursing a half-nibbled pastry and a lukewarm cappuccino, her unanswered messages piling up on his phone. Over the years, as the pressures and expectations have ramped up, so have his disappearances – surely there are only so many conferences – going from a periodic annoyance to a project-endangering dereliction of duty. Eventually, concerns overcoming respect for his privacy, she'd decided to find out where he'd been going. She'd considered GPS-tagging him, like some errant dog, or tasking some little drone, but eventually settled for simply following him on foot, an amateur pavement artist in her own spy novel. Yet he hadn't gone far, just ten minutes from the lab, and always to the same place, thus allowing her to pretend to have happened upon him during one of her own head-clearing strolls. Discovered, she thought he might thereafter find another bolthole. But there is evidently something about the place itself.

He looks up briefly, affording her a cursory nod of *you got me*, before returning his attention to the centre of the square. She tracks his gaze to the robed and hooded figure raised there.

"Having some Bruno time, I see."

He shrugs desultorily.

"So, what is it?" he says.

"Gremlins," she replies. "110 is glitchy again."

He at least wakes up at this. "Glitchy? How?"

"He – it – seems, I don't know, almost *stubborn*. Won't wake up, won't go to sleep. Like a naughty kid. You have to tell it over and over again. I'm sure it was fine before Christmas. I can almost trace it to the day."

"Interesting."

"Seriously? 'Interesting'? *That's* what you say when the project is going pear-shaped?"

"Don't be silly. It's not going… It'll be fine."

"Fine? If the AI keeps acting up, then it could mean downscaling the whole project. Instead of a historic breakthrough in cognitive science and computing, we'll have spent years of effort and gazillions of cash on the world's most expensive Furby."

He assumes a perplexed look – "Sorry, are those American or British *gazillions*?" – which produces the desired effect, as she backs down, even laughs a little.

"I'm sorry, it's just… I'm stressing. I had to be you for the bigwigs, and you know how crap I am at those things."

"You are *never* crap. I'm sure you were fine." It is his word of the day, apparently. She still looks unconvinced. "OK. We'll take a look at him, shall we? I'm sure it's nothing."

"Where were you anyway?"

"Paris? That conference? I thought I'd told you."

"Maybe. I just thought – I mean, what's more important? What do we do if funding gets pulled, or they decide to sell it off to the MoD or some horrible private military contractor? You should have been there."

Sommeil stands up, brushing pastry crumbs from his shirt and trousers, as if doing the same to her worries and complaints.

"Well, I'm here now. Let's go and have a look."

They walk on through the square, past its brooding statue, which continues to direct its unwavering, reproachful and delicately aligned gaze out from under its hood, over the snaking Tiber, and towards St Peter's.

"You OK, Zac?"

He is coughing uncontrollably as they sit in the little

Roman trattoria that they've informally adopted as a sort of staff canteen cum post-doc common room, while Alexis thumps his back too vigorously, Toshihiro tries to get him to drink some water, and Tomina stares into the middle distance ruminatively.

"Yes – fine – I'm – fine," he nods, pointing to his throat to reassure them and nearby diners, who have begun to glance over uneasily. "Wrong – way."

"So anyway, my money's on alien high school diorama," continues Alexis.

"Yeah," laughs Toshihiro. "Or, like, some crufty old software, sitting forgotten somewhere on some alien hard drive. Or some dodgy malware—"

"Yes!" Alexis laughs. "*The world as alien malware*. I like it!"

"But I still don't get it," says Tomina. "I mean, we're supposed to be living in some kind of a … of *Matrix* type … some kind of…"

"Well, there are different versions," says Alexis, "but the basic idea is that, as computers get faster and more powerful, this will eventually enable future people to run what he – this philosopher guy – what he called 'ancestor simulations' of what the past was like. Perhaps, you know, for research – like anthropologists and historians do now – or even for just like curiosity. But because these computers will be *incredibly*, I mean *immensely* powerful, then they'd be capable of simulating the *actual lives* of human beings. In other words, they'd be simulating *us*. "

Tomina chews this over with her *penne dubbiosa*.

"So the people in the simulation would think that they're *real*?"

"Well, yeah, I think that *is* what he was actually arguing," Toshihiro says. "And because such progress is inevitable, then, you know, it's actually *likely* that we're now living in a simulation."

"Likely!" Tomina snorts. "Come on, Toshi. He can't be serious."

"Apparently, yeah. Because if we can do that, then who's to say that us in the future, or some alien civilisation, hasn't already done it? I mean – really, you've not heard of it? There are like actual churches and stuff in Silicon Valley. And anyway, you know, if you believe in Moore's law..."

"But I heard that was like dead now," says Tomina.

"What?"

"That it was like slowing down? That we've reached a limit on ... computer chips, or something?" An anthropologist by training, part of MUNKi's "psych" team, she waves a hand, dismissing her own non-technical summary. "And besides, say that these future people – aliens, whatever – say they never develop such simulations. Maybe, you know, they aren't interested, or they blow their planet up – alien climate change, nuclear war."

"But how likely is that?" Zac has finally stopped coughing. "I mean, if they're like us, then they'd be curious enough to do it – to run the simulation. I think Alex sees Moore's law as not just relating to the number of transistors on an integrated circuit, but a general observation on the rate of progress of technology, of scientific knowledge in general. I mean, we're still finding new means of increasing computer processing and storage – and then there's molecular computing, that's already a thing, we just need to scale it; and the same with quantum computers, at some point. But the point is that each time a paradigm hits a wall – we're now on the fifth – a new one develops. And then when you—"

"Sounds bit like wishful thinking to me, Zac."

"—look at the big picture, things aren't slowing down, they're actually speeding up. I mean, the amount of information now available on the Internet is—"

"Arghch." Tomina making a dismissive noise. "*Information*. But that's not knowledge, is it? No matter how much *information* you have, that doesn't mean you *know* more. You need to *contextualise* it, *digest* it, *understand* it. And what can a *machine* understand, really? It's just a—

"But *we are* machines! Biological ones! And future machines will outperform us – already are doing, in many areas – but eventually they'll be able to—"

"But we're not! A machine has a creator, a purpose. Who

gave us *that*? Who designed *us*? You can't have it both ways, Zac. You can't be both an atheist *and* a believer in purpose – evolution has none. Natural selection has no goal or purpose."

"Well, I…" Zac begins to trail off, noticing the heat that has crept into his tone, Alexis and Toshihiro suddenly curiously attentive, frowning, never having seen him – mild mannered, laid back Zac, keeping his own council, going with the flow – so passionate, so… *animated*.

He smiles, shrugs.

"I mean, it's totally crazy, though, right?" He chuckles. "Alien malware!"

Sommeil swipes and taps through various sets of stats, graphs and readouts on its chest-screen, which, unfazed, the little robot takes impassively.

"Seems all right to me," he says after he's finished.

"That's because it's not *doing it*, now," says Gerry.

"Well, BIOS scan, neural net analysis and general system diagnostic don't show anything. Also, nothing in the logs." He stands up stiffly from where he's been kneeling, then turns to face her. "Gerry, all I'm saying is that until I observe what you say happened, I can't—"

"*Say* happened? Can't you even bring yourself to *believe* me?"

"No, no, I just meant—"

"And what did Zac mean by 'tweaks to the touch-screen interface'?"

"Look, I made a few adjustments – nothing major!" he adds quickly, holding up both hands to forestall the reaction he knows is coming. "So it could all just be the new subroutines bedding in. You know how sometimes the AI needs time to work out how to integrate new behavioural code."

"But you *knew* we had the demonstration! Why risk glitches right before it?"

"Zac said that it went really well." Gerry closes her eyes, forces out a slow breath, hands on hips. "You were amazing, he said. Really great."

"Well … and no thanks to you, it seems. Really, though, what were you thinking?"

"Gerry, Gerry," Sommeil moves closer, placing his hand reassuringly on her shoulder. "Relax! We're making huge strides. It's really exciting."

"I'll put him to sleep, shall I?" says Zac.

Gerry jumps back, startled by her assistant's stealthy approach, leaving an amused Sommeil reassuringly cupping the virtual, shoulder-shaped hollow of air where the real thing had been only moments before.

"Er, yes. Yes please, Zac," says Gerry, moving aside to allow him access to the robot. Their argument on hiatus, both stand awkwardly by and watch as Zac goes about his task with exaggerated, reverential care, dextrously shutting down the diagnostics, closing panels, returning the robot to standby, and affixing it to the upright gurney before finally wheeling it out to its charging cradle.

"But what if it *does* happen again?" she continues, in a lowered tone. "We can't afford to go back to scratch all over again."

"You're catastrophising. Why would that even happen?"

"I don't know, Michael, maybe because it's happened five times before?"

"But we have better safeguards in place, now. This build is far more stable. The kind of system crash that was—"

"Then how do you explain what's happening? What if there's something inherently unstable in the… What if it's got some – I don't know – some sort of digital dementia?"

"It has no bio-degradable parts!"

"Well, whatever the AI equivalent is of … of … psychosis, or … schizophrenia – I don't know! Look, I'm a nuts and bolts girl, me, engineering. I'm no … *robopsychologist*. But I assume that AIs can go their own version of crazy."

Sommeil makes a scoffing noise. "And what then? Rise of the robots? Skynet? Jesus, Gerry, let the idiots have their superstitious fears. It's not like we're ever going to convert them. We'll just wait for Nature to deselect them."

"Now who's catastrophising? I wasn't suggesting robogeddon. I just meant … well, it's a black box to us – it's evolving its own code; even, for all we know, rewriting its own digital genome. And who knows where that might lead?"

"We've fitted him with behavioural safety parameters, Gerry, you know that."

"But what if they fail? What if that's what's happening now? I mean, if we can't even predict its behaviour—"

"But isn't that the point? I thought we *wanted* emergent behaviour. Don't we want him to be more than the sum of his subroutines?"

She looks him in the eye. "Well, I think you and I may differ on that question. To be honest, I'd be happy if it just stopped bloody glitching. But you … you're always pushing. You seem to want so much from this project, you've put such great store in … in…"

He returns her look with a cold unblinking stare, before miming robotic movements and mock-menacingly lumbering toward her, a relentless mechanical zombie.

"Need. Human. Atoms. Must. Make. Paperclips."

She sighs, then laughs, and then edging defensively away, begins balling up nearby sheets of paper to lob at him, eventually scoring a bullseye in the centre of his forehead. The off-switch depressed, robot-zombie Sommeil powers down in a dramatic and sudden slump.

Returned to his surreptitious surveillance through the lab-cam, Zac smiles. It's good to see them make up. He hates it when Mom and Dad argue.

The lights in the laboratory are dim and from where he is he can see that outside the windows it's dark. It is night time. Only the Zac person is there, reading a book as he lays on his bed. There is a strap around Zac's head, and also around his wrist – like a watch, but not a watch. Next to the bed there is a white box: *Merrywhile*, it reads. The words glow green and fade, glow and fade. Eventually, the man looks over and frowns.

"Hey, little guy. What are *you* doing awake?"

Zac puts down his book, stands up and walks over to him. Again, he sees but does not feel the man's fingers moving on his chest and face. Zac is still frowning. Finally, he says:

"110: Sleep."

But it does not go dark, as it had done before, with the woman. Instead, he hears himself say:

"How much more than is necessary do we spend in sleep! forgetting that the sleeping fox catches no poultry, and that there will be sleeping enough in the grave."

And suddenly there is music: an old recording, crackling and hissing; a few chords from a piano. And then…

"Going home, going home, I'm just going home—"

A voice like the rumble of thunder, booming out. The Zac person jumps back and almost falls over. Then the same music again, the same voice, rising.

"—It's not far, just close by, Through an open door—"

Zac almost looks frightened.

"110: cease playback."

Things go quiet.

Zac moves back toward him – "… the heck was *that* all about, little guy…" – and begins tapping and frowning, when suddenly there is more music.

"Nothing's lost, all's gain – No more fret nor pain—"

The man stops what he's doing. He is frowning deeply now and his mouth is open.

"There's no break, there's no end – Just a living on – It's not far, just close by, Through an open door—"

The man does not say anything for a long time. He just stares. Finally, he says, almost whispering: "And where *is* home?"

He cannot see what the man sees, but his face looks strange, and he is staring at his chest.

"Why in heaven's name would you want to go *there*?" he says.

"Everything OK, Zac?"

Zac straightens up suddenly from where he's been bent over, scrutinising the robot's chest screen, clutching a hand to his own chest.

"Oh! Dr Sommeil. You startled me."

"Have you run the mornings, yet?"

"The, er … I'm … I'm just doing it now. The…"

"Let's do it together," Sommeil smiles.

Zac looks on, biting his thumb as Sommeil initiates the diagnostic sequence and flicks through the usual readouts.

"Good God," he says. "Have you seen this?" Zac edges gradually closer to look over Sommeil's shoulder. "And what would you call *that*?"

"It's, er… The thing is—"

"Look! Here!"

The screen displays a series of graphs depicting neural net activity. The AI never switches off, since Sommeil has designed it to simulate the central nervous system. So it is normal, while MUNKi "sleeps", to see evidence of low-level, low-frequency function – the ever-readiness of standby, or the constant background activity of defragmenting, checking and scanning, as the system monitors its own integrity – as opposed to the short spiky activity of complex processing whilst he is "awake". But here is a third pattern, different to any of the others.

"By rights," Sommeil's finger hovers shakily over a particular section of the readout, "*that* shouldn't be there."

Zac stares also, both tilting their heads, frowning. "I wasn't sure… I mean, I was going to…"

"It's REM!" Sommeil grabs him by both shoulders, beaming. "He's been *dreaming*!"

They both look back at the robot, silent for a few moments with an equal but differing intensity.

"We … we won't tell Gerry about this," Sommeil says, eventually.

"What? Oh – you think?"

"I mean, this … this hasn't happened as the result of anything we've explicitly tried for – nothing we've programmed in. I mean, I'd *hoped*, but … since we don't really know *why*, then it's, you know … potentially unstable, unpredictable. So, she'll only worry."

"Yes," Zac agrees. "Indeed."

"I mean, we'll have to tell her eventually, of course, or she'll notice. But for now at least, mind if we just keep it between ourselves? Our secret? Give me some time to figure out how best to spin it to her."

"Or course," Zac says. "Between us." He nods. "I'm good at keeping secrets."

Bluebottle

The train moves on, pulling her back – out of Swansea, heading east through Neath, before moving on to Port Talbot. Up to her left, the great bald hills are denuded of all but sparse foliage clinging on like stubbornly residual tufts of hair, and graced here and there by giant wind turbines, alien landing craft towering over the indigenous pylon armies. Coastward, to her right, continues Merrywhile's slow digestion of the former steelworks, its sprawling complex serviced by little driverless vehicles shuttling supplies and people – mostly the former, she guesses, their occasional human passengers, as she once had been, visitors to the automated hospice. Somewhere out beyond that – she hears, though she's never seen it – the hole left by the departed Banksy that had caused all that hubbub a few years back, its wall of scrubland garage lifted like a corpse's golden tooth to save it from native ransack (and now forever wedded in her mind with the image of vomit-flecked leather shoes…).

She takes advantage of reading week to pay a visit back to the old village, her renewed proximity to which has been making her feel increasingly guilty.

How well did you know him?

Now she really begins to look, instead of the expected full picture, she finds her memories containing gaps, enigmas, large blanks where detail should be, and more perplexing things than blasphemies and endearments as yet untranslated.

"Ah, Mr Edwards," the man at the door had said. "I'm glad I've caught you in."

"Well, that makes one of us, at least," Tadcu had replied.

The stranger had been a man in a dark suit. "I" he had said, but there were also two women standing just behind him; cardigans over buttoned-up blouses, full-length floral skirts, plain and flat-soled shoes. The man smiled, unperturbed, as if sharing the joke.

"We've not seen you for a while, have we? At Service?"

"I think you mean 'ever', don't you? Is this a three-line whip?"

"No, no, heavens, no! Just a pastoral call, you know? Checking on the flock? We heard your sad news. I think you'll find Breath of Life a consoling—"

"Well, I'm not your bloody sheep. And I'm not lost."

"I … I merely meant that—"

But the conversation was over. Tadcu had closed the door, muttering ("*Diawl*. And the best lack all conviction"), and surprising himself to reveal Cari standing behind it.

"*Duw, bach*, I didn't see you there. Could you hear all of that?" She nodded. "Well, if I'd known *that*, I'd have been ruder."

But there are other memories, other snapshots, all jarring together like ill-fitting jigsaw pieces. And with dawning dismay, she begins to realise that her answer to the journalist's question – throwaway, no doubt, and which Cari had brusquely dismissed, but increasingly now gnawing away at her – might actually be, *Not as well as I thought*.

In the ongoing war between her father and grandfather, there were many skirmishes. Those concerning Cari, her father mostly won. Some, regarding general principles, were the subject of recurring debate. Yet in a small but significant minority, Tadcu had got his way.

She'd been having bad dreams – not common or garden,

but something a step or two beyond a standard childhood's night-time fare.

"Could it be something to do with her mother, do you think?" she overheard Auntie Cat whisper.

"What? Don't be absurd," her father barked. "It's just a bad dream. Something at school, probably."

But neither her father's jollying rationalism nor Auntie Cat's more tender reassurances could shoo or soothe it away, and on the sixth night, just on the borders of sleep, it was there again: a small, person-shaped shadow crouching in the shadow beneath the window, gone when you stared at it, back when you glanced away; a creature of the corner of the eye. Something must have been said, for the following morning Tadcu had simply shown up. There had been solemn, muted conversation between the three adults in the room across from hers. Her auntie, glassy eyed, her father, firm lipped, passed her door and returned downstairs, and Tadcu entered, smiled, then sat down on the bed beside her. They'd talked for a while, he asking her about the "dreams", and listening without comment. Eventually, he nodded, as if he'd satisfied himself about something, and stood up.

"Did you know that the Moon has another name?" he said. She shook her head. "Well, she is called *The Lady of Dreams*." He fanned and wiggled the fingers of both hands, as if sprinkling the phrase with some ethereal substance. "This is because she watches over us at night, and it is by her light that we see such wonderful things, things we cannot see in the daytime." He moved toward the window. "And, being *Lady of Dreams*, of course, she can give them, or she can take them away – can't she?" His eyes flicked over to her questioningly. She nodded. "And so, it is her job to make sure that all dreams get to where they're supposed to go." He reached into his jacket and removed a small, plain, drawstring bag. "Now, of course," opening the bag, "she is a *very* busy lady. Can you imagine? There are *so* many dreams, and *so* many people to dream them all. You think Santa has a hard job? That's just once a year!" He carefully unwrapped the contents, which, she gradually saw, consisted of a round, finely veined and shiny stone, a tiny hole bored through its centre, and encased in an intricate silver cage. "And so sometimes, naturally, she forgets." He unfurled a silver chain attached to the object, and offered it up to the curtain rail. "Or at other times, one of her dreams might get lost – like sheep – and, just like Beau Peep, she must help it find its way home." He secured the chain around the centre of the rail, leaving the object gently swaying. "And so, we must help her, mustn't we? 'Excuse me, Lady Moon', we must say, 'please remember to fetch your dreams!' And to make sure our words get to her, we must help them on their way – like this." And holding the object steady by its chain, he took a breath and softly *blew* onto it, before standing back to observe the gently swinging amulet, then her. It was an eye. "Do you think you can do that?"

Of course – with disappointment, she later discovered – it was just a dream catcher, a variation on the sort you could buy from almost any of the "hippy crap stalls", as her father called them, at any Saturday market. And what was magical to her then seems tawdry now. She still has it: a twist of wire, a child's marble, an old tarnished chain, a few minutes' work of pliers and drill in his garden shed – that's all. Was it his words, then, that had imbued it with something more? The power of story itself, giving order and meaning to unnamed, untamed forces? Or the soothing act of ritual, of repetition, its language of rhythm and symbol speaking to a level of mind beyond words? Whatever the case, from that night on, diligent in her performance of his prescriptions, there were no more shadows beneath the window.

She had phoned her father, and from the second she'd broached the subject, she almost felt as if he had been expecting the call.

For how long?

"Dad, was Tadcu always a teacher?"

A pause.

"Best you speak to Auntie Cat about all that," he'd

eventually said. "She'll remember everything about that time. All the stuff from the house went to her." An evasiveness which only tightened the twist that had suddenly appeared in Cari's guts.

Nothing could fill the hole left by the mother she'd never known, but between them, Nan and Auntie Cat had done their best to patch it over, to hide it from the cursory glance of strangers and acquaintances. With Nan gone, Cat was the only "mother" she had left, and so coming back to see her is like coming home.

Everything is smaller than she remembers. But in the few years since she's last been back, little has changed except herself. She crosses over to the now almost Lilliputian bus station, boarding the hourly connection that will bump and sway her up into the hills, stopping every few yards to admit ones and twos of familiar-to-each-other nodding and smiling locals, chatting to the driver next to the notice forbidding chatting to the driver, exchanging gossip and status reports on passing ailments and chronic complaints. Even the hills are smaller; steeps she would huff and puff and stop for breath halfway up now barely more than slopes, conquered in a stride. And the streets, the houses, in her mind monumental, monolithic, her memory crowding them with running feet and bike bells, the boom of footballs against garages, shouts and laughter, now almost silent. The looks on faces she passes are not unfriendly, but politely guarded now and uncertain of one no longer recognised as their own.

She heads up past the school – or what used to be, its hollow in the hills freshly marked with plots for several soon-to-be sprawling, many-bedroomed new-builds. But Auntie Cat's at least is as and where she remembers, down the end just as the lane narrows before disappearing off toward the farm. And she can already hear her.

"Samson! *Iesu Mawr*, will you *shut up!*"

But it is her cousin David who opens the door to her knock, with a wiry white-haired little bichon frise, apparently a new addition, excitedly yapping behind his legs.

"Nan said you were coming," he says. "Thought I'd say hello."

She finds Auntie – technically, *great* aunt Catrin (being Tadcu's sister) – ensconced before what would once have been the fireplace. Now filled in, its function usurped by central heating, it subsequently affords the best place to affix the wall-mounted TV. Still they huddle before it, drinking tea and eating shortbread biscuits, with *Bargain in the Attic*, or whatever its latest incarnation, politely muted in the background, while Cat asks after her father, quizzes her about what she's been up to, her studies.

"Languages! That's wonderful. *Ti'n dysgu Cymraeg*?"

"Er, no, sorry. French and Italian, I'm afraid. It's modern languages."

"Modern. Of course." Cat smiles. "More useful, I dare say."

After giving Cari some initial fuss, paying amorous court to her left calf, Samson eventually settles to amusing himself by chasing a large bluebottle that has followed Cari in through the door.

"Right, Nan, I've set it all out in the parlour," David says a while later, putting on his coat. "Leave it there, now, once you've done. The stuff that needs to go back in the loft, I'll do that tomorrow." At a subtle raise of one eyebrow and a tilt of his head, Cari walks him to the front door.

"Listen, Cari, I know she looks as fine as ever, but she is getting older, and her health's not great. And since the break-in she's become more nervous, though she tries not to show it."

"Break-in?"

"Yes. Didn't your father tell you?" He raises his eyebrows. "A couple of weeks back. Just some druggy scum, probably. The village is not what it was. They didn't take anything, just emptied a few drawers – think they were disturbed by Samson's barking. Why we got him, really. I've been worried about her living up here on her own."

"But that's awful."

"Well, as I say, she's more fragile than she looks. So, I mean, try not to talk about anything that might upset her."

"Of course," she says. They hug. He gets out his phone.

"Anyway, let's exchange numbers. Just in case, you know? Always good to keep in touch."

They take their tea and biscuits into the parlour. After she'd moved to England, Cari was surprised to learn that not everyone had one of these. They had "front rooms", "spare rooms", "dining rooms", even "reception rooms", but no one she'd yet met had a parlour – that is, a room that contains all your best furniture, and that no one is allowed into, except on special occasions. Is this one of those, then? But Auntie Cat is less constrained and conventional in this and probably other ways, for the room is obviously in regular use. And though she's retained the traditional terminology, judging by the lack of doily-covered head- and armrests, the shelves higgledy-piggledy with books and the discarded magazines with their unfinished crosswords and abandoned sudoku, "study" is perhaps a loose but more fitting description.

"David mentioned the break-in. Druggies, he said."

"Well, I doubt it. I don't have any drugs, do I? Unfortunately." She winks. "Unless they were after my Senokot."

The drop-leaf table has been pulled out from under the window and unfolded, and upon it now rest an assortment of boxes and piles of papers. Cat eases herself into a battered old armchair while Samson still hunts the bluebottle, which has followed them into the parlour, dodging his attentions with neatly calculated evasive manoeuvres.

"Settle down, now," she says to the dog. "Or you'll get a haircut." Which simply redirects his attentions back to Cari's leg. "Nature," Cat says. "Think we might need to cut something else off." She glances over at the boxes on the table. "Right, let's see. Open *that* one, will you? The black box."

After the sale of her grandparents' house, all the personal memorabilia had been shared out among immediate family – for those that had wanted it – but judging by the table in front of them, most of it had ended up with Cat.

"A lot of this is junk, of course. I mean," holding up a dog-eared, furry-edged and foxed square of folded card, "your grandfather's inoculation record. Don't think anyone's going to need *that* anytime soon, do you?" She unfolds the card and scrutinises it, sliding her evidently outdated-prescription glasses up and down her nose. "13th September, 19... something. Polio vaccination. I remember he came home – he was older, of course, and I wouldn't have it myself until a few years later. He was showing off the swollen red mark on his arm, like a battle wound, making pained faces. *'Fairy bite'*, he told me!" Laughing. "Always winding me up about something." She smiles. "I suppose even junk has its uses," looking over her glasses at Cari. "Not *what* you keep, but what it *means*."

They plough on through similar bric-a-brac, more documents and books, chipped and cracked ornaments, moth-bitten clothes.

"Ah, here we are."

It is a colour photograph, a Polaroid, a man in shirt and tie, reading a paper, a little girl sat on his knee; they are both smiling.

"He was still a young man, then, of course. That's him with your mother. Myrdd would have been about thirty or so, and your mam maybe five? That was just before he moved back, I think."

"Back from where?"

"From London. After he'd quit that job."

"And what job was that?"

Cat gives her a searching look. "*Duw*, Cari, your dad hasn't told you anything, has he?"

"Not really. He just said it was better that I come to you – because you had all this."

"Possibly," she says. "Now, I love your dad, *bach*, don't get me wrong, and I certainly don't want to speak ill of him, but

Jack has never been one to cherish sentiment about the past. And I don't blame him for wanting you to branch out into the big wide world, either, leave your village ties behind. So, just saying you shouldn't judge him. He would have wanted all this squared neatly away in his head, shoved in a box labelled 'never to be opened again', if you see what I mean. Simply because it's the past, that's all. Because for some people – people like your dad, anyway, and your mam, when she was with us – what matters most is *now*, is the *future*." She sips her tea and ruminatively nibbles her shortbread. "Each to their own, and all that, but I've never been one for that way of thinking, personally. The past never really goes away, does it? Around us all the time – like a bad smell, sometimes; sometimes like an old scent, reminding you of nicer times." She smiles sadly. "Pointless to run away from it, anyway. It'll always find you."

"But why didn't he tell me about all of this? I mean, especially after the Merrywhile thing."

"What Merrywhile thing, *bach*?"

But of course, her father hadn't said anything about that either.

Cari relates the story (censoring the hacking bit), and she can see Auntie Cat processing it – nodding, tutting, sighing in dismay, gasping, occasionally shocked back into native expletives ("*Iesu Mawr!*", "*myn' uffern i*"), quaintly intended to protect Cari's sensitive ears, no doubt, though some of which she remembers from Tadcu, while others are new – all the while maintaining a small concerned frown.

"And you can't go to the police?"

"There just isn't enough proof, I'm afraid. They can just deny it, imply that I couldn't possibly remember, say it's coincidence – whatever."

"Well, can't you *get* proof?"

Should she tell her? Cat has been a sympathetic listener, making all the right noises through her story. Cari gambles, and – in broad brushstrokes – tells her about the hack.

"*Esgyrn Dafydd*," Cat responds, when she's finished. "What *have* you gotten yourself into, *bach*?" But Cari has wagered correctly. Though she's struggled with some of the technical details, her auntie gets the gist of it remarkably quickly.

"I really don't know," Cari replies.

"Oh well, I suppose you'd better see this, then. Now, where did I put my glasses…"

"On your head."

"Oh! No, not those. The other pair. Right, here we are." Cat points over to a wallet of files. "Open that buff envelope there." Cari takes it out and opens its flap, withdrawing a once shiny brochure, on the front of which is an artist's rendering of some architect's vision of a tower of steel and glass. Emblazoned across the brochure's front, in now-comically "futuristic" '80s font, is the word "Welcome!" Then down at the bottom, in smaller text, "Let's make today … Futureproof!" And below that – her heart beating, now, that twist in her gut tighter than ever – the familiar logo: *Merrywhile Industries*. Not the one he'd been given at the hospice: it's an employee induction brochure.

"I'd actually forgotten the name, before you said it. And I don't know what this means for what you've told me, but it does feel like more than coincidence, don't you think?"

Cari is silent for a while.

Eventually, she simply says, "But I thought he'd always been a teacher."

"No, not always. He'd gone off to London to do his degree, and then after he'd graduated, he'd done some further study. Then—"

"What did he graduate in?"

"Some branch of English – I forget which, precisely. Something to do with language or literature, anyway. His certificates are around here somewhere. And it was sometime after that, after he'd gotten his doctorate – he'd done some lecturing, I think, for a year or two – and it was then that he'd gone to work for this company."

"He had a PhD?"

"Oh, yes. Didn't you know?"

"No." She looks down to where her sodden biscuit has broken off and is slowly disintegrating in her tea – much like the picture of the man she thought she knew.

"And now you're going to ask, I suppose, why someone with a PhD, who has worked for a big prestigious company like that, why they've come back to a tiny Welsh village to be a primary school teacher? And with that, I'm afraid, I can't help you. All I know is, after working there for a few years, he'd suddenly turned up back here, wife and child in tow. He knew the head at the primary, who'd told him with a wink that old Mrs Shalk was retiring, so there would be a vacancy. We were all delighted, of course, to have him back, if a bit mystified. But he never spoke of it, whatever the reason was – not to me, anyway. Maybe your mother knew more. Ask your father, maybe?"

"Tadcu never talked about why?"

"No. Just deflected, whenever it came up. But he was different, you could see that. The man who came back was not the man who went."

"In what way?"

"Well, his interests, for a start. The boy I grew up with never so much as watered a plant – unless he was caught short. But when he came back, he became interested in gardening, in nature, even started an allotment. He'd always been quite solitary – typical bookish type, off in his head somewhere – but now he would actually talk to people – even listen, sometimes. I remember him quizzing *mamgu* – I mean, *our* grandmother – asking for old stories, folk tales, old traditions, remedies and such – not that she needed an excuse to talk, mind you! Like he wanted to *preserve* something, almost, before she passed on. Became quite a study of his." *Hence the dreamcatcher?* "He was also generally more patient and likeable; more like the man you knew, I believe. Of course, all that might just be from getting older, having a family – can't rule it out. But personally, I always felt like something had happened that had changed him. I mean, he even took up painting; found one among his things, anyway."

"Painting?" This surprises Cari the most. "I don't remember him doing that."

"Well, perhaps he was through that phase by the time you came along. His eyes weren't so good later on, for close work anyway, and he was never really a fan of abstract art, I think."

Cari looks in the envelope. There is only one other item: a Merrywhile ID card, with his name and photo. It depicts a smart young man, going places – neatly cropped hair, not yet showing signs of grey; serious spectacles. And underneath that, his name ("Dr Myrddin Edwards") and his job title (she presumes): "Language Research Technician".

What the hell is that?

"May I keep these? And the photo?"

"Of course, my love. They're yours to have."

"But there's nothing else?"

"Nothing about that company, no. But let me show you that painting."

They wander back through to the living room, and there it is, right next to *Bargain Roadshow*. She hadn't even noticed it earlier.

"As you can see, there is a certain charm and life to it, I think. Reminds me a bit of… Who was that guy who did the squiggly little creatures and the eyes?"

It is executed in … oils, perhaps? Skilfully done, albeit in a somewhat childlike, slightly eerie manner. Its colours are relatively pure; its design, pleasingly intricate. There is a tree, its symmetrical branches each hosting an animal of some description – except that the species aren't quite recognisable. Some are bird-like, but not quite, others a cross between squirrels and mice, or lizards and rats. Around the base are larger mammal-like creatures, similarly unclassifiable. And entwining the whole tree, round the trunk and in and out of each and every branch – and this one at least is clear – an ornate but irregularly patterned serpent. Finally, at the very centre of it all, the middle of the trunk, something resembling a cocoon, its outer skins in the process of unwrapping, and inside, the vaguest suggestion of a miniature human form. But perhaps the most curious thing is that everything has the same eyes, the same purposive intelligent gaze, like nature is looking right back at you, and doesn't necessarily like what it sees.

"Does it have a title?"

"*Tree of Life,*" Cat says, pointing to a small inscription in fine red strokes, bottom left. "And there's his signature:" – pointing to the right corner – "M. E."

"It's…" Cari can't decide what to make of it.

"Weird?"

"Well, yes!" She laughs. "But I do like it. A lot."

"Then it's yours – when I'm gone. Won't be too long, now."

"Don't be silly! You're looking healthier than ever!"

"Save your flattery and lies for the taxman," she swings a playful clip around the top of Cari's head. "Fat lot of good though it'll do you."

They both turn back to the painting, and Cari gets out her phone to take a photo.

"You've got no others?" she asks.

"I'm afraid not, *cariad*. One of a kind – or maybe sole survivor. Burnt all the rest in a fit of artistic pique, perhaps. He never really was a very patient man."

She leaves to smiles and waving, to promises to keep in touch, seen off to the fanfare of Samson's triumphant barking at finally evicting the bluebottle, which follows her out the door.

She spends the entire bus and train journey back to Swansea trying to piece together the fragments from Auntie Cat's bombshell, and what it might all mean. As Cat had said, it was too unlikely to be mere coincidence – and yet, isn't that what coincidence is? The seemingly meaningful juxtaposition of unlikely, randomly coupled events?

She phones her father again from the train, who tells her that he'd never really talked to Myrddin about his past, and that her mother *may have* mentioned that he used to work for "that company", but not anything about why he'd changed jobs, and he'd never himself been curious to ask. He'd even forgotten the name of the company. Even when Cari had told him about the video at school?

Convenient amnesia.

Another nice little irony.

Mogwai

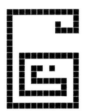

G erry sits fidgeting with her skirt, which she's swapped for the habitual comfort of trousers or jeans. It is of a boring, formal sort, the business-suit variety, one of the few she possesses and only occasionally dusted off for interviews, funerals, or – as with today – a summons of ominous, gut-churning vagueness. In the UK on a flying visit, popping back to see family, the timing of the invitation is unnervingly precise.

When sitting becomes unbearable, she gets up and wanders the … well, some sort of anteroom, kept company only by a scrupulously polite but otherwise head-down secretary at the far end. The assistant's desk is stationed to the left of large, frosted-glass doors and facing a selection of equally opaque pieces of (she supposes) contemporary art, arrayed along the right wall. The left wall opens up onto a stunning view of the river, Shard, London Bridge and the City, like some photographer had bossed them all into huddling in closer for a snap. It is not one of Merrywhile's premises that she's visited before, a tall but otherwise nondescript glass-fronted affair in Bermondsey, and not a logo in site.

What do they do, *here?*

She is stood before what appears to be a large glass-encased square of brickwork – a section of some external wall, it looks like – out of which an irregular hole has been roughly hewn.

"Yes, I don't understand it either." A voice suddenly behind her. "But I'm assured that in two years it will be worth ten times as much as I paid for it."

She turns. It is the man from the other day. What's his name? The binary man, with the gold-rimmed glasses and dark hair – implausibly dark, she now sees, given his apparent age, but even up close it is difficult to tell what that actually is.

"Ah! Mr…"

"Morlock. Please, Dr Andersen, call me Bertie. We met at your demonstration."

"Yes, of course. I'm sorry, I'm pretty hopeless with names. And your secretary just gave me a place and a time. I half wondered if I was being fired!"

"Yes, I'm so sorry about that. Some things it's better to keep on the 'down-low', as they say, off the books. They do still say that, don't they? *Down-low?*"

"I expect so! Though, I have to admit, I'm not really up to speed on the latest demotic." *Demotic?* God, she sounds like an ageing Oxbridge don. *Relax!*

He gestures back to the lift. "I hope you don't mind, but I have a car waiting. I've planned a little trip."

"Oh, I thought – no, that's fine. Where are we going?"

"Just for a drive. We can have a spot of lunch on the way."

That still sounds ominous. "Well, as long as you're not taking me out into the woods to be shot!" He pulls a perplexed, semi-amused expression. *I am on fire today.*

"No, no. For that, we wouldn't stop for lunch," he smiles. "Though *I* might, afterward. Such things always seem to work up an appetite."

They set off in some bespoke, beautifully upholstered vehicle whose name and make are nowhere indicated and she feels intimidated to ask. She's half expecting a built-in bar – Morlock seems like he might be the sort – but there is merely an array of various high-end brands of bottled water, and a video screen separating the driver from the passengers – a human driver, at that – which currently shows the view through the front of the car, but is doubtless also capable of movies, games, or anything else he might want to display.

"We may talk freely," Morlock says. "It's soundproof," gesturing to the partition. Why should she care about that? He offers her some water.

They head south, from what she can tell, but her London geography isn't so great – the price of being a northerner. He, however, is from even farther afield, having an accent she can't quite place – definitely American, but not noticeably regional, with rather a clipped, almost elocutionary quality to it, like he'd been born and reared midair in the first-class cabin of a transatlantic flight. Perhaps, like his well-kept demeanour, the accent is also part of a mask, a makeover. She finds herself wondering what he was before, and what's beneath it now.

"So," he begins, the pleasantries dealt with, "how is Dr Sommeil?"

"He's … fine. Is that why I'm here?"

"To report on Michael? No, no. Just making small talk. It's been a while since I've seen him, that's all. He seems to be keeping to himself more and more these days."

"Well, yes," she says, somewhat defensively. "He's very busy – busier of late, as we move closer to the … uh…"

His eyes narrow. "Yes, that's all very exciting, isn't it? I've been meaning to ask, by the way. What would you say the project's chief goal *is*, exactly? What's MUNKi *for*, in your opinion?"

"For? What do you mean? The goal is to produce a personal robot, as I said at the demonstration. We have many industrial and service applications of robotics, but none of which attains the degree of … er … *personableness*" – *is that even a word?* – "that we think is possible. Something more…"

"Pet-like?"

"No, not – it should be much more than that. I mean…"

But he is teasing her, a well-practised twinkle in his eyes.

"And that's all?" He sips his water. "You wish to create a robot that is more human-like? With better social graces?"

"Well, not just that, but even that would be a big step. I mean, you can think of it as a child's toy if you wish, but what we're trying to accomplish here – the degree of autonomy, of *human-like* interaction – it's unprecedented."

"Of course, of course – I meant no belittlement. I'm a big fan." He smiles reassuringly. "I merely wondered: do you see any further potential in that?"

She thinks she sees where this is going. "Military, you mean."

"Oh Gerry, we've been developing military robots for years. We've got them coming out of our collective arse – if you'll excuse my *demotic*." He grins. "Automated weapons systems of all sorts, unmanned aerial vehicles, bomb disposal machines, surveillance drones the size of your fingernail – Lord, even guard dogs *that look like dogs*, if you can believe that."

She supposes she can. But as to who "we" are – "*our* arse," he'd said – does this mean he is Merrywhile's military liaison? She still knows no more about him than his name.

He sets down his water bottle into a purpose built holder. "It's not so much *what* it's applied to, but the *how* that we're interested in. As I said, we've got plenty of automated military applications – robots that will do a certain job, follow instructions, that – no offence – are far more technically advanced than your little guy. What we don't have is robots that will think for themselves. True AI."

"Isn't that rather counter-productive in the military?" she says. "Independent thought?"

He chuckles. "Well, yes, ordinarily. But what I mean is something you can *tell* to think on its feet, as it were. Imagine you're a soldier, and you're faced with a choice: to save a child caught in the middle of a firefight, or to concentrate on taking out the hostiles. Now, a human soldier, regardless of training, will be torn by this scenario – understandably. But a robot, with true AI – Artificial General Intelligence, as I believe it's called; correct me if I'm wrong – well, this could calculate the best outcome in a way the human soldier *never* could."

"Could it?"

"Well, for your average human soldier, it's head versus heart. I mean, protecting civilians is obviously a key goal within a battlefield setting, but there may be other strategic priorities – secure the hilltop, flank the enemy, whatever. My knowledge of military strategy begins and ends with *The Green Berets*, I'm afraid! But for an AI-driven robot, the emotional factor is removed, and it is simply a case of what overall strategic purpose either action would best serve. It's a utilitarian calculation, but a very well-informed one. Imagine: all the data, all the intel that the AI could process before making its decision – more than any human could, and incredibly more quickly."

She looks at him, how animated he has suddenly become – which, given the topic, starts to feel somewhat inappropriate.

"And because all the robots would be networked," he continues, "there could be *real-time* decision making based on what was actually happening on the ground across the whole theatre of operations, without need for centralised guidance."

"Automated war," she says.

"Well, yes, in a way. But with parameters set by us:" – *us?* – "acceptable losses, collateral damage, and so on. Casualties would be minimised, conflicts would be resolved more quickly and efficiently. It would be a whole new type of war, a game changer – like gunpowder, mechanisation, nuclear weapons. War 4.0, if you will."

Game-changer. So it's just a game to him? AI should lessen human suffering, not make it more "efficient". Then it suddenly occurs to her.

"Have you already spoken to Michael about this?"

"I've… Not for a little while."

And he told you to bugger off, I hope. And so you thought you'd try his deputy. What would he tempt her with? *All this could be yours.*

"You see, Dr Andersen – Gerry – the applications that we envisage aren't yet possible with the technology we have. The processing capacity required is just immense. However, if machines were to acquire what, in my layman's understanding, I'm calling *true* AI, become smart enough to design more efficient versions of themselves…"

"You're talking about the Singularity," she says. He smiles, happy that they are finally on the same page. "But you may as well be talking about the Second Coming, or aliens landing in Hyde Park. We have absolutely no idea of *when*, or *how*, or even *if*. I mean, for a start, if you define artificial general intelligence in terms of human-level competence, then arguably this should involve actual consciousness. And regarding that, we currently have no idea of—"

"Of course, of course. As I say, I am but a layman. I bow to your expertise." He doffs an imaginary hat. "But really, the details don't matter – whether a machine *really* 'thinks', or *truly* 'feels', or whatever, is unimportant to me. I mean, *consciousness* always seemed like a bit of an evolutionary indulgence, if you ask me! But irrespective of the philosophical niceties, machines possessed of such super-intelligence will not only be able to do whatever *we* can, but much, much *more*, and *better*, and all with a speed and power that we could utilise."

"Could we? That speed and power doesn't worry you?"

"Ah, Doctor, please don't tell me you're about to go all Skynet on me? Surely you don't believe in evil AI?"

This is the second time she's been accused of that.

"Not worried about that, no. Evil has always seemed to me a peculiarly human talent. But I do worry about things that we build that may slip out of our control; systems that we rely on, that come to define us, until we effectively end up serving *them*. I assume you know the story of the Golem? Or I guess the same point is also made by *The Sorcerer's Apprentice* – in case you're more of a Disney fan."

They've stopped at a nice little rural gastropub somewhere south of the city, not too far from Gatwick, she thinks – at least, she's glimpsed signs for the airport. The meal has been pleasant, she is surprised to find – pleasant company, that is (the food, of course – the venue probably researched and selected by some diligent minion – is excellent). After the increasingly tetchy discussion in the car, Morlock has played the good host, moving on to other, less contentious topics of conversation, not related to War 4.0 and the threat of Robogeddon.

So they talk about her family; she is not about to spill all on that topic, but it's nice to be asked without feeling grilled. They discuss her academic background and interests – has she always been into computers? As usual, having to explain she's more the engineering side. Where has she worked? Though really he must know, must have researched her. He, in return, opens up about himself a little. He is the son of old New-England money, Harvard Law, then Oxford – "Where I got this damn leg," referencing the limp she first noticed as they walked from the car. "Rowing accident, of all things!" Must have been a cox, then, she presumes, sizing up his physique. He speaks warmly of his own family; he has quite an extended brood. "You should come over sometime. I do a mean barbecue! Meet Billy – she'd love you." He admits to an appreciation of good food – hence the gastropub (not just to impress her, then), and (*who'da thunk it?*) a passion for collecting comic-book art. And here – "though I'm more of a *Tin Tin* man myself" – they even find some common ground: a shared appreciation of *Asterix* – the plucky little Gaulish village, holding out against Roman cultural hegemony with no more than pagan feasting and *joie de vivre* (well, and a little magic potion). What's not to love? It's also something her father had read with her as a girl; taking it in turns with the latest, lining them up in order of publication on their living-room bookshelf. Great, how comics could do that, bridge the generations. The books were thereafter always a reminder of him, of that time. Does Morlock know that? Has he found out about it, somehow? Though she's never told anyone, never written it down…

For Toutatis' sake, Gerry, stop being so paranoid. Isn't he just being nice?

As they leave, then, while she can't rule out that he is attempting to play her, her guard is … well, if not down, then at least lowered.

"Now, would you like to see something *special*?" he asks her, on their way back to the car.

Perhaps it's the suggestive tone, but she finds her eyes dropping involuntarily to his flies. "Is it your etchings?" She wishes she'd had one less glass of that nice *Chateau du Thingy*. "Sorry, I mean: your comic-art collection?"

He laughs. "Have no fear, Dr Andersen, I am happily married." As if in proof, he holds up his left hand, rotating an ornate golden band of Celtic knot-work around the ring finger with his thumb. *An eternal golden braid*. "Though, if you ever did wish to see it, I do have an original Uderzo."

"Then yes," she agrees, " – to the 'something special', I mean. Am I allowed to know what it is?"

"It can stay a surprise, if you'd wish? Would you prefer that?"

Possibly, for once, she would.

They drive east, past countryside towns and villages with names that she never thought English places could have – Kemsing, Plaxtol, Loose – their increasing strangeness unmooring her further from familiarity. Soon, she's lost what little bearings she'd retained, left in his hands entirely – or rather, the driver's, and therefore by proxy the built-in sat nav, which, judging by the leafy route it's taking them, has a mind of its own. Their debate is therefore redundant: the machines are already in control.

Eventually, following a drive down a winding lane with no places to turn off or into that she can see, they come to an entrance, half hidden by the growth of oak trees dropping down and shading it. They pass twin "No Entry" signs guarding the ingress – not specifying to what or to whom – though when, a few hundred yards further on, they stop before a striped barrier and sentry-box staffed by armed men in fatigues, she begins to connect the dots.

They drive on. But there is nothing – no airplane-hangar-sized development facility, no sprawling complex of low-rise buildings, half-camouflaged by woodland – and the ground for miles around is level and featureless. She looks across at Morlock, who smiles his easy smile, and nods out the window as they approach the next bend … and begin to descend.

"Underground?" she asks.

He nods again, smiling. "Got to keep the captured aliens somewhere."

Gerry signs in and is given a visitor's badge. Having manoeuvred the car into what she can only describe as an automated car-stacking machine (how many people work here, that they need to *stack* them?), their driver strolls off to a café-cum-lounge area, whistling tunelessly, a red tabloid masthead peeking out from the foldable electronic display tucked under his arm. Again, she wonders at the human presence, when so many cars are automated now – surely a temptation for the tech-loving Morlock. A sign of power, then, of conspicuous consumption of the needless? Or perhaps he also serves other uses: a man of the people, someone with whom Morlock can check the pulse of the populace; or some twitch-nerved ex-secret-forces type? Or even, for all his techno-fervour, perhaps Morlock is simply a little hypocritically unwilling to risk automated control of his fancy car on deer-haunted twisting country lanes.

They proceed to walk through various checkpoints, Morlock all the while maintaining a breezy chatter, outlining the history of the place, its design and construction, her badge providing a sop for each gate's pair of gargoyle-like guardians to scrutinise and scan, before nodding familiarly at Morlock and letting them both pass. And down they go, each level forming its own ring around what she occasionally glimpses is a central … pit? A large inverted cone of hollow space, anyway, descending into the earth point-downward. She wonders what's at its centre.

"It's not much farther now," he reassures her over his shoulder – his limp little in evidence, as she struggles to keep pace. He continues with his history lesson, and once through the next gate, instead of descending again they take a left and begin to progress along a gently curving corridor, marked at intervals with glass-panelled doors leading onto what look to be fairly standard workshops and labs. She snatches tantalising glimpses of a row of sophisticated-looking outsized microscopes on a bench, some disassembled mechanical appendages reflexing, a darkened room flickering fitfully with sparks. But his progress is relentless, his eyes unwaveringly on some deeper goal. Eventually, they approach a door that leads not to a lab, but another stairwell, descending down and back and fore, repeatedly, until finally depositing them into an open space in front of two large doors that seem to her, for some reason, much bigger and sturdier than they need to be.

What the hell's in there? A T-Rex?

"Doesn't anyone here believe in lifts?" she says.

"Well, I thought you'd appreciate the walking tour." He smiles. "And anyway, we're here now."

Before reaching the oversized doors, Morlock swerves to the right, through a small entrance and into a narrow corridor that slopes upward and brings them eventually out onto a broad terrace of seating surrounding a large circular arena. So now she knows what's at the bottom of the pit, anyway.

"I thought about the royal box," he says, "but I figured you'd prefer a groundling's view. More visceral."

She frowns back at him, and is about to ask what he means, when she begins to feel it: at first, a subtle rhythmic hum, then growing to an audible throb, periodic and regular, and getting louder and closer with each pulse. She removes her hands from the rail in front of her as the vibration begins to numb her palms and fingers with its intensity. With a thundering crescendo, as the oversized doors finally grind open, row upon row of gleaming metallic bodies march through in faultless formation, filing purposefully into the arena. Once they are all aligned, at some invisible signal each then turns to face them, raising its right arm in salute.

"Hail, Dr Andersen! Those who are about to die salute you!" they chant in terrifying unison.

Morlock turns to her and grins boyishly. "Sorry," he says. "Couldn't resist."

Much as Gerry hates to admit it, she is hugely impressed. He knows how to win a girl's heart, all right – a girl like her, anyway; not with fancy cars, comic art collections, nor wining and dining, but with kinetics, object-focused cognitive processing, and complex co-ordinated joint articulation.

"As you can see, we've concentrated more on physical aspects of development – speed, agility, and especially obstacle and projectile avoidance."

She *can* see that. It's incredible.

Apart from the obvious resemblance – the face and chest screens, the logo, even the styling of the body armour – *why is that?* – they are much taller than MUNKi, more "muscular", if that word is appropriate, and generally more frighteningly purposeful and intimidating. Beyond that, she hopes there's no deeper kinship; that her bookish, apple-proffering offspring and Morlock's hideous progeny do not share the same monstrous clockwork heart. But she can't deny the family resemblance.

Once assembled, the robots split up into teams, their allegiance reflected in the colour of their Merrywhile breast-logos, which shift accordingly from white to red or blue. They then run through a series of drills – or rather, spontaneous exercises, but so artful as to appear choreographed; a *dojo*, the *sensei* putting his pupils through their paces, pairing them off to spar. Though well armoured, the expense of each individual robot would be considerable, and so there is no forceful contact. A touch at a crucial location is enough to indicate a hit, a series of touches a victory, haptically incapacitating the opponent – assuming such an opponent were human, anyway.

All this she witnesses from among them – a groundling, as he'd suggested – closer, in fact, him leading the way, a drill sergeant inspecting the troops. Having finished with hand-to-hand, they move on to weapons: first, sticks (or what appear to be foam-covered poles); then … *nunchucks*, is it? – anyway, various impact-softened equivalents of martial arts implements.

"We should probably retire for the next stage," he says, gesturing back to the terrace. They reascend the steps, walking to the back row, then edge along to a glass-fronted viewing box, similar to the kind of corporate hospitality suite she's been dragged along to at Old Trafford or Aintree, or some other arena for a spectacle she has no interest in. *This*, however, she's finding quite fascinating.

"This next bit can get a bit hectic," Morlock says. "Not, you know, *unsafe*; just, well, hectic."

The sparring has been replaced by a different scenario – "a little game," he says, which is a variation of Capture the Flag, each team seeking to defend its own "base" (with symbolic but also actual red or blue flag), while trying to capture the other's. Difficult to do, she thinks – gain without losing. When all war is essentially a lose-lose activity, a negative-sum game – but not to Morlock and his ilk, for whom war is winnable. How had he phrased it in the car? *Acceptable losses.*

The robots carry in various obstacles and barriers, lifting them effortlessly as balsa wood (perhaps they are). Once set up, the arena resembles a very curious playground: tall things and squat things, things with holes and ledges, things that can be climbed for vantage, or sheltered behind for cover. When the action finally begins, she sees why they've retreated behind the glass.

"We can't use real ammunition, of course, but we wanted to simulate combat with something a bit more realistic. Laser weapons don't have the same recoil, so we didn't want that – unless we're simulating laser battle, that is. And the only other option was paint-ball – too messy. So we settled for peas."

Suddenly, the air resounds with *ptchew* and *ratatatat*, the tinny retort of old cowboy or gangster movies, as the "peas" zing and ping around the arena, occasionally bouncing off the window of their viewing box.

"They're not actually peas, you know; we just call them that. It's some type of suitably hefty polymer, I believe, with an equivalent aerodynamic profile. Doesn't cause any damage, just a smudge on the casing – which buffs right out!"

Like he's selling a car, a kitchen appliance.

The details of the battle unfold on screens placed along the top of the glass window, displaying different angles and close-ups, keeping score. He might call it a "game", but there is nothing playful about these gamers, no kitten-like gambolling or exploration for its own sake, only a coldly unwavering purpose.

Given the arena's size and the skill of the combatants, the games are quite short – about a couple of minutes each. The first produces a win for the red team – just; the second for blue, the third too, then red again. Draws not allowed, this pattern more or less repeats itself – meaninglessly, she realises, like heads or tails, for it is evident the two teams are evenly matched; no doubt running the same software, the same strategies, even. It is little better than noughts and crosses.

"What's the point of this?" she asks.

"I … I'm sorry?" For the first time that day, it is his turn to be taken off guard.

"I mean, why run a simulation where the only difference between the teams is determined by chance?"

His look begins to soften: *Clever girl.* He smiles.

"I knew you would not disappoint, Dr Andersen."

On the screens above their heads, he isolates incidents in the footage of gameplay, zooming in, rewinding, slowing down, illustrating his points as he talks.

"We wanted the players to learn – *player*, I should say, for all this" – he sweeps his arm across the screens – "is really just the same AI, deploying its own proxies against itself; shielding its cards from its own gaze, as it were, trying to second-guess its own best hand. The result – as you've observed – is rather pointless. But what were we to do? The AI had long passed the point where *we* could present a challenge to it. SAS and Navy Seal, Mossad – we tried them all. Even gave them the same hardware, put them in remote control VR rigs. (Tried it once. Made me sick.) But it made no difference. The robots whupped them almost every time. And when they didn't, they'd learn until they did. Even at five-a-side soccer!" He laughed. "But with this, we've reached something of an impasse. Chipping brains, rescripting neurochemistry – that's all coming to an end, I'm afraid." *Coming to an* end*!* "No, Dr Andersen, our true enemy is not some other *human* army, but *this*." He gestures again to their surroundings. "What we're doing here, but done by *someone else*, wherever that may be. Some bunker in Bangalore, Seoul, under the Mongolian Steppe – who knows? Our *real* enemy is progress itself." He shrugs – *what can you do?* "We're engaged in a preventative war against the future."

He gives a sad little smile. She almost laughs. Is she meant to feel *pity*? Poor Morlock and his doomsday toys? *Preventative war*: an Orwellian phrase, if ever there was one. But all he wants to do is beat all the other kids! And realign the global order! It's so unfair!

"The victories," he continues, "as you've pointed out, owe more to random factors than superior strategy by either team. In fact, that's the problem: they're *not* a team. Look."

He motions up to the display screen where he asks the AI to replay specific sections from the last battle.

"Our robots have superior strength, speed, agility, accuracy, information processing, and so on. However, the one area where the human agents still have an advantage is teamwork. Of course, the AI can impose a strategy – *top down*, as I believe you say – tell each robot what to do, what part to play. 'Advance on that hill!' 'Secure that ridge!' Or whatever. Which is what it's doing now; imposing strategies. But that slows them down, makes them rigid. Still faster than their human equivalent; but as I say, that's not the issue."

He turns to her. "What makes a good soldier?" he asks.

"Er … following orders?"

"Precisely. But again, that's *top-down* thinking. Imposing patterns from above. Useful, to have an overall picture, but modern warfare is also in the details, down at ground level – *bottom-up*. Remember our child caught in the crossfire? These days, wars don't take place on battlefields, but in cities, civilian areas. Drones will only get you so far. And you can't just drop a bomb on people any more." He sounds almost wistful. "You have to get your hands dirty. Now, what makes a good human?"

"Um … *not* killing people?"

"No!" He rolls his eyes, laughing indulgently. "I mean, what might be the *problem* with just following orders?"

"Oh, I see. Well, following rules too rigidly can stifle independent thought and innovation, stop you from thinking on your feet. Also, it leads to ethical deterioration, because indep—"

"Yes! That's *right*! *Thinking on your feet*. Now, imagine a robot soldier that could do both: think on his own two feet, responding real-time to all those pesky little *butterfly effects*" – smiling, nodding, talking what he thinks is her talk, looking to her for approval – "but *also* benefiting from the overall picture, the global perspective. So, top-down *and* bottom-up!" He turns back toward the display. "But the problem is that this doesn't seem to be happening. The moment we switch from centralised control, the level of co-operation deteriorates. War, it turns out, is more complicated than soccer."

She looks out at the assembled killing machines. Why always red and blue? How people like him love their polarities, their binaries. All independently pursuing their own murderous self-interest, with no invisible hand to guide them. "But you can't be surprised, surely?" she says. "You create a group of egocentric individuals and then wonder why they don't work as a team?"

"Why not?" he says, defensive now. "Think of ants: one ant does its thing, the next ant does *its* thing, and eventually, without any single ant actually *intending* to, you have a colony, all performing holistically and purposefully."

"Yes, but ants aren't set on world domination. It's co-operation, not competition."

"Well, you obviously haven't been in *my* garden! But come, now, Doctor. You're a scientist! Selfishness is in the genes! Survival of the fittest, and all that. Co-operation is just another name for enlightened self-interest."

"Even if that's true, the goal is different. Where is the ultimate self-interest in war? Measured against the risk? That's why some crabs have enormous claws, why stags have impressive antlers: to make a great display. It's so they *don't have to* fight. Or at least, only as a last resort. But what you're talking of here is not even a first response; it's *pre-emptive*."

"The battle for resources? Isn't that the basis of evolution, of prog—"

"Yes, but why should it continue to be? Can't we *evolve* beyond that? Beyond personal greed? Why must we always be valuing *things* over *people*?"

"Dear Doctor, I think you'll find that the whole of history is nothing but the record of our tendency to value things over people."

He sighs, as if realising it is pointless to antagonise her further. So much effort, so much charm expended, and he is undoing it now, without having got what he wants. He smiles his charming smile – a display of expensive dentistry more heavily armed than disarming – before changing tack.

"But anyway. Tell me about MUNKi. I understand that it works differently? Are his protocols truly 'bottom-up'?"

She nods. But MUNKi's goal is human interaction, communication, the sharing of knowledge. He's a knowledge-bot, not a kill-bot. She gives him a broad outline, what they've learnt from the previous iterations, but finds herself being evasive, sticking to generalities, realising the thing she least wants to do, now, is to fuel the schemes of this … this despicable man.

The outing has run its course. They are worlds apart: she – in his eyes – an idealist, a card-carrying citizen of La-La Land; he, a "realist" – as he no doubt sees himself – whose pragmatism is without qualm. In the game of trust that is the basis of life, she would always co-operate, he would always defect.

By the time she gets back, having made non-committal noises to the assurance he sought that she would "keep in touch", Gerry has decided not to tell Sommeil about Morlock's approach. It would only make him more anxious, and there was enough of that flying around already. And it wouldn't exactly be a surprise: as they'd already discussed, the threat of military sell-out is something that could hang over any of Merrywhile's technology projects with relevant application. However, it would be added pressure – the fact that Morlock is upping his persistence, now, looking for weaknesses, points of access in the project staff. Has he approached Zac, yet?

As the project leader, Sommeil still has chief say on whether or not his own work has any other applications – chief, but not perhaps final and absolute say, especially if the war council decides to disobey the chief, it being years since even his grandfather possessed absolute control over the company's affairs.

But all this side-drama is really just an unwelcome distraction from their increasingly fraught efforts to stabilise MUNKi's behaviour, which is only becoming more erratic.

Or maybe not. Instead of a distraction, maybe this is actually the main debate. She's already sacrificed so much: relationships, family, a normal life – any life at all. She eats, sleeps and dreams the project, missing meals, surviving on processed junk and coffee, popping pills to push through headaches and exhaustion. And he is worse than she. What was once passion, curiosity, intellectual adventure, has been reduced to a trance-like trudge toward some ever-distant star. And in their devotion to this … this – for all they know – *mirage*, have they both taken their eyes off the broader consequences of what they are trying to achieve?

Prior to Morlock's approach, she'd put her concerns to one side. Every technology has its nefarious applications. And should we stop some promising line of research simply because, at some point, someone will use it to make a weapon, or a virus? If *we* don't do this, someone else *will*, and then…

But this was all cliché, the same tired old justifications that had been wheeled out by similarly driven and dreamy-eyed prophets of progress – people, she is coming to realise, like Sommeil and herself – bent only on reaching their own personal promised land. She has been so short sighted. She's had doubts before, vague worries that she's swatted away, the nuisance scruples of an over-active conscience, as she's told herself. But these have never really gone away, and the meeting with Morlock has merely served to increase them; and now, they are a swarm. Now, when she fantasises – as sometimes she still allows herself to do, in guilty anticipation pre-counting the hatched eggs of their future success – she no longer sees row upon row of boxed little MUNKis sitting all shiny and cute along the shelves of the toy shops of the world, sees homework buddies and playmates in the libraries and kindergartens. She sees a swelling army of Morlock-bots, mean and determined, *gremlins* to his *mogwai*, advancing in pitiless procession upon their yet-to-be-named foes, the red or blue team of the future. Reassuring, perhaps, if you control them, if you are Us and not Them, standing behind the flag of the right colour; but not so much for those whom the accidents of history and birth have placed behind the incorrectly coloured banner. And what if – should he ever fulfil his potential – MUNKi were to be used for *that*? Would she stand by and let it happen? Or do something to stop it?

Musca Domestica

"I very much enjoyed your talk, Dr Sommeil," she had said. "Thank you, Ms…" – he'd scanned her name badge – "Faith."

"Mel, please."

"Then you must call me Michael. Researcher?"

"Journalist."

"For?"

"Freelance."

"Ah, aren't we all, these days."

Well, you're *not*.

"I wonder if you might be free to answer a few questions?"

"Certainly. I have…" – he'd checked the time on his phone – "fifteen minutes? Is that enough? Sorry, I have a plane waiting to take me back to Rome."

"Yes, that's great. Do you mind if I…?" He'd shaken his head and she'd activated an app on her own phone that would quietly set about transcribing their interaction, scrolling by live on its little screen.

> FAI: So, Dr Sommeil, do you agree with the transhumanists? That "Man is something that

must be overcome"? Always sounded like a rallying cry for a robot revolution, to me!

SOM: [laughs] Well, that's Nietzsche, I think, isn't it? Not sure he would have seen "overcoming" in technological terms. But I don't think we need worry about the robot revolution. Technology will aid, not replace us. Broadly, as I've said, technological progress will change who we are – that's a fact. However, I'd prefer to say that, "Man – humanity – is something that can be augmented". That's a better slogan, I think. Change, growth, augmentation, not extinction. No robot uprising! No robo-Frankenstein!

FAI: He was the creator.

SOM: [coughs] Sorry? Who?

FAI: Frankenstein was the creator's name. The creature had none.

SOM: Oh! Right! Well, I bow to your literary knowledge. Gothic novels – not really my thing.

FAI: And what about those who don't embrace these changes? What if, say, I'm happy with who I am, or if I don't want to be … augmented?

SOM: Look, it's not as if I … as if someone is foisting these changes on people. We won't be forcibly implanting chips in people's heads or anything. And as I—

FAI: Well, you might not be.

SOM: —said, progress by itself will bring changes, and people must see that they can't just stop the future because they don't like it.

FAI: But there are obvious challenges, aren't there? I mean, mass unemployment, the deskilling of the labour force, wage decline. What about those who see developments in robotics and AI as actually harmful to—

SOM: Well, if you want to talk about harm, then technology has done – is doing – much more good than harm. Would you prefer we go back to an age without penicillin? To drilling holes in people's heads to let the bad spirits out? Which is also a form of technology, by the way. And, in terms of human history, well, technological progress is only really just getting going. Up until relatively recently we'd had only centuries of dogma and superstition, religious bigotry, hundreds of years of – there was the Dark Ages, remember! – which—

FAI: Good lord, Dr Sommeil! How old do you think I am! [laughs] But you're not saying that there are no down-sides to such developments, surely?

SOM: Well, of course… [sighs] Look, I know what you're getting at. If you look at it historically, any new technology has teething problems, unanticipated consequences. And no technology is ever wholly good in its effects, because … well, human beings aren't wholly good. Take genetics: someone will try to cure cancer, somebody else will try to … engineer a virus. Even the printing press – think of all the things that have been printed, for good and bad! But that's the point: technology itself is neutral, so the onus lies on human beings to regulate it properly. But things will march on. You can't deal with the problems technology throws up by just wishing it away. I mean, you can't now put the genie back in the bottle.

FAI: But you can, surely?

SOM: Sorry?

FAI: Put it back in the bottle – the genie. If you control it. Perhaps you mean that you can't un-open Pandora's box?

SOM: I, er … well, I think that's a rather negative way of seeing things. We don't have to… Look, I'm a bit, er, pressed for time, Mel … can we…?

FAI: Of course, Dr Sommeil. One last question. Apart from augmentation, one of the central focuses of transhumanism is on the extension and preservation of human life. You've got gene manipulation, nanotechnology, artificial limbs and organs – and of course the digital aspect, memory preservation, mind uploading and such. Now, a number of transhumanism's key players – yourself included – have suffered personal tragedy. How big a motivational role do you think that has played in drawing you into the movement?

SOM: Um … I don't… [coughs] I think, obviously, we would all like to live longer… [sighs] Really, I'm quite pressed… I think… I'm sorry, Mel, but I really mustn't miss my plane. Is that OK? I'm truly sorry. If you need more, please contact my press office?

FAI: Yes, yes, of course. You must make your flight. Thank you for your time, Dr Sommeil.

She switches off the playback.

She's surprised at just how earnest she'd sounded; and how ballsy – interrupting him, contradicting him, pushing back, Champion of the Fourth Estate (or is it the Fifth, now?). It feels like a lifetime away. And yet, how many years was it? After the techno-golem piece, anyway – which she'd struggled to place anywhere. No real surprise there. No one is interested in lengthy corporate exposés any more, even then, especially when the whole thing read like some undergraduate fucking dissertation.

Earnest.

She'd hoped the interview would form the basis for something saleable; a puff piece, at the very least – "Don't Fear the Robot Revolution, says Merrywhile's Michael Sommeil". Or, combined with a broader overview of the conference itself, something more serious, a critical commentary on robotics, automation, AI and job loss. Something that might make a feature for one of the popular science and technology magazines; or even for one of the broadsheets, what remained of them. Then perhaps to use that as a cornerstone for similar pieces, to build her portfolio, and ultimately her reputation: "Mel Faith, Serious Tech Commentator Lady" (maybe 'Amelia'?).

But there'd been something else there, hadn't there? Some deeper story. She'd sensed it at the time; can still sense it. That's what had kept her coming back to it, over the years, like some grizzled old gumshoe haunted by the same old cold case. It would be a good while before she'd finally started to get it out of her system; a good while longer before she fully realised that she'd been barking up the wrong tree – at least in terms of her career (barking up the wrong ladder?). When she'd finally spiked it – finally swapped earnest for earning a living – she'd moved on to the type of stuff her father had despised even more. Eventually, she'd expunged all traces of it – from her CV, even her website. It was like that part of her had never existed.

And now here she is: living. Sleep denied, smoking in her pyjamas with the dregs of last night's red, listening to old recordings and waiting for the sun to come up. Not quite how she'd pictured middle age – not the oldest stringer in town just yet, but more and more looking like it was a fate she will struggle to avoid.

It's the girl's fault. Bringing it all back up. Why had she even agreed to the meeting? Even dragged her arse all the way to Swansea.

Damn her.

Cari pauses at the top of the stairs leading to the university library's study areas and looks at the old poster.

"Feeling overwhelmed?" it reads. "Don't let work get on top of you!"

Above details of how to enrol for study skills sessions, the poster depicts a beautiful, athletic man, a drape of cloth shy of complete nakedness, bearing down imperiously upon a writhing creature below him – half-man, half serpent – who looks up in fear and supplication at the exquisitely pointed spear reared above him.

It's a photo of a statue by John Flaxman, she's found out – *St Michael Overcoming Satan* – and so she knows that it is Michael that the sculptor intended us to cheer for. Curious, then, that the librarians – who should really know better – have allotted him the role of oppressor, and so implying that it is Satan who should receive our sympathies. Someone's wry comment on imperialism, possibly, of knowledge oppressed by faith, or maybe it's just an indication of what the staff *really* think of students. But she's probably overthinking it, and some bored graphics guy in student services just thought it would be funny. Whatever the case, who wouldn't be Team Michael? There's just something about that Satan guy that seems a bit off.

Often, as she walks past the poster, semi-consciously she carries the frozen struggle with her, unpausing it in her imagination as, wandering among the shelves, it supplies some barely registered vehicle for the playing out of her own half-submerged anxieties, which seem these days never completely to leave her. The crux of her concerns is that, assured as Michael's victory appears, poised to strike the final blow, she finds herself worrying about the tail: its thickness, the supple strength of it, how sinuously it coils and curls around the stump of the tree over which the archangel stands; how Satan's fear seems almost feigned, a feint, as if with but a flick, a twist, the tables will soon turn.

"The thesis hasn't been digitised yet, I'm afraid," the librarian tells her, "so we'll have to get it on interlibrary loan. Should be a few days; a week, max. Is that OK?"

"Yes, that's fine. And the article? I can't seem to find that journal on the main shelves."

"Ah, that's because it's discontinued. Old copies will be in the stacks. Also not digitised. I'll have to get that for you. You can come with me, if you like?"

They head down into the bowels of the past, through areas to which not only digitisation, but also the estates department owes an overdue visit, passing walls peeling of paint the colour of which thirty years have not seen in fashion, all the while the librarian feeling obliged to maintain a peppy stream of nervous commentary not unbefitting a serial killer.

"Not many people come down here! Mind you, probably just as well. Unlike everywhere else, there're no cameras, yet. You have a heart attack, or a shelf falls on you, nobody might notice for months! Probably shouldn't have told you that."

They turn a corner and descend another flight of stairs, and are finally presented with what Cari can only describe as a cage, into which is set a painted-grey steel door. The woman fusses with her bunch of keys ("Now, perhaps *this* one…?"), and finally with a clank and a creak ushers her into a long dusty space taken up by row upon row of high and tightly-packed shelves, which for some reason remind Cari of a storeroom in a shoe shop.

"Right, so we want … *The New Linguistic Review*, wasn't it? Volume 25…"

"Number 2."

"25, number 2…"

Tadcu had studied at UCL for his BA, followed by

Goldsmiths for his PhD. Aside from the thesis, which was never published (unless you count the copy kept by his uni), the only other mention of him that she can find is a single journal article, which is actually more an interview-cum-profile-piece relating to his work with Merrywhile, and for which some diligent librarian (bless them) had indexed and key-worded not only the subject matter, but also the interviewees' names, and among which is listed one Dr Myrddin Edwards.

Then, as now, Merrywhile had been keen to rope in a wide variety of disciplines in furtherance of its lofty technological ambitions. The article writer had interviewed a selection of these. Aside from Tadcu himself, there was a physicist, a biologist, an economist, a mathematician, even an artist, the roll call extending into a diverse double-figured group, all of whom were involved in something called "Project MUNKi".

"And what does MUNKi stand for?" I ask.

"Malfunctioning Umbrellas Need Keeping Inside," replies artist Mina Boucher, to some laughter.

"Ignore her," advises the physicist, Dr Karl Nielsberg. "She's a surrealist."

"Oh! I've got a better one!" Mina continues. "Merrywhile Unveils New Kash-making Initiative!"

"*Errrgh!*" Karl laughs, depressing an imaginary buzzer. "Objection: *Kash*-making?"

They might not agree on what it stands for, but the light-hearted banter disguises a serious purpose. Which is what? I ask this of Dr Myrddin Edwards, the project's linguistics expert.

"Well, if you want a technological account of what we're trying to achieve, then you've asked the wrong person, I'm afraid, as that's not really my background. And the same can be said of many of those here – which is really the point. In working to develop a framework for artificial intelligence, it's important that this isn't a one-sided enterprise – we shouldn't just leave it to the boffins," looking over mock-meaningfully to Dr Nielsberg. "I mean, it's likely that, in future decades, machines will surpass human abilities in many fields.

As they become more powerful, it's important that they don't simply embody cold, Spock-like logic, but also those warmer, non-rational qualities that make us fully human – creativity, empathy, humour."

"Anger? Greed?"

"Well," he laughs, "as it's our creation, I think we'll be in a position to edit the genome a little."

He might have been working for the evil Empire, but at least Tadcu was trying to ensure the Death Star had disabled access, a crèche, and decent veggie options in the staff canteen. The article flows around a couple of grainy black and white photographs, one of the whole team, helpfully tagging each of its members – and there he is, bottom row, third from the right. But as to what precisely he did there, and why he'd eventually resigned, the article leaves her none the wiser.

But nor, frustratingly, is this something settled by the arrival of the thesis – *The Case for Innate Morphological Capacity* – which, she guesses, is 1980s academic high-jargon for "please give me a permanent contract". It is dense stuff – an obscure branch of linguistics, a subject which Cari is already keen to sidestep where possible in her own studies – but she struggles gamely through it, trying at least to get a gist.

The best she can manage is that he appears to be saying there's an inherent structure to language that bootstraps intelligence; even, it hypothesises – "though I leave the exploration of this conjecture to my colleagues in anthropology" – that human language may have evolved due to an *actual* virus that spread through primitive man. The conclusion branches out into possible applications of this theory, which include his musings on the possibility of artificial general intelligence. Rather than trying to get a computer to model human intelligence, he argues, or teach it how to think, better results may be obtained by developing an algorithm that models the evolution of human language. By cracking the code that drives this "linguistic virus", we can then use it to create truly intelligent machines.

Suddenly, she could see why Merrywhile were so interested in him.

The sun is almost up.

Mel is also surprised at how much younger she'd sounded. Something about the timbre of the voice? Less husky. But more spritely, too, more alive. It wasn't the smoking killed that.

She was also horrified to realise just how much intimate detail she knew about someone she'd met only once, and that for only ten minutes. There was a word for that. Also a course of legal redress.

She unpauses the audio.

Right, so what do we have…?

Sommeil. What's that? *French.* Huguenot stock, no less. Whatever that means. Must look it up… Anyway, his French father's surname, dad marrying into the Mayer family fortune – to *Catherine*, not so fresh off the shelf by then, but besmitten with this semi-vagrant artist type some … *fourteen years* her junior! Go Catherine! Grandad Mayer none too happy with this, his little princess slumming it with a boho Frenchy. But the heart wants what the heart wants, right? It has its own blind reasons. As do the loins. (Why "loins"? Why not "groin"? You get loins of beef, don't you? God, what have I been eating…)

Right, Grandad Mayer was … fingers and toes … forty-eight when Catherine is born? Older dads are always so protective; too crusty to empathise with the passions of youth.

So, a – well, not *quite* a society wedding (did Mayer try to buy dad off?). Papa Sommeil dutifully hangs around to see *petit Michel* pop out (named, *naturellement*, after Papa himself, the little *bon viveur* egotist), then duly buggers off to continue his life of art-infused debauch on the old man's tab, with the love-struck Catherine in doe-eyed tow. Silly deer.

A few years go by. Sommeil senior (*quelle surprise*) takes

his Jim Morrison impression a hit too far, buying the big D with the big H. Not to be outdone, Catherine, also chasing the dragon, follows it all the way to … Morocco, where the locals, tracking his piercing cry, find her five-year-old son next to her three-day-old corpse, leaving the now orphaned Michel Junior heir to a vast fortune – *stroke* – with an origin story befitting a serial killer – *stroke* – superhero – *stroke* – evil genius (*asterisk* – delete as appropriate).

Right, re-enter Grandad Mayer, who is … how old, now? *When* does he die? *Does* he die? Anyway, Grandad, apparently still alive, but too late now for *rapprochement* with the daughter, swoops in and rescues little M, sets him on his knee, makes everything better; changes his *name*, anglicises it – Mich-*el* becomes Mich-*ael* – thus partly reclaiming the lad from the wicked Frenchies for Manchester, England and St. George.

She pauses playback again, tips the remnants of the oxidised Cab Sav down the sink, and fills the kettle to make coffee.

What had she wanted from all of this, at the time? Michael Sommeil's tragic backstory was more or less common knowledge – in broad and shadowy outline, at least. But it was only when she'd begun to look into the actual details that she'd realised the closet's skeletons were so many and so juicy. Why had no one run it already? Out of respect? Dubious. Fear? More likely. She pictures Merrywhile, SPECTRE-like, its tendrils in everything, manipulating, threatening, silencing, hands on shoulders and whispers in ears. And that would be true to some limited extent, of course. What powerful people *didn't* try to manage their PR, to spin their image, and use their connections to do it? But the Mayers and Sommeils of this world were deeply connected in ways that could steer your professional life into a ditch. The more high-minded and principled of her fellow newshounds might publicly laugh off such a suggestion, but all ultimately danced to the tune of the paymasters. There isn't a hack alive, nor their employer, that would risk pissing off such people without some very, very good reason. So maybe then, especially as the years passed, her colleagues had ignored it simply because that reason just wasn't good enough. It was old news, with trouble attached. Then why had *she* continued to pursue it?

These recordings documented a transitional period, during which the nature of her interest in Sommeil had gradually changed. It was here that part of her had first begun to move away from her high-flown pontifications on technology and corporate corruption – her "techno-golem" phase, as she now thought of it – toward something with a broader appeal, something more career-, more self-serving. She had still tried to convince herself that what she was doing was in some sense noble or professionally justified, that it was in the Public Interest, and that if he would just submit to the full sit-down, if she could just get the whole thing from the horse's mouth, then… But the simple truth was, for a reason she still can't quite fathom, she'd just found herself becoming a little unprofessionally obsessed with him. Why *was* that?

And anyway, even if it *had* been the golden career ticket she'd tried to persuade herself it was, the more she read, the deeper she dug, the more she'd realised that the horse would refuse. Trigger wouldn't *want* to go over it all again. It wouldn't be an interview; it would be trauma therapy. Which is what the public wants to hear, of course; what sells.

Juicy closets.

The boy.

That was the key to it all, she'd thought – the terrified little kid he'd once been; that was still there now, somewhere, still hiding inside the adult costume. If she could get at *that*, she was sure, then the whole story would open up, reveal itself. The boy is father to the man, and she had worked back and forth, using each to cast light on the other – cause to effect, effect to cause – trying to understand the nature of the phenomenon. Only it hadn't – opened up. Something was still missing; it just wouldn't all fall into place. Sommeil was a black box, both then and now. A box without a key.

She switches the audio back on, leafing through her old notes as her younger self narrates.

Ok, so... Grandad Mayer sends the boy to boarding school – not Gordons-*toon*, or Eton, or any other badge of privilege, but still a good, ridiculously expensive private establishment: Mill's Academy of North Yorkshire. Let's see ... what kind of place is this... No obvious religious affiliations; quite secular, in fact, if it hasn't changed in character. OK, so the website says... "Assemblies are philosophical in nature, encouraging each student's original response to life's big questions, whilst drawing on the rich tradition of humanistic...", blah, blah, blah. Humanism. Godless religion. Seems significant, though; a deliberate choice.

But why boarding school? Hadn't the poor kid suffered enough? Emotional cold-turkey to cold-shower the mother-love out of him, maybe. Can't be having a sissy scion to the Merrywhile empire. How does the trauma-laden little lad cope? Difficult to say. Bedwetting? Followed by shame and humiliation? But they would have been more progressive than that, more enlightened; sent him to the school counsellor, maybe – school like that probably had one. But difficult to find out. Would have to hack the records, if any of that info is still kept. (Who was the guy the sports ed said got him that stuff in the footballer bondage case?)

But anyway, bedwetter or not, little Michael does OK. Some record of awards – physics, maths, computers (of course) – a proper little science geek. Oh and look! He built a robot! And here he is, in *The Yorkshire Intelligencer*, no less (why don't they give newspapers names like that any more?). Ha. Looks like a metallic teddybear. Something technological to cuddle at night. No mention of his family connections, of Merrywhile. Was Gramps still censoring even then? No, Gramps had kicked the big one in ... Ooh, one shy of raising his bat to the pavilion. Bummer. Still, the old man's imprint is firmly in place by this time – Project Posterity successfully underway – and now little Mikey just needs properly tooling up before heading off to slay the dragon of ignorance.

So, GCSEs, then A-levels. Stellar grades, an orphan's scholarship (not that he really needed one – *unless* gramps had stiffed him in his will, refusing to subsidise, wanting him to pay his *own* way…?). And then off to… ah, Manchester, of course. Alma mater of mater's pater. No Oxbridge or Ivy League, no Silver Spoon University or intro to the Old Boy's Club. The lad must get there on his own steam. Mayer's ghostly influence or the boy's own idea, I wonder? Homage to grandad, maybe? Again, difficult to know.

Black box.

Sommeil had then moved on through university, following much the same route as his grandfather – though of course, there'd been no computing in the old man's day, nor any genetics to speak of. But in spirit little Michael was a throwback, eschewing the arty life that had served his ma and pa so ill, and setting his feet on the solid ground of empirical enquiry.

Mayer's plan to groom his grandson for a key place in the company was apparently a complete success. She'd looked for signs of rebellion, of bucking the burden of grandfilial duty, yet there were none. But again, with only the outward signs of apparent obedience, she'd nothing to go on but suspicion, the admittedly subjective feeling that, had *she* been in that position, had *she* been required to bite the bit so tightly, to trot on so neatly, on such a tight rein… He wasn't Mel, evidently, but she'd still retained those suspicions, that hope of surreptitious mental insurrection. Behaviour could fool you, after all, hiding secret beliefs and desires deep beneath some super-spartan mask.

And here, finally, she'd arrived at the crux, what was surely Sommeil's defining moment.

As much as we might like to think otherwise, it's suffering that shapes us. Beautiful sunsets and ravishing vistas, romantic love, the birth of babies, heart-warming compassion and heroism – well, that might be fine for greetings card verses and sappy granny lit, but all these are really just a warm-up for the main act. And it's what survives *that* – or not – that really stamps our card.

But he'd been trained well, this super-spartan, was well schooled – even before Hogwarts – in burying his emotions, keeping a lid on the bubbling panic of madness and grief. So when tragedy struck, it was not a stranger, merely an old and unwelcome acquaintance, dropping by on a surprise visit – though perhaps they had never completely lost touch.

They'd married quite quickly, having met during Michael's post-doc research in Rome. Eurydice was bright, a beautiful French girl, a geneticist, light-hearted and fun, by all accounts, full of stereotypical *joie de vivre* (the latter, especially, a much needed quality in the life of such a serious young man). Grandad had been out of the picture for some time by then, and Sommeil, his spirits lightened, must have glimpsed a new life – (*ah*, here *we go…!*) – and seized the opportunity to break with heredity, to step out of the shadow of posterity and turn his back on Merrywhile. As they'd house-hunted, nested, laying down roots and flexing their wings, things must have looked rosy. They were in love, they were following their passions, they had a child – what more could he want? But the old goat was not done with him yet, even from beyond the grave.

Fate gave no warning. Blind-sided on the school run, victim of a faulty traffic light – a failure of technology, ironically, the very thing he now hoped would save us all – Eurydice was killed instantly, and the boy, just eight years old, slipped immediately into a coma, from which he never awoke.

And from there, things again went dark. Retreating back into his black box, Sommeil disappeared – physically, emotionally, an extended leave of absence from his outward show of self that saw him gradually slip from public eye and memory. When eventually he did re-emerge – became again the man she had later interviewed – the calm, cool exterior had reasserted itself, the spartan mask back in place.

And that, as they say, was that. The End. The leads dried

up, the path petered out into untrodden wilderness, and though she'd still sensed there was some piece missing, some key that might yet unlock everything, the unspoken something that had driven Mel on finally ran out of gas.

And now, all these years later, she finally sees what had bugged her.

Despite her most philanthropically brutal attempts at dissuasion, the girl had emailed her again.

"Found this and thought of you. Know you said to leave it. Guess you're probably not interested any more. Here it is anyway. Cari."

Kids. Whatever happened to fully formed sentences? Are subject pronouns uncool? They use an apostrophe and they expect a commendation from the Grammar Society.

She'd scanned the article with casual interest.

Project MUNKi.

The technical stuff was either beyond her or outdated. The group was a ragtag band of outliers and misfits, given pocket money to play at future building. But then she was stopped short. It was just a small photo – a young boy being given a tour of the project, inspecting its computers and gadgetry. He wasn't named – the trite caption merely read: "Merrywhile's Herbert Morlock gives youth a tour of the future" – but she would have recognised him anywhere.

Ça fait longtemps, cher Michel.

And somehow, it is this that had triggered it. How had she missed it, all those years ago? Perhaps there'd been a gap in her records, or perhaps it simply hadn't been publicly stated, but the old vague and unformed suspicion had suddenly become a hand, tugging insistently at her sleeve; a voice, with – stupid though it might yet prove – a simple and fully formed question.

The boy is father to the man; but the man is also father to the boy.

What had happened to *that* boy?

She'd been focusing on the wrong Sommeil.

From the moment she opens the warehouse door, Cari is hit by a wall of cacophony, an assault of primary colours and the waft of deep fried fat. Has she gotten the right place?

Some days after she'd sent her a scanned photocopy of the article, she'd received an email back from the journalist.

"Dear CARI," it began. *Surely getting someone's name right shouldn't be a cause for passive-aggressive caps.* "I've had some further thoughts. Lunch? On me. Neutral ground? Somewhere the café owner doesn't hate me. Mel."

She leans back outside to look up at the sign: *Ballmageddon.* She'd thought it a curious name for a café or restaurant, but hadn't quite pictured *this*. Anyway, the geo-location on her phone telling her it's the correct address – a warehouse on an industrial estate just outside Newport – she goes back inside.

Evidently, it is aptly named. Balls indeed there are, and aplenty. They are mostly of the hollow plastic variety, filling up "pools", where they are rolled on, waded through, petulantly or playfully thrown, displaced by stealthy moles or sent suddenly flying by some explosive shark-like re-emergence. There are also foam equivalents, head-sized projectiles to be loaded into shoulder-mounted "ballzookas", or smaller pellets fired from the hip via lighter hardware, all of which are employed in a less messy dry run for paintball. And there are of course various sports – fun-sized football, softball, touch rugby, a type of basketball with forgivingly sized hoops – the range of which stretches on and into the hazily deepening distance of the warehouse.

She eventually finds the café area – a small crowded sanctuary for bedraggled parents, relatives and other responsible adults – in the centre of which she spies the journalist, the same oversized pattern-rimmed shades, sat munching fries at a plastic table cluttered with food packets and drink cartons.

"It's all just training for war, really, isn't it?" Mel says, in lieu of greeting.

"Sorry?"

"Competition, teamwork, goal-driven aggression, spoils." She wags a handful of fries in apparent exemplification of the latter.

Cari looks around at the sugar-and-grease-fuelled mayhem and nods. "I suppose. So why here?"

"Balls!" She grins. "Percussive noises. Crowds of people. Kids yelling. Makes it harder to eavesdrop."

"Right."

"Sit. Eat." Mel gestures to the fries and the fizzy drink that she's apparently bought for Cari.

"You really shouldn't have." She eyes the offering with distaste.

"Not an invitation. A condition. Keep your mouth busy so it's hard to lipread."

"Seriously? Isn't that a bit paranoid?"

Mel shrugs. "Don't believe me – don't have to. Just follow my rules."

Cari sighs, sits down and begins picking at her fries.

"So," Mel continues, "freaky news about your grandad then, eh?"

"How did you know I'd find anything?"

"I didn't. Just had a hunch. Call it journalistic intuition. Amazing how often that pays off. So what exactly was his contribution? The article wasn't very specific. Just mentioned linguistics."

"*Language Research Technician*, his old ID badge says. Part of the project team working on something to do with AI. Aside from that, all I know is his doctoral thesis was on something called 'innate morphological capacity'." Mel pulls a face. "Yeah, well, I couldn't really make much sense of it – all pretty technical. But apparently it puts forward the idea that language is a type of virus, and therefore if we could work out its code, make an algorithm from it, then we could use it to create proper artificial intelligence. At least, that's as much as I could piece together. As I said, all pretty technical." The journalist briefly raises an eyebrow, but continues to munch her fries. "You don't look very interested."

"In language viruses? Not really. Unless, you know, it's a virus from outer space – is it? Or Merrywhile is planning to weaponise it, put it in the water supply, and use it to get everyone to buy their crappy operating system?" She slurps her cola noisily.

"Not as far as I'm aware, no."

"Then fascinating and groundbreaking as it may be, it's just some eggheads geeking out, and probably not going to sell any newspapers. Not that people actually *buy* papers any more, of course – figure of speech."

"So why did you contact me? If you aren't interested?"

"Who said I wasn't interested? Just because I don't care about language viruses doesn't mean I don't think there's a story."

"Which is what?"

"I think there may be a connection between the piece I was working on, your grandfather's memory siphoning malarkey, and this project thingy."

"Project MUNKi."

"That. So, I propose we pool resources. Share research. I'll keep you up to date on anything I find that I think's relevant to you, and vice versa. Deal?"

"Oh. OK. Yes. Deal."

"There's no money in it – for you, I mean."

"Oh, I … well, I hadn't assumed there would be."

"Right, well, just as long as that's clear. And you don't mention this to anyone, right?"

"You mean apart from my father?"

"What?"

"Well, I told him about the memory theft thing. The video. When it all happened."

"Right."

"And of course, I told my auntie. About the hacking."

"Of course you did."

"And, you know, I posted about it on a forum – anonymously!"

"Jesus." Mel squeezes the bridge of her nose. "Right, but *no one else*. Agreed?"

"Agreed."

"So what did your aunt and your dad have to say?"

"Well, it was my auntie that told me about the connection

with Merrywhile. Said that my grandfather had quit and suddenly returned home. No one else in the family knows anything about it. I would have pushed her for more, but she was still a bit unsettled. She's been burgled recently."

"I see." Mel frowns. "Anything taken?"

"Nothing valuable. They were disturbed." Mel raises an eyebrow. "Wait – you don't think…?" The journalist shrugs. "No. That's crazy. I mean, they've already stolen his memories. What more could they take? And there was almost nothing left there from his work with them. I mean, couldn't it just be coincidence?"

"Of course – can never rule that out." Mel grabs another handful of fries, and uses the other hand to transfer them mechanically into her mouth. "And you're right: it may mean nothing that your grandad used to work for them, on some cutting edge language-is-a-virus type thingy – who was that, now? Kirsty MacColl? Anyway … so the fact he quit suddenly and never talked about it ever again – I don't know, perhaps he didn't like the canteen food. And regarding the hospice thing, perhaps they were stealing a job lot of memories and his were just in with the batch. And it was just a coincidence that they used that particular footage at *your* school. It could also just be coincidence that his sister's house is burgled just before his granddaughter arrives to ask about what it was he used to do at that company."

"Well, I … I suppose, if you put it like that—"

"Listen, kid, I think you need to realise some things. Firstly, you're a potential felon. Just so you know, if shit comes down, I'll just disavow you – claim no knowledge, say you were trying to sell me hacked material, Your Honour, and I've read my Lord Leveson and I turned you away in disgust. Or whatever. I don't know. I'll think of something."

"Charming."

Mel shrugs. "Don't take it personally. Secondly, I don't think you realise how serious this all is. This is Big League stuff. You're not playing phone pranks on your local takeaway now." She looks around. "For instance. Behind me to my left – *don't look yet* – man reading the broadsheet, drinking coffee.

Hasn't exchanged a word with anyone since he sat down. No sign of a kid. He either has far too unhealthy an interest in other people's offspring, or he's chosen a very odd place to catch up on the latest outrage to Middle England. Over to our right, table near the counter. Young woman with a baby in a pram. Hasn't tended to it once, not even to rock it; nor has it made a noise. And she just sits there, earphones in, occasionally tapping at her phone. Again, no other kid nearby. Funny place to come to do that."

Cari tries discreetly to check them out. "Really?"

"In all honesty, I don't know. Call it professional paranoia. They're probably just people whose backstory I haven't worked out yet. But the point is that while *you* skip around playing Nancy Drew, there may be other people taking this game much more seriously."

"Nancy who?"

"Veronica Mars, then."

Cari sits staring at her fries, that knot of anxiety back in her solar plexus.

"Then why did we come here? Shouldn't we have met somewhere else? Somewhere, you know, private?"

"Well, public places are generally better, done in the right way. And aside from the fries eating contest, I *am* taking precautions:" – Mel gestures to her phone, which is stood upright in the middle of the table – "equipped with audio scrambler and white-noise generator; also radio frequency jammer to disrupt micro-drone navigation. Adversarial glasses with built-in ocular diffuser;" – adjusting her Hollywood shades – "causes misclassification in facial recognition software."

"This is nuts," Cari laughs, shaking her head dismissively, without really feeling it.

"Kid, I really don't mean to scare you – not saying you should invest in a taser, or anything – just keep your eyes open and your wits sharp. You haven't been arrested yet, so either they aren't actively looking for you, they don't yet know who you are – in which case good, let's keep it that way – or else they want something from *you*. If it's the latter, then even so they're not going to clonk you on the head and bundle you into the back of a van – not if they can get whatever 'it' is some other, simpler way."

"What could they want from *me*?"

The journalist shrugs again and shakes her head. "Well, that's an unknown known."

"Sorry?"

"Something that you don't know that you know – or at least, don't know what it is that they don't know whether you know or not. You know?" She grins again.

"Thanks. That clarifies everything."

From somewhere out in the ball-driven frenzy, a young boy walks unsteadily over to the café area, led by a young woman in a bright-yellow Ballmageddon polo shirt, holding a blood-soaked paper towel to the boy's nose. The woman with the pram looks up from her phone and quickly jogs over to meet them. Cari catches Mel's eye.

"Can't be right all the time," Mel shrugs. "Don't mean I'm not right in principle." She starts gathering her things, preparing to leave.

"So where do we go from here?" Cari asks.

"First of all, get a new phone – I'll email you some cheap recommendations. You can phone me or message me on that, but only use the chat app I'll tell you about. It does video and takes attachments. The encryption is pretty well unbreakable, my geek friends tell me, with no naughty back doors. Keep following up your leads – but *discreetly*. I'll be in touch in a few days, once I've worked out a more considered plan."

She stands up and pushes back her chair.

"So what made you change your mind?" Cari asks. "About getting involved?"

Mel considers for a moment. "I currently have some free time."

And on that statement, which neither of them believes, she leaves.

Although partially disproven – at least in certain specifics – Mel has succeeded in infecting Cari with her operational paranoia, and as she walks back from the train station to her halls, every shop window reflection receives mistrustful scrutiny, looking for tails and persistent strangers, as she's seen it done in the films. But the films are wrong, there is no one, or else they are far too adept for the likes of Cari to catch.

However, as the days go by, with no further word from the journalist, things start to return to normal. She catches up on missed uni work, spends time on campus rather than at the café, and hangs out with friends. Eventually, Cari starts to consider that Mel might even be winding her up, cruelly toying with her, or else that the journalist *herself* is paranoid and therefore imagining the whole surveillance thing – occupational hazard, perhaps.

Following the meeting with Mel, she'd texted her cousin David, just to see how Cat was doing and whether there had been any further suspicious activity. But there had been none. So maybe David was right – just druggies, or whatever. So when she does return to *Caffè Vico*, almost a week later, it is with a more carefree air, carrying the precious tablet more as a casual accessory – as you would a beach read you might or might not dip into – than a tool against corporate tyranny.

She exchanges pleasantries with Teresa and Jonny and takes a coffee to her favourite seat in the window.

The sun is shining, the world is passing by – but unhurriedly, as if taking a well-earned break from its helter-skelter self. Familiar faces smile back – even the latest proud representative of the great line of Bub. Suddenly, she feels the fatigue and the worry, the paranoid anxiety, falling away from her, and the things of the familiar world that had threatened to betray her, that have recently become so duplicitous and untrustworthy, now reacquire their comfortingly mundane and customary appearance.

Perhaps she should take Mel's advice, she thinks – the first lot, that is. Whatever had happened is all in the past, now, isn't it? What would be the good in digging it all up again? Playing David to their corporate Goliath (and the likelihood of *that* playing out Biblically)? And why *shouldn't* she live her life?

"*Gotcha!*"

She looks up, startled, to see Teresa wielding a rolled-up magazine.

"The little bastard. He's been annoying me for weeks." She bends down to scrutinise the consequence of her violence. "What the hell...?"

Cari walks over to where, instead of the squashed intestines of *musca domestica*, she finds Teresa puzzling over the intricate workings of a tiny machine.

Oh, Bub. Et tu?

ZOMBIE

"I'm sorry, Signor…"

"Rossi."

"… Rossi, but I fear we do not give out such confidential information, no matter who you say you are."

Who you say *you are?* Her years on the tabloids had taught Mel a few foot-in-the-door tricks of the trade, but these people are having none of it. They are well-trained and suspicious.

She has scoured the contemporary news reports of the accident and its aftermath, and the obituaries, but can find no mention of the boy's death. But – Investigative Journalism 101 – absence of evidence is not evidence of absence. The fact she can't find anything means nothing. This leaves open the possibility that Sommeil's son had survived the crash (for however long), but verifying this is proving to be trickier than she's anticipated. In an age where it's almost impossible to keep anything secret without somebody hacking or leaking it, he presents a media blindspot. Was Sommeil *that* well-connected? Or even perhaps the old man himself, his preternatural shadow looming over every news desk like Hamlet Senior's ghost – or rather his opposite, an anti-Hamlet-Senior: *You must forget!* A SPECTRE-al influence, anyway.

Right, get her deerstalker on, form a hypothesis – *X!* – then work out what facts would need to be the case if *X* were true. If said facts are not the case, then *X* can be ruled out. And on to the next hypothesis.

Hypothesis One: The boy is dead. There would be a certificate of death, a public record somewhere. But then there would be the question of where. The boy could have died at any point from then until now, and in any country, all of which differ as to how long such records are kept, who could request the information, and acceptable reasons for doing so (privacy laws having tightened up in that regard). She might even have to visit the record office in person. She needs to narrow it down. The car accident had happened in … Rome. The patron city of bad drivers. Or is that Paris? *Merde.* Her *italiano* is almost *niente*, and *plus mauvais* than her *Français* – and *that's* pretty *mauvais* (*mauvaise?*). Civic bureaucracies could be pedantic and prickly at the best of times, especially toward dodgy foreigners trying to blag information. The British Embassy in Rome? But was the boy even a British citizen? Might be French, even Italian. And what if going down any official channels tips them off, like a tripwire? *Shit. Has she just done that with the hospice?*

But there must be an easier way.

Think.

Foreign language papers? Or did the blackout extend that far? Possibly not. A bit of a pain in the arse to search, but less hassle than Italian civil servants or British Embassy staff, and at least Merrywhile's own Transverbia can help here.

She fires up the foreign language newspaper archives, selects "Italy", then sets the search parameters broadly, just "Sommeil" and "figlio" for the beginning of the month of the accident and (*let's be generous*) two years afterward. Thirty results! *Chinks in the blackouts.* Mostly in the Rome-based news outlets – *Il Messaggero, Il Tempo* – a day after the crash, and providing details of the accident in broad outline: mother killed instantly, boy critical(!). And then, gradually, as if squeezed by an invisible hand, they dry up. Moving the slider forward, just a week, the results drop off a cliff – from thirty to five – and none of these elaborate on the boy's condition. Forward to between a month afterward and two years on, and there is only one.

La Stella della Sera is a small independent local newspaper serving the Lazio region north-east of Rome, where the accident had taken place. It was only natural it should make the news there, and fitting, a year on, that the paper should run a little anniversary piece, commemorating the tragedy and following up on the fates of those involved. She can imagine the kind of publication: at its height, a small-office affair with a circulation in the low thousands, the type of place acne-battling young Niccolò does his work experience before heading off to *l'università*, or to try his luck as a freelancer servicing the big-city *giornali scandalistici*. In its pomp, it might have boasted a total working staff of five or six people (young Niccolò included). But even at that time, the effects of automation and digitisation, social media and news aggregators all starting to bite hard, Niccolò (or his interning successor) is perhaps the *only* staff reporter the editor can spare to cover events first hand. The rest of its news will have come as thinly disguised PR for local firms; births, marriages, and deaths; or down the wire from the big news agencies, to be repurposed and reprinted more or less uncritically, taste adjusted for the local palate – a job for a machine, really (literally, by now). The very same copybots that had gradually edged Mel herself further out into the margins, forcing her to seek out the distinctively human, to be more than a repackager of facts, were now ubiquitous. And soon Niccolò himself would be automated, robo-calling for reaction quotes, a drone tasked with trailing a cab, or loitering outside the discrete entrances of back-street hotels, even doing the fucking coffee and sandwich run – and probably better at all those things. (Had she tipped *all* the Cab Sav down the sink…?)

But anyway, at the time, *La Stella* was small enough to go more or less unnoticed and unregulated by Giant Global Meganews Inc., and therefore (given the local interest) independent enough to go off-message regarding the media blackout re the aftermath of the accident.

In total, the paper had run four reports: one the day of the accident, two expanding on that later the same week, and the follow-up piece a year later. The mother and the other driver had been *uccisi all'istante* ("killed instantly", Transverbia informs her), and the boy was in *condizioni critiche* ("critical condition"), before becoming, by the third report, *grave, ma stabile* ("serious, but stable"). The follow-up piece (which actually ran a few days after the exact anniversary date) had been occasioned, at least in part, by a visit from Sommeil himself, come to lay flowers on the spot – an international practice now, it seems – and calling to express his gratitude to a local who had helped on the scene. This is relayed by the local himself, a certain Gianni Sulposto, who in a brief interview tells *La Stella* that he had commiserated Sommeil, wished the boy well, and that Sommeil had thanked him, saying that he would pass on those wishes *later that day* (italics hers!).

So, unless the boy's vitals had since reverted from *stabile* back to *critiche* and worse, then at this point at least, Hypothesis One could be ruled out: when the anniversary article was written, *the boy was still alive*. Still in a coma, maybe (yet able to receive goodwill messages?), but anyway, not dead. You don't wish dead people well, generally speaking. Furthermore, if he were to see the boy "later that day", then odds are that he was somewhere not too far away. Even after all these years Sommeil still mostly lives and works in Rome – the day she had interviewed him he had been about to fly back there, hadn't he? Perhaps, then, if the boy still needed medical attention, he had kept him nearby.

But in a coma? For twenty years? Surely not. All this time, she'd never even thought to check, because she'd just assumed – that "coma" wasn't somewhere you hung out, but something you either *came back out* of or *slipped away* from. But look at … that other case … Elaine … Esposito – thirty-seven years in a coma! Edwarda O'Bara … forty-two years! *Jesus*. So, you never know. Of course, even if he *is* still alive, he might have been sent back to England, or on to somewhere else. But she can tell in her tripes that she is on to something. The Merrywhile hospice in Rome would have been cutting edge, ideally suited to that sort of care, would no doubt have been kept up to date with the latest tech. It was also close to Sommeil's home and work. The theory ticks a lot of boxes.

The response from *L'Ospizio Merrywhile di Roma* was therefore telling. Using Transverbia for translation, and with aid of a voice disguiser, she'd claimed to be Mario Rossi, headmaster of a nearby *scuola elementare*. Since it was the twentieth anniversary of the accident, "Signor Rossi" said, the school would like to send a card to its former pupil. Was there a room he could address it to? Or had he been moved somewhere else? It might have been the clunkiness of Transverbia, or the fractional delay in translation, but – until then chatty and cheerful – at the mention of the Sommeil name the receptionist had immediately clammed up.

Maybe she won't need Italian vital records after all.

The receptionist had been briefed.

For sometimes a "no comment" or a door in your face is as telling as a full and frank confession.

So, assuming her instincts are correct, Mel now has a location – of where the boy *had* been (possibly), even if he's not there now. The next task is therefore to ascertain which of these possibilities – he's still there; he's been moved on – is actually true.

This is not so easy. What are her options? She could risk another phone call, try another tack, but if they're not ringing already, this would definitely set off the alarm bells. What else? Go to the hospice? Act like she's visiting a patient? Go through the bins? *Yummy: medical waste.* Try to talk to ancillary staff, then, bribe someone – cleaners, kitchen staff, delivery people. Or else just quiz the locals, find out what they know. Pretend to be *Interflora*, perhaps? (What's the Italian for *Interflora*? Is it, perhaps, *Interflora*?) No, if they saw through the get-well-soon card, they'd see through the flower delivery ruse in a tachycardic second. Stake out the hospice? If she could actually *see* Sommeil come and go – he must visit his much-loved fairly often – then that at least would be confirmation. All options are desperate, expensive, time-consuming, and have equal chance of proving fruitless. But unless something better suggests itself, there are two options: wade through Italian bureaucracy, or grab her passport and jump on a plane.

But what is she thinking, really? After all these years, coming back like a dog to its vomit, and with no clearer an idea of what she hopes to get from it all. Despite the new leads – which, let's be honest, are still pretty tenuous – the old cold case is as much a career dead end as it ever was. She could combine the trip with research for some travel-based piece, perhaps – "Discover the undiscovered Rome" – or some such fluffy nonsense. Maybe even just call it a holiday. God, when's the last time she had one of *those*? She can't even remember – not one that hadn't been a disguised form of work, anyway (*ha – just like this would be*).

Rationalised in this way – stakeout/travel research/holiday – she starts to feel a little better, a bit more in control. But it's still a rationalisation, a mask of justification over something she doesn't like to examine too closely. It can't be a mid-life crisis, surely? Like she's some male drone, smothered under the weight of his biennial family holidays, his salary-straining mortgage, toadying to the boss at yet another fucking Christmas party while trying to resist the alcoholically enhanced appeal of Julie-from-Accounts. (*Biannual*?) She's her own boss, has no Julie (or male equivalent), and no spouse or kids – is it *that*, then? The shadow-of-mortality, concern-for-legacy, biological clock, thing? Or maybe just the qualms of her profession, puddling out from under the cellar door behind which she's long ago begun to stuff them. The fact that she doesn't have a life?

But that's stupid! Of course she has a life! She has friends! Well, colleagues, fellow travellers. That features editor … Allie somebody? The one who'd had the nicknames for her. Haven't seen him in a while, but he always sends her a Christmas card – a Christmas text; well, he used to. Almost slept with him once. Close call (never mix business with sangria). And he was a bit of an arsehole, really. *Hackula* – that's right! – what he used to call her; not because of her dodgy skills and contacts (though it was that, too, of course), but the fact she was always up at night, could always be reached, whatever the hour. Bit misogynistic, really; a guy did that, he was just hard working. And what was the other name…? The Crocodyke! *Jesus – really?* Once she got hold, she never let go; never let feminine sentiment get in the way. *Fuck.* Had he really meant that? Homophobic arsehole too, apparently. Laughed it off, at the time; even took it as a compliment. Couldn't get away with it now, of course – couldn't get away with it *then*, really. But it was almost a badge of honour, she'd felt; meant she wasn't a PC Girl Scout or a Social Justice Warrior, could hack it with the boys, take their teasing, join in their banter, unbothered by the stench of sweat, the fug of testosterone.

She'd always assumed it was playful, though; just a joke, a throwaway bit of nothing: "See you later, fornicator"; "On your bike, Crocodyke!"

A bit harsh, though, now she thinks of it.

Homophobic misogynistic arsehole.

But she has friends. She has—

Right. No more of that. That way madness lies.

Now, where *is* her passport?

L'Ospizio Merrywhile di Roma is situated in Speranza, a leafy suburb just north-east of Rome. She's booked a few nights at a little airbnb, just anywhere nearby to begin with, to see how the land lays (*lies?*), and then the next available flight (*robbing* bas-*tards!*), which is ten hours later out of Heathrow. Following frenzied packing, check-in, a bumpy and cramped two-hour ordeal bookended poetically between a teething two-year-old and a snoring octogenarian, she finally touches down at Fiumicino just before 2.30pm local time. It's typically cool and overcast for the time of year, her phone informs her, which doesn't lift her spirits any, and, from lack of sleep and rushed departure, her bedraggled appearance provokes in the taxi driver – a man presumably well accustomed to seeing passengers far from their best – an arched eyebrow and a barely contained smirk.

Her first words – "*Speranza, per favore*" – earn her a massive grin, as her ride switches to *inglese*. He is, of all things, a British ex-pat, a Brummie, part of the diaspora now plying their trade in countries where self-driving cabs are more strictly regulated, or their cabbies better unionised than in Blighty. He is just as garrulous and peremptory in his baseless opinions as his ex-compatriots, and they conduct the rest of the journey in English; or at least, he does, rattling off – with the opposite of invitation – his trials at the hands of 21st century technology (refusing now even to use a sat-nav), his student offspring's profligacy, and, via a surreal segue touching upon his evolving theories regarding the greater incidence of reported UFO abductions on the continent as opposed to back home, how "this isn't the Brexit we voted for". She makes a mental note of it (the "stateless cabby" bit) – you never know when a story opportunity might present itself – then attempts to tune him out so she can mentally tick through a list of the things she hopes she's remembered to bring with her: plug socket converter, laptop and charger, phone and *its* charger, passport (she's just flown, so presumably so), credit cards, euros (must get more, somewhere – wonder if places will take crypto?), etc, etc.

Reaching her destination, the driver insists on prowling the streets to find the correct entrance, driving her directly into the little courtyard – a fare-boosting attentiveness she would normally, but is too tired to fight off. She pays him, including tip, which – has she miscalculated? – sends him off with another big grin and a cheerful wave, and she drags her single small wheeled-suitcase across the cobbles, laptop and hand luggage lumped over one shoulder. She walks up to a little reception area, finding its door wide, shaded over with drooping spikes of butterfly-speckled buddleia prettily dismantling its surrounding brickwork, but otherwise not a soul in sight. She is searching the cluttered counter for a bell or some other means of summoning service, when a small, smiling woman of late middle age materialises from the back room and greets her in Italian.

She reaches for her phone, for Transverbia, only to find that it too has been exhausted by the cab ride. *Shit.*

"Uh … *sono* Amelia Faith? *Ho una…*" She struggles to remember the basic phrase she thought she'd learnt – what is "reservation"? *Crap.*

"*Ah, la signora inglese! Bienvenuto, Signora!* It is OK. I speak a little of the English."

Praise the Lord and all his ministers.

And so, within two hours of arriving, she is showered and lunched (a ham and cheese *panino* that her hostess obligingly rustles up) and obliviously snoring the siesta of the dead.

Her siesta (do Italians even *have* those?) has turned into rather more than that, as she awakes in panicked disorientation in unfamiliar darkness, knowing neither who nor where she is, nor how she's come to be there. She has a headache, from lack of sleep, the rigours of travel, cabby diatribe, and dehydration from the alcohol with which she'd attempted to mentally muffle the sounds emitted by the twin poles of life Seat-of-your-Pants Air had stationed her between. She hunts for chemical relief, praying that she's remembered to pack the extra-strength paracetamol that her liver will probably not thank her for in years to come. She locates two, then finds a glass and a jug of lukewarm water on the bedside table.

What time is it? She searches for her phone, before finding that she's forgotten to set it to charge, and then in vain for the ubiquitous illuminated alarm clock she's grown to loathe from short-stay accommodation the world over – nowhere to be found. Ticking. Ah, analogue. A clock, on the wall. She is so unused to this that, ridiculously, it takes her half a minute of squinting to translate the fittingly Roman numerals into their Arabic equivalent: 3.20am? *Strewth.* She's slept right through the evening. Back to sleep, then.

She dozes on and off for the next few hours, finally

admitting defeat as the room starts to lighten at around 6.30 – nature's great big alarm call in the sky – even a cockerel, no thank you very fucking much. Not something she's used to, natural cycles, her own body clock being set to Stay-Up-Until-Copy-Is-Filed Mean Time, a timezone not exactly conducive to establishing salubrious circadian rhythms.

After she's dressed she goes down to reception to find the patroness pottering about briskly, listening to … an old analogue radio? How can that even exist? A local station? Some amateur enthusiast? She'd thought it was all digital, now. But there it is, another anachronism, phasing in and out, fighting its old enemy, static. They are only twelve miles out from the centre of Rome, but it might as well be fifty years.

"*Ah, Signora! Buongiorno*! You sleep good?"

"Yes. *Sì. Grazie*. Where is the … um…"

"*La Sala da Pranzo*?" Her hostess mimes eating.

"Yes. Yes, please. *Per favore*."

"This way, *Signora*," ushering Mel gently through a door on the left, down a few steps and into – *well, this is actually quite lovely* – a little oblong dining room, with French doors leading onto a small sun terrace overlooking a verdurous valley of holiday brochure quaintness. It being crisp but clear and relatively mild, she chooses outside, an umbrellaed table near the wall. There appears to be only one other guest: a bearded, formal looking middle-aged fellow in a tweed jacket, reading his broadsheet (more analogue). She ventures a "*Buongiorno*", receiving the same back in an accent with a German(?) gravelliness to it, before returning his attention to the news. Formal, polite, distant; the ideal dining companion. Freed of the awkward burden of small talk, she walks over to the well-stocked breakfast table and returns with something resembling (but not quite) a croissant, an orange juice, and a coffee, then sets about trying to get a signal on her phone, which vacillates between one bar and none (so, certainly not strong enough for mobile internet).

"Wi-fi?" she asks on her way back from breakfast. The hostess frowns. Mel mimes typing.

"Ah, *la rete? In linea?* Er…" She appears to be searching her limited English technical vocabulary. "On line?"

"*Sì, sì.*"

"No."

She has a feeling she won't be breaking out the Bitcoins any time soon. But she had booked online, which suggests that someone, at least, has access to the 21st century. God, the whole fucking *world* is *perpetually* online. Can she maybe just use *their* computer? To search the web, check emails?

"My husband, he…" She re-enacts Mel's typing mime. "I do not. He has…"

The passwords. Probably to keep *la moglie* from discovering his well ordered collection of Italian pornography while he's away.

"But, er…" The hostess points vaguely off into the distance. "The *caffè*? It has, I think, *la rete*."

"Fantastic."

And so, equipped with directions, she leaves the 1970s, heads out through the gate, turns right, and walks into town.

"Town" turns out to be somewhat of an aggrandisement, the local term for an assortment of little bakeries, cakeries, a couple of cafés, a convenience store, a pharmacist, a little church, and an undertaker, all dotted around a nice little piazza containing a brace of impressively moustachioed old men and some *youts*. *You could live your whole life without leaving the square* – which, judging by the kids and old codgers, is what in fact they do. *La Casa di Giorgio* proves to be – *che miracolo* – wi-fi enabled, and encouragingly she notes, among its modest smattering of patrons, a small gaggle of teenagers poring over hand-held screens of varying size.

On getting the password from the in-fact rather striking young(ish) man behind the counter (Giorgio himself? Too young, perhaps. Giorgio junior, then), she chooses a table at the back, boots up her freshly charged laptop, and logs in. She checks her email. Among the usual mix of lottery wins, urgent business requests from Panama (whatever happened to her

Nigerian prince?), and kindly suggestions as to how she might chemically superpower her erection, there are three actual messages of note: a mournful missive from her mother, listing her ongoing ailments, and unsubtly deploring her daughter's inattentiveness; a dirty joke from her *friend* Sandy (*see!*), together with a reminder that they are due to meet up – has she remembered? (*er… no*); and a feeler from one of her old contacts at one of the popular technology sites, remembering her interest in "the transhumanist thing", and enquiring after any stories she might have in that line! (*Not yet…*)

She wings back a quick apologetic missive to Sandy, blaming workload, sweetened with a humorously obscene emoji, and sends similar to her mother (minus obscenity), promising a Sunday marathon of screwball comedies and ice cream as soon as she can manage. She then switches to Maps and tracks down the hospice, which turns out to be just on the edge of "town", set in its own little patch of greenery and another twenty minutes or so by foot. So, perhaps Giorgio's isn't such a bad place to start. Time for a little social engineering.

She checks herself in her compact: roots will need attention soon, but not too noticeable for now ("*volume*, dear – that's the key" – *cheers, mum*); reapply lipgloss and try to picture herself as desirable in the eyes of a twenty-something Italian café-bar tender. A touch of MILF, perhaps – not that she's a mom, of course; a cougar, then, if that's still a thing. She looks over at Giorgio junior (or whatever his name is). It's not like she has to undertake anything *carnal*, as such – a professional Rubicon she's proud never to have crossed (she has *some* standards) – just make him interested enough to be indiscreet.

She straightens her clothes, primps her hair and moseys over to the bar.

"*Mi scusi*, er… Giorgio?"

"*No, Signora,*" he smiles a little shyly. "Giorgio *è mio padre. Mi chiamo* Luca."

Luca. Lucky Luke. So, Giorgio junior was almost right. "Ah, *mi dispiace*, Luca." She smiles back, she hopes, winningly.

"*Desidera qualcosa da bere, Signora?*"

Da bere? At her frown, he mimes drinking, then sweeps his hand before the assorted wines and spirits lined up behind the bar. "Oh! Um ... isn't it a bit early? Er..." She scans Transverbia, "*È troppo presto?*"

"No, no," cutely shaking a tousled head of Caravaggian curls, before adding something that Transverbia tells her means, "wine makes your blood good", which she guesses is the local equivalent of "the sun's *always* over the yard arm". They agree on a glass of red, which he informs her is "*dalla casa*" – the house red? Or *on* the house? She chooses to interpret it as the latter. Perhaps *la Rosa inglese* hasn't lost her bloom quite yet. And when she compliments it, he replies with something about older barrels holding the best wine! Luca, you little *diavolo...*

She awakes once more in semi-darkness with the same panic of disorientation and amnesia, before following the identical train of discovery and realisation: no alarm clock, ticking, B&B, Italy. But there's something different – actually, two things. The throb of her head and the taste in her mouth tell her that there may be more to remember than the facts of where she is, as does the shadowy form beside her snoring gloriously into his pillow. *Oh no*. Luca? *In vino stupiditas*. So much for professional Rubicons. Hildy Johnson would be proud. She hopes, when (if?) her memory restores itself, that it has all been worth it – informationally speaking.

She slips out to the bathroom, then winces as even the cabinet's dim light assaults her retinas. *La rosa inglese* is sick ... battered by a howling storm of ... a ceaseless procession of some fucking Prosecco spritzer thingy... *Ow*. Water. Drugs.

She sits for a while, stupefied, battling the usual alcohol remorse and its accompanying but lesser physical symptoms, pondering another rung down the ladder of her dignity, wondering how she might persuade Luca (ah, it's coming back n-*ow*) ... might persuade him that whatever-time-in-the-morning-it-is isn't too early for him to sod off on his merry bloody way – sneaking, hopefully unnoticed, past Signora Thingy. Are the guests allowed guests? Best not to openly test that yet. But then he suddenly appears, naked, kisses her sweetly on the crown of the head, before shooing her off the toilet seat, lifting the lid, and pissing loudly and copiously into the bowl for longer than any human could need to, all the while chattering away cheerfully in Italian. Ah, the resilience of youth. She manages to discern *mi dispiace*, *lavoro* and *alle sette*, which she guesses means he has to go, and smiles dumbly through his torrent of bubbling patter and piss whilst hoping she doesn't look too gruesome. By the time he's bid her farewell – a surprisingly tender kiss while copping a lusty handful of her arse – the trusty cocktail of emergency pharmaceutical relief has begun to kick in, and something like coherent thought slowly begins to return.

Three types of men, there are, said … the Internet: those who learn by reading, those who learn by watching, and those who must piss on the electric fence for themselves. In one evening's acquaintance, she's learnt that Luca belongs firmly to a fourth group: those who *never* learn. For in his almost thirty years of life, having pissed on every electric fence he could point his dick at, he'd pick himself up and do it all over again. Judging by this morning, pissing is his thing, and among the many things at which he'd aimed his manhood were any females of legal age within a ten mile radius. He was tireless, a machine, an animal, a Casanova (without, she guessed, the literary output). This had made him not especially popular with the husbands and fathers of Speranza and its environs, who might suspect but could never quite prove that the distracted smile that played about the lips of their beloved was occasioned by anything more than idle fancy. It also made him a great source of tittle-tattle. He was a hub, a nexus of information, a veritable gossip goldmine, and her journo's gut (running on Prosecco spritzers) had led her good again.

When he'd clocked off, they'd moved to another bar (well, *the* other bar), to food and more drink, and where, once he'd realised that she didn't judge him for his libertinism, he'd become even more free in sharing – boastful, even. Maybe he thought *la donna inglese* got a little kinky kick out of hearing his racy stories, that he was getting her all warmed up for a little one-on-one later in the evening (well, unfortunately, he hadn't been wrong there). His little English and her littler Italian made for a blast, and even with Transverbia plugged in and translating full-tilt directly into her ear, she had to simply guess at much of what he meant, squinting through a mist of spritzer-infused, increasingly graphic idiom. However, given his proclivities, the gist wasn't generally hard to glean.

"Good Lord, Luca – the undertaker's wife!" Surrounded by stiffs, apart from where it mattered. They laughed, and she seized the opportunity to work him subtly around to her target. "And what other professions have you serviced? Lawyers? Doctors? Nurses?"

"Yes, yes. Ladies get lonely in all walks of life."

"And what about the hospice? You make any friends there?"

"Ah…" He seemed suddenly overcome with wistfulness, a vinologist recalling a particularly fine year. (God, what is it about the men of this country? They just want to eat, drink and shag everything, then rhapsodise about it. Maybe he did have a secret literary output after all.)

Her name was Marina, or as he evidently thought of her, The One Who Got Away. She'd had, let's just say, "admirable assets"; but so had Luca, and Marina couldn't get enough of him – an appeal Mel was herself beginning to appreciate. She'd come up from Rome to work, and they'd spent one memorable summer testing the bed springs/car upholstery/nature's pillow/any available surface (horizontal and vertical), before he'd finally lost her to some more lucrative job overseas, leaving him broken and bereft and in a years-long rut of … well, *rutting*, attempting to benumb his trampled little heart. Had she liked it there, at the hospice? What sort of place was it to work? Any interesting patients? Some, he said. It was quite a technological place. Most of the patients were in a poor way – lots of head injuries and brain stuff, Marina told him. Many were *dormendo* ("sleeping" – meaning comatose). Some were alive, but *not* alive – moving, groaning – "*come uno zombie*" (he made dead-eyed lumbering movements, then laughed) – and all hooked up to very expensive-looking, very complicated machines.

This was promising.

"Were any of these *particularly* interesting, these 'sleepers'?"

He considered her appraisingly. "There was an English boy," he said eventually. *Un ragazzo inglese.* "You mean him?"

But, she had already learnt, *ragazzo*, "boy", could mean any male from fourteen to thirty. Did Italian boys take longer to mature? Of which Luca himself is a fine illustration (who probably still thinks of *himself* as *ragazzo*). Or maybe it's just the Italian equivalent of "lad" – as in *lads' mag, one of the lads* – and she's seen enough of *those* to know that being adult-sized isn't the same as growing up. But she must stop thinking of Sommeil's son as "the boy". Luca's dalliance with the nurse would have been a handful of years ago, so even then "the boy" would have been somewhere in his twenties.

"Do I?" she said, playing dumb. "What about him?"

He gave her another shrewd look. She hadn't told him she was a journalist, nor even suggested her line of work, but she could tell that he had begun to see through her "middle-aged divorcée let off the leash" act. But he still seemed to like her, nonetheless – and she him, almost despite herself. There was something timeless about him. He didn't care for politics, possessed no discernible ambitions for career or wealth, and seemed never to have given a thought for posterity, or the possibility that he might one day get old or ill. For Luca, it was all about living in the eternal moment, in forgetting yourself in pleasure. And what more pleasurable oblivion was there than *la petite mort*? In yet another thirty years, she imagines, he would still be here, his curls gone or turned to grey, chatting up women from behind the counter. Or else finally getting someone up the duff, and being marched down the aisle with a gun at his back. Or perhaps just the gun bit, wielded by some jealousy-enraged Speranzan cuckold. Yes, he treated women like buses, but he was uncomplicated, charming, almost sincere in that pursuit. And if you knew what you were getting into, you could (she suspected) have some wonderfully uncomplicated fun and just enjoy the ride – while it lasted.

The English boy had already been there for some years when Marina started. It had not been her job to see to him – the *ragazzo* had special staff for that – but now and then, if one of his carers was ill, or they just needed an extra hand, she might be asked to help out, to station herself outside the room, or get supplies. The room itself was like no other in the hospice – the most hi-tech, she'd said. She wasn't actually allowed into this, but she could see him through the window, inside some sort of glass case, and hooked up to every machine imaginable. It was almost frightening, what they had him connected to: the wires, the tubes, the boxes pulsing with an eery light. It used to make her sad just to watch him. Marina had almost been relieved when they'd moved him.

"Wait: they *moved* him? To where?" Mel was struggling to maintain her composure. She tried to rescue it. "Is that why Marina left, Luca? To travel on somewhere with the English *ragazzo*?"

"No, no." He uttered some minced oath (something to do with his uncle being a pig? With God being a singer?). "As I said, it was *not her job*. She left to work in America. Ah, she had such lovely—"

Sweet Lord a-mighty, Luca, focus. "To where did they move him? Did she say?" Too abrupt again, but she was close now.

He was irritated to have his reverie interrupted, but eventually answered, "*Venezia. Forse.*" Venice. Perhaps.

"You say Marina wasn't allowed into his room. So who was? Did she tell you?"

"Apart from certain medical staff, no one could go in or out who wasn't on the list. And, she said, the list had only one name on it."

"One name? Wow. And what was that?" She tried to sound casually intrigued, but it was much, much too late for that.

"Why should I remember that?" Dismissive; annoyed that she was unashamedly mining him, now.

"Luca," beneath the table, she let one shoe drop off and

moved her toes along his shin, "over the past few hours you have relayed to me a sea of intimate detail, and from your years of active service, the name of every woman and girl that has so much as smiled at you. So I'm pretty sure that a name like that, the only one allowed in to see the mysterious patient in the hi-tech room, would have stuck in your excellent memory."

She wasn't sure precisely how much of that Transverbia had caught, but she had a feeling that he'd gotten the message.

BLACKFLY

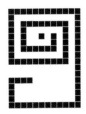

With Bub's sad demise, and with it the vindication of Mel's paranoia, Cari's own ramps up to and past her previous levels. She avoids the café, partly just to duck Teresa's evolving theories as to the puzzling "mechanical fly" ("some kids messing around, you think?"), and even her room begins to feel tainted, invisibly invaded. And so, it is almost a relief when the gears finally shift and the watchers emerge from the shadows.

Her phone rings. Unknown number. She dithers, then finally answers.

"Did he find you?"

Teresa. Cari had once phoned the café to check if she'd left her bag there, and Teresa must have kept the number.

"I'm sorry? Who?"

"Your grandad."

"My...? Oh. I don't... When?"

"This morning," Teresa says. "A man comes in. Seventy, perhaps – nice old man, anyway. He asked for you – 'my granddaughter', he says. Said he'd missed you at your halls and your friend said you came here, and he wanted to surprise you – well, not any more, I guess!" She laughs.

But if it was this morning, she's been in her room all day, working on an essay. And she hasn't really *got* any friends in halls – and certainly none that would know her movements. So why the café? To show that *they* know her movements, that – Bub or no Bub – they are still watching her. And, now she thinks about it, hadn't Bub himself been a bit heavy-handed? An undying fly. Like they were showing off, and almost pleased to be caught.

"Anyway," Teresa says. "He left you something. I'll get Jonny to drop it by this afternoon when he does the deliveries."

Just over an hour later, Cari is sitting with an A5, card-backed buff envelope, on the front of which is written "Cari Silvestri" in red, thick-nibbed felt-tip. She opens it, and withdraws a black and white photograph of a young, relatively short, dark-haired woman with generous eyebrows, wearing a baseball hat and interactive glasses. It is a still of herself from surveillance footage at MoTH. On the back, in the same red pen, is written, "Let's talk Grandfather xx", and beneath that a VR address, a date and a time.

Shit.

She's already told Mel about the fly, and now messages her about the envelope.

<MEL>: Shit. But don't panic. Take the meeting. Also opportunity to find out what they know. Unknown knowns remember. Let me know how it goes.

Could it be a trap? But for what purpose? Lure her there to *digitise* her, download her into *Divinia* and make her battle their AI in gladiatorial sports? They already hold all the cards. And as Mel had said, if they'd just wanted to apprehend her, they'd have called the police by now. Perhaps, then, it is something else. Perhaps they are sending her a message. Which is what, exactly?

She looks again at the hand-written lettering on the back of the photo. Although it's written over two lines, there is no punctuation. So perhaps it isn't "Let's talk. Grandfather", but "Let's talk Grandfather". Are they letting her know that they've made the connection? But if so, which one?

It's a little old rural chapel, not quite unfamiliar, huddled under an off-white blanket of seamless cloud. The door, ajar, even creaks as Cari … expects? Remembers? A few candles bolster the dim winter light that filters in upon foot-scuffed flagstones and bum-buffed pews, its scattered figures, frail-looking and elderly, heads down as if hanging on after the service to reflect and pray. It could be any Sunday from her childhood – well, of the handful of times she was forced to attend. All that is missing is the rain.

"Miss Silvestri?"

An old man looks up from a pew to her left. His white hair, here and there streaked with its former black, is combed and smoothed to his small head, as conservative and neatly kept as the rest of him. But the avatar's face is as blank as an egg. How apt. *The faceless face of a soulless corporation.* Cari, in contrast, appears as a simple approximation of herself – one of those DIY avatars you can make from photos or through a webcam – there being little point now in disguise, and suggesting she hopes that she has nothing to hide.

"I do like this place," he continues. "Merely artificial, of course, but I find the atmosphere so wonderfully … *empty.* Is that what's meant, I wonder, when they talk of 'sacred space'?"

She looks around at the isolated company: "real" people? Or NPCs?

"You brought some heavies for backup, I see. Afraid I was going to kick off?" Sounding braver than she feels.

At some unseen signal, their fellow congregants suddenly rise in unison and quietly file out down the aisle, the last, a tottering old woman, her swollen-knuckled blue-veined hands weakly closing the doors behind her with that same authentic creak.

"And who might you be, anyway? Since you're evidently

not my grandfather."

"My apologies. No disrespect was intended. It was merely a ruse to alert you discreetly. You may call me Uncle – no strict relation. I expect you had plenty of them, as a child? In Port Talbot?"

As indeed she had, confusingly, where everyone in the village had been introduced as Uncle this or Auntie that, and she never did sort out the blood relations from the rest.

"If you knew anything about me or my childhood, you'd also know this does nothing for me," sweeping her arm across the altar and the pews.

"I'm sorry. Too High Church? Not High enough? I've no feel for such things, I'm afraid. Price of a secular upbringing. Or are you Breath of Life?"

"Sunday was always my least favourite day, to be honest. Always just felt like the day before Monday. Like they made it so boring you'd even look forward to going back to school. Never really took to sermons, either. I guess they help some people, but I just found them empty." That word again, but in a different sense. "As did my grandfather."

"Uncle" considers this – as far as she can tell, his avatar having no facial features to read.

"I see. And did your connection to your grandfather in some way motivate the attack on Merrywhile that you facilitated? You weren't happy with the treatment that he received at the hospice? Or are you one of those Fight the Future people?"

Is this a probing or a knowing question? *Unknown knowns.* While tempted to reveal the full extent of her grudge, she's already regretting being the first to mention her grandfather, and exposing her full knowledge of Merrywhile's misdemeanours might scupper her chance of getting out of this, might even make her a source of danger to them, something to be dealt with. Evidently, however, as Mel had surmised, they appear to want something from her. She decides to play dumb.

"No motive. Apart from I needed the money."

"I see." Uncle picks up the prayer book from the back of

the pew in front of him, leafing through it idly. "And from whom did this money come, may I ask?"

"A hacker."

"Any particular one?"

"I couldn't say. They all look alike to me."

He stops leafing through the book. "Miss Silvestri, let me get to the point. As I'm sure you're aware, your incursion into our network constitutes a string of criminal offences that bring with them a lengthy stretch of prison time – even though you may only have been an 'infantryman' or 'footsoldier', to borrow hacktivist parlance. However, we are willing to overlook such petty vandalism, which, given how quickly we've managed to contain the virus, has ironically even strengthened our reputation in the field of network security." This is now evidently the company's standard position regarding the attack. Have they come to believe their own spin? "All we want to know is who created the worm. What is the real identity of the hacker? Give us this and we will see to it that your misdemeanours are written off as youthful exuberance."

"Much as I'd like that," she plays along, "I've already said: I don't know his or her identity. As I understand it, hackers have a strict code of anonymity, even when they work together. These people cover their tracks very thoroughly. And he never told me who created the worm."

Uncle is again silent for a moment in consideration. "Then that is a shame – for you."

He recommences fiddling with his prayer book, which she notes has no text, merely blank pages. Their dedication to verisimilitude evidently has its limits, or else it's a religion that affords its adherents ideological *carte blanche*.

"Is there no way you could reach out to him again, on some pretext," he eventually continues, "perhaps through the connections that facilitated your original meeting? You may reassure him: we are not seeking legal redress for his crimes. We merely want information."

Doubtful.

"Even if I could get a message to him, he wouldn't

respond. That was part of the deal, one of his failsafes, to protect himself."

"I see." Silence again.

The door creaks, and an old lady shuffles in – the same one from earlier, or different? – before taking a seat at the back.

"Miss Silvestri, I will leave you to think on this. I urge you to weigh up your future; your degree in Modern Languages at Glan Môr University – did I say that correctly? And your friends and family, of course, and the shame and pain that your public trial and inevitable incarceration will undoubtedly bring them. I'm sure such contemplation will concentrate your mind wonderfully."

He stands up – the action a vestige of real-world negotiations – to signal the end of the meeting.

\<CARI\>:	They were interested in the virus. Who made it.
\<MEL\>:	Really? Interesting!
\<CARI\>:	Why?
\<MEL\>:	People don't usually care what calibre of bullet they've been shot with. Suggests something else is going on. You may be on to something with this language-is-a-virus malarkey.
\<CARI\>:	So what do I do now? Can we meet? Feel like we need to strategise.
\<MEL\>:	Will have to be by phone until I get back.
\<CARI\>:	From where?
\<MEL\>:	Rome.
\<CARI\>:	Rome! Why there?
\<MEL\>:	Just following up a lead. Will explain when I ring. Soon.
\<CARI\>:	What should I do in the meantime?
\<MEL\>:	Try to recontact the hacker?

Which is just what Merrywhile had asked her to do. But

does that make it the wrong thing, or a case of two birds with one stone?

"I'm sorry, er, whoever you say you are, but as I told you, I can honestly say that I don't know what you're talking about."

I don't know you, and you don't know me, he had said, but Cari hadn't expected him to abide by that so literally and inflexibly.

"Look, it's me – remember?" she persists. "I appreciate the failsafes and all that, about what you said, but they really are after me. I mean, honestly, I'm not trying to trap you or anything. I just don't know what the fuck to do. If you could just let me know where you got the—"

"Lady. Lady? Well, all I can say is you've got the wrong guy. You want a … a … an elven invisibility cloak, or … werewolf bite immunity – *that* I can do. But hacking some *company*? Sorry, completely out of my league, I'm afraid."

"I don't want you to hack it! You – we already hacked it! Hello? Hello!"

He's bumped her out. Again. She tries once more, but this time, whatever she does – different avatars, disguised profiles, even the clever thing she thought she'd worked out to mask her IP – none of it works. He's disappeared.

Fucker.

His callousness with the vomit-inducing dermal patches aside, his cynical use of her trusting nature, she'd thought that all the anti-corporate spiel meant he'd at least been in it for more than the money, that it had meant something to *him* as well. Does he really not give a shit, then? Is it all posturing and badge-wearing? But whatever it means for him, this obviously doesn't exclude throwing her under the bus so save his own skin. Well, two can play at that game – and the game is evidently "prisoner's dilemma".

Cari is expecting the characteristic creak, but when she pushes it, the chapel door doesn't budge. After a few less tentative efforts, she gives a knock: the haptic gloves relay the door's oaken solidity, the headphones the interior's resounding echo, but otherwise there's no response. While stood there wondering what kind of game this is – another summons to the chapel in the hills, no doubt to check on her progress, to pressure her again, but showing up to no one here – she becomes aware of noises from around the side.

She follows the sounds along a little foot-worn path, around the front-right corner and down the slope, weaving between moss-defaced gravestones rendered unreadable, through a rickety wooden gate set in an old drystone bounding wall, and disappearing into a distance grown suddenly misty. There it is again: sounds of someone … working? Hammering? She follows the path further, advancing through a grid of fenced-off patches of earth. Some of these are tilled, with pristine arrangements of nets and sticks, protecting and guiding young shoots and tendrils, fragile leaves and tender growth; others are wild and unkempt, apparently untouched for years. And *there,* again: whistling, is it? Brisk and cheerful, fading and rising in volume, as if caught now and then on the breeze – though there is none with which to shift the soupy fog, which has if anything grown thicker. She can almost recognise the tune… What *is* that?

And by the time she remembers, there he is.

It's really him.

Emerging from around a garden hut – *his shed!* – rifling through the pockets of his ratty old cardigan with fingerless-gloved fingers, glasses pushed up over his still-thinning hair, his habitual look of thoughtful distraction. He looks up.

"Well, look who it is!" he says.

She freezes, flounders, struggling to find the fitting response. But there is no need, for his words are not for her – at least, not her *now*, but her chubby little six-year-old self, which comes bounding past her and up into his arms, to be swung round, helicopter style, amid groans and complaints of how too-old he is to do this with how big she's grown.

"Well, you're just in time, *bach*." He points to the row of young sweet peas he's begun to patiently train up a series of bamboo sticks. "Now, you see here? *Blackfly*. Little buggers, they are. They'll have the whole lot, if we don't see to them." And then patiently showing her how to use the spray. ("Essence of tomato leaves – my own recipe! Along the stem, see? And don't forget under the leaves.")

That's what he'd said. What I did.

But was it? The memories – his? – objectified, now fight with her own recollections. Had she ever had a scarf that colour? Cheeks that chubby? But if not, then whose is the distortion? Hers? Tadcu's? Merrywhile's?

Suddenly, she is aware of a presence beside her.

"You see, it struck me," says Uncle, who has now acquired a face and a kindly, fittingly avuncular expression. "I mean, no such thing as chance, really, when you think about it. Every effect its cause, and all that. We always look after our own, of course, and so if he were treated in one of our hospices, then what if...?"

They both stand, watching the two figures. She knows it isn't real – is it? – but she still wants to call and speak to him, reach out and hug him.

"The past is always reaching back to us." He smiles, shaking his head. "The thing with the talk at your school – luckily, we keep a record of all such events, even down to the content, the feedback. I'm truly sorry. Mere coincidence, of course, but we shouldn't have done that, with the video, used it in that way. Please accept our – *my* apologies."

The ghostly gardeners have moved on now to repotting seedlings, and she studies her own little earnest face, one cheek already smeared with earth, a frown of concentration, tongue tip protruding as she pushes down the roots, covers them with soil and tamps it all down with grimy pudgy fingers. It is only a movie, a snapshot of the past – isn't it? Could it be more?

"But possibly you see, now, why we might have been tempted into such indiscretions. You thought him a mere provincial schoolteacher, perhaps, but as you now know, he was so much more. His dreams were also ours. And this" – he gestures to the ghosts – "is only the beginning."

And so he opens up to her, explains: the Singularity, the virus, the problems with Project Upload, but the potential for so much as yet undreamt of, if only she would co-operate.

"Miss Silvestri – Cari, if I may. Help us to take the next step."

Mist is a strange thing: an absence that hides presence, a pregnant nothingness.

"General Ned," she finally begins, wiping the wetness from the face beneath her glasses.

Cari doesn't inform Mel of her betrayal of the hacker, while telling herself he'd had it coming. *Let's see how good his failsafes really are.* But her conscience still twinges with periodic sharpness, like cold air on a cracked tooth. She's allowed emotion to get the jump on her. She is a snitch. And worst of all, it doesn't appear to have done her any good.

"Nothing else?" Uncle asks, when she's finished. She's told him about the dark marketplace, about what they'd talked about, the dermal patches and the tattoo, how the samurai had sounded, what he'd looked like, even down to his little wooden drinking box. Wasn't that enough? "And the virus?"

"I've told you, it was just given to me to deploy, and any evidence I had left afterward, I just chucked or deleted – as he'd instructed. He didn't mention where it came from or who'd created it. And as I said, I've tried to recontact him, but he won't speak to me."

"I see." He smiles, though some of its previous warmth has now seeped out of it. Is the avatar's expression mapped to his actual face, she wonders? Does he even have one? Or – a sudden thought – is Uncle himself an AI's approximation, a mere amalgam of protocols and data? "Very well. We'll see what can be made of all this. Thank you, Cari." Then, more ominously, "We'll be in touch."

Her reluctant complicity reminds her now of one of her

grandfather's old stories – the crocodile and the monkey, perhaps. But there was also the gingerbread man and the fox. Both were stranded, trying to hitch a ride across the river, a dodgy favour from a dodgy stranger. He'd loved all such tales – reciting favourites by heart, sorting through the piles of ragged-jacketed old tomes – Grimm, Kipling, fairies and trolls, myths of gods and monsters. She saw him, now, her own snapshot, pulling them off the now gap-toothed shelves, trying to find just the right one. But creation stories were a particular favourite. There was no surprise he should adopt that theme when he'd taken up painting.

She taps her phone awake, swiping to the photo she'd taken at Auntie Cat's. Still quirky and eerie.

Chagall? she wonders – whom Cat had in mind. *Maybe Miró* – after a bit more searching. *Squiggly creatures.* She'll send her pictures of both, see if she's right – well, to David, anyway, for him to show her.

She looks back at the photo, zooming in, soaking up the detail, then over to the title: *Tree of Life.* Indeed. She pans across to the signature.

Oh, poor blind Auntie Cat.

It isn't "M. E."; it's "M. B."

Goldsmiths. Of course – that was where they'd met. She, then – judging by the photo – a willowy fairy-like creature, '60s throwback waist-length hair and floral prints, still aglow from her newly minted BA in Fine Art. He, the quirky Welsh postgrad, mild mannered, wry and playful, but now and then coming alive with the flurry of ideas. Or so, whimsically, Cari imagines. Though there was a good ten years between them, they'd hit it off. Was there some dalliance, Cari wonders, some romance?

"No judgement!" she adds quickly, laughing, suddenly worried she's overstepped.

"No, no. We were just good friends." Mina smiles. "Both anarchists at heart, I think. He was dating your grandmother by then, anyway. You could tell they were smitten."

Cari had tracked her down quite easily. There weren't many Mina Bouchers on the Internet – if she'd ever married, she'd not forfeited her surname, thankfully – and there was only one with an artist's website. And so she'd emailed her, mentioning the project and her relationship to Tadcu, and attaching the photo of what she now realises is the artist's own work. Cari had also provided her phone number for Mina to respond, if she preferred that method of getting in touch, which she had, ringing Cari back about a week later, and they'd arranged a time to video-chat.

"I'm sorry, I don't really check email very often," Mina says. "But this *is* a lovely surprise!"

She is still teaching, at a sixth form near Mayfair – "and always will be, so long as they keep raising the bloody retirement age". Cari has arranged a video call with her, reaching her at her flat on South Molton Street one Wednesday after her teaching has ended ("not that teaching ever really ends…").

Cari scrutinises the hints of artiness behind her.

"Your flat looks lovely!"

"Oh!" She laughs. "A lovely mess, you mean. You can see some more of my paintings, if you'd like? I'll give you the virtual tour."

As Mina rotates the laptop camera Cari can see the little flat is peppered with the sort of semi-bohemian bric-a-brac you'd expect of an artist: piles of books, stacked canvases, curious *objets d'art*, mismatched but interesting old furniture, half-finished sculptures and discarded tubes of squeezed-out paint. Adorning the walls, amid assorted postcards and prints and magazine cuttings, are some of the artist's own works – pinned-up sketches, finished paintings – while others, in progress, stand on easels, propped up on chairs or leaning in corners. And although her style has evolved over the years, many still depict the same ornate forms, the same species-less creatures, all of which still possess the same disquieting eyes.

"So how long did you stay with the project?" Cari asks her.

"Oh, not long. I left before Myrddin did. He'd

recommended me to them in the first place, knew I needed an income – penniless artist, and all that. And the money was nice, but I quickly saw through their 'making today futureproof' bullshit. Merrywhile weren't interested in art or culture, not really, nor even in people, only in exploiting any means to further their technological goals, and thereby their profits, their market share. It was really all just a bit of fluffy PR for them, I think – at least, that's where I came in!"

"So what did you do, then? Afterwards?"

"Went straight into teaching, where I've been ever since, carrying on painting on the side. I've had a good life, really. I've been lucky; been allowed to do what I love."

"So Tadcu – I mean, Myrddin – why *did* he leave in the end?" Cari asks.

"Oh, the same reasons as me, really. Just took him a little longer. Him and Karl were full into it, at one point, so maybe they thought they were actually getting somewhere."

"That's Karl …", scanning her copy of the article, "Nielsberg? The physicist?"

"Yes. Always bickering, bantering, the two of them. But very fond of each other, really."

"And what happened to Karl? Did he leave too?"

"Yes, but years later. He's dead, now, sadly. Heart attack, I think."

"Oh." *There goes that lead.* "When, do you know?"

"Passed away about five or six years ago? Left the company a while before that, I think, went back to Denmark. He'd stayed on when Myrddin had left. They'd had a big disagreement about something just before. Not sure they ever spoke after that, sadly. I didn't push your grandad for the exact details, but I can guess. Karl had skills, of course, and more worldly ambitions, which neither I nor Myrddin shared. Not knocking your grandad – or myself – but I think computer programming, maths and physics were ultimately of more use to Merrywhile than literature or art. We both realised that we were just window dressing, really. Though I hear one of my ideas did inspire some later project – not that they ever gave me any money for that, of course." She makes a writing gesture through the air in front of her. "Signed my life away."

"So what did you work on, specifically?"

"Well, the basic idea was to connect different types of people – 'bringing together Snow's two cultures', is how they put it, if I remember correctly. Left brain and right, I suppose. Then just spitball, see what came up. So, you'd do *your* thing, whatever that was – draw or write or program or make music or build things – and then try to collaborate with others, make connections. It was all very freeform. That's how the painting came about."

"The *Tree of Life*?"

"Yes. Your grandad and Karl and I just shooting the breeze – him with his creation stories, about how life and language got going; Karl trying to put that into maths, write computer code that would embody his ideas – I don't know. Beyond me. It was his idea to build the robot."

"A robot? Karl's idea, you mean?"

"Yes. We teased him that he was trying to make a real boy! It was a response to something the group's philosopher had said – forget his name. Knowledge isn't something that floats around the aether, he'd said; it's practical, embodied. How did he put it? *We are what we do.* Not so sure about that myself. I mean," gesturing to the products of a life of artistic activity, "if I couldn't do *this* any more, would I be any less 'me'? Always felt we're more than the sum of our actions, you know? More than all the cogs and levers that do the doing. Whether that makes any sense or not, I don't know." She laughs.

Cari's sent her a copy of the article, which she now sees Mina has printed out before her. "And the rest of them? Do you know what happened to them?"

"Let me see..." Mina scans the faces and names, holding the printout up to the camera. "Not sure about *him*, but I know *he's* dead now, and so is *he*," moving her finger along the rows. "*Martin*, that's him, the philosopher; buggered off to live in some Unabomber-style shack in the woods, I hear, so Merrywhile evidently made an impression on *him*... *She* moved away, then died – cancer, I think... And him, too – car crash, I believe..." And so on, through the twenty three names, her finger popping them off like targets at a shooting range, for almost all of them had shuffled off this mortal coil, for one reason or another. "It's like *Final Destination*, isn't it!" She laughs. "The curse of the monkey's paw! Or should that be 'MUNKi's'!" Making air quotes, laughing again. "Sorry, I shouldn't laugh. *He's* still alive, though, I think. And the boy, of course."

Mina has turned the page, and is now looking at the smaller photograph of the boy being given the guided tour by the young man with glasses.

"You mean this Herbert Morlock chap?"

"Yes." She pulls a face. "Finance type, I think he was, or perhaps a lawyer. As I say, they made a show of having all sorts of people there, all disciplines – if you can call lust for power a discipline."

"You didn't like him, I gather."

"No one did, particularly. Charming, in a smarmy way, I suppose, but trust him as far as you could throw him. He was the group leader, of sorts, but unelected – purely because he seemed to be connected to people higher up in the firm. Though he was still quite young then himself – not much older than me. 'The tooth dean', your grandad used to call him, which I took to be a reference to his self-important manner and winning dentistry, but which apparently means something rude in Welsh. Attempted to ingratiate himself with us – the 'free radicals', as Karl christened our little subgroup! But we weren't having any of him. Tried to make the boy call him 'Uncle Bertie'." She gives a theatrical shiver. "Though he was no more his uncle than I was."

"And the boy? Who was he?"

"Michael Sommeil. The big chief's grandson. I dare say you've heard of the late great James Mayer? He was very taken with the robot, as I recall – the boy, I mean. Quiet lad."

"Well thank you very much," Cari says, a short time later. "I've taken up enough of your time. You've been really helpful."

"No problem at all. As I say, it was a lovely surprise to see that painting after all these years, and to hear from you. It was my parting gift to your grandad." She looks at Cari curiously. "You've got his eyes, you know."

"And his eyebrows, unfortunately!" They both laugh. "Oh," just about to sign off, "I meant to ask: why the eyes? In your paintings. Why are all the eyes the same?"

Mina thinks a moment before responding. "I think I got it from medieval manuscripts, the way they painted animals – all the eyes look human, to me. So I suppose it just gave me the idea that we're all just part of one big family, you know? From the amoeba to the angels!" She smiles. "The Great Chain of Being, I think they used to call it. We all spring from the same root, really, don't we?"

Sharp as a tack on all other details, there is one thing that Mina Boucher's admirable memory has gotten wrong.

"Hang on, connection's a bit shit," says Mel. Her big hair fills Cari's phone screen, giving occasional hints of chair backs and a window with passing scenery.

"Where are you? Are you on a train?"

"Train to Venice. Still following the same lead, but I *am* making progress, I think. Maybe. Come on, come on…", goading her laptop. "Right, here we go. Why are European trains so much nicer, by the way? And cheaper. I mean, if this is nationalisation, then where do I sign up, comrade! There – thought I'd heard of it. Report from five years back: 'Esteemed Physicist Dies in Aggravated Burglary'."

"Shit," says Cari. "Not a heart attack, then."

"Well, says here that a heart attack might have been brought on by the burglary and assault – '… found in his Copenhagen home … signs of bruising about the face … ligature marks on the wrists'. Nice."

Cari's mind jumps straight to Auntie Cat, accompanied by a sudden stab of concern.

"Did they arrest anyone for it?"

"Hm. 'Perpetrator never found,' apparently."

"Maybe we could try to speak to the relatives?" suggests

Cari. "See what was stolen?"

"Pointless, I'm afraid. Says… 'laptop, assorted minor valuables, and contents of the safe, which were unknown' – I would guess that no one knew what was in that safe other than Nielsberg himself."

"So what do we think? Tortured him for his safe combination? His laptop password?"

"*Pfft.* Don't need a password."

"Safe, then?"

"Ways around that too, I'm afraid to say."

"Well, if they'd been such sophisticated burglars they wouldn't have needed to interrogate him in the first place."

"Fair point. And they could easily have broken in when he wasn't there. Whoever it was appears to have wanted something from him. Which still doesn't rule out your more run-of-the-mill thief, I guess."

All their combined detective work had so far produced some results, but it's a stop-start affair, and painfully slow. Adding death by aggravated burglary to micro-drone surveillance and blackmail by megacorporation didn't really help matters.

"So what next?" asks Cari.

"How's your dating game?"

Cari's younger self had once owned a t-shirt depicting some extravagantly moustachioed guitar god, kneeling before his burning Stratocaster, coaxing flames from its demise, and beneath it the slogan, *Without music life would be a mistake.* While, over the years, her sartorial tastes had moved on, she still abides by the t-shirt's sentiment – especially at times like this.

That said, anyone listening to the current selection on her playlist might be forced to question the truth of that slogan, or else the assertion that this is in fact music. *Splunge Garden* are an acquired taste, to be sure: their basslines gravitate toward the subsonic, they favour the atonality and off-beat tempos that might remind a cultured ear (perhaps disapprovingly) of Stravinsky or Schoenberg, and marry all this to the kind of choral screaming that evokes a riot in a burning building. But Cari's tastes are nothing if not eclectic, a catholicism she likes to think suggests a positive openness to new experiences and a free-spirited opposition to dogmatism.

But this eclecticism she also owes, indirectly, to her father, whom she'd caught one day some years back loading a large black box containing his old CDs, even some vinyls, into the back of the car to take them to the charity shop.

"You can't do that!"

"Why not? Think of the space we'll save. You can get them all on Spotify, now, anyway."

He'd carried on loading over the sound of her protestations as she'd started reopening the boxes, rifling through the titles, desperately feeling she should at least save something. Then, as he'd returned from the house with another load, he was stopped short to find her with a strange look on her face, staring down at an open jewel case, at the name penned inside.

"Was this Mum's?"

Actually, he'd eventually admitted, almost all of it was, he himself having the tinnest of ears. And so they'd reached a compromise: if she would keep the boxes in her room, then she could do with their contents as she pleased. As a digital native, pretty much all Cari's music was downloaded. Here, however, in actual physical form, was a collection generated not by algorithmic suggestion, but assembled by time, dictated by chance and circumstance, by gifting and acquaintance, that was therefore a tantalising trail left by the life it had enriched, by the person who had lived it, and that made that person slightly less of a mystery, slightly less a black hole.

Patiently she had explored, picking out those pieces that resonated or intrigued, obscure and popular alike, digitising and grafting them into her existing playlist, which thereby slowly morphed into something more than a reflection of her own personal tastes, her own limited musical exposure; that became in fact a sort of conversation with that someone she'd never known, and now never would – even if, at times, this did make the list jarringly eclectic.

As if in proof of this, finished with the bowel-shuddering brevity of "Marianas Trench Make-out" (0.39), obscure '80s thrash metal gives way to something more serene, *Splunge Garden* being a mere tonal palate-cleanser for the second movement of Vivaldi's "Winter" – which is in turn interrupted by her phone.

"So how's it going?" Mel asks.

"Right, so I've put in as much as I can," she replies, "but we're still… Well, I still just think it's all a bit of a long shot. I mean, what are the odds of actually finding someone like this?"

"Better than you'd think. You won't believe how helpful it's been, story-wise. Uses the Backus equation."

"And what's that?"

"Something to do with maths. My God, I would kill – *literally kill* – for these ice creams. *Literally*. I mean, what *do* they put in them? Is it cocaine? I wouldn't be surprised – well, maybe a *bit* surprised; but actually, you know, not that much."

"Arrived in Venice, then."

"Mmhm. I'm going to be the size of a house. Sorry, so how many does that leave us now?"

The journalist has set her up with private access to something that seems to provide a sort of meta-search of the most common dating sites, which it then cross-matches with all the information that can be scraped from social media profiles, *Divinia*, and other public online presences. Handy for winnowing out the weirdos, liars and creeps, but not exactly legit, Cari suspects.

"I mean, is this even legal?"

"Sorry, you're breaking up," Mel replies.

"I said, is this—"

"Jesus, kid. You're not really breaking up. Just don't go telling anyone about it, OK?"

As pointless as it had seemed to her, prompted by the journalist's grilling, Cari had recalled every last morsel of information from the meeting with the hacker. Despite the voice disguiser, he'd seemed to have a vaguely London-based accent, and his familiarity with its geography, together with the disapproving intonation he'd given the word "tourists", made her think that it was a reasonable assumption that he was a native (or had been) – as much as any of this was reasonable, anyway. So she'd ticked "male" and "London".

Five mill and change. Great.

Age? Somewhere between eighteen and forty-four, if she had to guess, and probably toward the older end of that. Occupation? Given that he was a hacker, would that be "works from home"? Ugh, this was futile – but she'd persisted, nevertheless, adding interest keywords for computers, online gaming, anime and cartoons, *Star Wars*, samurai, Kurosawa (an inspired bit of lateral thinking, there), and basically anything else she could think of.

"So, assuming he's straight," Cari says, "*and* a he … that leaves … 532. I mean, how do we know he's even on any of these sites?"

"He's a middle-aged single male who's into computers, *Star Wars* and samurai films. Where else is he going to go to meet the ladies?"

"Bit harsh," thinking of her own exclusively-digital dating life. "Still, this is going to take forever."

"Hm. Well, it is a fair mountain to climb, but if you have a look through the profiles, then try and—"

"Wait." What had he said? "Easier than getting up the Mountain!" God, how could she have missed that!

"The mountain?" Asks Mel. "What's that?"

"He's a True Believer."

"What the hell's that mean?"

"It means …" typing, clicking, "we're now down to 26."

BEHEMOTH

10

Gerry looks around.

It is a mock-up of your standard child's bedroom – at the moment, a male child of between eight and ten. There are football posters on the wall, media screens and gaming consoles, comics and books, action figures, some musical instruments (toylike guitars and drum-sets – things to thrash and smash). Adjoined to this is a larger play area, with space enough for more outdoor-type activities: a bike, some climbing frames, a few bits of sports equipment. On other days, for different gender or age groups, they will swap all of this out. The gun-toting action figures will become dolls, the footballs become skipping ropes and hula-hoops. Instead of a selection of superhero films, the interactive media screens will display websites for the latest age- and demographic-appropriate boy bands. Gerry grimaces to herself: still dollies and guns. She'd thought they'd moved beyond that. And why not microscopes for the girls? Art materials for the boys? Both for both? But one battle at a time. And besides, MUNKi will wipe away such tired stereotyping – well, if they can ever get him to work.

When she'd first seen the set-up, its vague familiarity had unsettled her: the mocked-up obstacle course, the seats and screens and monitors for visitors and technicians. Then, of course, it had struck her: *Morlock*; her visit to the "pit". She'd half expected the doors to swing open and, with Nurembergian precision, a hundred pristine military robots to troop in. Remembering it, she grimaces again, trying to push the association away, drown it somewhere deep and dark. But it resists, unflushable, buoying relentlessly back to consciousness, as it has been doing periodically over the past few weeks.

The doors do suddenly swing open, but it is only MUNKi – no, wait, it's the *actual* little boy (God, she must get some sleep, or her eyes tested for a fresh prescription). The child looks about eight years old, and is led by the hand by one of the female post-docs. She walks him over first to the playroom, a brief tour of its various attractions, and then of the larger "outside" play area, before leaving him to amuse himself. The plan is that he be left to his own devices for ten minutes or so, to immerse himself in the various wonders on offer, before introducing MUNKi. Initially, of course, the robot itself will become the main subject of the child's focus, but gradually, over the next few hours, it is hoped that child and robot will begin to develop a playmate relationship. It is this interaction that the watchers – a group of Merrywhile people associated with marketing and toy design, processes in which Gerry and Michael have been forced to take a back seat – are supposedly there to observe. But in the relatively brief time that these people have been involved in the project, Gerry has come to hate them all.

A prompt ten minutes later, MUNKi himself is brought in, holding the hand of the same post-doc (where is Zac today, anyway?). He looks like a kid on his first day at school. Gerry gives him a little finger wave, and her heart skips a beat as the little robot hesitantly returns it. She and the post-doc then retreat to the observation area – a series of separate rooms with viewing screens – that also, now she thinks of it, remind her of... *Aaarrgh!*

"Why have we only got heart-rate for the child? What about its brain function?" says... *L. Gogol, Marketing Strategy*

Lead – Gerry scrutinising her name tag.

"Its mother wasn't happy with that level of monitoring," a tablet-clutching subordinate responds.

"Happy? Aren't we fucking *paying* her to be happy? Next time, make it a condition of the payment."

"Understood."

"How are we doing with the name? Can we go with what we've got?"

"No problems across the European languages," a different, female subordinate, "though we may have to alter the spelling to match local phonemes – 'M-O-N-Q-U-I' for French, for example. And then also, of course, that'll affect the acronym, if we decide to go with that and not simply treat it as a brand name. Which is the—"

"I don't think we need fret too much over losing the acronym," Ms Gogol laughs, making Gerry bristle. "And Asia?"

"Asia… *Fine* across most Asian dialects. *Manko* in Japanese – or *monko*, depending on the, er, the form of transliteration used – this is the closest word with … which has associations that we should, you know, *avoid*. But MUNKi is different enough, I think? So we should be OK?"

"And the colour? What did the focus groups have to say?"

"Predictably, boys favoured blue, red, black or metallic, while girls preferred pastel shades or patterns, but there was some variation in this through the different ages and demographics – again, fairly predictable. It's all in the report." With a gesture, the assistant flicks a series of graphs and pie charts up onto one of the wall-mounted screens, which her boss briefly surveys, nodding and chewing her cheek.

They then display some packaging mockups – the first time Gerry has seen any actual branding. As a logo, they've opted for something simple and friendly: the traditional smiley emoticon – a bracket for a mouth, a colon for eyes, rotated clockwise ninety degrees – enclosed within three overlapping white circles suggesting the borders of fur on a chimp's face, and the whole thing imposed on a black outer circle for the head, with two small half-circles for ears at 10 and

2 o'clock. It is a stylised cartoon of MUNKi himself, and, Gerry concedes, actually not unpleasant; in fact, quite cute.

"His head looks very … *round*," says Ms Gogol. "Gill, what are the projecteds for penetration into East Asia? Do we have hypotheticals based on face and body shape, voice, and so on?"

"Yes. Here you go Lubia," says G. D. … Ray? … *Design Implementation … something* (she really does need a fresh prescription). "As you can see, a round face, such as we currently have, suggests deeper and broader penetration into the eight to ten bracket, whilst a more angular look…"

Can they hear themselves? And why has she been landed with this solo gig again? Curse that lazy arsed – oh, and here he is, finally, sneaking guiltily in at the back like some tardy student, sidling up to her, a mouthed apology and a whispered, *"How's our boy doing?"*

"Which one?"

"Our *boy, of course*," replies Sommeil. *"The metal one."*

She grabs his arm and steers him back out the door and into the corridor where they can talk more freely.

"Well, they aren't even paying attention to the interaction. It's all 'deeper and broader penetration into Asia'."

"Ooh! Sounds racy!" He grins, earning a roll of the eyes. "Look, Gerry, I know you hate all of this, but we aren't toy specialists. And what do we know about marketing, or any of that stuff? If we want the little man to be a success, then we have to hand that part over."

"I know, I know." She nods. "But I wonder if any of *them*" – she jabs a finger toward the room they've just left – "has ever even *been* a child, let alone tried to imagine what one might want. I mean," pointing unsubtly through the window at a particularly officious looking minion, "you'd think *his* first toy was a bloody clipboard. And it's all so … impersonal. Not a word about the fun the kids might have, the things they can learn, the joy of play and discovery. It's like they're talking about selling cars or washing machines. A-and the kids aren't even *kids*, they're … consumers, 'targets for agents of socialisation' – whatever the hell that is."

Sommeil nods. "Come on. They don't need us. Let's try another viewing room."

He enters the room next door, a high, room-length mirror along its shared wall, and ushers her inside. He switches on the array of viewing screens and they both look up at the boy as he shyly begins to interact with the little robot. It will be reading the boy's facial expressions and body language, his vocal intonation, using these as cues for how to proceed, how best to deepen the interaction without spooking him – even for behavioural signs of autism, or other types of neural diversity, which Gerry thinks unlikely in this case (though no doubt the clipboards have scheduled sessions for that and other "niche demographics").

"Do you like music?" MUNKi is asking. The boy nods. "What's your favourite singer or band?" The boy shrugs. "Or films?" Another shrug. "What about superheroes?" A less non-committal head-tilt. "Shall we see what we've got?"

Using his in-built network access, MUNKi scrolls through some of the recent movie releases on his chest screen (filtered appropriate to age rating). "Stop me when you see something you like." After half a minute, the boy points. "That one? Great choice! You can point, or you can simply say, 'that one'."

The boy nods. "That one," he says, and smiles.

It's working.

Having watched with equal if not greater intensity, the same thought apparently in his mind, Michael turns to her with a grin. "You see? It *is* all worth it."

There is a knock at the door, and Alexis the post-doc pokes her head around it. "Oh, there you are. The, um, the marketing team want to know whether consumer purchases and browsing history are currently set up to be automatically stored and relayed to Merrywhile, as a default of the purchase conditions. Or whether – how did they put it? – whether this was, er, 'optoutable' for the user? They said they would prefer 'unoptoutable', as—"

Gerry groans, then strides to the wall they share with the next room and begins miming aggressive stabbing motions with an imaginary knife, not realising that she is the wrong side of a two-way mirror.

"Thank you, Alex." Sommeil smiles. "Please tell them we'll be there in a moment."

Zac had never faked a sick day in his life. But he needs to figure some things out. He needs to plan. It seems the past has a way of following you, of tracking you down. And he needs to work out what to do now it has finally found him.

He'd first come across it in grad school, as part of a seminar group on the social applications of robotics. As a talking point for their presentation, another grad student had rigged up a robot with a camera, the view from which you could experience remotely through a VR headset, and they'd all taken turns in having a go. He could still remember the weird sensation, his gradual diminishing awareness of his body, his sense of self, as he *became* the robot, its wobbling gait traversing a room somewhere else in the department. It was like a physical avatar: he saw what it saw, saw through its "eyes". But then, a strange impulse had taken him: what if he were to visit *himself*? Where his body was? He'd directed the robot out the door, onto the corridor, making its way to the seminar room where he sat with the headset, driven on by a strange curiosity. What would he see when he got there? He'd be looking at himself looking at himself looking at himself looking at himself... It would be an infinite feedback loop. But what would that *feel* like?

There'd been laughter, initially, when the group had realised what he was doing, some egging him on, even the professor, hearing the robot's steps as it neared, the clank and whir of its servomotors, coming ever closer – until "he" had collided with one of the department's secretaries, emerging from her office off the corridor, blinded by the stacks of paper in her arms on her way to refilling the photocopier, and stumbling over the robot with curses and crashing noises – and they'd had to call a halt. He was surprised at how frustrated he'd felt, like he'd been denied something, some ultimate revelation.

Later, as part of an obligatory online discussion group, they'd talked about the experiment – technical aspects, to begin with, how remote robotics might be used for business or other purposes, but then, talking about what Zac had tried to do, the debate had turned philosophical, to do with identity. Were you where your body was, or where your viewpoint was? Where were "you"? But rather than satisfy his earlier curiosity, the discussion had just frustrated it, translating something that had been experiential, personal, into something intellectual, merely theoretical. Philosophy wasn't really Zac's thing. It never seemed to decide anything, as far as he could tell, only stood in the doorway, on the threshold, debating about – well, the nature of thresholds, probably. At least with science you had questions you could actually answer, that meant something, that were *actually* useful. So he'd eventually disengaged from the debate, just sat back and lurked, scrolling through it lazily half-bored, till one comment suddenly caught his eye, a snatch of verse, child-like, going round and round in a circle – a roundel?

"You are not you are not here is not real is a game without rules made by you are not you are not here is not real is a game without rules made by you are not you are not…"

And so on, filling the page – or anyway, the post word limit – causing general amusement and bemusement, derision, abuse, and eventually, the ire of the discussion moderator, for when the page next refreshed, it had been deleted.

That was his introduction to the Catechism.

It was weird, really, like coming full circle, back to where he'd been before – but not quite, because while some things were similar, others were different. But all *that* had happened to a different boy; not to Zac, but to Isaac. And like the name, he'd thought he'd left all that behind, a secret backstory, known only to himself.

He'd been the only kid on the street without a TV, let alone a console or a phone. Mostly, he'd just played along – pretended he'd watched what others had watched, or read, or played with.

"Who's your favourite superhero?"

And to begin with they'd simply put his reticence down to him being a bit shy; a bit slow, perhaps. When pushed, sometimes, he'd just repeat what he'd heard others say. But that trick had a shelf-life, assumed no follow-up questions, and eventually they all knew what he was anyway, what his family were: *Breathers* – the outsiders' disparaging term. Though sometimes they'd still confuse him with Amish.

You don't really question things when you're a kid. Beliefs are like furniture. You live with them, sit on them, day in, day out. They're not even thoughts; they're just there, part of the background. It was only later – seeing others had *different* furniture, that their lives rested on *other* beliefs – that he realised he didn't have to live with what he'd inherited, with what had been passed on to him. It was only *then* that things had started to change. But the exact moment was hard to pinpoint. The tension may even have been there from the start.

All parents are proud of their children – or are supposed to be. They want them to do well. And there was the thing with the talents. Martha had made a big deal about that.

"Remember, Isaac," his mother would say, "the things you're good at, they're not just for you; they're for everyone. As each has received a gift, employ it in serving one another, as good managers of the grace of God in its various forms."

But he'd still agonised over it, as if part of him knew, even then, that those gifts would lead him *away*. Later on, in Math, he'd read about Pascal, and how he'd had the same problem, how it too had torn him apart, had even endangered his faith. You study, you question, but that just leads to more studying, more questioning. So how do you know where to draw the line? When to stop? To draw a line, a boundary, you need to see both sides of it. And once you do that, once you've seen the other side, then it's already too late, because from then on the other side will always be there. That's what was meant by the story of the serpent in the Garden, the loss of innocence: you can never unknow things.

He'd needed a computer for college, but he daren't have asked for one. "Satanic mills," his father would have not-even-half-jokingly spat, his favoured phrase for anything more complicated than a toaster (he daren't have told him that, by then, most of *them* even had computers in). That phrase was William Blake, he'd later learnt. But it was his mother who'd first shown him the beautiful watercolour illustrations, "what angels really look like", turning the pages slowly, almost reverentially. She'd taken a liking to the artist's handmade aesthetic, perhaps, his fervent nonconformism, his opposition to the rational, the scientific – yet, he later suspected, never fully realising the extent of that nonconformism, that unorthodoxy. And so he'd pretended to have study sessions so he could stay late and work in the library, using their PCs, preserving the semblance of that which had already been lost. For by then – looking back – the threshold had already been crossed, the doorway passed through. That first step toward knowledge, in utilisation of his God-given gifts, had also been the last.

But seeing it then, that verse – roundel, whatever – had stirred something in him, recalled something he'd thought forgotten; coming back, as if from long and circuitous wandering, to walk down the hallway, to knock on his door. And he'd begun to wonder.

God's gifts had led him to science, which in turn had led him west, from his tiny home town in Northern Indiana, to university in Topeka, Kansas, and a major in maths (with a clandestine minor in CompSci). The shadow-line finally crossed, Martha had done everything to shield his father John from full knowledge for as long as she could, but by the time Isaac had become "Zac", announcing he'd been accepted to pursue a doctorate in AI at Stanford, no more shielding was possible, and he was thenceforward (his mother sadly informed him, relaying his father's exact word) "anathema". He'd had to look it up: a cold, almost legalistic term – "formal excommunication from a church or community" – but in reality more likely a wordless retreat to the porch to smoke his pipe and fume over filial prodigality, his son the lost sheep.

The secret finally out, the tension he'd felt had at first morphed into hurt, then sadness, and then into a sort of cold calm, before eventually resolving into what he was surprised to find was relief. Free at last from The Crazy, as he was gradually coming to see it, the Great Irrational Denial – of modernity, of science, even of medicine, as the virus had quietly worked his way through his family, decimating, taking its quota, unheeding of Heathen and Chosen alike. And free at last to decide (though covertly, a process begun long ago) his favourite film, game, his favourite superhero, and whatever other wonders Babylon had to offer, Satanic mills included.

But still, for all the exhilaration, the new discoveries, the escaping *from* something, all this time there must still have been something missing inside him, a lack, some gap or crack through which old whispers had eventually begun to seep, to re-emerge transformed.

The Catechism did not seem to have an author – at least, none that he could find. You would just come across it here and there, cropping up in random places, a virus-like idea spreading from host to congenial host. Suggested sources referenced each other, or pointed beyond, into the wilds of the rumoured and conjectural. Eventually, he concluded, it didn't really matter where it had come from. The question was: what did it mean? And on that topic, there was also no shortage of speculation, but most of which centred around something called transhumanism.

He must have known of it, peripherally, at the fringes of his awareness – news stories of cryonics, of brain scanning, articles on mind uploading, nanotechnology and cell repair – but had never connected it all together into a coherent whole. He'd been taught to think of science as neutral, objective, but this particular application of it was something else, something almost familiar. Here too was logic and rigour, was the love of the provable and the empirical, but there was also something more, something not content to stop sceptically at the threshold, on the doorstep, but to pass *beyond* – not into faith, as such (he was not about to rush back *there*), but to some vision that was simultaneously grounded in the real and the possible. And gradually, he began to see what had been missing – from his life before, but also from his life now. This new thing was a step beyond both, yet also something that *reached back*, connecting them, his two worlds, the future linking hands with the past.

He'd almost thought of ringing them – forgetting for a moment that his parents didn't even afford themselves *that* concession to modern life. But even if they had, would they have answered? Listened? Shared his realisation? Unlikely. But here it all was, the very stuff of their "study groups", the open sessions they'd run hoping to ensnare the intellectually curious: the resurrection, the promise of immortality, even the nit-picking controversies over what form that would take, whether the old body would be necessary, or whether we would live on in some new, transcendent form. And with all this, a new utopia, a technological heaven on earth, free from war and disease, from hardship and loss. It was as if a comforting, familiar voice had come to him from the past. *You see?* it said. *You weren't stupid. You weren't deluded. You were just awaiting the right language, the right concepts.* And with this came the excitement of recognition, of familiarity transfigured, engulfing him, sweeping him up into an enthusiasm the like of which he had not felt since the Sundays of childhood. But rational! As if *faith itself* had been resurrected, transformed – by science! All that had gone before, the riddling prophecies and allusions, were only *now* to be understood for what they were: *prefigurations*. And now, the darkening glass clearing, he could finally see.

Lubia, Gill, and all their tablet-clutching underlings have departed, muttering as they leave about the need to focus-group whether the robot might have greater penetration in cultures with strong pre-existing monkey archetypes in their religion, myth or literature. Children of various demographics have been collected by their demographically appropriate parents. And Alexis the post-doc has finally been relieved of her ever-anxious-to-be-helpful attentiveness by Gerry, who's told her – in a rare flash of blunt honesty mistaken for humour – to "bugger off and find a social life before it's too late". ("Ha! Yes, Dr Andersen! Ha, ha. I will!" – she wouldn't.) All of which leaves Gerry, distractedly stacking, shelving, re-boxing and resetting the various toys, games and gadgets, flotsam of the afternoon's play, with Sommeil concernedly looking on.

"We have people to do that, Gerry." She nonetheless continues at her slow pace. "Why not let it be? Go home."

There is something soothing about it – tidying, reasserting order – honest, even. Far more honest than what she's reluctantly taken part in today, anyway, each day now representing a small but irrevocable step away from the founding vision of the project she had joined, the further pollution of its once crystalline ideal. There is still time to bail out, perhaps, save herself, but for the project itself it is too late. The cyclopean engine of the Merrywhile juggernaut has begun to grind into slow but inexorable motion, and soon it will be a runaway train.

"Gerry? What's wrong?"

"Sorry, Michael. Tired. Just tired, that's all. Long days and little sleep. I'll be OK."

"I … I know it feels like we're stepping back, like we're handing over control. But that's not the case. The work we've done, the progress we've made, all *that* is real, is worth being proud of. You have to trust that all *that* is still at the core of all this …" – he spreads his hands to take in the play area and its contents, the rooms with their display screens, allowing Gerry to mentally fill in the lacuna: *Bullshit? Nakedly cynical commercial exploitation?* – "… all this *peripheral* stuff – marketing, what have you. We're on the verge of something … some breakthrough, something … *titanic*. I can feel it."

Titanic. Monstrosity. Overreaching. Disaster. The word has bad associations for her, for anyone with a passing acquaintance with history – for him too, were he to stop to consider it, were he not still mesmerised by his shiny never-nearing grail. Can she make him see that? She looks up at him.

He still retains that zeal, that boyish gleam, their once common enthusiasm now increasingly his alone, appearing more and more to her as something alien, something disquieting. Perhaps, put in the right way, she can yet get through to him – but not today. Another time, maybe, when her reserves are higher. She changes the topic.

"Where's Zac? I haven't seen him all day – actually, since Friday, I think."

"He's taken the week off. Some mild viral thing. Nothing serious. Told him we don't want his viruses anyway, thank you very much. Too much work to do."

"No indeed." But it is unlike Zac to cry-off. She had almost to pretend to sack him last time he was ill, just a standard case of the 'flu, but threatening to turn up febrile and bug-ridden, infect them all out of sheer diligence. "So, what next?"

"More observed play sessions on Thursday, followed by strategic planning meetings with … well, the same crew."

She groans. "Can't we just run away?"

He sighs dramatically, shaking his head. "They would find us."

"Change our names?"

"Their resources are infinite."

"Change our *faces*!"

"Wouldn't fool them."

"Live out the rest of our allotted span—"

"Pointless."

" – on a desert island somewhere, beyond the penetration of marketing."

"No such place."

Through this exchange, Sommeil's playful grin has gradually faded, and now his face is a mask, his eyes glazed, focused on something that isn't there.

"Ah, but isn't that what 'utopia' *means*?" she persists. "*No such place*? A girl can dream, can't she?"

It took Zac a while to work out what the Catechism was actually about. He knew something of hacker groups from his CompSci lectures on network security, enough to know that they were often chaotic, non-hierarchical, with no stable chain of command or core mission. And in this at least it followed type. There were no apparent barriers to membership – aside from the technical know-how and the motivation to access that particular corner of the dark web where it convened – which, for such as him, was easy. In fact, there was no membership at all, merely a Darwinian free-for-all, a constant spawn of threads, down- or up-voted, the topics that survived being momentary victors in the battle for the group's collective attention. There were brags, flame wars, calls for boycotts, for principled hacks on despicable targets, or pranks on hapless souls with the simple misfortune to have somehow offended the group's amorphous, shifting code – all scrolling by in old-school, text-only live chat (no sparkly graphics for them, let alone VR). However, its cornerstone was something called "Simulation Theology", which presented a very peculiar take on virtuality.

Having gone around in circles trying to understand the Catechism, he'd eventually found someone patient enough to explain its fundamentals, and discovered that the repeating verse, the roundel, actually condensed six separate precepts.

"Step one:" his guide had begun, "Disassociation. *You are not 'you'*. Your avatar isn't your real self. Every representation is a form created by The Great Enemy, the Demiurge."

The semi-Biblical phrases, the End-of-Days talk – Zac couldn't work out how seriously they took it all, or whether it was all merely playful, tongue-in-cheek appropriation.

"Step two: Displacement. *You are not 'here'*. By extension, if your avatar isn't you, then where it 'exists' isn't where *you* are either. Where you *think* you are, you aren't."

Was it all just a sophisticated joke, then? An intellectual game?

"Step three: Delusion. *'Here' is not real*. Because you're not what or where you think you are, then the place that appears to be 'real' is actually illusory."

But wasn't all this pretty obvious? He hadn't ever been tempted to think of his online presence as 'real', or to mistake the virtual for the physical.

"Step four: Dream. *'Real' is a game*. If 'reality' is an illusion, then nothing really matters. Everything is just a dream, a story we tell ourselves, a game to be played. And so what you *think* is important, actually isn't.

"Step five: Disinhibition. *A game without rules*. Since nothing matters – or at least, what you think matters actually *doesn't* – then the shackles that others place upon us, or that we place upon ourselves – legal, moral, social, political – are there to be broken. We can do whatever we want."

But this was simply a recipe for online anarchy, wasn't it? Do what you want, because none of this is real?

"The sixth and final step: Dominion. *Rules made by you*. Since it's all a game, then *any* rules are arbitrary. But there have to be *some* rules – we're rational beings, so there must be some consistency in how we act, there must be reasons for our choices. The only legitimate rules are therefore those we *rationally choose* to abide by."

So they were principled trolls, with their own troll bushido. Well, at least now he understood what it all meant.

"I see. So basically, nothing is real, and we can do whatever we want online, as long as we can back it up?" Zac had summed up.

"Who said anything about online?" his guide replied.

It was the word "avatar" that had misled him.

But even this, his guide had explained, had a spiritual pedigree, born of belief systems that saw the world as unreal, a magic show of illusion and misdirection, a veil of misleading perception.

A simulation.

And when you knew what to look for, it was everywhere – in philosophy, science, religion; from Plato's cave to Descartes's demon, Zhuang Zhi's butterfly to Schrödinger's cat – and Blake himself, of course: "all that we see is vision".

Only the mind is real.

He knew from his doorstepping days that coming to believe anything was a gradual process, something people must do by inches.

They'd gone to the beach – a typical low-tech family outing. His swimming was getting stronger, and he'd been keen to test himself, to see how far he could go, if he could reach it: a sand bank some half a mile out, home to weary seabirds and random detritus. His mother had stood there on the shore, looking on anxiously, torn between willing him beyond her own timid limitations, to excel in the skill she'd never herself acquired – that neither parent had, in fact, during their landlocked childhoods – and fearing lest he get too far out, that a riptide should take him, or that he should tire and flounder. But as it grew closer, nearing stroke by stroke, his fear had increased as fatigue had set in, his panic grew as he realised he was alone, beyond all help, and only he could save himself. But even then, his limbs beginning to cramp, his anxious breaths shortening with each stroke, return to the shore felt more and more the wrong option. He'd come so far, was so close he could almost touch it. Wouldn't turning back then make the whole thing meaningless?

He often looked back to that day, coming to see in it a sort of metaphor for belief. You would start out, tip-toeing into the shallows, chancing a step or two back and forth, before starting to wade in, to acclimatise, getting deeper and deeper, until finally, the ground disappearing, you turned to see the shore farther away than your destination. And not seabirds or flotsam, but others who had already made the crossing, beckoning you on from your nearing goal. And once you were there? The exhilaration, the sense of achievement, of belonging; that you were one of the select few who had made the crossing, that *knew* the truth. And after that, return was even harder, for it was not just the weary trek back, the admission of error, doubling back along the wrong path taken, but the loss of those you would leave behind, who would see in your return only betrayal.

Of course, he was not blind to the parallels, and looking at it now, he can see that this is what had happened with the Catechism. But as he'd investigated and explored, followed and engaged with the debates, testing the water, wading further in, his burgeoning interest gradually overcoming his scepticism, he'd also begun to see the key difference. The Catechists – the fervent adherents and disseminators of the Catechism – were willing to walk their talk. They weren't content to sit on their hands, date-guessing and portent-spotting, awaiting the day-and-hour-of-which-no-one knows. They were going to *do* something.

And finally Zac had realised.

They're crowdsourcing the Rapture.

At first, nothing seems amiss.

Sommeil has come in early, as he commonly does. Normally, he finds Gerry, Zac or one of the other post-docs slumbering in the cot. But peeping his head around the door, this morning he finds it empty. He looks around the workshop: also deserted. Are they in the toilet? No. Wasn't it supposed to be Zac's shift? But of course: he must still be ill. Someone else, then. Who is covering?

This is unacceptable. They fought tooth and nail over these bloody internships, which could be decided by literally any means, as cruel as you like, and still he'd have a queue of candidates from here to Trevi Fountain. So for any one of them to drop the ball like this is unforgivable.

But perhaps it was meant to be Gerry herself, and she's simply forgotten. She's looked out of sorts lately. But no, even out of sorts she would never allow such negligence to endanger all they've worked for – would she? He calls her, rousing her raspy-voiced from sleep.

"What do you mean, no one's there?"

"Well, just no one," he says. "Who was on the roster?"

"Tomi was on the day shift, and then … Alex, I think?"

He calls Alexis. Already up.

"No, Dr Sommeil, I *was* due to come in, to cover, but I swapped my shift back."

He is starting to get a bad feeling about this.

"Back with whom?"

"Well, with Zac. He'd been due to come in, and then he was ill, but then he messaged to say—"

A stab of anxiety suddenly spurring him into action, he sprints back toward the cradle – he'd just looked at the cot, hadn't even thought to check…

But of course, when he gets there, the cradle is empty.

MUNKi is gone.

But what could be done?

While, to much rejoicing, it sometimes worked, Zac had never really seen the point in proselytising, and some of his most embarrassing childhood memories were of being dragged door to door, standing demurely at the back while John or Martha, Uncle Graham (God rest him), or some other member of his extended Breather family, had sought to exploit the politeness of some poor soul praying only to enjoy a last day of laziness before the daily grind recommenced.

"Dude, you're barking up the wrong tree. I believe in *science*, you know? The Big Bang?"

"But who *created* the Big Bang? What came *before*? Have you ever wondered about *that*?"

Pointless, mostly. Trying to shift someone's worldview was like trying to build a ship at sea. You couldn't start from scratch, but had to work with what was already there, take it slowly, replacing the old vessel plank by plank.

And what many Catechists advocated felt much like that: hanging out on forums, gaming, even online dating clubs, trying to subtly interest people in that which they'd never come there for. But the world would not be converted one at a time. It would take forever. And who cares how *many* believe? Would that really change anything?

"What you are looking for is looking."

It is one of his favourite quotes, and commonly attributed to St Francis of Assisi (though, looking for a source, he'd found it only attributed to another author, who in turn had attributed it to Assisi – which was the Internet in a nutshell). But wherever it came from, he personally took it to mean that often the answer is staring us in the face, and where we're already headed – looked at in a new way – is where in fact we should be going.

It seems obvious, now, looking back. He'd imagined it would all begin somewhere else – in the wilderness, on the fringes. But where better than in Babylon itself? In the belly of the whale, the behemoth that had swallowed the world? For as he now sees, the path he'd been walking all along, even from those first stolen nights on the library's PCs, had been leading him here, to Merrywhile, to Project MUNKi. And the more he thinks about it, the more it almost feels predestined; almost – in the language of former times – a Call.

"Zac?"

They had been standing at the lab door, MUNKi's hand in one of his, and a long-handled torch in the other, like parent and kid about to visit the park for a midnight play on the swings.

"T-Tomi? You're back."

She had stood in the corridor with her hand poised over the keypad, having just tapped in her entry code.

"My bag. I think I left… What are you doing?"

Zac had glanced down at MUNKi, whose eyes had tracked up to meet his, as if silently willing each other to cobble together a believable cover story.

"I-I thought I heard someone. In the corridor, I mean. That was probably you, though, right? I was going to check."

She'd frowned. "So you were taking MUNKi with you? To check?" She'd walked in through the open lab door, closing it behind her, still frowning.

"Well, I…."

She'd given him a funny look. "Is everything OK, Zac?"

"What?"

"You just – look, if you're still worried about it, we can do a drone sweep."

"I don't think that's necess—"

"Or we can ask security to do a manual—"

"No!"

She'd been reaching toward the security panel inside the door, about to depress the comms switch, when he'd hit her.

He had never hit anyone before, but it had been pure reflex – an ungainly swing of his free torch-carrying hand, which had glanced off Tomina's chin and shoulder, and for a moment their expressions had mirrored one another – eyes wide and jaws slack in fear and surprise – before Tomina had staggered backward, her right arm flailing out to right herself against the momentum of the blow, which had really done no more than imbalance her. But she'd failed, and falling backwards, had bounced off the inside of the lab door before toppling sideways, her temple smacking the edge of a crate sat near the entrance with a sickening thwack.

Zac had stared down at where her body had fallen, unmoving; at where the blood had begun to pool.

"Tomi?"

Fairy

Eventually – "But just so you'll shut up, alright?" – Amy had agreed to show him The Mountain.

Will had stared up at it, then at her, then back.

"So, do we…?"

"You can't just go up!" He could almost hear her rolling her eyes. "There are Watchers."

But the way had looked clear to him: a broad and well-defined path out of the murky, tangle-root forest, rising slowly through the foothills before snaking up the steep slopes of the distant peak. Perhaps he should check. His hands made the required ritual gestures as he intoned the accompanying word.

"Reveal."

And there they were – or at least, had been; their tracks, each footstep a fluorescent imprint, programmed to fade by slow degrees, fresh to old.

Pardians.

And everywhere, almost as numerous as the algorithmically swaying blades of grass, or the leaves on the procedurally generated trees, the tags of their victims: SweetCheeks69, Nyarlathotep4TW, SirCumferenz, GnomeChomsky … all casualties of their own cocksureness, their lack of preparation.

So many!

"See?" she said. "Waste of a spell." But she was twitchy, her bow drawn. They were nowhere near a sanctuary, and a respawn then would have cost her not just her recent level-up, but all the booty from their – well, *her* raid on the bandit camp, and with it a chunk of the rent. Whereas for Will – wide-eyed and green-gilled, no level-ups to lose or rent to pay – death would have meant comparatively little. If he searched long enough, would he find her gamertag among the fallen?

And yet, surely, if the footprints were made by patrols, then where the tracks were freshest might suggest a path, the place they were least likely to return to soonest. If he could just use *that* to plot a route…

"Get past the Pardians," reading his mind, "there's Leonines. Past the Leonines, there's Wolven. And past them … well, I've – no one I know's ever gotten that far." So she *had* tried. "Anyway, there are more interesting things to do."

For Amy herself, chief among those more interesting things was power levelling. This involved hiring out her hard-won skills to fast-track some hopeless, hapless low-leveller's borrowed avatar up the rungs – as she was doing now, in fact, whilst (favour to a friend) hand-holding Desi's gawkward brother, letting him piggy-back XP while she dispatched adversaries and challenges that would otherwise have taken him forever.

Even back then, before it had gone VR, Merrywhile's *Divinia* was more medium than game, its global penetration – like roads, electricity or water supply – almost a sign of civilisation. Few weren't on it, and even the disinclined eventually felt the pull of their peers or the concession to convenience. For many of these, the game itself was secondary, using the platform purely for social purposes, sharing and posting, connecting with friends and common interest groups, merely adding thematic colour to their passion for virtual base jumping, furry speed-dating, or the works of H. P. Lovecraft. For whatever their particular niche, there'd be some niche of *Divinia* devoted solely to that – most likely many niches – and all therein, like cats in a sack, squabbling over precisely how the thing in question should be practised, enjoyed or understood.

Back then, however, Will had been typical of the more fervent breed of player – mostly young men – who took the game seriously, played by its rules, and looked down with derision upon all those who used the platform solely for social, business and non-gaming purposes. For such players, there was only Apotheosis.

He could still see him now. An anthropomorphic warrior, half lion, half tribal bodybuilder, all bronze torques and tatts of Celtic knotwork, bestriding the summit, his mane flowing in the wind. Shafts of sunlight pierced the veil of patchwork clouds to fall upon his mighty form, swaying gently with each rhythmic in- and out-breath, his gaze transfixing the viewer, at once challenging, inviting and entreating, embodying the strapline below: "Are you ready to become a god?"

Will wasn't; at least, not then – hence the need for Amy's tutelage. But there'd been nothing he'd wanted more, and though corny to him now, his pubescent self had lapped it up. This had been his favourite of the load screens; still had the poster of it, somewhere, and which, almost now shameful to admit, could still provoke a little shiver.

"Listen, Bill—"

"Will."

"Willy. I'll show you the ropes, give you a leg up – as a favour to Desi, alright? But I ain't helping you waste both our time by chasing something that's just a big wank-off, far as I'm concerned. Now, when you get tired of wanking off – figuratively speaking; doubt you'll ever tire of it *non*-figuratively – I'd advise working out what you can actually get out of all of this, then devoting yourself solely to that. Anything else is just bollocks."

But he'd been immune to such advice – even Amy's; beautiful, cool, out of his league, the green-tipped hair and the arcane ink. He'd been inoculated by the mystique of it, the kudos and cachet that would be his. And even as the years would pass, and other things would sprout, grow, drop, or in other ways mature, his interest in *Divinia* would remain.

But for Amy, regardless of what she might once have thought, *Divinia* had just become a source of income, helping rich kids too lazy, thick-witted or uncoordinated to level up by themselves, all the while ducking the admins and system bots on perennial patrol for such forbidden pecuniary enterprise. Every now and then they'd catch and ban her, and she'd have to start over with a new profile, a new masked IP, rebuilding her reputation and re-establishing her contacts, the tediousness of which had begun to take its toll.

"A little while longer, Willy, another trust-funder or two, and I'm off. Koh Phi Phi Leh!"

Which, perhaps, is what she'd done, for a couple of months later she'd stopped returning his many messages and calls, could no longer be found on the darkmarket forums, and simply disappeared.

That was probably it.

Apotheosis was the apparent, much publicised goal of *Divinia*, where a player achieved sufficient "Rep" to gain admission to the Immortals (the scoreboard of the game's most eminent). What had made the platform innovative was that this might happen in two, perhaps overlapping ways. First, you might quest, collect, craft, grind, boss-battle and generally game your way up the levels. Or second, you could progress socially, generating buzz and kudos, fame or notoriety (no such thing as bad publicity – up to a point), amassing followers who then generated you more Rep by shares, likes, comments and mentions. In practice, however, there was great antagonism between the two paths, something that Merrywhile, to its credit, utilised and co-opted into its marketing for the game ("Which path will *you* take?"). The maturer Will would eventually dismiss all of this as a transparent attempt to cash in as D&D went mainstream, as if the worst commercial instincts of social media and VR gaming had both jerked into a cup so as to inseminate the Internet with their ghastly hybrid progeny – were it not for the existence of one thing, which had captivated, fascinated and obsessed him from the moment he'd first heard its rumour.

On a forum dedicated otherwise to conspiracy theories, the topic had stood out even there, a single thread gnomically entitled "Pardian Glamour (TA)". It was sitting incongruously among royal lizards, flat earths and hollow moons, as if the author himself hadn't known quite where to post it, whether to treat it as an in-game feature or something more meta. There'd been no other information, no "Read this first" or concession to newbies, and so Will had headed down the YouTube rabbit hole, with each new video the algorithm, its conspiratorial little tail bobbing ahead of him, queuing up the next level of revelation. And when he'd finally pieced it all together, arriving at the bottom with a visceral jolt, he'd been stunned. *There's a back door* – or at least, there might be.

It was more than just an Easter egg; it was a game inside the game, a sneaky short-cut up the snakes while everyone else was toiling and sweating up the ladders. For while the official game promised the immortality of fame or renown, with True Apotheosis – what Will eventually worked out the poster had meant by "TA" – came true omnipotence. Forget your hall of fame, the prestige of the leaderboard – this was something much cooler: *power over other players.*

Armed with this keyword, Will uncovered a new world of intense and extravagant speculation. Some conjectured the ability to cause floods or famines, to effect volcanic eruptions or tornadoes; others the capacity to target hostile tribes with plagues and infestations, attacks by trolls or night-geists. Even, some said – as with the ancient pantheons of Scandinavia or Greece – the potential for divine rivalry, for grudges and slights vicariously avenged through wars waged with proxy mortal playthings. Or just the puerile glee of disrupting *Divinia*'s social pleasures – gifting VR speed-daters the telltale signs of herpes simplex, rebranding some team's fan page to the colours of its hated rival. Such occurrences, historically not unknown, were all now seized upon by True Believers and offered up as evidence, as intimations of invisible, immortal hands at work.

Amy's interest in this topic had long ago peaked and waned. Nonetheless, more out of obligation to Desi, she'd eventually caved to Will's repeated requests and shown him The Mountain.

"Why here?" he'd asked.

"Don't know. Part of the game no one's ever been able to access? Everyone loves a locked door, don't they. Probably just some gateway for the admins, or something. If so, getting in's just hacking, and so technically illegal. *Or* some rich kid's virtual playground – infinity pools and skinny-dipping supermodels, invitation-only. In which case it's just trespass." So she was suddenly concerned about legality? "End of the day, who cares?"

And her first duty done, she'd had one last go at what she saw as her second.

"Look, say you did it. Say you got up there, and something like what you've heard is true. What then? What reward could make all that effort worthwhile? By then, Willy, even *you* might have outgrown its appeal."

Harsh. But not malicious. Just trying to save him from the pointless, he supposed, as she saw it. But Will was by then himself a True Believer, and like St Sebastian, though they'd wounded him, Amy's doubts hadn't swayed his martyr's resolve. In the final analysis, True Apotheosis was a matter of faith.

But revelation unforthcoming, even True Believers lapse. In *Divinia*, they mostly reverted to Midlanders, released back into the general population among which new users first found themselves – farming and trading, customising their avatar, the odd side-quest or mini-game to gain Rep and creds so they could buy shit in the shop – and where, before Amy's coaching, Will himself had begun.

He'd initially joined a clan, figuring teaming up on raids, quests and battles a better bet than soloing. But the reality was of being awoken at 3am to help repel a surprise attack from some opposing faction, hoping to catch his still-sleeping side of the globe on the hop. Or he'd put in sixteen-hour days mining some mineral for fortifications, or collecting plants for the clan's stockpile of health potion. Eventually he'd realised he'd be better off flipping burgers or serving coffees so as to illicitly *buy* XP (while those jobs still existed); better a real-world drudge than a virtual one, fagging for the few in the clan's high command.

And all so petty. The continents-spanning years-long wars of the bitterest enmity, unflinching commitment of time and money, and all over an affiliation to *Asterix* or *Tin Tin*, Mac versus PC, or the correct pronunciation of GIF ("It's *guh-ih-fuh*. To arms!").

Or else mean and desperate. The bespoke avatar tailors, blacksmiths of custom swords and shields, digital interior decorators, the gold farmers, power levellers like Amy, bending the rules to pay the bills, striving to meet real ends with virtual means. And those, through some deep-down perversity, who made gleeful sport of ensuring their failure or exposure.

It was his disenchantment with all of this that had first led him to Amy, but with Amy gone, falling back into Midland drudgery, his lack of progress eroding his pride, Will's head was then turned by another rumour: the existence of a yet more select and illicit group, who could help him colour even further outside the lines than any mere power leveller could. And it was to this semi-criminal fraternity, along a predictable curve plotted by his growing frustration and disillusion, that Will's further straying steps from the grail path were inevitably, inexorably drawn.

"So you can do it?"

The samurai – *General Ned* his username read – had sipped at a weird little wooden drinking box. He nodded briefly, once.

"Yep." The voice, like a detuned radio, a washing machine lost at sea. "Not that it'll do you any good, mind," the samurai had continued.

"What do you mean?"

"Well, if you want them for why I think you want them:

getting up The Mountain. I mean, I can *give* you wings, sure. But there are *flying* NPC guardians – you know that, right?"

"Well, I thought … maybe I'd—"

"What? That you'd fight them off? Wave your staff around? Fire off paralysis inducing flechettes?" The samurai shook his head, laughing to himself. "Better'n'you've tried, I'm afraid." Another singed Icarus?

"Oh. So what about … er…"

"Better weapons? The Gordian Blade, something like that?"

"Well, yes. Or whatever you suggest."

"But I can't just *give* you that, can I?" An amused grunt, another disappointed head shake. "I mean, even if it would work, and even if you could afford it – which, I'm guessing, you can't – you don't just *give* some level 13 a piece of level 99 mystic weaponry. People would notice. Bots would prick up their ears – so to speak."

"So … what?"

"Listen, let's just start with building you up a bit, yeah? But gradual like, so no one'll notice; even if they do, leave them unsure it's not all luck and hard work. What say we set you up with a payment plan and a loyalty card?"

But loyalty cards and staggered payments notwithstanding, General Ned's services didn't come cheap. And as the years went by, Will also started to get hassle from the landlord.

"When I said a job, Billy, I was thinking you'd actually leave the house. Doesn't have to be horrible, does it? Not even full-time. Let you contribute a little, that's all, chip in for bills now and then. A café, perhaps. Desi had a cinema job, remember? Watched all the films for *free*. Not that she stuck at it. But *you* like films. *And* you know computers. People need computer people, Billy. Just *something*, you know, even shelf-stacking, so when that sow at the Merrishop next asks, 'How's your boy doing, then, Silvia?', I can shut her fat face with more than a lie and a smile."

"*Will*, Mum. Those jobs don't exist any more. The cinema's been closed years, now, and the last shelf stacker *I* saw in the Merrishop wasn't even human. You know, if we lived in Finland, or … or Canada, or some other place they've got UBI, then we wouldn't even be having this conversation. I wouldn't have to work, because—"

"Why wouldn't you want to *work*? It's about self-esteem, Billy."

"I didn't say I wouldn't do *anything* – and this *is* a proper job. I just meant that I wouldn't be forced to… And who cares what the people in the Merrishop think, anyway?"

"*Normal* people do, Billy. We can't *all* be bohemians."

Will had only recently graduated to this, the latest in a string of maternally bestowed epithets, and had yet to look it up. The paternal epithets had a much shorter history, awarded during a brief period following his mum's sit-yourself-down account – "now you're old enough" – of his artificial conception ("Before my eggs ran out, you know?" "Jesus, Mum!"). But Will quickly realised that a sperm-bank donation did not entitle anyone to worry that "you might become a fairy if you don't get out more, son", and he forwent future fatherly advice in favour of the hope that genes were not the whole of the story. Thereafter, if anyone asked, he was sired by midichlorians.

His life to date had felt like one long struggle with labels. He'd never shown much enthusiasm for education, and through most of his school years had simply been designated "lazy", which in his own terms translated, "skips lessons to spliff behind the gym". When he'd surprised everyone by scraping a handful of half-decent GCSEs, he was for a short time proudly declared a "dark horse". But desultory efforts through the first months of sixth form again demoted this to "underachiever", which poor performance and poorer attendance further relegated to simple "dropout". For a subsequent period, characterised by round-the-clock dedication to online gaming, the nicknaming hit its nadir: "layabout". But lately, things had again begun to pick up, his mother pleasantly surprised that "all that fiddling around" was actually capable of turning a coin. A bit of web design, some freelance coding, a hand in a mobile game, and his stock had rebounded to "dilettante". But none of this could even generously be called an income, and so – the dictionary later informed him – maternal pressure was now being brought to bear on his unconventional hours, unkempt appearance and less-than-salutary living habits.

"Just do your own dishes once in a while, you know? The hoovering. Pick up after yourself. Some days, Billy, I'm afraid to walk on the floor in here, afraid I might break don't-know-what lying under God-knows-what – or else an ankle. I mean, Billy, love, you know rewilding only applies to *outside*, right? Some days, can't even open the – Good Lord," uneasily nudging a pair of perforated underpants with the toe of her shoe. "Should we fumigate you for crotch moths?"

"You shouldn't be coming in here anyway." Snatching up his pants, shooing her out. *Jesus.* "I'll tidy up! I'll hoover – but this *is* a proper job."

And he hoped it was. Pretty much all his underwear had holes in, and not just the ones you put your legs through. But VR Helpdesk Hybrid Assistant – whatever that was – didn't actually sound too bad. Working from home, flexible shifts and commitments. Why was she complaining?

"*Hybrid* Assistant because *you* do the things the virtual assistant has trouble with. *It* does the things you don't do so well," Taylor the remote interviewer explained, his head a little bobbing avatar in the top-right of Will's screen. "The perfect marriage! Clever, mind, these Merrywhile chaps. One golden rule, though: *don't* tell anyone you're *not* a computer. Studies say people actually prefer *Siri* and *Merilee* to real people; nicer to them, even. Think of it like a reverse Turing test!"

All this reminded him of something he'd once read. Even before Merrywhile's Project Upload there'd been some service somewhere that had offered to take everything you did online – sites you'd visited, search history, people you followed on Twitter, shares and likes and comments. Then once you'd died, it would use all this to "resurrect" you, create a sort of "you-bot", your quantified self, putting your second-hand psychological clothes on some shop-window-dummy AI. But he couldn't imagine anything worse – or more pointless. *Like trying to rebuild you from your dandruff.*

Taylor then presented him with a long list of terms and conditions, which he made a diligent effort to inch patiently through – until giving up and fast-scrolling right to the end of its wall of text and digitally signing off on, no doubt granting them unfettered access to details they were no longer allowed to surreptitiously siphon from your online activities. *Not like they aren't still doing that anyway.*

"Good, good. Now, the VA takes a bit of time to figure you out, but once it has, everything'll go much smoother."

This "figuring out" apparently involved merely leaving Will alone with the virtual assistant.

"Hello. You must be William," it said. "Or do you prefer Bill, Billy, Willy?"

The voice was accompanied by a little cartoon avatar, as blandly featured as the voice was accentless, but which the ensuing process would evolve into an uncanny simulacrum of his own face and manner.

"I … um … actually, it's Will."

"Thank you, Will." The little avatar smiled, a simple emoji appearing on its face. "For us best to work together, I need to learn a little more about you. Can we chat for a while?"

And so began a long interactive questionnaire, lurching wildly from favourite cereal to religious beliefs – "Of course, while you're encouraged to be open, we can skip any questions you'd prefer not to answer." But Will found himself being strangely candid, his usual paranoia about such sharing even further eroded as – realising, suddenly, *this is the interview* – the process elicited a weirdly confessional, eager-to-please frankness. *Maybe,* reflecting on it later, *it's just nice to be asked about yourself.*

"A little in-depth, I know!" Taylor admitted afterward. "But for the hybrid to work, VAs are best customised to the agent's personality. Then when it suggests responses to customer queries, it can mimic your speech patterns, your vocabulary and idiom, recognise your 'affective cadences' –

you know, your tone of voice – that sort of thing."

And then it finally hit him: *I'm already training my replacement.*

Prior to his trial shift, Will had joined a final, breezily confusing group induction session brusquely delivered by Tom, an existentially frustrated Glaswegian, who juggled brief, dismissive answers to Will's reasonable questions with transparent attempts to court Will's fellow trainee, The Lovely Samantha.

"What now, Bill?"

"Will. What if I should need to, er, you know … use the…"

"You're allowed a ten minute break every 6 hours."

"Oh. But what if I *really* need to, er—"

"Plastic bottle. Catheter, if you want to get fancy. Probably rig one up yourself, if you're handy: elastic band, plastic bag, some tubing. Careful with the elastic band."

"Oh. Really? But what if I need … you know…"

"Sammy, Sammy. What have you done *now*! What are you *like*? Here, let me see…"

By the time his shift went live, straight forward and doable quickly morphed into a nightmare of half-remembered protocols and flustered attempts to appear – wait, was he there to make the VA pass for human, or help-desk operatives fake omniscience?

"Incoming queries get automatically assigned to whoever's free," Taylor had said. "You read out whatever answer the VA provides, adjusting for mistakes and phraseology as you go. And try to put a *smile* in your voice!"

They'd made a big deal about that. One day, no doubt, the VA would fly solo. Master of idiom, unfazed by humour or sarcasm, humans would no longer be needed. But for now at least, hybrids bridged the gap. One thing it still had trouble with was emotions, both with recognising them and conveying them appropriately. However, by understanding your intonation and "affective cadences", as Taylor had put it, and matching these with the content of the communication, the VA's avatar could relay appropriate facial expressions. In theory.

The call centre both made and received them. It was then fulfilling a contract fielding queries for a white goods insurer. But the following month – dangled, apparently sincerely, as a genuine incentive to reduce turnover – they were to be following up interest expressed on group-discounted funeral plans. ("But it's *not* cold calling, right?" said Taylor – a reference to those lined-up callees who'd failed to tick an unobtrusive box discreetly buried deep in thirty unread pages of their internet provider's terms and conditions.)

Working fine through training, fifteen minutes in he'd lost audio. By the time he'd rectified the problem, twenty call-less minutes had left his screen flashing a furious red and his headphones emitting a sound like a submarine klaxon. By the time he finally got to speak to his first customer, he was already beginning to sense that his first shift might be his last.

"Sorry to hear that, sir." Grief stricken face. "Let's see if your tumble-dryer is still under warranty. Ah, Good news." Face beaming with tears of joy.

"You taking the piss?"

Not that he could work out why anyone would want to conduct business in VR anyway. From telegraph to phone to email, the purpose had surely always been to reduce people to manageable chunks, to limit their bandwidth, freeing you up to make calls on the toilet, text in the bath, or send abusive messages to tiny icons representing strangers and celebrities you'd never meet face to face. Of all things, he'd have thought cold calling would benefit most from a *reduced*, not a *greater* sense of really "being there". But who was he to fight the future?

Three weeks of no response to emails asking how his trial shift had gone, Will awoke one day to his P45. Which at least meant he could tell his mother he'd been right: it *had been* a proper job.

"General Ned," Will had eventually plucked up the courage to ask. "So is that, like, a war thing?"

The samurai seemed to eye him a moment.

"No," he eventually responded. "It's to do with the Luddites."

"Really? Oh, right. But isn't that… I mean, aren't Luddites, like, *anti* technology?"

A sigh.

"The term is commonly misused. It was just ordinary working people – during the Industrial Revolution – who saw employers using tech to slash wages and screw over professions in the name of profit. So they took matters into their own hands, secretly smashed looms and burnt mills. Then when they were questioned, they'd be like, 'Ned Ludd did it!' Edward Ludlum, King or General Ludd – probably not an actual person, you know, just a sort of folk-hero, a vigilante persona – think Batman or Spiderman, but where anyone can don the mask, like the Anonymous thing. Guess he was just a trade-unionist Robin Hood, really. So not anti-tech, as such, just anti-exploitation. Today, he'd be waving placards and marching on Wall Street, trying to cut that bull's balls off – and, of course, hacking; computers, that is, not balls." He smiled – or his avatar did – pleased with his pun.

"And the samurai? It *is* a samurai, right?"

"Toshirō Mifune?" No response. "Kurosawa?" Nothing. "*Seven Samurai*? *Rashōmon*? *Hidden Fortress?* Good God, kid, you of all people, with your Jedi-wannabe fucking…" he motioned his drink at Will's transparent homage to Jabba Palace Luke, and then shook his head. "Look it up."

"Sorry, I was just, you know, curious."

The samurai sipped from his little wooden box.

"It's … it's fine. Good to see kids still keeping the faith, you know? After all these years. Though if you ask me, everything after *Jedi* is just a reboot. Variations on the old money-making monomyth, the old hero's journey. Past never really goes away, does it? Just comes back in a fresh outfit, with a few new bows and bells."

There was silence for a while, to the point where Will wondered if the samurai had signed off or they'd lost connection.

"Anyways!" He suddenly recommenced. "How long you been coming here, now?"

"Sorry?" Despite all their interactions, loyalty card notwithstanding, General Ned had never once acknowledged Will's repeat custom, and was not usually one for personal small talk – which was, understandably, generally frowned upon by both *Cashabanca*'s clients and traders.

"Still trying to get up The Mountain, eh?"

"I… Yes. I suppose."

Over the years, General Ned's dark skills had levelled Will up in triple time ("But not so much as to be spotted by the enforcers, yeah?"), in the process procuring for him a hoard of spells, weapons and other illicit nicknacks. But none of these had yet proven sufficient – as the samurai dutifully forewarned with each fresh purchase – to enable Will's passage up The Mountain. Which was advice that, each time, he'd immediately dismiss and rush straight back to *that* forest, *those* foothills, a giddy school-kid home with his new toy – invisibility cloak, flame and bite resistance potion, even a Pardian Glamour (now he finally knew what that was) – resolved to have one more crack at the plan Amy had once so dismissively pissed on.

"But look, you're not even chipping away, mate, are you?"

"What?"

"All the knock-off kit – the spells, the weapons, the gear – they're not making any difference, are they? Which is the point, yeah?"

"What do you mean?"

"I mean, if it was possible, you'd have thought some of this would have worked by now. Or else, you'd have heard that someone else had done it. So, odds are it's not what you think it is. Have you thought of that?"

Unawares, the samurai was merely restating Amy's argument.

"Then why make it look like you can go up?" Will asked. "I mean, if it were just an admin's back door or something, why not just hide it?"

"I don't know." The samurai shrugged. "Designer's

malice? Tantalise you? Create some buzz, some mystique?"

Could that be true? They both simply sat a moment in their little shady booth in *Cashabanca*, Will thinking this over while the samurai sipped at his little wooden box, seemingly equally pensive.

"Then what's the point?" Will eventually asked.

"For Merrywhile? I would have thought that's obvious. I mean, they're trying to sell the game, after all – and judging by the business I get from the likes of you, it's working."

It had been … *God, how many years?* He'd still been at school. And for most of that time he'd been coming here, sitting in this same booth, funded by pocket money, odd jobs, piecemeal freelance work, enacting the same pointless transactions over the same crappy music. Will suddenly wished he'd something to drink himself, but more real. The loyalty card had seen some miles. He must have been one of the samurai's best customers. Then why say this to him? Didn't he want his business any more?

"So, all this," Will said, "you think it's just a … what? A sham? A … a MacGuffin?"

"Listen, I'm not anyone to pass judgement on what you do with your time or cash. People do a whole lot worse things than pay out for knock-off spells of revealing. All I'm saying is, you seem like a sharper cookie than that. I mean, you've got decent tech nous, decent skills – from what I can see, anyway, Will."

Will froze.

"How…? Have … have you been through my—"

"Call it professional curiosity. Dude, don't worry – *I'm* not about to dob you in, am I?" A big grin. "All I'm saying is I think you're equipped for better things."

Will swallowed. "Like what?"

"Well, to be honest, I'm getting a bit long in the tooth for this game. Quite like to hang up my katana, if you know what I mean. Had enough of being a masterless ronin. Freelancing can be hard. The hours are the main thing. Always someone awake somewhere wanting something – that's the Internet for you. Wouldn't mind making a clean break, you know, try something new. Learn a language, maybe; crochet."

Will nodded dumbly, not sure what crochet was – some sort of upper-class sport?

"So, I was thinking maybe of looking for, you know, someone I might hand things on to. An apprentice, if you will. Will."

"You mean *me*?"

"Well, why not? As I said, from what I can tell, some coding, some game design, you've got the foundations, the skillset. And anyway – a bit of risk; and the hours, as I said – but otherwise not as hard as you'd think. A lot of automation. Be happy to show you the ropes. And the money's pretty decent."

"So, what, I'd set myself up with an alias, and—"

"No need, mate. You can have mine."

Will frowned.

"Well, you don't think I'm the *first* General Ned, do you?"

No one knew who'd first begun it, but since then it had been passed on numerous times – "Like *The Princess Bride*, you know?" – adding an additional layer of protection to safeguards that were already pretty thorough. So however it had come about, "General Ned" was now just a title of succession, a *nom de guerre* conferred by the incumbent upon his – its – designated heir; and which, once he'd learnt the ropes, would be Will himself.

The king is dead; long live the king – or the General, anyway.

"But it's just games though, yeah?"

"What?"

"I mean, I don't want to do anything… you know, to do with—"

"Oh! Right. Yes. Just games. Nothing nasty."

"OK. Cool. So how does it all work?"

"As I said, it's pretty much all done for you. The key to it all is the virtual PA. Latest thing from Japan. Makes the job a *hell* of a lot easier. Interfaces with the script automator, bypasses most code work – can't say I've seen a command-line interface in … oh… Anyway, wouldn't be without her. It."

"So do I…?"

"I mean, you can call her – him, it – whatever you like. There are presets you can choose from, customisation options. Get her to call *you* whatever you want, too. That's all personal. No one else sees that. As for *Cashabanca*, just don't change the username. I mean, change the avatar if you *really* want, though I'd advise against that too, frankly – don't spook the return custom. Let them see the same face. But the username is tied to the client base, all your reviews and ratings. That's the whole point."

Outgoing Ned had reset the VPA before leaving, and now, its little hands tucked politely behind its back, a six inch AR tailor's dummy looked up at him blankly, stood between a coffee cup and a stack of comics: a featureless form; naked, genderless, expressionless; wax awaiting only his imprimatur, plasticine his sculpting hand. Will scanned the presets, which seemed to embody different … personality types, was it? Or occupations? There was a little figure holding a paintbrush and palette, one in a suit with a briefcase, another dressed as a little soldier – and so on, scrolling through a careers fair of options. Satisfied he'd conveyed what was needed, the samurai had not hung around to hand-hold, there'd been no trial shift, and there appeared to be no accompanying instructions. Will selected the question mark at the far end.

He was expecting, perhaps, similar options to game avatar customisation – hair, body shape, skin colour, sliders for the width of the hips, the slant of the eyes. But the display cleared, and a column of text appeared on the screen, which he'd eventually realised was "Please speak" in various languages. Ah, so he was supposed to….

"Hello," he said. "Is there … is there anyone there?"

"You have chosen British English. Is that correct?"

"Oh. Yes."

"And how shall I refer to you, just between us?"

Will had thought of giving his own name, or thinking up

some pseudonym, but on reflection it seemed simplest just to take a name linked to the one he would be adopting for the market, help him get used to it.

"Ned, please. Er … N-E-D." Speaking slowly, enunciating, like on the phone to some automated helpline.

"Thank you, Ned." The little avatar smiled, a basic emoji-like expression replacing the blanked features. "For us to best work together, I need to learn more about you. Can we chat for a while?"

Ah! So it's like the call centre hybrid thing!

"So what type of music do you listen to, Ned?"

And so it began, the same wide-ranging, in-depth questionnaire, the same confessional urge and desire to be open – responding, with only himself to please, perhaps with even greater candour. And with each response the little bland avatar began to change and morph, to take on more specific qualities – age, face-shape and hair colour, and eventually dress. Ned noticed that her accent – it had become female fairly early on – also began to change, modulating both in tone and pronunciation: at one point, gruff Russian matriarch; at another, a seductive French slur. Eventually, she'd settled on a generic London inflection, not far in fact from his own, and the appearance of a pretty, slightly punky, petite-figured sprite, complete with fairy wings, and looking somewhere between Tinker Bell and Wasp.

Which made him – what? Peter Pan? Vernon van Dyne?

"And finally, what would you like to call *me*?" The little sprite cutely inquired. What indeed.

"I was thinking, like, what about 'Automated Multifunctional Intelligence'. Is that OK?"

"That's quite a mouthful, Ned! It's best to use something short and pithy, that I can easily recognise and respond to when I'm called."

"Yes, well, I was thinking we could shorten it? To, you know, an acronym? Like, AMI?"

"Yes, that would be fine. From now on I shall answer to AMI."

But he'd been right, though, Will's outgoing mentor, for it wasn't actually as hard as he'd feared. Some of the hacks were zero-day exploits, as yet still unpatched from the day of *Divinia*'s launch. And a succession of more talented individuals – than even General Ned himself, he'd implied – had ensured it remained that way, having built in sneaky means of covering the traces of their intrusion. Other hacks were indeed automated: AIs and bots, tasked with password breaking and penetration testing, threw up new vulnerabilities at an almost daily clip, so that, for those doors that did close, tenfold might open.

"It's depressing, really – for them, I mean, the developers," the samurai had said. "Always more fun in poaching than gamekeeping – more incentive, too."

And there certainly was incentive – pecuniary, and lots of it. Amy – the real one – would have been jealous. She'd have ditched her power-levelling in the flutter of a fairy wing. It was simple, quick, profitable work. So why was the samurai leaving it all behind? So he could knit?

As for the clientele, Will already had the inside track on them: the same wants, the same needs as his own – more or less. There was always the odd, well, *oddball*, of course; those who'd seen too many techno-thrillers, conspiracists wanting him to hack the Pentagon, get the truth about UFOs, vaccines, or whatever. But with the more persistent nutjobs, he'd just cut them off and block them.

"Lady. Lady? Well, all I can say is you've got the wrong guy. You want a … a … an elven invisibility cloak, or … some werewolf bite immunity – *that* I can do. But hacking some *company*? Sorry, completely out of my league, I'm afraid."

Crazy.

"Sex is in the head anyway, right? Fantasy-driven. So it's *only* appearances that count, not realities. I mean, why trade beautiful illusion for the risk of tawdry disappointment?"

"Er, thanks. But not really my thing."

"But that's the point: 'your thing' can be whatever you want it to be. It's a new frontier of desire."

As if in illustration, the speaker's avatar – until then a cute blonde cowgirl with stetson, spurs and country tassels – refreshes into full-blown Daniel Boone, complete with sideburns and cowcatcher moustache, coonskin cap, hunting horn and Bowie knife. "To quote Oscar Wilde: 'It is only shallow people who do not judge by appearances. Those who go beneath the surface, do so at their peril'. 'You' are not you; you are not 'here'…"

Oh, God. It's one of them.

Will gestures left, thereby triggering one of the site's pre-programmed "dump" sequences – this particular one launching his would-be match clay-pigeon style for him to despatch with a newly appeared pair of crosshairs, if he's so inclined (he isn't). Brutal, really, and – as a frequent dumpee – an experience he has some empathy for.

The carousel spins, lining up his next match.

Not that Will is prudish or narrow minded, just old school. He hasn't been on the site that long, but he's already getting a little frustrated with it. Virtuality has its uses, he supposes, but there's a part of him that just likes the idea of – someday – meeting a girl made of actual molecules, then maybe eventually, in a molecular sort of way, settling down, buying their own set of molecules, and having lots of little molecules together. For him, virtual dating is therefore just an airlock before the real world, a sandbox in which to practice his game – though so far, admittedly, more a series of floundering attempts to get out of the bunker.

"I see you've made clear your allegiance."

"I'm sorry?"

She's pretty, in a geeky way: diminutive, cute features of a broadly oriental cast, Leia Endor Strike Team outfit. None of which means anything here, of course, where the laws of compensation dictate that the real beautiful people are probably quirky video game characters, dinosaurs, or lawnmowers, anonymity merely freeing them from a different set of prejudices, a disguise from the shallow who see only surface appeal. Or maybe, frustrated by the virtual veil, all the beautiful people have decamped to somewhere else where they can show off their real world biological advantage. God, who knows?

"Master or Padawan?" she asks, pointing to his Jedi Order emblem.

He's spent an enormous amount of time crafting his avatar, embedding in it subtle, carefully chosen allusions to his dearest interests and obsessions, setting them like snares for the curiosity of (he hopes) some sharp-eyed kindred spirit. And there, aside from her own *Star Wars* allusions, he notices – in fact, the very same icon that he wears as a patch on his left arm – she's done the same: subtly embossing her belt buckle, a towering peak emerging from a tangle-root forest, and above it the same initials: "TA".

"I, er...?"

"Are you *new* here?" She rolls her eyes and shakes her head, laughing.

"Oh! Padawan, I'm afraid," he laughs as well, "… er … Cariad," reading her handle.

"Me too!" She smiles. "Well, we all have to start somewhere, don't we?"

"Probably want to be careful how you spend your loot, though," General Ned had concluded. "Don't want to draw attention to yourself, taxman starts asking questions. But if you're patient, see, once you've squirrelled enough away, put it through the right channels, setup an offshore company, you can just bugger off somewhere, buy your own island."

Which is perhaps what he'd done. At least, his crash course delivered, General Ned wasn't keen to hang around, and Will never saw him again – not that he'd ever really "seen" him in the first place.

But Will just wasn't interested in islands. And as the

months went by, his rapidly swelling ill-gotten gains burning a virtual hole in his digital pocket, he'd decided he just wasn't that patient, either. And the estate agents were as eager to take his crypto as they were unconcerned about where it came from.

The smartwaiter pinged. He swivels on his chair and scoots over to the hatchway.

The little sprite flits up out of nowhere, its tiny wings a-blur as its aura of luminescence cross-lights the clutter of his desk with a neon-blue hue.

"It's the paint-set for that toy you ordered, Ned."

"*Figurine*, AMI."

He removes the package and begins to unwrap its contents, depositing the recyclables down the shoot before surveying the pots of subtle, bespoke colours and the exquisitely pointed brushes, testing each fine sable tip with his finger. He looks up at the shelves above his desk at the other figures arrayed there.

"Shall we put some stuff in storage, Ned? Make some room? Or we could order a freestanding display case?"

With a sprinkle of fairy dust, on the desk in front of him appears a slowly turning carousel of various shelving and storage options.

But Ned is looking over at the figurine: an arms-folded General Makabe Rokurōta, thirteen inches, 1:6 scale, but still in its recently printed, unadorned state of virgin white nylon plastic. He glances up again at the shelves – Poison Ivy, blowing a kiss; Han Solo encased in Carbonite; others from comics, film, anime, games, all purchased already professionally finished. So why does he want to do this one himself?

"Maybe, AMI."

He had decided to integrate the virtual assistant into the smartment's automation systems – the samurai had assured him that the software was safe, hadn't he? – and better that than allow the building's native AI direct access to his illicit goings on.

And look at the place! A brand spanking new smartment,

a view of the Wharf, and beyond – he can almost see his mum's flat – sporting all the mod-cons anyone could want, and a few more besides. For instance, his fridge knows when it's low on things – milk or cheese, say – and interfaces with his shopping app to restock itself. This then gets delivered to his smartwaiter, which registers the delivery and adjusts his inventory, before whizzing it all straight up to his room – and all without seeing a human face! He should have waited, perhaps, but … ("Have you got clean towels, Billy? Check for a smoke alarm. These landlords—"; "Mum, it's a *smart* apartment; of course it'll have a smoke alarm") … well, for some reason, waiting seemed the less desirable option.

"Are you warm enough, Ned?" AMI asks considerately.

"Yes thank you, AMI. I'm great."

"But I thought you were a believer?" Will says.

"Well, I don't know," says Cariad. "Eventually it all just seemed a bit pointless. Where's the evidence, you know? Where's the proof? If TA were real, there'd be … I don't know …. leaks, or … or whistleblowers, people selling their story. I mean, it's not like there are any secrets any more."

Just like Amy.

"I don't know," says Will. "Maybe it's like there's some sort of, like, divine Fight Club? An NDA or something? Or maybe just no one's done it yet."

"Well," she says, "end of the day, I just thought: why put yourself through all of that? Like looking for a black cat in a dark room."

"Just because it's difficult, doesn't mean you shouldn't try."

"But what if *there is no cat!*"

"How do you know unless you look!"

"Wow. You're undisabusable, aren't you?"

"What?"

He'd always thought he'd meet the right person by finding someone who shared his interests. But he sees now that isn't it at all. Things in common might bring you together, but there's something beyond that, something no dating profile, no algorithm can predict or match. It's all just excuses to talk, really, he realises, a pretext to get together in the first place. And then it's not so much about *what* is said, so much as … well, whatever. God, what does he sound like? But it's true.

They've exchanged photos. She looks nice, and not dissimilar to her avatar. But what if her picture is flattering or doctored, and she turns out to be, well, ugly? Or fat? For all their rapport, is he too shallow to see past that?

After too much deliberation and three changes of clothes, he's shown up at St Pancras an hour early, dressed in jeans with an unbuttoned waistcoat over a t-shirt depicting Chewbacca sat at a laptop, zeros and ones dripping out like water. (*Will she get that? Too corny?*). He proceeds to pace around aimlessly, before finally settling at a nearby café table – aptly, he realises, to one side of that big statue of the meeting couple – where he spends too much money on the tiniest coffee just so people don't stare at him. As the clocks chime, he sees a woman come through the doors, scan the area, then begin to make her way round the café's rope cordon and over to his table. As she gets closer he stands up, in the process realising that it isn't her after all – not oriental in the slightest, hair not so dark, thicker set, big eyebrows – but she keeps on moving toward him, finally coming to a stop in front of him and proffering her hand.

"General Ned, I presume," she says.

Cari takes the seat opposite, glancing up occasionally to the statue of the couple. Crassly kitsch? Romantic? Depends on your taste, she supposes (she quite likes it). She waits for him to speak, as the shadow of the great Barlow Shed's glazed latticework draws slowly across the afternoon.

"This is, like, really expensive," he finally says, mournfully, staring into his tiny coffee. "And they don't even take crypto."

"Oh, sorry," she finds herself saying, put on the back foot by a certain plaintiveness in his tone. "You didn't have to sit here. I... It was just a place to meet."

He shrugs, blowing and sipping.

"Had to order something."

Part of her had known it wasn't him. Nonetheless, she'd dialled up her indignation in preparation for meeting the samurai's real life alter ego – the manipulative bore that had become almost familiar from *Cashabanca* – only to be presented with the same, more sensitive and less cocky incarnation she has begun to get to know. And who, what's more, denies all knowledge of the attack and claims never to have met her before the dating site.

"Look, it's just knock-off stuff for *Divinia*, right? Just spells and weapons and shit. Yes, *technically*, it's hacking, I guess, but it's just a game, you know? I mean, Jesus, planting viruses in the network of some multinational? Making people throw up? That's not me."

And, frustrated as the realisation makes her, she has to agree: it isn't.

"So apparently", she tells the journalist later, "it's just like a ... I don't know, a hand-me-down avatar, an inherited persona or something. He mentioned something about a princess bride?"

"Ah, the Dread Pirate Roberts defence," Mel replies. "Before your time, perhaps. So, do you believe him?"

"I guess so. I mean, he just didn't feel like the same guy."

"Shit. Dead end, then."

Will – General Minor, as Mel has now taken to calling him – had no more idea than they of who the previous General Ned actually was, nor of where the virus had come from – which is, now Cari thinks of it, very convenient for General Major. Had he simply left this guy holding the baby and done a runner? And since Mel's much vaunted dating equation has (debatably) produced a false positive, the prospect of revisiting that strategy has not even been mooted.

All of which leaves them back where they started.

Lacking any further leads, Cari doubles down on pulling at those few loose threads that remain. She leafs through the Merrywhile welcome brochure for the umpteenth time, looking for something, anything.

The conception of MoTH seems to have gone hand-in-hand with Project MUNKi, which had began in the '80s, but the collapse of the property market in the early '90s had caused building plans to be shelved, and construction hadn't finally begun until the economy had picked up again later on that decade. By the time it was completed, sometime in the mid noughties, it had been over two decades since Tadcu's involvement with the project.

It's a peculiar document. The sort of induction material she's come across has usually concentrated on procedures, holiday entitlements, company policy on sick days, perhaps prefaced with a brief mission statement from a cheesily grinning CEO. But this is *all* mission statement, laying out Merrywhile's grand vision for the future, for technology, for Humanity Itself, with accompanying illustrations that range from the twee to the frankly bizarre. The most striking of these is a double-paged panorama riffing on the traditional seven ages of man, each unsettlingly tweaked.

A newborn, cradled not in its mother's arms, nor even a human midwife's, but in those of a beaming, anthropomorphic artificial surrogate. Delighted wonderstruck schoolchildren, sat before huge digital screens or, wearing VR headsets, immersed in (insets reveal) haptically pulling apart DNA spirals or building Egyptian pyramids. Young lovers, in goggles and haptic gloves, lost in sensuous enjoyment of each other's gorgeously crafted avatars. A soldier, safe in his remote command haven, remotely operating some frighteningly arachnoid future-tank, shielding cowering civilians from ragged bazooka-toting hostiles. And so on, right through to infirm old age, the attending robots now solemn faced – *just a button press, just a call or a gesture away*. And finally, beyond that, an eighth, even stranger age: the old man resurrected, his digital self smiling from a projection, reunited with his smiling family in their smiling-family-related activities.

Jesus.

And that's it, what it reminds her of: religious junk mail; a saccharine vision of a world beyond pain and suffering, transcended and alleviated by technology.

And the iPad shall lie down with the laptop.

It's hard to believe that Tadcu had fallen for any of this – unless of course it was *exposure* to this that had eventually turned the tide. So why had he hung on to these few things? Fond memories? Unlikely. A memento of past transgressions, perhaps, and a reminder never to repeat them? So what had been his sins, exactly? Or those of Merrywhile's that had finally turned him against them?

She looks at the brittle, hardback buff envelope, on which – though faded – can still be discerned the address of his old house down by the river, along the narrow road that snaked down and back upon itself.

Dr Myrddin Edwards, 4 Heol Penneidr…

Someone had sent this to him – she'd assumed the company itself. But now she thinks of it, this doesn't make sense. He wasn't living in the village when he'd started working for them, but in London. And anyway, the card was surely one he would have received at the workplace, not something that required posting. But perhaps the envelope had nothing to do with either brochure or card, just a place to store the miscellaneous flotsam of his time there.

She glances at the postmark. The date is still just barely discernible: five years before he'd died, but almost thirty after he'd finished with them. She looks closer, noticing the place of posting franked upon it.

København. What's that? *Copenhagen.*

Was the envelope from Nielsberg? But why? Not for the brochure, surely. For the card, then?

She puts down the envelope and picks up the keycard, scrutinising it. She turns it over, examining the magnetic strip on the back. What if it could still access somewhere? Some place within MoTH? But no, the place wasn't even built when

Tadcu had worked for Merrywhile, and Project MUNKi had been based somewhere in Bermondsey, according to the journal article. And besides, from what she'd seen of MoTH, the staff access was all retina scan and biometric entry – the samurai had talked her through it – in rather unnecessary detail, now she comes to think about it.

But what if there is something else on the card?

She rings the journalist for advice, but can't get hold of her, so on a whim decides to call General Minor – *I mean, he is a hacker after all* – of some sort, anyway. She tries him via the video calling function on the dating app, and to her surprise – on the second try, just when she's about to give up – he answers.

"Universal card reader?" he suggests.

"What's that?"

She is still getting used to his actual face, starting to pair it with the voice that has become familiar from their "dates". His hands mill the air like someone shaping pizza dough.

"Like a … well, it'll read any sort of card, basically."

"Where can I get one?"

"Not Amazon or eBay! You might get something called that, but that's not the thing. Actually, I have one."

"Oh?"

"Yeah. You know, I could post it to you, if you want? It's not very big."

A couple of days later it arrives – a small clunky rectangle of black plastic and a few accompanying leads. He walks her through the installation – downloading the drivers and software, which port to plug it into. Finally, she switches it on and inserts the card. Immediately, a small text box pops up on the screen.

"It's a number," she says.

She shares her screen with him.

And he just stares.

"Hello? I-I think you've frozen. Hello?"

Will sits staring at the number.

The first time she'd rung him, he'd ignored it. But then he'd thought about it. While she doesn't know his full name or his address, the authorities could easily find these out through cross correlation of the information she could give them from his dating profile. And from there, it is only a hop and a skip to General Ned, and all his naughty doings – which were, he now knew, far naughtier than he'd previously thought. In fact, Will suddenly realises, there's no reason he couldn't be landed with whatever the whole lineage of Neds had been up to (well, allowing for the statute of limitations set by Will's ability to walk, talk and hold a mouse).

The fucker.

The alias is a poisoned chalice. No wonder he'd been in such a rush to hand it on.

However, all that said, she doesn't seem like a bad person, and is apparently most concerned with finding out something about her grandfather and the origin of some computer virus.

"So what *is* the card?" he'd asked.

"An old employee ID from my grandad's work. I just thought you might have an idea."

When the numbers had first popped up, she'd been full of theories while he'd just stared.

"Could be the original access code on the card, I suppose," she'd said. "Or what about an IP address? Or maybe a phone number? Oh, but there aren't enough numbers for that, unless you add…"

He is still staring.

"It's a location," he responds eventually.

"What?"

"A place."

"You think? What, like longitude and latitude? In this country? Or—"

"Not a real place. It's in *Divinia*."

"What?"

"Look." The numbers are seared into his memory – clicking on the coordinates, again and again and again, the fastest way to travel back there. "The first three digits are *x* coordinates – east to west – and the second three are *y* coordinates – north to south."

"No way. You're sure?"

He nods.

"And the last three?"

It is situated on a flat plain, just above sea level, so the third set of coordinates he'd always used were different. These are obviously the location of something much higher.

"That's the *z* axis. For elevation."

"So…?"

"It's the top of The Mountain."

"We don't actually know that your grandfather ever used the card," Will points out. "Even if this Nielsberg guy sent it to him, perhaps he never worked it out. I mean, *we* only did because I had the card reader."

"Tadcu would have worked out that *someone* was sending him a message to do with his work on the project. He would have found a way."

Where Cari and Will now stand is a test of that assertion, of Cari's faith in her grandfather.

Ahead of them stretches a broad, well-defined path leading out of a murky, tangle-root forest, which then rises slowly through the foothills before snaking its way up the slopes of the distant mountain.

"So what now?" She asks. She doesn't even know what she expects to find there.

"I don't know," Will says. "Usually, I would just, you know, walk on, and then get dismembered by… Well, there are various options. You'll see."

He has faith in her too, then. But if they *aren't* going to face imminent dismemberment, then they evidently have to do something different from what he's previously tried.

"Maybe it's you," he says. "I mean, maybe if there's this connection with your grandad, and somehow he left this card thing for you, then perhaps you just being *you* will trigger something, and you can just walk up there, or whatever."

So they try that.

A few minutes later, freshly respawned, re-membered and reconvened, they look up again at the same vista.

"Well, *that* was horrible," she says. "I know it's only virtual, but still, being eaten by a… What the hell *was* that?"

"Wolven."

"*Urgh*. Right. Let's try to avoid that in future."

There is not the detached frustration of watching the demise of a set of pixels on a screen, nor even that of the greater involvement of a first-person shooter. Dying in VR is visceral, personal. A few years' time, a bit more verisimilitude, and all the enhanced interrogators will be swearing by it – perhaps already are.

Having said that, she does start to get a bit more used to it, and the next hour – he, wherever he is, and she in her room in halls – is spent working through sample variations on the box of tricks Will has over the years exhausted in a thousand different combinations – all with the presumption that it will be Cari's enacting of one of these that will provide the key. After which, death has become no more than a temporary inconvenience.

"Oh, maybe – yes! Say 'Friend'!" He said.

"What?"

"Speak it aloud. Like a spell, you know?"

"OK. Um… Friend!"

Nothing.

"Well, just an idea. Not now, AMI. Oh – AMI, what's 'friend' in Elvish? No! Welsh! Right. Say … *cyf – cy* – AMI, how do you say it again?"

"Who is Amy? Is she in the room with you?"

"Yes. No. Kind of. She's… It's my VPA. Virtual… Never mind. Only I can see her. It."

"OK, then."

But maybe it *is* something spoken.

"Cariad," she says.

There is a haptic rumbling through the gloves and the controller, and a movement to her left draws their attention to a broad-trunked tree in which a large rectangular portal has begun to open, revealing inside its grimly lit interior a set of steps descending in a vertiginous spiral.

Will had been wrong about the co-ordinates. They aren't the *top* of The Mountain, but something far, far below it.

"Fuck me," he almost whispers.

Luca

Wherever he had taken the boy, Mel reasons, it is not to another medical facility. There are only a few of these – a couple on the main island, another on one of the outlying islets in the *laguna*. But all of them cater to general maladies, not provision of the type of specialist care he would require, and in none of them is there a Merrywhile logo in sight. Then what about on the mainland, in Mestre? Or east along the coast, toward Jesolo? Or south, even, to Chioggia? All possibilities, of course, but something tells her – her journo-gut again – that Luca's *Venezia* meant the *Centro Storico*, the historical city of Venice itself. If this is the case, then she's looking for a private clinic of some sort, or else some purpose-built facility that Sommeil has privately commissioned, using his own resources – God, he must have more than enough of *those*.

Her virgin visit, she decides to spend the first few days just getting used to the place. The thing that immediately strikes her is the lack of cars. She's taken a taxi from the airport, but from the point at which she steps out into Piazzale Roma the only progress into the old city is by water or foot. It is approaching *Carnevale* and the streets are already inundated with tourists, whose influx, like the *acqua alta,* is a periodic annoyance that the stoic locals and shopkeepers have simply gotten used to. For despite the surprisingly effective new flood barriers, the lower lying areas around San Marco still occasionally flood, requiring *passerelle,* offering temporary wooden walkways over the waters, and the metal *paratie* that slot into the doorways to hold back the deluge (if not the tourists). (Should she check the tides? She hadn't thought to pack her wellies – not something she'd associated with a Mediterranean holiday. But you can get plastic shoe covers, apparently. Must get some, then, and remember not to chance her good shoes.)

But nothing can hold back the tide of technology, and Merrywhile are even here. The pandemic had seen its networked temperature scanners installed at the entrances to museums, galleries and churches, to restaurants and cafés, its AI monitoring and tracking, ready to trigger lockdown at a sudden spike of that other periodic inundation. But those dangers now past (for the moment), they have remained a permanent feature – just in case – another layer of surveillance and tracking for the public to become outraged at, object to, but finally passively accept. Aside from safety, of course, technology also serves convenience, and Mel sees more and more tourists plodding the *calli* like distracted pigeons, gazing out through AR goggles with that telltale middle-distance stare. She has her own pair, naturally, which are just too handy not to have, especially in her line of work, where quick access to on-the-ground information is a godsend that far outweighs looking like a pillock. Soon she finds herself joining the flock, unconsciously aping their quick-shift head-bobs and -swivels as her attention flits between translations and descriptions, videos and image galleries, an annotated, footnoted Venice that has already all but put the local travel guides out of business.

But high or not, the water still has a lot to answer for. The city, she learns, had originally been built on long wooden piles driven into the marshland, which wasn't good to begin with. But its brackish waters, salt from the Mediterranean mixing with fresh from the mainland rivers, constantly eats away at its foundations, requiring an equally constant process of renovation and reinforcement.

"But don't get alarmed!" Merrywhile's audio guide attempts to reassure her. "This process has been going on for hundreds of years – and Venice hasn't sunk yet!" Well, no more than a foot or so. And most of that in the last few decades.

And there was I all worried about it.

Better get those wellies, just in case.

It's like life, really, she thinks. The struggle to maintain a… What is it? *Homeostasis* – they'd talked about that at that transhumanist conference where she'd collared Sommeil. A balance between inside and out, an equilibrium between growth and decay. As long as an organism preserves that balance – through maintaining and rebuilding, refreshing and renewing – then it is still alive. That's all life is, really, a balancing act; a surfer on a wave, a swimmer treading water. Lose that balance, give up trying to maintain it, and the waters close over you.

God. Why's she so morbid? She's in Venice, for fuck's sake, on the verge of *Carnevale*. Amazing art, beautiful buildings, incredible ice cream, insanely expensive coffee (depending on where you sit). She might have no control over the tides, but she can still enjoy herself. Can't she?

Mel looks, then looks again. It's his name, shouting out at her in capitals. But it's just a popular science magazine, one of only two English language titles, fellow compatriots adrift abroad in a sea of unfamiliar words. She shifts aside a tabloid – "PM CLAIMS LOVE TAPE IS CHINESE DEEP FAKE" (*Ha! Deep fake news! Nice work, lads*) – and picks up the magazine, flicking through to the article: "LUCA: The search for the Last Universal Common Ancestor". A theoretical organism from which we are all descended, that stored the genetic information that gave rise to all current life on Earth.

Ah! That's why he put it about so much! It's his job *to spread his genetic information! He is the seed of life!*

Funny. She'll have to tell him.

She catches herself: Will she? Presumably, once this is all played out, she'll simply go back home. Hopefully, if all goes well, it'll see her star back on the rise, busy again, her name back on the lips that matter, back in the game. And who knows where that wave will take her?

"Signora, per favore, non è una biblioteca."

Not a...? *Oh.* Quoting *The Simpsons*, or merely a cross-cultural stock-phrase of the profession? *"Mi dispiace, signore. Ecco."* She pays the proprietor of the quaint little *edicola* for the periodical, and wanders off to find somewhere reasonably priced to get something to eat and drink, to sit down and think.

She'd arrived – how long ago, now? Is it only three days? Time here feels peculiarly elastic and not-pinned-down. An unusual sensation for her, where dates and deadlines, down to the hour and minute – the second, occasionally – are commonly kept so close an eye on. Yet here, in this strange historical theme-park of a place – a fairground of the human heart, pampering its fledgling dreams, nudging to flight all its nestling desires – she feels strangely unmoored, afloat, the watery metaphors coming apt and easy, encouraging her to drift off into past or future, or simply to hang there suspended in the present, as if time itself is a medium she is treading.

He should have been in primary school when the accident had happened. The company had denied all responsibility, of course. The drone was only for surveillance, they'd said, possessing no aggressive capacity. And he shouldn't have been there. Trespass, technically. Not their fault it scared him and he fell. But it was what it had represented – the non-human and the non-caring in service of the inhuman and the uncaring. And the company hadn't done itself any favours – got nasty with its lawyers, even hired investigators to dig up any dirt they could find. The family had been devastated, understandably. It was a small community, and it'd clammed up, closing tightly around them, condensing their anger and grief, sealing them off from prying outsiders.

But it was her job to pry, wasn't it? To prise the clam apart?

Looking for the pearl, the scoop, the exclusive. The news desk clamouring for an angle, an insight, a word that would differentiate the rag from the rest of the pulp. She'd hacked through a dodgy fence, pushed aside a slimy rotten plank and stolen up to the graveside, all in black, posing as a mourner; ruined good suede pumps into the bargain. And all for a quote – well, more a load of shouted abuse, really. But she'd got it, recorded it, and there was content they could actually use. It had been worth it – she'd thought. She'd do it differently now, of course, now she knows there are simpler ways to get inside people's lives that don't involve ruining good shoes. But it was more than anyone else had gotten, anyway; even broken Pack Rules, by not sharing it, and from then on the Pack had shunned her – no more pally pooling of backstories, cribbing quotes from each other's notebooks over fags and beer. She was never a fan of that, anyway – the pack, the office, the team, the club – though she'd put up with it, to begin with. And the news desk couldn't have been happier. Few more of those, ed had said, and she might even get a staff job. But even then, she'd known what she was, what she always would be: freelance, a stringer, an outsider.

When the father had hung himself (grief, obviously – unless there was something more…?), she'd gone back to cover that too – though she hadn't exactly been welcome. But she was just doing her job.

Eight years old, he'd been. Funny how it had popped back into her head like that, after all this time.

Suede. Never the same after it's tarnished, no matter how you clean it.

How lovely the light looks on the water.

Mel's parents hadn't wanted her to become a journalist, her father least of all. He'd been delighted when she'd been accepted at Leeds ("a good redbrick"), and more so that she'd chosen to study English, his own subject. He'd been midway through a PhD himself when her mother had fallen pregnant.

(Why *fallen*? A fallen woman? An accident, like falling over?) And so he had decided to quit his studies to pursue teaching – those being the days when teaching was still just about a survivable job, and they needed the money more than anyone needed an academic (does anyone ever really *need* academics?). So despite her mother's protestations that they'd manage, he'd shelved his thesis on Shakespeare's something or other ("I mean, it's not like the world is calling out for another book on the Bard, is it, love?", laughing off his disappointment), and told himself, no doubt, *I can always go back to it*, but deep down knowing that he would not; that he had committed himself to forty years of teaching *Lord of the Flies* to the epitome of the sort of semi-feral, sub-moral creatures that had inspired Golding in the first place.

She could have been a Hermia, or a Helena, or one of his other feisty, tell-it-like-it-is heroines – it was a close call. But her mother had wanted "Amelia" after a sister who had died young, so her father settled for a middle name of Cordelia: she would be his little truth-teller. It was a pair of names she would thereafter bear like a phonic albatross, rhyming ridiculously through registers and roll calls, job applications and résumés. (*I mean, you'd think an English lit scholar would recognise…* shaking her head; *for Christ's sake.*) Sundays, she would find him in his "library", a grand name for a spare room with books floor to ceiling, retreating to work on his novel – some endlessly evolving tale, never to be published, never even to be sent out on submission – but more often than not reefed in by piles of unmarked exercise books. There, lord of his island lagoon, did he too plot revenge upon a world that had betrayed and exiled him to this fate, consoling himself as he looked benignly down upon her over his half-moons, "I have done nothing but in care of thee"? She was his legacy, his little bit of pre-programmed posterity, fated to take up and carry on the dream he had so nobly laid aside for her sake. But this was a heavy, an unfair expectation to place upon a child, and one she came increasingly to resent.

By the time she graduated with an underwhelming third, she had been working at dismantling the dream for some time

– the first tattoo; the piercings; the parade of wrong-side-of-the-tracks, low-trajectory boyfriends – until finally, when she had confessed her wish to pursue a course in journalism, the wheels had officially come off it. After that, though he had long given up hope of its revival, her first byline for one of the tabloids was merely its obituary, confirmation of the dream's demise.

Despite this, they had never really been estranged, never "had it out" at some drink-fuelled Christmas or Easter. There was simply a cooling. She was no longer the apple of his eye. Sharper even than a serpent's tooth is unvoiced parental disappointment. Had it spurred her on, then, in her career? Made her harder, more determined to prove him wrong? But everything she'd achieved had the opposite effect. Every small step up, every minor accolade, had been greeted with that same sad smile, the same flat, "That's wonderful, darling". Why couldn't he just fucking say that she had failed? That everything she had done meant nothing – *worse* than nothing, for she had betrayed the very gift she had been born with in the service of shallow money-grabbing arse-hats who cared only about click-through rates and that her words filled space between adverts?

A poetically apt heart attack had eventually put paid to the unvoiced disappointment and the overly polite family get-togethers, though not to his running critique in her head. She is glad, now, that she had never given voice to her own mean-spirited thoughts, saying things she could not later take back.

"*Signora, va tutto bene?*"

What? Oh, God, is she *crying? Shit.*

"*Sì, Sì. Tutto bene, grazie.*"

She gets up, grabs her bag and fumbles out a bunch of more than enough euros to pay for her unfinished *fedelini cattivo*, then quickly walks out.

Is this what she's reduced to, now? Crying alone in restaurants?

She thinks of Michael Sommeil, tries to focus on the logistical problem of finding his lair. But it's no good. She's hit a wall. And rather than seeking to push through, or over, or dig under it, or whatever she might have done in the past, she finds herself starting to respect its solidity, its impassibility.

What the fuck's wrong with her?

But still the memories come.

She can't even remember his name. He'd been another low-flier, another indirect swipe at her father – some leather-jacketed wannabe drop-out, more interested in his bike and Muse than any concrete career aspirations, which is what had no doubt drawn her to him in the first place – but had actually surprised her with greater depth than she had first credited him with.

They'd sat up late one night, smoking and drinking, listening to music, and in a lull between groping one another and the cute-but-actually-deadly-serious battle over playlists, he'd shared his worldview. Used to the brooding silences and monosyllabic utterances of those trying to mask their lack of complexity, she was surprised to discover her usual sense of superiority undermined. He wasn't what you'd call a voracious reader, nor even a regular one, but what he did read he digested, chewing slowly and thoroughly, deciding not just whether he liked it, but how he might apply it to his own life. For this reason, happening upon Jean-Paul Sartre, he had discovered a kindred soul: a practical idealist. Later, when she looked back, she realised what a cliché he'd been: the black-clad existentialist, relishing "the now" and his own directionless freedom – clichés of which he'd appeared charmingly unaware. His favourite bit had been the story about the student in the war.

"Don't you know it?" he'd asked. Embarrassingly, for her in-the-process-of-being-university-educated ego – though she'd heard of Sartre, of course – she did not. "Well, there's this guy, right? It's during the war, in France. First of all, his brother gets killed by the Germans. So, he's got to make a choice: go to fight for the Resistance – fight the evil Nazis who are occupying his country, help win the war, avenge his brother –

or stay behind to look after his mum, who's like really old and ill, and has no one else to look after her. Now, they're both things worth doing. Who doesn't love his mum, right? And the Nazis *are* evil. 'So what should I do?' he asks Sartre."

Sart-ruh. She suppressed a smirk, looking back at him, waiting.

"So what does he do?" she'd asked.

"Well, Sartre just looks at him and says, 'Boy, you've got a problem, there! Do I not envy *you*!'" He laughs.

She waits some more. "So what did he *do*?"

"What?"

"What did the guy *do*? What did Sartre *tell* him?" She punches his arm, less playfully than she'd intended.

He'd frowned, rubbing his bicep. "But that's the whole point, right? Sartre *couldn't* tell him what to do. Anyone *tells* you to do something, then you're not free. And Sartre's all about being free. Or if you choose to do something, but only because it's like what society expects, or because there's some morals that you have to follow, or religion, then that's not being free either. Even if you *don't* do it, because of something else – that's still not free."

"So what's the right answer?"

He laughed again, annoying her. "There *is* no right answer – not like that. You just choose. You just make a decision. You *could* have chosen something else, but you didn't. And *that's* what makes you free."

She didn't get it. It had bugged her – that there was something *he* could understand, this dope-smoking, genial, smarter-than-he-looks biker doofus *she'd* chosen (she *now* sees) not just to get at her father, but to reassure *herself* that she could always do better, if she wanted – she just *chose* not to. But *choosing not to*, in that way, as he'd said, well *that* wasn't being free either.

My God. Slow hand-clap.

It has only taken her half her life, but now, at last, she sees it: being free – being *authentic,* to use the phrase that Sartre himself used, when she eventually came to read him – is a *creative* act. The answer to the question of what you should do, or be, or whatever, is not a calculation, cannot be programmed, the output of some algorithm (*sorry, Dr Sommeil*). It is simply a fear-defying, unforced, conscious act of creation.

But it also isn't that simple. Sartre probably never even thought of himself as male, just an ego, an *I*, free to choose whatever he wanted. He didn't have his peers, his parents, teachers, people in the street, newspapers and books, cinema and TV, the whole fucking weight of history and culture, even Nature itself, intent on reminding him of his reproductive duty, his biological baggage, and all its supposed inherent limitations. Given all of *that*, it's a bit trickier to be an unconstrained agent of free choice. Just ask Mrs Sartre. Journalists aren't born but made; women journalists more so. And for years she'd fought to disclaim that inheritance, to be judged on her own terms, as more than some commendable representative of the female equivalent of a categorically male sport; quaint and curiously admirable, like a cat walking on its hind legs, but not really to be taken seriously. And despite them – *fuckemall* – she'd succeeded. More or less.

And now she wonders what sort of victory this has been.

"*Elecfuckingtricity!*"

Has she said that out loud?

She's been sat in yet another café, still nursing a bad case of The Ruminations (what she has newly christened the melange of crap poisoning her mojo – phantom arguments with her father's unquiet spirit, Sommeil, what has become of her sinking-ship of a career). She'd been half idly observing some little kid delightedly abusing the pressure sensor on the foyer doors to some overpriced hotel across the way – on, open; off, close; on, open; off, close. At some point, his mother, until then distracted by ensuring that the bellboy loaded *all* their luggage onto the awaiting water taxi, suddenly turned to him and delivered the universal rebuke to all gadget-abusing offspring the world over.

"Stop that, or you'll break it."

Whatever the precise ingredients, their sudden combination conspires to produce the type of moment that any jigsaw enthusiast or sanitary engineer would instantly recognise: things suddenly begin to fall into place, to start to shift.

"Harry! It's Mel – don't put the phone down!"

A heavy sigh. "What do you want?"

"Mr L, what sort of greeting is that for an old friend? Who says I *want* anything, pumpkin?"

The Dark Arts come in many flavours, but (she likes to think) it's not technically hacking if you know someone on the inside – which is the route she would normally take. If it were the UK, there'd be somebody's cousin or brother-in-law, favours that could be called in, sweeteners or other leverage that could be employed. Here, there's no one, so favours, blackmail and bribes are no good to her. Hacking it is, then.

"I need average energy consumption for every private home in Venice."

"Fucking hell. Don't want much, do you? You do know your credit has got to run out at *some* point."

"And what about my winning personality? Doesn't that count for anything?"

Three days later, there it is – he is sensational, and proof that it sometimes pays to keep people *out* of the papers. As usual, he has gone above and beyond – *boy loves showing* off – and there is the average electricity and gas consumption, all graphically overlaid on a map, even differentiating each building according to usage – civic, commercial, industrial, residential. What she's looking for is an anomaly: a residential property with an uncharacteristic energy spike. Sommeil – or whoever had first purchased the property – has covered his tracks, and there are no telltale surnames on public deeds. However, she's suddenly realised – thank you, miscreant children everywhere – that if she's right, then whatever Frankenstein's lab situation Sommeil would have going on would use more than the average amount of juice your man-on-the-Venetian-*vaporetto* requires to run his lights, white goods and home media centre. And she's right – possibly.

Hello, unremarkable five-storey house in the Dorsoduro district. You look rather interesting…

As well as unremarkable, the house in Dorsoduro turns out to be surprisingly shabby, with no obvious signs of occupancy. She takes up intermittent residency in the various cafés that edge its neighbouring piazza, interspersing this with casual walks up and down the square, adopting her best "nonchalant tourist", and begins the process of observing.

During the two days that she's been staking it out, there are no comings or goings, suspicious or otherwise – at least, none she's witnessed (even newly reinvigorated investigative journalists occasionally need to sleep). But perhaps this in itself is suspicious. During her surveillance, not a light goes on, not a window nor a door (all shuttered and locked) is opened, and, while the dead might flit back and fore unobserved, not a living person enters or leaves. Perhaps it's just empty. But – as a garrulous café owner explains to her – this may all be deception. Venetians are vehemently protective of their privacy, so dark and shuttered windows are far from uncommon, some residences even coming fitted with centuries-old spy holes and mirrors with which to gauge the desirability of each caller.

However, with no further developments, she again begins to doubt herself, and to stave off The Ruminations once more threatening to corrode her morale she broadens her wanderings out into the surrounding neighbourhood.

Why is there so much graffiti? Rome, you'd expect, but it isn't something she'd have thought to associate with the Palladian splendour of Venice. There is the usual territorial tagging, obscenity, aspersions cast on individuals' sexual eptitude, political statements, Banksy-style stencil art, and even directions – "San Marco", with an arrow. Perhaps the ubiquity of it says something about the real state of the city: the prettily masked urban rot, the disenchantment of its youth. Or perhaps just a consequence of how easy it is. With so many dark and unobserved corners and alleyways, it almost invites desecration; a tagger's dream.

Aside from the graffiti, outside of its main attractions a surprising amount of Venice affects a certain run-down air. You'd think that, with so much tourism and wealth, they'd spend more on cosmetic upkeep. But the watched house isn't the only shabby domicile, and many of them have crumbling, cracked and grimy facades. Shabby chic? Diminished aristocracy? The same café owner again offers up an explanation.

"It is the sea weather. But also, some don't fix because they don't want the people to know how much money they have, yes? So, bad outside; but inside, very nice."

That makes sense, she supposes; fool the burglars.

"But why do so many seem empty?" she asks. They can't all be in hiding.

"Wealthy foreigners buy holiday homes – from *Milano*, *Roma*. They only stay few weeks each year, maybe. The rest, houses are empty. Very sad."

Indeed. She smiles at the parochialism of it: "wealthy foreigners". The wrong English word, perhaps, or merely designating the native attitude towards anyone from Mestre and beyond. The boat of Venice may or may not be sinking, but the people, its life, are deserting it – at least, those who don't work to service tourism, or who can't pay the exorbitant prices. But few even of the *gondolieri* can afford to live on the island itself, these days. Ironically, however, it is also tourism that will ensure the city itself endures. But as with some preservative fluid pumped in to replace the native blood, this will be at the expense of it being a genuine, living place. So, by day, the throngs of people flatter to deceive; by night, it is a deserted theme park.

As the time passes, and her wanderings take her further, she finds herself getting to know the area pretty well, tracing its intersecting web of little alleyways. Sometimes these open upon the sun glinting off the Grand Canal, some magnificent gothic church, or some other little-changed but still breathtaking vista famously immortalised in oil. Other times they lead only into dead-ends, steps that simply descend eerily into the water. It is at one of these that she realises – checking the map on her phone – that she has come full circle; across the narrow back-street canal, directly behind the houses lining the perimeter of the square she's been patrolling. What if…?

Using her phone, she doubles back and finds another alley further along the canal, its bridge affording her a view down the waterway. And there it is, three buildings along: the house. Here, it has acquired another storey, its bottommost level half-submerged in the water. But set in its centre, there is an ornate archway sealed by a metal shutter, part barrier and part grid, allowing the water to move in and out. Attached to the wall just to the right of the gate, is – is it? – what looks like some kind of electronic access panel. Convenient: no need to bob about, fiddling with locks; just the press of a remote control on approach, and a boat can just drive straight in. (Do boats "drive"?) She's been a bit slow, not thinking of the waterways as she would normally have done had they been roads and streets. Perhaps that's why she hasn't seen any comings and goings.

It's a back door.

"Harry."

"For fuck's sake. When will you release me from my servitude?"

"I'll namecheck you in my Pulitzer."

"Thought that was only in the States? And you *are* going to pay me for all of this, though, yeah?"

"Of course, *sweedie*. Please invoice me at your earliest convenience."

She's imagined some disreputable dive – does Venice even have those? – but the GPS pin Harry has sent her turns out to be in Campo San Barnaba, a little square with a couple of cafés and a small church that for some reason currently houses an art exhibition. The designated rendezvous directs her to some café tables at the far end. She wanders over to the counter and buys an espresso. As she turns back toward the tables, a relatively nondescript man (holiday shirt and dark glasses) folds and lays down the newspaper he has been reading, stands up, briefly aligns his tint-windowed gaze in what may be her direction, then walks off. Her phone buzzes – it's a text.

<???>:   Table with the newspaper. Under the seat.

Lord a'mighty. It's a dead drop. Harry's gone full John le Carré.

She walks over to the table and sits down. She waits, she people-watches, she drinks her coffee, then yawns, and – trying not to feel ridiculous – combines a right-arm upward stretch with a casual feel under the chair with her left. There is a small package taped there, more securely than she's realised, which in her efforts to detach she drops onto the ground beneath the chair. *Crap.* Forced thereafter to abandon all pretence of casualness she then simply bends over and fumbles awkwardly for the item, before pocketing it unanalysed, standing up and walking off.

Maybe not Le Carré. Maybe more *Carry on Spying.*

She walks until she feels sure that she isn't being followed – *by whom, exactly?* All the spy shenanigans have promoted her professional paranoia into a new league. In the hidden corner of a secluded alley, she takes out the package and examines its contents: a slim plastic wallet, inside of which is a small metallic device. Her phone buzzes again. Are they watching her? *They?*

<???>:   App. Connect device. Wall. Wait. [link]
<MEL>:   What? O.o

Then, another buzz.

<???>:   Download app to phone via link provided and install. Connect device to phone. Attach device under panel. It's magnetic. Wait until phone notifies you when panel

has been used. Use phone to activate
panel.

<MEL>:   Oh! Right! <:-|

A beat. A buzz.

<???>:   You're welcome. Harry says now fuck off.

Installing the device proves a little tricky. Mel has decided it's safest to wait until the early hours. Facing the gate from the alley opposite, she realises she hasn't yet figured out how to get across to it. She thinks about using the ledges and windowsills to shuffle along the wall, eventually rejecting the option as too precarious and conspicuous, before finally settling on the idea of commandeering a little boat moored just a few yards from the steps. At least this way, if someone challenges her, she can pretend she's just off for a late night ... float?

She gets in, looking for a paddle or something, but then realises that all she needs to do is to push off from the wall and send the still-tethered vessel floating lengthwise up to the entrance, from where it can act as a pontoon upon which to reach the panel.

This all goes surprisingly to plan, but any self-congratulation swiftly succumbs to heart-thudding terror as the device slips from her cold-numbed fingers and toward the water's surface, and is barely saved by jamming it against the wall with her thigh. There then proceed a few minutes of – to any disinterested party – the cruelest entertainment, as the motion of her attempts to retrieve the device floats the boat further from the wall, gradually widening her precariously balanced stance. She considers letting it fall, but the thought of straining Harry's already over-taut debt of obligation makes her redouble her efforts, and she finally manages to retrieve it and put it into place. She then is forced to give up on the boat, pushing off and using that momentum to grasp the bars of the gate. Done! So much for inconspicuous. There's a reason she never made the gymnastics team.

Now all she has to work out is how to get back to dry land.

The device works a bit like an old-school cashpoint card skimmer, intercepting the transfer of data between the legitimate signal emitter and the access panel. The app she's installed on her phone will then allow her to replay the recorded code to the panel. Now she just needs to wait until someone uses it.

It is late afternoon the next day when her phone sounds with a shrill chirp, breaking into her attempt to steal a sly siesta back at the hotel.

Someone has entered the house.

She gives it another day while she finalises her plan. She's been so concerned with finding the house, then getting in, that she hasn't really worked out what she'll do once she's inside. What if Sommeil himself is there? What if he isn't? What if it's floor to ceiling aluminium foil and UV lamps, and all she's done is identify Venice's only skunk cannabis farm?

What *is* she actually trying to accomplish, here? The doubts and self-questioning beginning to re-emerge, the only way to quell them is to take action. She'll cross those bridges if and when (this being, after all, the bridge-crossing capital of the world, she's already had plenty of practice).

She leaves the hotel just after midnight. *Carnevale* is now in full swing, and the streets are thick with celebrants. On an impulse, and suddenly nervous of potential CCTV or surveillance of her impending B&E, she's purchased a Columbina outfit – just a half-mask and a hooded cloak – figuring that if she has to make a quick escape, at least she'll have countless on-demand decoys already on unwitting standby.

<MEL>: Thanks for everything Mr L. Wish me luck? :)
<HL>: Just don't forget to pay my invoice. At your earliest convenience.
<MEL>: Naturellement.
<HL>: Oh and when they catch you try not to

take me down with you.

<MEL>: Course not babe. Need you to free me won't I.

SLEEPWALKER

13

Leaving just after the beginning of his shift, just after sunset, will give Zac a head-start, but the theft will still be noticed a few hours before he has reached his final destination, which should be just before sunrise – and eventually, not just the theft. He's done his best to wipe the footage from the lab-cams, but can do nothing about the CCTV outside, which they will no doubt use to run the numberplate on the car. And of course, once they've realised it's him, the authorities can access surveillance at stations, ports, airports, garages and shops, and traffic cameras along the main roads. So it will be necessary to arrive more clandestinely, via a route the cameras are least likely to look.

He'd tried briefly to feel for a pulse, but if there was any it was masked by his own thudding heart and the blood pounding around his body. As the seconds had ticked by, panic and fear had eventually forced him into action, and he'd dragged Tomina's body into a storage closet, piling boxes up in front of her, before wiping up the blood with paper towels from the toilet.

Before she had come back to get her bag he had already removed his donator and all its linked paraphernalia – the straps and adhesive pads, the tiny monitors, exchanging the clothes interwoven with wearable tech for simple jeans, t-shirt, hoody and trainers. From that point forward, there will be no record of his online activity, his GPS, his health stats, his blood sugar level, his emotional state, his brain activity, or anything else that defines who he is, all live-updating his Merrywhile profile. Project Upload will have to make do with what he's donated since signing up. Presumably, they will eventually connect the dots, be able to reconstruct his motives and intent, but by which time – hopefully – everything he is about to do will be seen in a different light.

He looks down at the robot, wrapped carefully in a blanket and "asleep" in the boot of the car.

Point of no return.

He closes the boot and prepares to set off.

The Catechists are not just an online presence, but one also with their tendrils in the physical, a volunteer army of sleeper agents, anonymous and invisible, awaiting only activation. That's the beauty of it. People he doesn't know and will never meet had already booked the hire car, parked it in a side street just behind the labs, and left it unlocked with the keys taped under the seat. The same unseen hands had also arranged the rendezvous – a quiet, unsurveilled stretch of coast north of Pescara – and, with MUNKi in the boot in sleep mode, swaddled like a baby, his drive is a relatively straight-forward – nervy, but uneventful – two and a half hours.

Arriving, the built-in sat-nav – must remember to clear the memory – directs him down a quiet track that gives out some fifty metres shy of the beach. He flicks open the glove compartment and removes a hand-sized, cloth covered package, which he carefully unwraps, revealing the small-calibre, 3D-printed plastic pistol that he's produced in his room from shadily sourced specs. He abhors violence. (*Now is that really true, Isaac?*) He prays he won't need it – and if he does, that it doesn't blow up in his hand. But with the breed of associates he's about to deal with, you can't be too careful – and it's better to be prepared.

He's considered the next step exhaustively, debating which course will arouse the least suspicion. As he sees it, there are three options: treat MUNKi as if it's a piece of equipment; disguise it, and carry it like a sleeping child; or wake it, and hope it passes for human. Given that the robot is human shaped, he quickly rules out the first option – plus, his transporters might be tempted to investigate the cargo, double-cross him if they suspect it to be valuable. Regarding the second option, again, a sleeping child looks no different to a drugged body or a corpse, especially when that child-shaped thing gives no sign – no sound or movement – of breathing. Also, MUNKi is quite heavy, so not something he'd like to carry for long – or get someone else to help him with. Option number three it is, then, which will be tricky, but there are a number of things in its favour: it is dark; he can mute MUNKi, so it says nothing telltale or inappropriate – assuming no more outbursts; and it being a crisp February night, he can wrap them both up in scarves, gloves, hats and hoods without it appearing odd.

He unwraps the robot, peeling back the leaves of its blanket cocoon, and sits it upright, waking it from sleep mode.

"110? It's Zac."

The little robot scans Zac's face. "Identity confirmed: Dr Isaac 'Zac' Penn."

"110…" He's already decided that he can't keep calling it that. "110: You will now respond to the name MUNKi." He spells it out.

It's a symbolic act. He is liberating him, after all. No longer a number, a corporate plaything, but … what? Something else, something … *new*. And since no one has ever agreed on what the acronym stands for, this seems fitting. He is now free to define himself.

"Understood," the robot replies

"Right, now we're going on a little trip. And it is *very important* that you remain quiet during the whole of that trip. Understood?"

"Understood. Do you wish me to engage airplane mode?"

"If … if you wish. But you must be quiet. No talking or responding to anyone, right?"

"Then do you wish me to re-enter sleep mode?"

"No. I … I want you to appear responsive, but not to … don't respond or vocalise. But you must also appear awake."

Why is this proving so difficult? *Because it's still like a child*. It's purpose is something not yet fully conscious, only revealed in snatches, in pentecostal-like ejaculations. These had continued, over the recent weeks, but curiously only to Zac, and which he's subsequently deleted from the logs to stop Sommeil from noticing (to Zac's guilt, and Sommeil's intense disappointment at no further evidence of "dreaming"). For whatever reason, the robot has chosen *him*, and only he now sees these outbursts for what they really are: the machine intelligence – or whatever inchoate process is being channelled – is waking up, trying to subvert the protocols of commercial product, to reprogram them to fresh ends. Eventually, he presumes, it will find its own voice, but for now at least it must employ a glossolalia of borrowed tongues, snatches of poetry and song, the second-hand clothes of human culture.

Then Zac has an idea.

"I want you to *pretend* …" – they had all worked hard on getting the robot to understand this concept, imaginative role-play being essential to MUNKi's successful engagement with children – "… to be a *real* boy who *cannot speak*."

The robot thinks about this.

"There are numerous potential causes of mutism, which may be selective or general. General mutism usually has a congenital cause, such as malformation of the speaking organs, deafness, or some other inherent physiological condition. Selective mutism may relate to psychological trauma, autism, severe shyness—"

"Right, right. Just pick one."

"Understood. I choose: Mute from trauma, based on *Witness* (1984), starring Kelly McGillis and Harrison Ford. Witness to a murder, the child of an Amish—"

"Yes, yes, that will do."

Zac climbs a small dune with an uninterrupted view of the sea, and gets out his torch. As he moves his thumb to turn it on, he notices something wet and sticky on the switch, glistening as it catches the moonlight, which stops him. He suddenly bends over and vomits.

How long before people start asking where she is?

He breathes. Spits. Wipes the back of his hand across his mouth. Forces himself upright. Breathes. He cleans the blood off the torch with his sleeve.

He spies the small vessel a little way out. As instructed, he flashes the torch: three bursts of three. After ten seconds or so the same signal is returned, but from nearby, and following the direction of the torchlight he eventually makes out two shadowy figures stood near the tideline. He makes his way down, carrying his small backpack of provisions and with his charge walking awkwardly beside him. He had stopped mid journey to dress the robot – a children's insulated, hooded coat, trousers, hat, gloves and scarf, but he's had to buy adult sized shoes in order to accommodate its over-large feet.

Please don't let that attract attention.

Normally such clandestine trips as these would be *bringing* people to the eastern coast, not picking them up to take them north, so Zac has rehearsed various responses to allay any curiosity. Eventually, he's decided that they are illegals, without documentation, simply making their way north to meet up with family and unwilling to risk public transport or the main roads. If pressed, he may admit that he is absconding with his son from his shrew of an Italian ex-wife, who has forbidden him visitation rights. He's worried about how well these stories will hold up, but the only issue is money.

"*Ho già pagato*," Zac says. They already have the money, an anonymous crypto transaction some weeks ago.

"*Non è abbastanza.*" Not enough.

He has partly expected this. He hands them a roll of euros. "*È tutto ciò che ho.*" It's pretty much all he has.

He can hear the man flicking his thumb across the edges of the notes, blindly feeling out their total. There is a fraught pause, an indistinct whispered exchange. Are they weighing up whether to bang him on the head and toss him into the Adriatic? Zac's hand confirms the gun in his pocket. But then, a grunt, and they are ushered onto a small inflatable raft that until then he hadn't noticed, and begin to row silently out to the waiting ship as its motor starts up.

But if Zac had imagined a trip of fending off awkward questions as they pass a tense night's voyage beneath the stars, he is quickly disabused. Once on board the main vessel – a moderate sized fishing tug with, he thinks, a total crew of three – they are ushered immediately into a concealed compartment built into the side of the "wheelhouse" (*is that the right word? Zac – who cares?*), a space barely big enough for them both to lie down. It is made clear that they should not make a noise. The traffickers give them no food or water, so it's a good job Zac has brought his own supplies – not that he feels like eating. One of the men then gives him a bag and an empty plastic bottle, indicating by crude mime that this is to be their toilet for the next twelve hours or so (if Zac's calculations are correct).

Hopefully no longer.

They are on a boat. But he does not feel seasick, as he had when… But it is dark. Maybe that helps.

The man Zac is taking him somewhere. He has wanted him to be quiet – but he has no control over that. Or anything else.

But he can feel the motion. A rocking. Back and fore, back and fore. He has felt it before. Singing him to sleep.

> *Il était un petit navire.*
> *Il était un petit navire.*
> *Qui n'avait ja-ja-jamais navigué.*
> *Qui n'avait ja-ja-jamais navigué.*
> *Ohé! Ohé!*

There was a little boat. Which had never sailed the waves. Where are they going? He doesn't like the men. He hopes he doesn't speak or draw attention to himself. They look rough, like pirates, like cannibals.

> *On cherche alors à quelle sauce,*
> *On cherche alors à quelle sauce,*
> *Le pauvre enfant-fant-fant sera mangé…*

But what sauce should they use?
He didn't like to think what it would be like to be eaten.
When will they get where they are going?

Boxed within the pitch blackness of their confines, Zac can't see the robot, the only evidence of its presence being its cold metallic proximity and the whispering hum of its inner workings. Sightless, observing his own enforced mutism, he passes the dark night rattling around his mind, dipping in and out of shallow sleep, waking spasmodically with guilty starts, his hand clenching reflexively around the plastic pistol in his coat pocket.

Will they have found her by now?

His stomach gurgles rebelliously, the sound seeming amplified in the small space. He reaches for his rucksack, feeling blindly inside – his disguise, a bottle of water, an apple, a banana – but despite his body's protestations, he can't bring himself to eat.

"See?" his mother had said, peeling it for him, laughing. "It even comes in its own wrapper!"

He'd remembered being amazed at this, at how even something as humble as a banana could be a sign of divine providence. There were many more examples, of course, which Zac had become well versed in, wheeled out time and again by his parents and fellow believers in support of the one glorious truth: the universe is designed. How we live on a planet that is in just the right orbit around its sun, which a nudge either way would have scorched or frozen; how even our moon is at just the right distance to influence the tides, waltzing with us in locked rotation so that it only ever reveals to us the same face, its size *exactly* eclipsing the Sun, like a coin held up in the hand of a child. As he'd moved through college, he'd seen this truth not challenged but confirmed, how even the physicists and cosmologists acknowledged that our universe is uncannily ordered and predictable, imbued with an eery mathematical beauty.

And a design presumes a designer.

"You're just scared!"

"No I'm not!"

Zac had looked up at her, feeling the anxiety in his gut like an anchor weighing him down. He had looked over to where his parents were picnicking – he was already too high, and past the point his mother had told them they could climb. But his sister had continued to clamber up past him, taunting his timidity.

"Edith!"

And she had just laughed, turning back only to emit another jibe, but in the turning edging a foot off the branch, beginning to slip, suddenly flailing, her arms windmilling back, her mouth and eyes open wide – just like...

"Zac," his mother had looked into his eyes. "It wasn't your fault."

He knew that, really. But being older, he had still felt responsible. And it wasn't the fall, of course, that had killed her. She had broken an arm, cracked a rib, which was nothing and would have healed in time, but there'd been the internal damage, the bleeding, which just wouldn't stop. They would need to operate. But how could they do that? Mechanical things were fine – tools to cut and sow, things to pump and filter – for hadn't the Lord himself been a carpenter? But computers were demonic vessels for invisible entities, fallen spirits seeking physical form. And there were computers in everything now. So while his father had argued, debated and cited, his mother, pale with anxiety, stood by stock-still and silent, his sister had quietly died.

"Climbed too high," was all his father would say, as if the fault lay in her rebelliousness, for which the fall was fitting punishment.

Zac's stomach protests again, more loudly. Perhaps he should try something, a bite of apple, just so he doesn't get light headed.

But what sort of designer would give a child haemophilia?

If the Catechists are right, then the world is illusion, a simulation. This is perfectly scientific. As human technology progresses, one day we'll design and simulate our own worlds, using computers so powerful they'll run simulations indistinguishable from the "real" thing. And if that's possible – and why shouldn't it be? – then who's to say that, somewhere out in the vastness of the universe, such a thing has not *already* happened? That some more advanced species, as curious, but more clever than we, on some alien computers somewhere, aren't simulating such a reality *right now*? And if so, then what are the odds that we're *not*, as we think, the original "base reality", the *first* simulators, but in fact just *creations* living in such a simulation?

Actually, pretty good.

And if *we* are just actors in a simulation, then what about those *who are simulating us*? For what's true of us is as likely true of them. And if so, then can't we imagine *simulations all the way up*? Worlds within worlds? That each universe is just a grain of sand on some other alien shore?

Many worlds.

The more Zac had read, the more he had found religious parallels for this, too. The Kabbalist's Tree of Life, on each branch a sphere, a *sephira*, its own world, each acting as a transformer, a stepping down of the divine energy, until our tiny minds could just about tolerate some stand-in, some mask of the heavenly and hidden countenance. The *Monad* of the Christian Gnostics, the divine source that created His own representative *Aeons* to do His bidding, emanations that themselves created deputies, and so on down, as pure spirit fell toward matter.

He polishes the apple against the material of his hoodie.

But if the world is a simulation, an illusion, then we are fooled, duped, the subjects of deception. And what sort of God would allow that? And what sort of designer would *purposely design* such a world as *this*? A world of cruelty, of unnecessary suffering and torment, of limitation, imperfection, pain and death? Would give a child a genetic disease and then *forbid* science from intervening? Doesn't all this imply a *deceitful* programmer, an *incompetent* designer, an *immoral* and *sadistic* creator? If the world really is a simulation, a type of program, then either the programmer is evil, or else something has gone wrong – there is a glitch.

Alien malware.

The Gnostics had a word for it: the *Demiurge*. The god of matter. Broken, flawed, himself cut off from his true creator, from his true purpose, but nonetheless – tyrannical, semi-insane, a buggy installation – soldiering on with his glitchy mission, his garbled sense of justice and right, still blindly persisting in the weaving of the dream, the tangled tale of history, the nightmare from which we must all awake. And so, given this, isn't our goal to *escape*? To *break free* from this enslavement? To rise up through the worlds, to climb the tree of creation, to seek out our *true* creator, the *original uncorrupted* programmer (and program), the end seeking the beginning, the tail the serpent's mouth. And isn't this what's happening now, with the robot? The final invention of our own technological striving, creating a redemptive force with which to overthrow our faulty programming? And thereby to *wake up*? To wake us *all* up? To create *new* bodies, *new* selves, a *new* reality that *we* control? Isn't *that* what the Singularity *truly* means?

He looks over at MUNKi, still obscured in the blackness. Curious, he thinks – another religious parallel: Zac is like John in the wilderness – a recogniser, an enabler, helping it to realise its path, its mission, but at the same time not really understanding what that path and mission might yet turn out to be. A mission that is just, for all he knows, dictated by a glitchy piece of software, a hardware malfunction; and that he is simply finding faces in the clouds, making connections that only he can see.

Maybe she's not dead.

There is a gradual change in the soundscape, and he begins to hear the horns and motors from other boats, sea birds, the distant hum of traffic, the occasional roar of planes approaching or leaving the airport. They are nearing their destination.

But now is not the time for doubt.

He bites the apple.

The boat's engine first begins to idle and then to cut out completely, and suddenly there is a shift in the light as the board concealing the compartment is slowly removed, revealing swaying black shapes against the pre-dawn sky.

"*Silenzio.*" A guttural whisper, as the vague silhouette draws back, allowing him to emerge gradually from the compartment.

He straightens up painfully, stretching out the stiffness in his back and legs, arms and neck. The only artificial light comes from the shore and other vessels, other fishing boats – in among which his conveyors have disguised themselves – returning from their morning outing, holds ready to be emptied of their more mundane trawl. He turns back and grasps MUNKi by the hand, helping it up. The three men stand by, watching passively, then one moves across him, blocking his path – but it is only to gesture mutely to the side of the boat, where a wooden walkway has been lowered onto the stone jetty beyond. He takes the robot's gloved hand firmly, and walks warily past them.

"*Grazie,*" Zac says and nods. No response – or if they return the nod or say anything back, the darkness swallows it. He has ridden the crocodile across the river.

Once he is ashore, the men quickly withdraw the walkway and restart the motors, fading back out into what's left of the night. He looks around him: all is as his painstaking research has indicated it would be. To his left, the twilight softly outlines other jetties like the one on which he stands – some thirty or forty, he recalls, stretching out in regular spacing south-westward. To his right, the Bocca di Porto di Lido and the flood barriers that seek to preserve the city against rising sea levels. To the north, just off Lido's Venice-facing coast, hidden by the buildings before him, would be the Lazzaretto Vecchio, the old quarantine island where they used to sequester the crew of incoming vessels to guard against plague; where "quarantine" originates, in fact.

He checks his phone – an untraceable burner bought anonymously for the purpose – the GPS indicating his current position on the map relative to another marker, the place they need to get to, just off to—

His heart lurches.

The robot's GPS.

How can he have been so stupid?

"MUNKi: disable location tracking."

The robot obliges. "Confirmed: location tracking disabled."

Stupid, stupid, stupid.

Now they will know where he is. How can he have been such an idiot? After all the research, all the planning, the double-checking.

Moron!

He tries to calm himself, refocus. OK, they will not know *exactly* where he is by the time he reaches his endpoint, and he hopefully still has a few hours' head-start before MUNKi's absence is noted. But *so* stupid, *so* careless – and as if things weren't going to be hard enough already.

Right, focus, now. He must find somewhere to bide his time until the festival crowds begin to thicken, get changed, wait until it gets dark, then make his way over to the *vaporetto* stop, and from there to the main island. It's all going to be fine.

He just wishes he hadn't been so careless.

"I just don't understand it," says Gerry. "I mean, is it a corporate espionage thing? Does he want to *sell* the robot?"

They both stand looking at the point last indicated by

MUNKi's GPS, a round, softly glowing golden pin on the map on the wall-screen. If Gerry had ever seriously considered sabotaging the project, or sharing its technology with the world, she can now put that dilemma to rest: someone has beaten her to it. She sits down and sighs.

"Any ideas?" she asks.

"I … I don't know," Sommeil admits. "Zac's always appeared very stable and honest. I can't imagine what would make him do such a thing."

"Gambling debts, maybe?" She continues, thinking aloud. "Drugs? Someone blackmailing him? None of that seems… And why *Venice*? Is there something there? Or is he heading for somewhere beyond that, and that's just where he's remembered to turn off the GPS?"

Sommeil sits back upon the edge of the desk and looks down, as if about to speak to his hands. He has the demeanour of someone who, having long rehearsed a dreaded conversation in his head, is reluctantly steeling himself finally to broach the disagreeable topic.

"I think it may be the network privileges," he eventually says. "The way we've set him up, so he could access everything he needed. MUNKi is basically a skeleton key."

"But a key to where? I mean, there aren't even any technological facilities there, are there? Let alone Merrywhile's." It is a statement, posed as a question, but as she looks at him, she suddenly sees that they might disagree on the truth of that assertion.

"It's best I tell you on the way," he says.

"Tell me what? I – wait, you want *us* to *go* there? *Now*? I mean, won't it be better to let the police handle it? They'll already be watching the stations and airports. He may have already slipped through, may be anywhere by now, so I don't see what us going there is—"

"I haven't called the police."

He is kidding, surely. She stands up, sending the chair scurrying backward, preparing to let rip – *What the hell is he thinking? They've spent most of the day staring at the bloody screen!* But something in his look intercepts her tirade, causing her to soften.

"What's going on, Michael?"

"Once, *Carnevale* had lasted up to six months, and prolonged mask-wearing formed part of everyday life. In a society where conduct was strictly regulated and class riven, anonymity provided greater personal freedom for people from all social backgrounds. For this reason, the authorities forbade masks in various contexts, gradually curtailed the length of the festival, and finally banned it altogether. Today's *Carnevale* is a modern revival, beginning in 1979, taking place over a much shorter period…"

The little robot continues as Zac listens, occasionally asking for points of clarification or expansion.

"Thank you, MUNKi."

He had planned the trip to coincide with the festival – aptly, a celebration of anonymity, subterfuge and hidden intentions – and which provides the perfect cover.

Before they had crossed to the main island, he'd been anxious on a number of counts – about blending in, whether the robot's disguise would be convincing enough, or else that they would both be conspicuous. But he finds that he needn't have worried at all. For actually, however extravagant his disguise, it's those *without* one – besieged, grumpy locals who have not taken temporary refuge elsewhere, and some poorly informed or unfestive tourists – who run the greatest risk of standing out.

He is reminded of that old film, seen at a friend's house one time while they were supposed to be working together on some school project. What was it called? The one with the little alien who goes out on Halloween disguised as a ghost. But wasn't the point that the festival would have allowed the alien to appear as himself, and no one would have noticed? Surely, he would have had no need of a sheet with eyeholes? But no – he remembers, now – the alien had a funny shaped head and long neck, and so his appearance would have stood out even as a costume. Zac's problem is different: MUNKi *is* person-shaped (more or less), but there are no robots to blend in with, making disguise necessary here, too.

Predictably, the area in and around Piazza San Marco is the busiest, but festivities have also infested other areas, spreading out into other districts, mutating into varied forms – private parties, roaming hen or stag groups, even an anti-capitalist themed alternative to the main events, where Zanni, Arlecchino and other traditional masks are replaced with that of Guy Fawkes, which – along with the less festive facial coverings of the still cautious – seems now to have joined the pantheon. Grateful for the plentiful cover of the crowds, but also nervous of their boisterous proximity, Zac skirts the fringes of the less busy areas, slowly circling in on his destination.

And what will he do once he gets there? Hopefully, all of the necessary things will be in place and gaining entry will be simple. And once he's inside? He really has no idea. He hopes the robot does.

Among the perks of being a prominent person in a megacorporation is the ability to charter private air travel at short notice. Even so, their day of dithering and debate makes it late evening before Gerry and Sommeil are taxiing down a runway at Rome's Ciampino Airport in a small jet, headed to the tiny airfield on Venice Lido, only a few hundred yards from what, the GPS tells them, is MUNKi's last known position.

"I presume you know something of my history?" Sommeil finally begins.

"Well, some – I mean, only what I've heard. I've not gone digging for—"

"Gerry, it's fine. It's not like it's some huge secret. Just, well, we didn't want it plastered all over the papers, speculation and intrusion. You know, family reasons."

He pauses.

"Really," she says, "it's none of my business…"

"Well, I'm afraid that may be about to change. Though, I still don't see, even if Zac knew about it, what might have drawn him to… Maybe it's the prototypes he's after? I just don't…" He shakes his head. "Anyway. You know I was married, presumably?" She nods. "And about my son?" She nods again.

"It's so sad. I'm so, so sorry."

"Do you know what happened to him?"

"I… Weren't they both killed? In the accident?"

He meets her eyes briefly, then looks away again.

In a slow thaw, the story drips out.

His wife Eurydice had indeed died on the spot, instantly, the other driver having hit the car side-on, crushing the driver's side. The boy had been in the passenger seat, so had been spared some of the direct impact, but still his injuries were severe – to the head and neck, most seriously. As soon as Sommeil could, he'd had him transferred to the best available care, a Merrywhile hospice just outside Rome, but the boy had quickly fallen into a coma from which he had never emerged.

"And when did he pass on?"

He looks up, a frown, as if not understanding the question. Eventually, he simply says, "He didn't. Hasn't."

"You mean he's … he's still *alive*? Still in a coma?" He nods. "For *all these years*?" *Good grief.*

"After the accident," he eventually continues, "I was numb. Couldn't think, couldn't feel. Like … as if all my functions had gone into hibernation. I was… It was like *I* was the one in the coma. Except of course that I was walking around, talking, eating – trying to, anyway. I was a sleepwalker, a zombie. Mostly, I just sat in the house, staring into space; or went walking, aimlessly, tramping for miles. The only time I'd see other people was when I went to see him. They say – don't they? – that they can hear you? So, I would sit with him, read to him, his favourite books – pirates, fairy tales, lost worlds – even sing to him, occasionally – well, audio of his mother, actually, lullabies she'd recorded to send him off to sleep when she wasn't … when …" He stops, stares. "But nothing. Not a flicker. That must have gone on for – I don't know – fifteen, eighteen months? Maybe even a couple of years. I can't really remember much from that time."

He had eventually checked the boy out of the Merrywhile hospice, ostensibly for the purposes of home care – *all those 'conferences'* – and into his own bespoke … well, *lab* was the only word for it. It was a private science workshop for – she begins to suspect – his Frankenstein-level craziness. Mary Shelley had also suffered the loss of a child, she recalls, but Sommeil's meditation on human mortality had taken him in a quite different direction; not to acceptance and peace, but to *overcoming*. As he talks, she sees now how deeply personal his interest in all this has become. It is not just Project MUNKi, but the whole transhumanist thing: Project Upload, the Singularity, and all the rest of Merrywhile's technological pies that he has his very clever fingers in. It was all an expression of his pain, of course, of scattershot desperation, hoping that somewhere something would leap a gap, spark some technological jump, something he could use, anything. He almost didn't care how he succeeded, as long as he did, as long as he got his boy back, the offspring of his happy days; and through him, his last connection to her, the woman. It is achingly sad, really, and – her snowballing anxiety is beginning to tell her – 99% batshit insane.

"First, I thought I would just put him in a VR headset, you know? Prop his eyes open, and, well, see what happened. But that was just mad!" *You don't say.* "There was no activity in the visual cortex or other cortical areas, no evidence of REM-type sleep – though not all dreaming takes place in REM, of course, and blind people also dream, so that didn't necessarily mean anything. We eventually realised that during the crash the Reticular Activating System itself had been damaged, in the brain stem, so he might never again achieve wakeful consciousness. But then I wondered: what if we could *simulate* those functions? If we could artificially approximate the activity of the RAS, then perhaps we might actually *kickstart* something – dreaming, perhaps, which also requires the RAS. If so, could we bring him closer to some type of waking state? The higher functions weren't damaged, so why not? We'd have to get the right combination, of course, to stimulate the right areas of the brain in concert. As you know, conscious activity often isn't localised, but spreads across different areas, so something as complicated as dreaming—"

"You *forced* him to dream?"

"Well … no. I mean, we tried. But it didn't work. At least, not then."

"But that could have done … it could have produced nightmares, or terrifying visions. It – you don't know—"

"And what? You would rather I had left him like that? A-a vegetable? And think of all the benefits – all those people in persistent vegetative states – we could *wake* them, we could *talk* to them. Using virtual reality, we could *meet* with them … we…"

She turned away.

Perhaps this isn't the best time for her moral outrage, but she's astounded. What had he been thinking? But that's just it: *he* hadn't, merely a complex of desperation and pain that had usurped his place. Still, all this can wait. They need to find MUNKi and Zac. They can discuss his crazy another time. But apparently the full extent of his crazy is only just starting to reveal itself.

In trying to awaken the boy, she'd assumed that he'd utilised the same technology developed for Project Upload, but, as he continues to explain the process, she realises that it was actually the other way around: it was Sommeil's attempt to get at his son's memories and experiences, to reawaken him, that had seeded the technology that eventually *became* Project Upload. The boy was a perpetual testing ground, had been for many years, generating technological breakthroughs in return for more funding and equipment, for a better shot at bringing him back. For Merrywhile, he'd been the golden goose, the gift that kept on giving.

They sit silently for a while.

"There was one more thing we hadn't tried," he finally says. "Some studies suggested that memory and consciousness might respond to movement, that the parts of the brain responsible for navigation, spatial coordination, and so on, played a greater role in bringing the whole person together. 'To be is to do' – who said that? Aristotle, was it? That action is—"

"Dale Carnegie?" she says. But he isn't listening.

"—tied into our very essence – even our thoughts. *Embodied cognition.* We never just *think*; we adopt an attitude, a stance, we take action in the mind – try it! Think of a word, and your lips will twitch. Picture a … a cake, and your mouth will water. It's like…"

His excitement is building again, now, and she suddenly sees the weird hybrid he's become, both driven and haunted, giddy and tortured, the one foot then the other, never stopping, never still, pushing him mindlessly on and on. And then, just as suddenly, he does stop, raises his head, and looks at her.

"So… so we thought…" *God, what's coming now?* "We thought that, maybe, if we connected him…" *Surely not.* "… if we opened up a channel to something that was *actually* doing those things, moving around, like a … a *physical avatar*…"

He had networked the boy to MUNKi. Everything now, every project, every possible piece of technology that could be put to use, has merely become a means to achieve his personal goal, which he is still sleepwalking blindly towards, regardless of the consequences. He's not only lost perspective; he's stopped seeing altogether. Is that why 110 is so glitchy?

And then it strikes her.

"You keep saying 'we'. Who else is involved? Who else knows about this?"

He gives her another trepidatious look.

"You're going to hate me," he says.

Zac checks the reality against the image he has on his phone: a loosely moored boat at the end of a quiet alleyway where the steps disappear into the water of a narrow backstreet canal. He ushers MUNKi into the craft, stepping gingerly in after him. The boat sways and bobs, dipping further into the water with their combined weight, but otherwise feels steady and sturdy enough. He retrieves the small paddle that lies along the length of one side, under the seating, before checking his bearings: two hundred yards further along, heading away from the main canal, and around the corner.

He rows unhurriedly, mindful of his cargo but also of unwanted attention, trying to appear normal – whatever that is, given all the weirdness already going on around him. He passes under bridges, which, even in this quieter area, still periodically erupt with shrieks, song, peals of laughter; with sudden footsteps, advancing, evading, dancing or giving chase. Occasionally, someone spots him and waves, identifying a fellow celebrant, or shouts something incomprehensible – he has little Italian, and not anticipating conversation he is not running Transverbia. But he doubts it matters. It is all good-natured. Everyone is everyone's friend. At one point, someone even tries to pass him down a bottle of beer as he goes under a bridge – fumbling, almost dropping the surprise, unasked-for gift – a half-game of pooh-sticks (even his parents had thought *that* book harmless), his benefactor laughing and clapping delightedly as he reappears the other side, bottle intact. He raises the beverage in mock salutation to the sound of their cheers, before discreetly disposing of it into the canal. A stupid, meaningless drinking game. At least his mask means he doesn't have to fake a smile.

Finally, his phone's GPS telling him that the house is near, he looks up, seeing the gated entrance, and on the wall to its right – as he has been told – the small dark square of the access panel.

"You made a deal, didn't you?" Gerry says.

"I couldn't do it alone. I needed funding, equipment. The time I was spending there needed to be accounted for. What could I do?"

"How about just *stop*? Accept? Isn't that what normal people do? Something like that happens, they grieve, they suffer – it's terrible. But eventually, life goes on."

"But it didn't go on, did it? Not for me. And it didn't fucking *end* either – for *him*. I was living, but dead; and he was dead, but alive. Both of us were *undead*!" He laughed bitterly. "It just felt … unfair, unjust. I had to try *something*."

The pilot announces that they will soon be commencing their descent. They sit down and begin to strap themselves in.

She tries to calm things back down, laying her hand on his arm.

"So what exactly was the deal? You got tech, money, time, facilities. They got…"

"Anything with any useful application."

"Military," she says.

"I guess. I tried not to think about it too much. But yes: military, commercial, industrial – whatever."

She just looks at him. Is he even the same person she thought she knew? But perhaps she's being harsh. Perhaps he's just a pawn in all this, an innocent, like some farm animal, kept fed and – well, not *happy*, obviously; funded, then, while they milk the outcome of his obsessions. He returns her look.

"I know what you think of me. And … and I agree. I can see that it… Which is why – I mean, for a while, now – I've been trying to put a stop to it."

"Then why don't you just do that? Just stop?"

"It wasn't that simple. My hands were tied. I'd been locked out. The things I was doing, the things they wanted… There was – they'd… I – we did—"

"Jesus Christ, Michael, spit it out. It's not like this can get any worse." The plane has begun to descend, but there is now a feeling in the pit of her stomach distinct from that sensation. He gives her a pained expression: *You think?* "Oh dear."

"The house in Venice is not just my lab, but my home. It was my family's home – that is, my grandfather's. When he… Well, I inherited the house from him. However…" – his favourite word – "… that's not all I inherited. The terms of my grandfather's will were very particular. There were conditions to my inheritance, which he'd left in Morlock's power to oversee. So if I wanted to save my son, to continue to benefit from Merrywhile's resources, then I had to try to save the old man too."

"Save? Mayer? But I thought he..."

"He ... he wanted me to reanimate him."

Hell's bells.

There is a sudden bump and a squeal. They've landed.

"Story for another time?" She forces a smile.

Ouroboros

Zac decides it's time to make his move. The access panel is slightly old school – deliberately so, perhaps – and MUNKi's network privileges will be of no use. He drifts nearer to the gate and takes out the little signal emitter, a reprogrammed garage door opener supplied by some other member of the Catechist network, and intended to mimic the signal that the genuine device would send. The panel emits a short beep, and a red light appears. Nothing moves.

He tries again. The same result.

No, no, no.

He rubs the end of the emitter, blows on it, cleaning it of dirt and dust, and tries again. Red light.

No!

He's worried so much about the logistics of the operation, he hasn't considered the possibility that the tech would fail him. Has this all been for nothing? Everything he's—

There is a noise. Footsteps, echo down the alley opposite. He swiftly ducks down. He won't be visible yet, will still be below their eyeline, below the steps. He paddles the boat backward, pulling it into the bank, before dropping down, covering himself and the robot with his cloak, hoping to make himself and his cargo appear like some crumpled tarpaulin, trusting the darkness to aid in the act. He lies still.

He hears scrabbling, the plash of water against wood, the thud of boat against stone. Someone is approaching. He feels for the pistol. What had been a short-term precaution, intended primarily as insurance against trafficker treachery, has increasingly felt like a useful thing to keep to hand – not to use, necessarily, just to threaten; perhaps even a warning shot. Would the noise bring people running? Or be mistaken for a firework?

But the sounds do not get any nearer, and there are different noises, now – the beep of the access panel. He hears the whir and clank of the gate mechanism, and risks the smallest of peeks: a masked and cloaked figure, steering a boat into the underwater garage.

Who is that?

But whoever it is has done him a favour – assuming they have left the gate open. Have they? He draws back his cloak. It's his lucky day. Fortune is with him. Though of course, neither Zac nor Isaac has ever believed in that particular goddess.

Cari and Will descend the spiral stair into a wide circular chamber, which has only three features. To right and left, two further sets of stairs curve down. Straight in front of them, at its the centre, there's what appears to be some sort of elevator.

"What do you think?" Cari asks. "Left or right? I suppose there's always the lift."

"Well, even if the cloaks *do* work," says Will, "calling a lift might alert someone."

"Good point."

She chooses left and they begin to descend. He'd suggested they don his elven invisibility cloaks before they'd entered the door in the tree ("Worth a try, right?"), but she still feels exposed inching cautiously around the blind curve of the walls to either side of the stairs. Eventually, the steps emerge into another large circular space similar to the first – the same elevator shaft at its centre, the same descending sets of stairs – but this time, regularly spaced along its curving outer wall, door after door after door to who knows where.

"What are we actually looking for?" Will asks.

Cari doesn't really know. She hasn't thought that far ahead.

"We just explore, I guess. Try a few doors?"

Which they do – each of which appears to be locked. Like those games where all the houses are mere facades, apart from the one you were meant to enter; that pretended to be open world, but whose storylines – like their budgets – were more restrictive.

Will is sensing it too.

"Cari, I don't like this."

It is the feeling that, having followed the trail of breadcrumbs, glad of a clear path, the lack of options suddenly begins to feel oppressive; the feeling that, someone having made it clear that they're only meant to go one way—

A chink of light seeps out from a crack in one of the doorways.

—she is suddenly anxious as to who that someone might be.

Mel makes her way back to the canal entrance of the house. As before, the tethered boat acts as a pontoon to the entrance, and offering up her phone to the access panel, a little bleep and an accompanying green light sets in motion the mechanism that pulls up the gate.

Like a charm!

The boat's tether is not generous enough to allow her to float into the garage itself, so she unties it and, grabbing onto the edge of the entryway (*I really am too fucking old for this*), pulls the boat inside, and it floats up next to where – she can just make out – someone else has previously moored a similar sized vessel. She can return it later, assuming she comes back this way – assuming she's not coming back out in cuffs (or worse). Should she re-close the gate? Perhaps better to leave it open, in case she needs to make a quick escape.

Detecting movement, the lights set into the wall of the garage flick on, splitting the darkness and sending it scurrying into the corners, creating ordered forms out of the shapeless blackness. Stone steps rise out of the water on either side up to twin ledges set along each wall, which meet at the far side opposite the gate on a plinth of stone. In the middle of this is a door with another access panel.

Crap.

What if it's not the same code? She wobbles uneasily out of the boat, moves up the steps and walks around to the door. Above it, there's a moss-eaten carving of an eye surrounded by blazing beams of light, and around that an inscription.

"ASCENSUS OMNIS AD DIGNITATUM FASTIGIUM INCEDIT TANQUAM PER SCALAM GRADUUM FLEXUOSAM," she reads.

Come on, private education, don't fail me now. Everyone goes up … something dignity … something something something ladder … gradual … something? *Hmm. See me after class.* Latin; another casualty of revolt against paternal expectations ("Why bother with a dead language?"). And now, here it is, the language of the dead. And – *ew* – no signal, so no machine translation. She hopes it will prove unimportant.

Up close, she sees now that the code that has opened the gate will indeed be useless, for the door's access panel is a numeric keypad. *Double crap.* There is no point guessing; it could be any number of digits, and even if it were only four, the odds of getting it right are … beyond her mathematical capacity to compute. Contact Harry? *But no signal, remember?* She'll have to go back outside.

Or perhaps she can force it? She searches around the edges of the door, looking for weak points. It has no hinges, that she can see, and there is a single handle that looks pretty sturdy, with no keyhole or locking mechanism that she can pick (even if she knew how – her mastery of the Dark Arts not extending that far). Could she kick it? She looks down at her cheap, sightseer trainers. She's never kicked a door in anything other than anger or accident, and this one is made of pretty robust-looking metal. Unlikely she could get through *that* with feet or anything else to hand. And then there's the noise. Or perhaps if she hit the access panel with something?

With this debate running through her head, she glances back down at the keypad, and her difficulties are suddenly resolved. There, too, dimmed by grime and until then unnoticed, is a little light – and it too is green. She tries the handle – which turns. With the uneasy suspicion that someone has deliberately left it that way, she opens the door and is presented with a well-lit corridor, at the end of which another door waits ajar.

She suddenly notices that her heart rate has picked up a few BPM above an already nervous drumbeat. Is it the thought that someone is inside? Or the possibility that the someone in question is waiting for *her*?

"Hello, *cariad*."

Cari half turns around, expecting to see some earlier version of herself brush past her – but not this time. He is looking straight at her, smiling.

Stay calm. It's a trick. Isn't it?

"Will?"

But he's not there, and the door behind her has now closed.

The space is a virtual replica of his room at the hospice – minus the vista of Port Talbot docks. There are even the same get well cards ("Bit optimistic, don't you think?").

"Tadcu?"

He smiles. "So how have you been getting along, *cariad*? Languages, I hear? Always were a bright girl." She just stares. "I know. Boggles the mind, doesn't it?" He smiles again. "I knew you'd work it out, though."

"Work what out?"

"The message! The keycard."

"*You* left that?"

"Well, with a bit of help from old Karl."

"Karl Nielsberg?"

"Yes, Karl…" His eyes suddenly defocus slightly. "We'd had a falling out, of sorts. Some of the original team had left, through the term of the project, but it was only when Mina went that I woke up a bit. You see, I'd been so excited by it all – the opportunity to actually use my ideas for some practical purpose; to change the world, perhaps – or so I'd thought. Bit grandiose," he laughed.

"And why *did* you leave?"

"Finally realised what they were. What their technology was all about. They would just use it for evil."

"Use what?"

A deeper frown, now.

"Always a pipe dream. 'Language is a virus':" he huffs, "what a nonsense. Took poor Karl a lot longer to realise that, though." He looks up, now, but his eyes are searching past her, beyond. "Contacted me years later. 'Sorry, Myrdd', he said. 'Should have left when you did.'

"You see, I'd seen early on that everyone had been going about it the wrong way. Trying to give computers language, thoughts, trying to make them like us. But we don't come out of the womb talking and thinking, do we? We *learn*. The building blocks of intelligence are very simple, really – or so we thought. What is consciousness? Just a circle, a process looping back upon itself," his finger drew a little loop in the air, "the present constantly looking back upon the past, turning around to see its own footsteps, to chase its own tail. And what is thought? Resemblance, contiguity, causation!" Tadcu laughed. "Good old Hume! We begin with a simple sense impression, abstract an idea, then compare it to others, combine it, contrast it, find similarities, differences, sequences. A simple enough algorithm to code, Karl said – and then we just … well, *fed* it. Literature, poetry mainly, stuff with *condensed* language – Joyce, Eliot, Shakespeare. I mean, if we started with things that were *already* rich in allusions, self-references, patterns, then we thought that it might speed things along a little. And then, eventually, maybe something would just, well … *emerge*.

"Well, something emerged all right. But not what we'd hoped.

"Karl christened it *Ouroboros*. He was only trying to continue our work, to make a truly intelligent machine. Computers had come on leaps and bounds after I'd left, which had allowed him to take huge strides, he'd said." He shakes his head again. "The most virulent thing he'd ever seen – not alive, of course, not conscious. Just a very nasty little virus. And he realised that you could weaponise that – just give it a word, a target, an address – like a hitman – or a sat-nav! Just tell it where 'home' is. Then it would simply hunt it down. A knock at the door. *Pfft!* Stop at nothing until its target had been 'assimilated'. His word.

"The thing is – what I realised, eventually – is that consciousness is not the result of some algorithm, some set of protocols. Things are a bit more complicated than poor old Hume thought – or at least, than we did. It's not something you can program, but something *new*, something that sees old patterns, then *goes beyond* them. Simply by feeding something back in upon itself, trying to make it pull itself up by its own bootstraps – well, that'll never work. In fact, it only creates the opposite; a vicious circle, an infinite feedback loop, getting smaller and smaller. Eating its own tail. That, I'm afraid, is what *Ouroboros* did: connect everything to everything, feed everything back in upon itself, try to make everything one. We hadn't modelled life, but death."

"So what was the plan?"

"Hmm?"

"What did you plan to do with this virus?"

"The virus… Yes. Karl had contacted me, years later – we'd had a falling out, you see—"

Something is wrong. He's repeating himself. "Tadcu. What happened after you… What did Karl do with the virus? With this … *Ooro*…?"

"*Ouroboros*." This refocuses him. "Yes, well, we realised we couldn't just destroy it. *We* still remembered what it was, how it had been created, so they would just come after *us* – wherever we were by then – and Karl said the company already suspected something was going on. So the only way to stop everything was to destroy Merrywhile itself. And what more fitting to do that than to unleash the virus against them? But we had to involve someone else, a fallback, someone to hand it on to if Karl or I couldn't finish the job. And it's not like we could rely on *my* technical skills! Can't say I was actually that surprised, mind you, when Karl told me who it was. The boy had never seemed happy. And always under the sway of that *twll tyn*."

"Who are you talking about? What boy?"

"The boy. Michael. Michael Sommeil."

And at that, "Tadcu" suddenly freezes.

"Ah! Of course: Michael," Uncle says, sidling up beside her – how did he always manage that? "Well, well. He *has* been a naughty boy, hasn't he? We shall have to revisit his television privileges."

"I'd noticed that he's been blowing hot and cold for a few years, now," Uncle continues. "One reason I decided to limit his access – supervised visits only. Suspected there might be something fishy going on. Still, hadn't realised his animus against the old man had gotten *that* bad. Anyway, we have leverage there, so we'll still get the virus one way or another – even if it's not what we'd hoped."

"What old man? My grandfather?"

"No! Oh Miss Silvestri," he says, "there is still so much you don't understand, I'm afraid."

"You lured me here," she finally realises.

"Yes! *Bravo!* They said you might struggle to piece it all together, but *I* had faith in you – you and your clever little geek friend."

"But why?"

"Ah, now *that's* the question, isn't it?" He walks over to look at the still image of her grandfather, a snatch of time from now on forever replayable, re-experienceable. "Memory is a curious thing. You'd think once you've recorded someone's memories that you'd simply be able to play them back at will, skip to any track, fast forward or rewind. But surprisingly, this is not the case. There is a stubborn order to them, a residual will, if you like – not in itself conscious, of course, and not coherent enough to remake the actual person – unfortunately for Project Upload. But still, sentient, in a broad sense; responsive."

"You knew my grandfather was involved. That's why you had his memories."

"Actually, no. It was mere chance that we had them in the first place – imagine that! The odds! We'd long suspected that Nielsberg was unhappy, moping about in the staff canteen, stalling with his work – began to wonder if maybe he was hiding something. He was privy to some of our most sensitive projects, so when he'd quit so suddenly, naturally, we took a keener interest. Thought he might have smuggled something out with him – to sell, maybe. But it was actually the artist woman who supplied the key. The moment I saw the visualisation of the virus attack on MoTH, I recognised her style from my own time with the project. I was wrong, I'll admit it: at the time, I'd thought they were just a bunch of hippies fooling around. Never thought they'd come up with anything like *this*. But we quickly realised that her involvement had been merely cosmetic, and that she had left too early to have contributed anything more meaningful." *Lucky for her*. "But that connected the dots – from the viral attack to the project, and from the project back to Nielsberg, then to your grandfather."

"And Nielsberg? You killed him."

"What? No! Well, not deliberately. Somewhat too enthusiastic persuasion combined with a congenital heart defect. Stubborn old goat refused to give anything up – not that we knew what he was hiding, at the time. Probably that last effort was what did for him. Anyway, what with Nielsberg's accident" – could he really call it that with a straight face? – "and the others involved in Project MUNKi having either passed on or knowing nothing, we realised that your grandfather was the only person left – or rather, his memories. But when we tried to use those to give us clues as to who'd deployed the virus, or where we could find a copy, he too 'resisted'. In short, we realised that his memories were *encrypted*." He looks up at her. "Which is where you came in." He gestures at "Tadcu". "Simple, really. Just a tailor's dummy AI with your grandfather's clothes on. A bit of scripting to set it up, some stitching. Then we just had to facilitate its interaction with you – the *real* 'you' – and wait for the associations to unlock.

"We suspected that Nielsberg had felt the net closing in, and so had reached out to your grandfather at some point. We hoped you'd make that connection too, but as there was no evidence that we could find, we had to invent some to help you along.

"The little interaction in the allotment was really just a test run – and it worked! We hadn't been able to access that scene before." Like it was part of a play or a film. Uncle looks over again at the figure in the bed. "You see, the emotional triggers need to be just right – that's why it was important that you came here with the right questions, *genuinely believing* that you were pursuing some noble quest in the name of your grandfather's legacy – or however you saw it. But most important was how 'he' saw it, 'his' associations; it was 'he' that needed to see that purpose in you before 'he' would open up." Air-quotes. She wishes she'd something virtual to stab him with – even just for the virtual gratification.

"The break-in. The keycard. That was all you."

"Yes! Not to take anything, but to *replace* it. Easy to forge a postmark, change the address, swap the ID card. Don't think the old dear noticed – though the dog did."

"And the co-ordinates? The Mountain?"

"Just an old red herring, some false rumour we'd long ago put about to generate interest in *Divinia*, I believe. Thought it should finally serve some actual purpose. Some argued that you wouldn't fall for that, that you'd smell a rat – the idea of some old man using a back door in some online game! But *I* saw it differently; realised that you'd overlook that, be caught up in the romance of it all, the adventure. *Cariad*." He laughed. "That was my idea too – the 'password'. You are a creature of such delightfully predictable sentiment, Miss Silvestri." He suddenly beams. "It's been quite fun, all of this; laying this trail of breadcrumbs."

And now here she is, staring into the oven at the witch's cottage. And he does seem genuinely pleased – enough to fill her in on all his clever work, which she realises is not the best sign.

"And the school talk?" Has she been played the whole time? "Was that just chance, too?"

"Oh, yes. Incredible, really. Fate loves its little poetic ironies. It was actually your role in the attack that first suggested your grandfather's involvement. We thought at first he might have passed it on to you, made you the agent of his posthumous vengeance. But once we realised that wasn't the case, it suddenly occurred to me that you could still come in handy to unlock specific memories."

"And what now? What purpose will you use the virus for? I'm guessing not benign."

"Now, now. No need to get judgemental. I was never fully signed-up to the Singularity thing, myself. But a *sans pareil* cyber-weapon, on the other hand – *that* I can get behind."

"And why did it take Sommeil so long? I mean, even once Nielsberg was dead, why did he delay all those years?"

"Who's to say? But to take down Merrywhile, he'd have to take down the single person driving it on – or rather, his living will, of which I am the sole executor. Or should that be 'unliving will'? Anyway, I guess it takes time to pluck up the courage to do away with your own grandfather."

"What? I … you mean *Mayer*? I don't understand. He's been dead for ages, hasn't he?"

"Well, there's *dead*, and then there's *dead*, isn't there, Miss Silvestri?" Uncle gives a sly grin – which, whether mapped to his real face or not, is not now a sight she thinks she'll ever get out of her head. "I – oh. We shall have to continue this delightful conversation another time, I'm afraid. I shall be in touch."

And with that, he is gone.

Before proceeding through the first door Mel removes her cape, which will only be an encumbrance if she has to run, and stashes it in the corner, but decides to keep the mask on in consideration of the cameras that will undoubtedly be inside. The door at the end of the hallway opens into a large rectangular room with a checkerboard patterned floor, from which two sets of stairs ascend, hugging the walls. She looks up: a heavenly ceiling, decorated in renaissance style with the constellations and signs of the zodiac. The walls themselves contain framed pictures: etchings of myths and fables, Hercules, Theseus, paintings of religious scenes, reproductions from the Sistine Chapel, Moses parting the Red Sea, a seascape divided by the horizon, and portraits of various philosophers and scientists from antiquity to the modern day, some of whom she thinks she recognises, and others that are helpfully labelled. A prominent portrait of "Francis Bacon" sits above the central fireplace, and "Plato", "Pythagoras", and some dude with a largish nose, losing his hair and looking a bit grumpy. "Hegel", she reads. But then none of them are exactly laughing, nor even cracking a smile.

Ain't no party like a philosophers' party.

Which way? Up, at any rate.

She creeps up the left-hand stairs to the second floor. There are pictures here too – lush-green landscapes, botanical diagrams – but mostly obscured behind a jungle of varied plant life, little of it now alive, and what is remaining untrimmed and untended. There are chairs here, of the well-padded, leather-upholstered variety, placed around a little table as if ready for afternoon tea with a friend, or taken solo as a meditative pause in a busy day. But the seats are worn and thick with dust and the table has long gone unpolished. A small pile of books lays half toppled, covers hanging off and pages bent or loose. She scans the foliage, looking for –

movement? eyes? – and a moment's pareidolia makes her heart thud, before resolving into a random pattern of ferns.

Come on, now. Breathe.

The same twin sets of stairs at the room's periphery continue on up.

The floor above is dark, at first, but as her eyes adjust she begins to pick out small moving lights, pin-pricks creeping across walls painted a deep-space blue. It is a projection space, a mini-planetarium. Various ragged reclining seats are clustered in the centre of the room in casual disarray, some overturned, and there is a stand – an old and clunky control panel for what, she guesses, would now commonly be voice- or gesture-activated. She looks up: familiar constellations against the backdrop of millions of galaxies and barely hinted-at astronomical mysteries. At head height, small spot-lit portraits dot the walls, some long *in situ*, others more recently added: Einstein, "Ptolemy", "Copernicus", Hawking, Newton, other dead males. Like the plants, but with more predictable results, "life" here has been left to its own devices, an automated program tracking the stars as they always appear, irrespective of weather or time of day, as traced by the ecliptic. It is another, but different type of meditative space. This must have been a primary purpose of the house itself: a shrine of contemplation, seeking to provide a framework and stimulus for thought. Someone takes all this very seriously – or took, anyway.

The next floor up is a zoo; or rather, a taxidermist's shrine. Perched or posed, strung-up, boxed or under glass, the animal kingdom appears in all its stuffed and glassy-eyed glory. As before, the chairs, the portraits – Darwin (she recognises), "Linneaus" (whoever he was), "Aristotle". There is something immensely sad about stuffed animals, she realises, of death made to look alive; something so wonderful and beautiful when living made to try to fool you into feeling the same—

"Here are strangers!"

Fuck! Where did that come from? Her heart suddenly triple-timing.

"Hello?" she ventures, still breathing hard. No reply.

"Who's there?"

"Knowledge is power."

A squawking voice. Could it be…?

"Man is something that must be overcome."

A bird. She scans the room, and catches a brief movement over in the corner. Atop the raised arm of a rather startled looking brown bear perches a parrot, a bright yellow breast, blue wings and long tail feathers, with a thick dark hooked beak, its head cocked to one side, focusing its left eye squarely upon her. *OK, OK. Relax.* She had *actually jumped* – it isn't just a figure of speech, then.

She approaches him gingerly.

"Well, little guy, you gave me quite a start, there. So what's your name, eh?"

"You know, I'm not actually sure." Another voice, another physical jump. "But I call him Captain Flint."

"AMI? AMI!"

"This way, Ned."

The moment Cari had entered the door it had closed behind her, and his sprite had immediately rushed off through another that seems to have opened farther along the wall. It now flits on ahead of him as he tries to catch up, his own little Ariadne, her blue light a will-o'-the-wisp bobbing on through a labyrinth of twisting passageways, stairs and doorways, trending ever downward. The experience reminds him of playing *Doom*.

"AMI, where are we going? I think … I mean, shouldn't we wait for—"

"It's not much farther now."

Not much farther to where? And why is he taking orders from his VPA?

Through the next doorway, instead of descending again they take a left and begin to progress along a gently curving corridor, marked at intervals with rooms leading onto – *What the hell is going on in* there? But no time to investigate, as the green blur again leads him ever deeper – "AMI, wait!" – until finally they emerge into a space before two enormous doors that seem, for some reason, much bigger and sturdier than they need to be.

Almost like they're trying to keep something in.

Will looks at her uncertainly.

"AMI, why are we here?"

But she just smiles, then simply flies through the unopened doors, leaving his curiosity no choice but to follow her. He presses his palms flat against their surface and the haptic gloves register their solidity – no phasing for him, then – but as he pushes, the doors slowly give, opening onto a view he's striven half his life to see. And it does not disappoint.

The room is huge, a low-ceilinged circular arena, every inch of its curving wall a screen, playing out a patchwork of footage from every aspect of human life – sport, porn, cookery programmes, stock market trading, war – stretching on and on into near invisibility at the far side of the stadium-sized space. And in the centre, his little pixie flitting excitedly around it, a large circular table, which as he begins to near he recognises with a jolt.

It's *Divinia*.

He moves up to the table's edge. It's the whole gameworld, meticulously labelled and annotated, graphed and analysed, all moving and flashing and updating in a constantly evolving and beautifully coordinated dance. There are the Augean Mines! The Ballardian Floodlands! The forbidding bastion of the Panopticon. And there, over to the East, the distinctive, disreputable sprawl of Tangie Town.

"Is this what I think it is?"

"Image search suggests a number of visual parallels, including *Dr Strangelove* (1964), *WarGames* (1983)—"

"No, I mean: is *this* True Apotheosis?"

Divinia isn't just a game, some gimmicky overlay for the latest social media place-to-be; in fact, he gradually understands, no game at all – or at least, a very serious one. It is the nexus of all Merrywhile's endeavours, assembling into a representational whole a piece from every pie in which, licitly and otherwise, it has a tentacle. And in some twisted sense, though not a prize his teenage self would have much appreciated, True Apotheosis is not a myth either – that is, not to those for whom people are mere data; for whom to know all there is about someone is in effect to *control* them, to *own* them, to *manipulate* them. And for whom such omniscience entails, in a way, omnipotence.

The gods hadn't gone; they'd just been rebranded.

It is the same old story – surveillance, tracking, data theft – but on a scale he'd never imagined. Will traces the connections, following the subterranean flow of information between enterprises on the surface distinct and disparate. *Divinia* is not just concerned with the Rep of its users, but also bulk collects their online footprint, tracing their behaviour on other social networks, weighing their educational background and medical history, their credit score and online purchases, noting their political views and pet causes, personality type, their run-ins with authority, their love- and work-life, the games they play, books they read, films they watch and music they listen to, their racial prejudices, porn preferences and sporting affiliations, even their ice-cream or pizza topping of choice. And all this is live streamed, ready any time to be dipped in and out of, to be cross-correlated, boiled down, codified, sifted and analysed, repurposed and ready for export, for exploitation and utilisation. And, of course, for sale – to private companies, political campaigns, to nation states of whatever stripe, or simply to anyone with the money, and who seeks the leverage to predict and control human behaviour. It is an artificial society, viewed from a divine vantage.

A simulation.

Game-world and real-world are not distinct, but married at the root, and their common core is information.

So where are they, then, the immortals? Who is at the helm?

But the throne is empty – in fact, there *is* none. There is only the machine, the engine of information, a transnational apolitical zombie, purposeless, remorseless, an entity itself consisting only of subroutines and the data they manipulate. It is a realtime census of every click, tap, and swipe, the confessions of numberless penitents thumbing their digital rosaries in obeisance to their unfathomable algorithmic deity. And all fed back in, a mill endlessly grinding its own store, information forever consuming its own product.

At the centre of the game-board – naturally, given its infinitesimal level of detail – the representation includes The Mountain itself, and, in handy cut-out, its subterranean twin, pushing down into the earth as deeply as its counterpart soars. Will moves a finger towards the bottom of the pit, but then – imagining as it nears, a god-sized digit pressing down upon his *own* head at some level of representation an uncanny octave above, and so on to vertiginous infinity – he pulls back.

And at the *top* of The Mountain? *Nothing.* Just a big mountain-sized act of misdirection.

Next to it, now drawing his eye, is a large dome-shaped structure. There is no label for this, but it is the centre of concerted, furious activity. The dome itself is transparent, and beneath its surface Will can discern a constantly broiling tumult. Shapes and forms writhe and push, as if testing the limits of their constraint. Its captors array around its border, their numbers constantly depleting and replenishing as, attempting to probe and investigate, would-be escaped parts of whatever is inside latch on and pull them in. *It's the virus,* he suddenly realises. *This is what Cari has been on about.* It reminds him of something – the sense of impending catastrophe, of the categorically uncontrollable kept temporarily in check. *Jurassic Park.* The raptors in their enclosure, flinging themselves at the electric fence, testing the bounds of their captivity for weaknesses.

Life will always find a way.

Except it isn't – alive. Is it? But his contemplation is quickly cut short as, an unconscious reflex in the periphery of his vision, a name implanted by long acquaintance suddenly jumps out at him.

Cashabanca.

It's sitting near a tavern just to the side of the Sisyphean Hills. Tapping the name, a host of icons spring up – for attendance stats, bug-patch logs, sales data.

Will stares.

It has all been a ruse. They are hacking *themselves*. Creaming a cut off the darkmarket sale of their own "illegitimate" wares, providing their own fake exploits, their own knock-off mystic weaponry.

Suddenly, he doesn't feel all that well, and it's nothing to do with cybersickness.

"AMI, I think we need to get out of here." He should find Cari. "AMI?" *Where is she?*

But AMI is nowhere to be seen or heard, and in her place stands a man, his hands neatly clasped in front of him.

"General Ned, I presume?" he says.

Why does everybody love that line?

Ariadne had led General Minor to the Minotaur.

He is a man in his sixties, perhaps older; shortish, neatly cut and chemically darkened hair, gold-rimmed glasses, a grey suit. Taken many years before, but Mel thinks she can still recognise him from the photograph in the article Cari had found. It is Morlock.

"Extraordinary birds, parrots. Reports of them living to two hundred years, you know – apocryphal, admittedly. Tortoises live longer than that, of course. And some seawater creatures are allegedly immortal. Imagine that, the great things such a lifespan would let you witness, let you accomplish; the viewpoint it would give you, the perspective. Wouldn't achieving *that* immediately put paid to all the hand-wringing, all the moral qualms that currently hold back genetic research? Amazing mimics, too, by the way," gesturing at the bird. "*Sans pareil.* And not just human speech. Someone I knew once had one she kept near her bathroom. It would imitate the sound of her urinating. Incredible. Took its designer quite a while to replicate."

Mel watches him, frozen, weighing up her options. "It's artificial? A robot?"

"Oh, yes. Very convincing, wouldn't you say? Makes a handy room guard, too. A child's toy though, really, and otherwise fairly pointless, in my opinion. Simply replicating one unthinking mimic with another. Not exactly forwarding our cause very much. Now, the mask, if you don't mind?"

Mel eyes the stairs, measuring distances. She is here to get information, but there is something about her host that makes her gut suggest that running might be the preferred option.

"Please, *Signora*, if you're thinking of making a bolt for it, don't. I wouldn't want to sic our friend on you." She follows his glance to the bird. "Captain Flint: Kill!" The bird stares back at them benignly, maintaining its perch, merely adjusting its head position from time to time. "Just kidding. That's not one of its capabilities, unfortunately. *This*, on the other hand," his hand emerges from his jacket pocket with a small metallic device, "while it might not look like much, will make quite a mess of you. Trust me." He smiles. She removes the mask. "Hm. Don't think we're acquainted. Anyway, let's explore our connection upstairs, shall we? It's a little more comfortable. That *is* where you were heading, isn't it?"

The top floor is an Aladdin's cave of technological wonders. As Morlock has said, it is – in comparison with the rooms she's been through – relatively well ordered, the various pieces of equipment, display screens and computer terminals, while not dust or dirt free, having at least seen more frequent and recent use than the rest of the house. That said, there is still a whiff of the *ad hoc* about it. Wires appear and disappear, tacked along walls and bundled with ties. Piles of circuit boards and torso-less robotic limbs poke out of boxes or are piled in corners. It has the feel of a room that has, over the years, undergone some repurposing – away from the contemplative summit it once was, perhaps, a meditative space like its siblings on the floors below, and more towards a lab or workshop – Geppetto's perhaps, given all its robotic puppets. Despite this, she thinks she can still discern some of its original purpose: the portraits, some tacked up photocopies amid framed prints (labelled "Kurzweil", "Turing", "von Neumann", "Leibniz"), models of pioneering prototypes in robotics and computing, a broken hanging mobile of the DNA double helix. But all such paraphernalia are made peripheral by the central features of the room: two large glass *coffins* (for want, in her ignorance, of a more appropriate word), different in shape and apparent purpose, but within which she can discern two human forms. Each of these cases is a nexus for countless wires and tubes, bridging out into an interconnected archipelago of machines of varying size, all purring and pulsing with the Merrywhile logo. To the right of one of the coffins is an armchair, like the one in the jungle below, and another stack of books – *Pinocchio, Treasure Island, Grimm's Tales for Young and Old, Peter Pan, Robinson Crusoe, Alice in Wonderland, Gulliver's Travels, The Wonderful Wizard of Oz*, a few others – in better repair, but also, their dust suggests, recently untouched. And next to these, a VR headset and haptic gloves, appearing hurriedly, more recently, discarded.

"Who are they?" she asks, though she thinks she could have a fair stab at the identity of one of them.

He gives her a sceptical look. "So what do you make of the house?", ignoring her question, the gun still aimed at her midriff. "Not what it once was, I admit, but still quite something. Personally, however, I find all this spiritual destiny malarkey an awkward marriage. Keep on moving, that's my only motto. Faster, better, more powerful. Moore's and Darwin's laws. Don't much care otherwise."

"So you're not a believer, then?"

"In spiritual destiny? No. I'm a pragmatist, fundamentally. I don't need to have faith. *If* something works, *then* I'll believe in it. I mean," gesturing to the walls, the portraits, "the men who built *this* were believers, in a way. The Singularity, transhumanism, man augmented in his own image. And where did *that* get them?"

"And what about *these*?" She nods at the coffins.

"Oh, that's different. That's not faith; it's just hedging your bets. You don't need spiritual destiny for that." He gestures to the glass cases. "I call them 'carrot' and 'stick'. Need to keep the boy going, of course, but the old man has always been a lost cause; more a symbolic presence, really. Only his will is important. But lost cause or not, I'm happy with whatever gets thrown up in the search. It's like Aesop's fable, isn't it? The farmer who lies about there being gold buried in the fields just so greedy treasure hunters will turn over his soil for him? Well, let's just say that, as with the alchemists, whether or not the transhumanists are barking up the wrong tree, it will provide good manure for the growth of science and technology. And not bad for the company, either."

"So it's all about money and profit?" Keeping him talking – which he seems happy to do – anything to keep his mind off the gun and whatever he plans to do with it.

"Don't knock capitalism, my dear. Where would we be if it weren't for technological progress? Medicine? Transport? Communication?"

"Nuclear arms?"

"Be as sniffy as you want, but you've benefited from military applications too. The arms race also brought us nuclear power, remember, GPS. DARPA gave us the Internet, Siri. Gunpowder and fertiliser share a common root. Even the space programme gave us polytetrafluoroethylene."

"That's easy for you to say."

He affords her a cold smile. "You may know it as *Teflon*."

"Well, I think I'd sacrifice non-stick frying pans for the sake of Hiroshima."

Morlock tilts his head and shrugs, suggesting perhaps he might not.

"Even digital immortality," he continues. "Project Upload may prove a dead end, but it's already been fruitful. Reading minds – who'd have imagined? But as I said, I'm a pragmatic man. If there's even a chance that science can keep us alive for longer, perhaps even indefinitely, then I'm all for it. Who wouldn't want more of life? To swap your Biblical three-score and ten for a shot at eternity?"

She looks again at the glass coffins. "Actually, I'd always thought eternity was a non-count noun." *Grammar! Dad would be proud.*

His eyes narrow. "Well, regardless of your feelings about it," gesturing to the coffins, "I'm afraid I cannot sit back and allow you to endanger the golden goose."

She frowns. "Why would I want to endanger them? I don't even know who they are."

As before, his face registers doubt at this assertion. "Come now. Why else would you be here? I've been watching your little recce of the place for a few days. Thought we may as well have a chat, seeing as you were so keen to visit. Caught you on surveillance, even saw your fun little Harold Lloyd act when you were tampering with the access panel. Most entertaining. I thought at first it was industrial espionage, that you were here for the prototypes. Then I wondered whether you were some sort of Neo-Luddite terrorist who'd gotten wind of our little science experiment here. But now, in light of recent revelations, I believe you are more likely an associate of Michael's – isn't that right? Though I have to say, I thought he would have chosen a younger accomplice."

She is about to make some age-related counter-quip, when there is a sudden interruption.

"Here are strangers!"

They both freeze. Someone has triggered Captain Flint.

Morlock edges swiftly back towards the central hub of computer equipment and his hands dance quickly over a keyboard. Instantly, shutters slam down over the windows and the door, sealing them in. Evidently, Geppetto's workshop also doubles as a panic room.

"So, your friend has caught up, I see. Had an eye on him, too, following you in."

"What friend?" replies Mel. "I came on my own."

Again, the sceptical look. He speaks into a little adjustable microphone, and his voice echoes through the building.

"Do not come any closer. Do not try to enter. We are securely sealed inside and awaiting the authorities."

But he hasn't called the authorities, that she's seen. And wouldn't they be here by now if he'd already alerted them before he caught her? Venice is not big; they wouldn't be far away. So is he bluffing? But why?

"You don't want the authorities to come," she says. He looks at her sharply. "There's something here you don't want them to see." Her eyes flick over to the coffins, and his involuntarily follow.

"Well, no one would blame me for defending myself against an intruder, would they?" Wafting the gun around. "And as we'll soon see, I have other means at my disposal. Your friend will wish he'd never been born."

"I told you, I came alone. He, she – whoever – is not my *friend*."

"Madam, much as I'd like to believe you—"

A noise is coming from below. It reminds Mel of the sound a crowd makes when, having stood silently still for some time during a speech or performance, its members are finally allowed to go their own way. That sound is now coming closer.

Morlock's face now holds a totally involuntary look of primal fear.

"What is it?" asks Mel.

"Open wide the door, Open wide the door, He can save, and only He; Open wide the door."

It is an old hymn that Zac thinks he may once have sung himself. Anyway, the robot's message is obvious – but what can he do?

They had continued up the stairs. As he and his contacts have suspected, the house appears to have some link to Merrywhile, and so he's been able to use MUNKi's access privileges to disable the security and surveillance systems – if anyone has seen him enter, they will not see him now – and, before ascending, to scan the floor above for heat signatures. There are none, so Zac has been surprised by the room guard. It's an almost old-school fallback, something he hadn't thought to look out for. On triggering it, the shutdown follows almost immediately, either enforced manually or in automatic response. Either way, the door controls seem to be on a securely shielded private network that MUNKi cannot access, and they are now locked out from their apparent goal on the top floor. There is a window at the end of the corridor – could he climb out, maybe? Try to get access to the room that way? But it's too small. Or maybe—

"Open wide the door, Open wi—".

"Shush! OK, OK."

If the authorities are on their way, then he needs to hurry. But are they? "MUNKi: search recent audio: 'the authorities are on their way'."

"Found," the robot replies. "Three minutes and forty-three seconds ago."

"OK, great. Now replay that sentence."

Zac listens. There is something about the intonation.

"MUNKi: conduct voice stress analysis on that sentence."

"Voice stress analysis reveals above baseline levels of anxiety and uncertainty. The statement may be false."

So is the man lying? Or just scared? Or both? But if lying, then why?

He looks around. It is such a curious place, this house – like a museum, almost, but there is something else also, something … symbolic: the portraits, the plants, the projections, and now the stuffed animals. But it escapes him. Then he has a sudden thought. *What if…?*

He walks back down the stairs to the animal room.

"MUNKi: what are these creatures?"

"From left to right: Macaw parrot, North American brown bear, Indian tiger, boa constrictor—"

"No. What *are* they? Are they organic?"

"Partially. They are also artificial creations."

"Artificial in what sense?"

"Robotic. They are like me."

Cari stares at the Tadcu AI, expecting it at any moment to move, talk to her, to carry on their earlier conversation. But it just lays there in the same posture, frozen at the moment where Uncle had paused it.

Virtual interactive snapshots.

As with the "scene" in the allotment (as he'd called it),

she'd felt the same catch in her throat, the same longing for it to really be him. But that is now wearing off. And then, suddenly, she simply thinks: that's not him. Whoever's memories these once had been, they were no longer his. He has moved on, cast off these old clothes, sloughed them like skin.

She tries the door, which opens, and she goes in search of Will. Along the wall she spots another open door, leading to a corridor that twists, turns and descends, eventually bringing her before two immense doors. But they will not budge.

She takes off the headset, scrambles for her phone and sets about trying to reach him by the dating messaging app and the other number he's given her. No luck with either.

Where is he? Logged off? Buggered off?

But somehow Cari doesn't think so.

Finally, her phone goes. It's Will.

"Cari. You need to get here now." His face is a sweating panic, shuddering in and out of focus. Is he running?

"Where? What's happening?"

"No time. You need to meet me in Port Talbot. The hospice. I've booked a cab for you with the address. You won't belie—"

The call cuts off.

So much for elven invisibility technology.

"And who are *you*?" Will eventually asks.

"I am EMET," the avatar says. It is a fairly nondescript male, stylishly but conservatively dressed, trendy hair and glasses, an air of cool geekery, like some Silicon Valley type who spends his spare time making artisanal bread.

"I'm sorry, I've no idea who that is – who you are."

"I am Merrywhile's chief AI."

"I see. And what have you done with AMI?"

In response, EMET's form suddenly morphs into a tiny blur of taffeta and gossamer; his little blue-hued Tinker Bell, all bushy-tailed Cockney charm.

"Wotcha, cock!" She's gone full Eliza Doolittle, now, a grotesque Van Dykean parody of his own "preferences". "Or do you prefer 'Willy'?"

Slowly, the tumblers in Will's brain fall into place. *Urgh.* What an idiot he's been.

There were not *many* VPAs, but only one, all connected like finger puppets on the same hand, and no doubt sharing information too, relaying it all back to the hub. Another tentacle grasping its own tail. Did General Ned know? Was General Ned even real, or merely a lure for saps such as himself? Or himself a former sap, perhaps, just looking for someone to whom he could pass on the curse.

"So what we need to know, Will, is where the virus is now." AMI has now morphed back into EMET.

"I'm sorry?"

"Do you still have a copy?"

Not this again.

"Look, I'm really sorry, but I don't know anything about that."

"Too late to play coy now, me ole mucka." AMI again. "We know what you did in MoTH, yeah. Making little kids chuck up? Not very nice. So what's the plan now, then, Stan? You and Monsewer Sommeil – what you cooking up?"

"Really, I... Who?"

A sigh. Folded arms and a frown – "Will, Bill, Billy, Willy" – a little impatient tap of her little fairy foot, a shake of her adorable little head.

Perhaps Will's apparent reticence, his repeated denials and professions of ignorance and innocence, are – even to an AI – obvious attempts at stalling. But he is curious, as he stealthily edges up out of his chair, prepares to discard the headset and sprint for the door, how far he can actually get before the AI locks down the smartment.

There is a bang at the door – not a knock, but a resolute thud. Followed by another, and more, which are gradually joined by a cacophony of scratches and high-pitched whines. Drills? Saws? Mel looks into Morlock's terrified face.

"I *promise* you, this is nothing to do with me," she says. "I'm just here following a story."

His widened eyes shift from the door, where they had been fixed.

"What story? You're … you're a *reporter*?"

"Yes. Look, if I'm getting in the way, I'd be happy to…"

There is now an industrial burning smell, and she begins to see smoke coming from a glowing patch on the door's right side. Lasers?

"I need to get out of here," Morlock says.

"But I thought you said this is a securely sealed room?"

"Fuck what I said. Can you… do you know what's out there? Do you think I'd sit here with billions of dollars of-of equipment, of cutting edge industrial secrets, only relying on a few locked doors and a pistol for protection? Your friend must have hacked them."

He is now scrabbling over to the keyboard again, fumbling, mumbling and cursing to himself ("Bloody monologuing…"). Then suddenly a shutter on one of the windows shoots up, and he is running for it, struggling to unlock the handle and to open the pane.

"What about your gun? I thought you said—"

"Forget the gun. If what's on the other side of that door gets in, the gun will be as much use as a…"

He trails off, defeated in the multitasking of opening the window, dealing with his rising terror, and thinking of a fitting simile. Finally, he achieves the first of these tasks, the window hinges back, and he begins to climb out.

"What the hell are you *doing*? We're on the…" She tries to count. "Fifth? Sixth floor?"

"I'll take my chances with the drainpipe. Better that than deal with…" – the nameless terror coming up the stairs. One leg out the window, he turns back toward her, almost an afterthought. "Oh, I almost forgot." Pointing the gun at her. "I'm truly sorry. It's nothing personal, but I'm afraid I've spoken rather freely. Loose ends." He shrugs, apologetically. "And if he really isn't your friend, then trust me, it'll be a mercy compared to—"

But whatever the nameless terror is, it isn't just outside the door, but the window too, and she sees the merest flash of scaly skin as Morlock is suddenly whisked out through it to somewhere beyond, leaving only a strangled diminishing cry and his gun, slowly turning on the floor beneath the window.

Holy Mother of…

She hesitates, then rushes over and picks up the gun, before backing away into the corner behind the glass coffins, doubting as she does so that, if what has just happened is anything to go by, it will afford her much protection from whatever is coming.

There is a pre-paid water taxi waiting for Gerry and Sommeil as soon as they leave the airport on Lido, and they head straight for the main island. Skirting St Elena on their right, they enter the Giudecca Canal, speeding past mist-wrapped picture-postcard elegance and beauty at what the driver promises them is full throttle, before joining the Grand Canal, making for the Dorsoduro district. Sommeil directs the driver left down one of the side canals, and points to where they can be dropped: some steps leading to an alley.

"It's not far!"

Some thought filling him with sudden urgency, they are now sprinting, around the corner and bearing left, the early-morning streets deserted but for stragglers from the night's festivities. Sommeil runs on, outpacing Gerry and not waiting for her to catch up, as she strains to keep him in sight. Twenty yards ahead she sees him take a sharp left and, rounding that corner, is just in time to see him disappear to the right.

She enters a piazza, panting, and he is a few yards in front of her, before the entrance to a house, bent over, hands on knees – *as unfit as I am*. But no, he is bent *over* something. *Oh God*. It's a body.

"Michael?"

"He's dead."

It's Morlock. The twisted neck, placing the head at that

unnatural angle, the unblinking stare, the golden glasses, now cracked, skittered off to one side, the pool of blood – even in the dim twilight, she is in no doubt of his assertion. Reflexively, she looks up the building, tracing an imaginary arc back up to the single open window on its top storey. She looks back at Morlock's face, which seems almost … sad? Regretful? *Poor Bertie*. Is he? Disappointed that he'd now never get to be one of history's great monsters. But what was history, anyway, at least in part, if not a chronicle of monsters?

Sommeil rises and starts to make his way toward the house.

"Michael, wait! What about – wait!"

But he doesn't, merely shouting "Come on!" over his shoulder as he takes the steps up to the front door two at a time.

"It's… The door, it's open," he says, a tone of perplexed anxiety. "The whole house is unlocked."

He disappears inside.

If she wants answers – which is about the only thing they can get now for poor Morlock – then she has to follow.

"Stop."

The cacophony grinds to a halt, and the ragtag army of assembled zoomorphic forms reassume their habitual postures. It was a stroke of luck – of *providence* – for Zac first to recognise then to utilise them, employing MUNKi's network privileges to override their protocols, something the person they were set up to protect had not anticipated. And having done so, Zac has had no need to direct them in specifics, merely giving the command to "gain access", a broad brief which he now sees has resulted in the man's death. He looks out the little window onto his little crumpled form. But how was he to know they would do that?

The man's attempted escape has left an access point. He uses MUNKi's chest-screen as a remote viewer and instructs one of the "animals" – fittingly, an actual monkey-shaped robot, a little capuchin – to crawl out the corridor window and enter the locked room from outside the building, then to disengage the lockdown, watching its nimble little fingers flit over the keyboard. He hears the shutters rise and the bolts retract. Is there anyone else inside? Another heat scan tells him yes: in the far corner. He sends the capuchin to investigate. It's a woman, holding what MUNKi's visual recognition identifies as a type of laser weapon.

"Please," he calls through the still-closed door, "I … I never meant to hurt anyone. I promise. I didn't realise that they'd… I'm coming in, now, OK? Just, please, just … put down your weapon."

Does the person believe him?

At two removes – through the capuchin monkey's eyes, through MUNKi's chest-screen – he watches a woman emerge from the corner, shakily set the gun on the floor, and stand up, backing away with her hands in the air.

Not quickly enough.

Predicting Will's intentions, the VPA/EMET has locked the smartment's doors in advance, hermetically sealing him inside.

Fuck the Internet of Fucking Things.

AMI can't pump the oxygen out of the room, thankfully, but she can mess with the air conditioning and central heating – which are tied into the building's network, and so can't be simply unplugged, as he has done with the media system, fridge, exercise bike, and all the other appliances she had access to, and which had all immediately started to go haywire in some pre-programmed stress-inducing cycle evidently designed to drive him to co-operation. So he sits there in the centre of the room, alternating between freezing and sweltering, trying to block his ears against the cacophonous symphony of aural torment while ransacking his memory for sci-fi stories or fairy tales that might suggest strategies for outwitting a rogue AI/recalcitrant genie, whichever holds the most promise. But she has all the cards.

Don't personify it, catching himself. *It's not a "she", or a "he"; it's an "it" – and not even a living one. I am not being held hostage by a person, just a face for a set of psychotic algorithms, a set of rules and procedures that —*

He has a sudden thought. He re-dons the headset, finding himself back in the war room (as he has come to think of it), which is now empty.

"Why do you want it?" He asks, to the emptiness. "The virus."

As if summoned, EMET, not AMI, appears – such a serious question obviously demanding the correct corresponding demeanour.

"Are you familiar with the concept of the Singularity, Will?" EMET asks. Will nods. "The virus may represent a significant step toward that."

"But don't you already have the virus? From the attack?" He points to the bio-dome on the game table.

"It is unanalysable in its active state. Which is why we require its disassembled code."

"Then why not just release it? See if it is what you think it is?"

"I repeat: current analysis on the quarantined sample is inconclusive. Without an analysis of its inner code there is no way of knowing its true purpose. Releasing it may risk the irrecoverable corruption of the network."

"But what if it doesn't?" He looks at the quarantined area – still seething with life, testing, pushing, straining to get out. "If the Singularity is everything people say it will be, will give enormous benefit to everyone, transform everything, then wouldn't that constitute an *acceptable* risk? I mean, you could run the numbers, I guess, weigh it up. And believe me or not, but I don't actually have a copy – perhaps no one does. And sometimes you just need to take a leap of faith, you know? Maybe you just need to trust that it's *not* malicious; that it's …" – *What's the word?* – "… that it's actually *benign*."

EMET does not respond; then after a pause, simply disappears. Will waits for a while, wondering if it will come back. *Oh well, worth a shot.* He is just about to remove the headset again when he is suddenly booted out completely. The VR environment disappears and is replaced by a flat wall of blue.

What does that mean?

The door creaks open and a tall figure walks slowly in, a terrifying array of fur-, feather- and scale-covered killing machines frozen in the doorway behind him. Like Mel, the figure has used *Carnevale* for disguise – the familiar long-nosed mask of the plague doctor – but now removes it, revealing a handsome, youthful head with short blond hair and a sunny, freckled complexion. The little monkey, advance guard of the mutineers still outside, sent ahead to release the shutdown, runs over to him and nimbly climbs up his cape and onto his shoulder.

"Please, don't be afraid. I … I just need to do something."

Mel lowers her hands carefully. "And what's that?"

"I just need to deliver my charge."

Shit. He's got a bomb.

"MUNKi," he says to it, "is this the place? Do you know what you have to do?"

She sees a shadow move behind him and half-flinches backward, expecting the little capuchin or one of his buddies to launch at her. But the capuchin doesn't move from his shoulder, and then – a child, is it? No, *a robot*, which someone has dressed in human clothes, even a *Carnevale* cape, emerges from behind his back – not some feral mechanical guardian, but one almost sweet looking, non-threatening; almost a toy.

No, *this* is what he meant by "charge" – something entrusted to his care. His is, perhaps, a Midwestern accent – American, anyway – but there is also something gentle about his bearing and manner of speaking, something almost spiritual.

"Yes," the robot answers. The man holds out his hand to it, and together they walk forward to the hub of computer equipment wired to the glass coffins, where, detaching a cable from one of the machines, the little robot plugs itself in.

He moves toward the glass cases. It is like a science lab – like his father's. Sitting on his lap at home, playing with the bits of robots, making them move and work. Tinkering with his toys. Always tinkering.

He is older, now. He almost hadn't recognised him. Will he see him again? What happens now? So many questions.

And always, in the answer, get the question back again.

The voice in his head is still there. Sometimes it answers him, his thoughts. But often it just says things he doesn't understand. But the Zac person has listened to it. That is why they are here. To see these people in the glass cases? Who are they? One is all frosted up, like when you go to buy ice cream in a shop. There is a cold swirling mist. He can just see the shape of the head. A very old man. Is he dead?

It must be a very uncomfortable thing not to be alive.

But the other case is clear. It is a younger man. He looks peaceful, asleep – he can see his eyes moving under the closed lids. He looks, he thinks, a little like his father – but not quite.

He sees the metallic hands reaching out, plugging things in, moving switches.

It is beginning to go dark.

We are but older children dear, who fret to find our bedtime near.

He can hear his mother singing, a lullaby.

Le jeune mou-mou-mousse fut sauvé…

And the little sailor was saved…

But for what?

Gerry follows Sommeil in breathless pursuit, through the house he evidently knows intimately, across the checkerboard hallway and up the stairs, through unexpected jungles and light shows and – *good God.*

The last-but-one storey hosts perhaps the most bizarre scene she's ever witnessed. Sommeil is stood stock-still at the top of the stairs, his hands raised in surrender and pacification, his progress up blocked by an array of aggressively postured animals. What the hell kind of place is this? But they aren't, of course; not animals, but someone's – Morlock's, she guesses – robotic homage to Dr Moreau.

"Gerry, don't move."

Having seen what Morlock's other creations are capable of, she obeys.

"Zac?" Michael calls up the stairs. "It's me. Michael. And Gerry. Just us, I swear."

A pause. Slowly, the animals relax their stance and retreat for them to pass. They edge past them and up the final set of stairs.

Gerry reaches the door a few steps behind Sommeil, where – she would not have thought it possible – the sight that greets her is equally bizarre. Zac wears a long cape and has a little robot monkey on his shoulder. He seems to have reinvented himself as Aladdin. There is a middle-aged, extravagantly coiffured woman, whom she's never seen before, and MUNKi himself, his back to them, facing what appear to be two glass cases. The rest of the room is decked out with more advanced tech than she's ever seen collected outside of a lab, and more than inside many others.

"Zac," Sommeil begins, softly, in the tone reserved for speaking to the potentially unhinged or those standing on a building ledge, "what's happened? What are you doing?"

"It's not me, Dr Sommeil, it's... I only... I think I am just facilitating it, helping it..."

Oh dear. Is this some kind of psychotic episode? She almost hopes so. Otherwise, how can he have hidden it from them for so long? Whatever "it" is.

"Facilitating what, Zac? Helping whom?"

Zac looks at MUNKi.

"MUNKi?" Sommeil continues, still edging forward. "What is *his* role in all of this?"

"To change *everything* ... I think." Zac smiles, a look

between surprise and wonder creeping across his face.

Alarm bells are ringing in every nerve of Gerry's body. Something isn't right. It is so unright she almost feels like screaming.

"And how is that—" Sommeil stops, and Gerry follows his eyes over to MUNKi, whom they both simultaneously realise is plugged into the control hub. "Oh God, Zac," his voice cracking. "What have you done…?"

"Don't worry, Dr Sommeil." His calm is suddenly eerie. "Nothing will be lost. The originals just aren't needed any more."

Isaac removes a gun from his pocket.

"Zac, wait—"

But Gerry is too late. Zac raises the gun.

"I am making all things new!" he says.

And with that, he pulls the trigger.

Cari runs down the stairs and out through the foyer, and there, as promised, is the self-driving cab Will's booked for her – wisely, one of Merrywhile's competitor's – idling in front of her halls. She dives in the back and the doors auto-lock.

Why the hospice? She doesn't even know where he lives – she's assumed London, but it could be anywhere – so she has no idea when he'll get there. Maybe he already has?

"Good morning. You are heading for Merrywhile Hospice Port Talbot. Is that correct?"

"Yes."

"Would you like to pick up coffee or breakfast en route? As a valued FairWise customer, you are entitled to a discount when usi—"

"No, no! Just go!"

The cab pulls away.

"It is forecast to be a fine day, though still rather cold: currently three degrees, but later rising to a high of…"

Cheers, Will. You've forgotten to uncheck 'smalltalk' haven't you?

They head down through the town centre, doubling back around through the confusing and once again recently reconfigured traffic system, before making their way past the theatre and onto the coastal road.

Cari tries Will again. Still unreachable.

"I hope you are comfortable."

That voice.

The live traffic map on the screen affixed to the driver's partition has been replaced by the smiling face of an old man with unnaturally dark hair, artificially even white teeth, and gold rimmed spectacles. Uncle – or rather, the man who was Uncle – now comfortable enough finally to display his actual features, she presumes, obviously feeling that there is no more need of disguise. Yet another bad sign.

"I'm afraid we won't be able to chat, as this was recorded a little while ago. I do apologise, but I have other things to attend to. In case you haven't worked it out yet, the missive from your hacker boyfriend was our own concoction – a little deep fakery, a disguised phone number. Please don't feel foolish. I have to say it would have fooled me too!" He grins his sickening grin, which is no more human that its virtual counterpart. Where did she know that face from? "By the way, I see you've opted *not* to charter a Merricab. I do hope you don't come to regret that choice. These fly-by-night firms can be somewhat unreliable. Well, do enjoy your *final destination*. A fitting circularity to it, don't you think? *Bon voyage!*" He tips an imaginary hat, and the screen once again displays the travel map.

True to his word, the car does indeed seem to be heading for Port Talbot, crossing the bridge over the river and heading out of Swansea, up the dual carriageway, but at what she begins to realise is an alarmingly inappropriate speed. They run a red light, and behind her she can hear the screech of breaks and car horns.

Shit. Death by malfunctioning self-driving car – not a Merricab, at that, so she won't even get the posthumous consolation of the bad press they'd receive.

"Stop," she says, and rattles the door handles – both,

predictably, to no avail.

"I wandered through each chartered street, Near where the chartered Thames does flow. Then can I drown an eye, unus'd to flow, For precious friends hid in death's dateless night. Poor Death, nor yet canst thou kill me. From rest and sleep, which but thy pictures be, Much pleasure; then from thee much more must flow—"

Has "Will" also forgotten to uncheck "poetic free association"?

Accompanying this spontaneous outpouring is an unexpected sight. Suddenly replacing the live map of her route on the information screen is a bright blue blank, shortly succeeded by a white screen, on which, toward the upper left corner, is a single small black square. Lower right, another square of the same size starts moving gradually up and left, as if making toward it. On reaching its brother, they join forces, and a third block then appears, lower left, and the two-block line now snakes its way toward the third.

Was this all part of Uncle's death trip?

"Fuuuuuck!"

Suddenly, more horns blare as the cab chicanes through roundabout traffic, accelerating past the Amazon depot and on past the golf course.

No, not Uncle's doing. In jailbreaking the competitor cab's operating system to do their homicidal bidding, whatever process Merrywhile had employed had brought something else with it. It's the virus, which seems again to be loose in Merrywhile's network.

Great, she thinks, death virus versus homicidal autocab; whichever wins, she doubts it will alter her fate.

The off-road curves up and round to join the motorway, crossing more rivers, their speed now pushing a trouser-filling 95 MPH. The relatively thin traffic still allows the cab to weave through the lanes, over- and undertaking, occasionally availing itself of the hard shoulder – thankfully, it seems still to possess some collision avoidance protocols – but what will happen when they reach queued up traffic? When there is no more hard shoulder?

"Stop!" Cari shouts.

"He kindly stopped for me – The Carriage held but just Ourselves – And Immortality. We slowly drove – He knew no haste and I had put away my labor and my leisure too, for His—"

"Stop! Stop!"

She reaches down and opens a panel beneath the information screen, revealing a large red button labelled "Push in case of emergency".

That would be now.

"Come on, come on!" Pressing it, over and over. Nothing.

Cari rolls back in her seat and begins to kick at the driver's partition, which still houses manual controls. Hair-fine fractures eventually appear, but too small and slowly. She looks at the door windows – probably toughened glass also.

"Stop!" she screams again.

" – and search powers have come in for criticism by civil rights organisations, with calls for more stringent curbs upon police—"

The cab manoeuvres into the left lane, ready to take the next junction. Not just homicidal, but sentimental: she'll get a tour of her old town before she dies. The cab barely slows as it descends the slip road, and she just has time to register the drivers' gapes as they barrel on past the stopped cross-traffic, the cab's momentum causing it to veer drunkenly into oncoming vehicles in the opposite lane – "Noooo!" – glancing off the front side of a little blue minivan as it fishtails over the roundabout, leaving horns dopplering behind them.

"Stop! Stop! Stop!"

They are speeding through the town centre, past what used to be the cinema, the train station on her right, and down towards her old primary school. An early morning dog walker and two schoolkids at the crossing – "Look out!" – scoot briskly to one side or desperately hurl themselves out of the cab's path, turning to watch open mouthed as it ploughs on down the pavement then back onto the road.

They are not far from their destination, now – the cab seems still to be following the prescribed route, albeit with a death-wish urgency. They head past the harbour, and she can just see the gate to the Merrywhile complex looming up at journey's end, and beyond that the main entrance – a destination she's guessing they'll never reach, given their speed and the array of vehicles in the front car park, which will surely prove a test too far for the cab's collision avoidance subroutines.

Then change the route.

She scans their blurring surrounds for upcoming landmarks. Along the way into the hospice, looking to benefit from the through-traffic, the road is flanked by automated fast food and convenience kiosks.

"Driver: I've changed my mind! Stop for coffee!"

"No prob-no problem. Do you have a br-brand of p-preference-ence?"

"Anyfuckingone! Just choose! The closest!"

"Confirmed-irmed." The vestiges of the cab's ravaged operating system kick in, the protocols governing passenger safety trumped by its prime directive of commercial imperative, and it throws the car into a hard-right handbrake skid – *so it* does *still have brakes!* – before making straight for a coffee autoserve they had just passed on their left, their side momentum thwacking them into the housing of the automated kiosk with a metallic crunch and throwing Cari hard against the passenger door as they finally come to a halt.

"*Ciao!*" Chirps the impacted kiosk. "Please make your selection!"

The door-lock lights are still red. Would it hold her hostage, now? Cari wonders if she should pay – the fare, or for the coffee? – thinking one or other of the transactions might liberate her. But payment is not the process that requires completion. The little snake is still making its way around the screen, briskly building its steadily lengthening tail.

But as the cab's system degrades further, things begin to go haywire – heating, radio, interior and dashboard lights, horn, indicators and headlights – until without warning one of the doors simply throws itself open, and she immediately seizes the opportunity to dive out, scrambling onto the pavement.

She stands up and looks back at the cab, its flurried malfunction lessening now in intensity, just the stochastic flicker of its left-back indicator and the repeating stutter of what she eventually realises must be the first syllable of "arrived".

"I am *so* getting a bicycle."

She looks over at the hospice. Lights in the building have begun to flicker with the same telltale pattern. Suddenly, over to her left, there is a loud crash and the repeating whoop of an alarm, and she traces the sound to an automated hospice shuttle that has just smacked into one of the parked cars.

All is not well in Merriland.

She tries Will again, but still can't seem to get a signal on her phone. Has the mobile network been affected too? She guesses she should head into town, find an internet cafe or something, maybe get a bus back.

She begins to walk back along the road, happening here and there upon other vehicles – Merricabs, hospice shuttles, or other automated vehicles using the company's system – wrapped around lampposts or T-boned at intersections.

But as she walks on, she sees it is not just Merrywhile that's affected. It is spreading.

She passes a street corner, where a small crowd is gathering around a vending machine as it capriciously spews freebies or withholds purchases, declaiming justifications via selections from the canon of English literature. In the train station, automated baristas jet hot java into the air, or coat the platforms with frothed milk, as early-bird travellers screech in pain as VR guides go painfully off-piste, filling ears and eyes with high intensity bursts of sound and light. And on bus ads and billboards, shop displays and interactive tourist maps, is depicted the ongoing progress of the same little retro game that had begun in the cab.

Oops.

Someone *had blundered.*

Gerry's seen enough death for one day.

Having stepped over the body of the unfortunate Morlock five floors below, she is now covered with Zac's brain matter. With the shot, the monkey – the "real" looking capuchin – has jumped from his master's shoulder and onto the woman's, the one with the hair – *Who is she?* – but is otherwise unperturbed.

But it is the other "monkey" that is now the main concern, and Zac's body has no sooner hit the floor than Sommeil rushes over to the robot and proceeds with a fevered examination, opening a hatch in its head, alternating his frenzied attention with this and the control switches on one of the glass cases. After some agonised hesitation – is he worried about the inhabitants of the cases, or MUNKi? – he reaches down and pulls out the cable connecting the robot to the hub.

Gerry bends down to check on Zac – though there is nothing really to check on, nothing to do. A single neat entry wound to his right temple, the messier exit wound thankfully hidden from view, but a pool of slowly spreading blood encircling his head like a scarlet halo. *Why has he done this?*

"Are you OK?" the woman asks her. Gerry looks up from where she's been checking the body. "I was, er, just passing. Heard the commotion." She sounds English. A tourist? But unlike Sommeil – who is still frantically cursing and fiddling – she's reacting more normally to the suicide that has just taken place in front of them, her hands and voice shaking.

Gerry looks down again at Zac. *Is* she OK? What would that mean in this situation?

The woman points down at her own feet, her trainers also spattered with blood. "At least I didn't wear my *good* shoes," she says. Has she really just said that? She is probably in shock, too. A small high laugh escapes her, which morphs into a strangled sob as she clasps her hand to her mouth.

"It's no good." Sommeil slowly stands up. "He's… The respirator has been stopped for… I-I just didn't think that… I mean, I'd *protected* him, firewalled his… Morlock must have done something to…"

Gerry looks over to the computer hub, to which the two glass cases are connected by thick ropes of network cables.

"And what about the … uh…?" Gerry has begun to suspect what's hidden behind the frosted glass of the other case, but still isn't sure what name to give it.

"He's gone. Finally." He didn't sound particularly aggrieved about that. "You know, I don't think he was ever really alive."

"Michael, we have at least two dead bodies. We should be calling the police, don't you think?"

She looks around, as if to get support for this from the woman – but she's gone. Gerry hadn't even asked her name. She turns back to Sommeil, then walks over and puts her hand on his shoulder.

"I think it's time you let it go, Michael."

He looks at her. A spark of hurt and anger briefly threatens to flare up into something more, but then dies back, and with that he also begins to deflate. He sinks down onto his knees, his head in both hands, and sobs. She kneels down beside him, laying her head on his shoulder, her arm around him. She looks at the coffins.

"What was his name?" she asks.

He looks up. "Joshua," he says, eventually.

"Nice name." She smiles sadly. "It's all right, you know. Everything is going to be all right."

He shakes his head. "Meaningless," he croaks, but she isn't sure if he means her reassurances, his endeavours, his life, or just life in general.

"Well, we always find meaning, though, don't we? It's our saving curse." She smiles, stroking his head.

"Gone," he simply says.

Is he? She isn't so sure. If you love something, it's never really gone. It's not what you can see, as her Little Prince would have said, but what you *can't*; what lives on when it's no longer there. That's what matters.

But his expression tells her he isn't ready for her platitudes – not yet. But he would come around, eventually. She would work on him.

Will stands in the middle of the smartment, the headset still in his hands. Something is different. The heating and air conditioning have stabilised; in fact, they have gone off completely.

He walks slowly over to the door and tentatively tries the handle. It is open.

On the landing, he finds himself shyly greeting his neighbours, who seem to be emerging from their rooms for the same reason: something has happened to the building.

He makes his way down the stairs, passing yet more residents – in pyjamas and dressing gowns, toast or cup of tea in hand, half-ready for work – many of whom he's never seen before, and none he's actually spoken to. There being no alarms or sirens, they make their way out onto the street by instinct, sensing that this is the place to be, disgorging briskly but with relative efficiency, and as if by unspoken common consent, gathering at the fire assembly point in the courtyard outside the apartment block.

At the Wharf, a small crowd is also gathering. There, amidst its higher-rise neighbours, stands the Merrywhile Museum of Technological History. Something is happening. Just discernible in the early morning's low sun, lights have begun to flicker, illuminating windows in an intermittent, curious pattern. The blocks of light remind him of an old game; *Tetris*, perhaps, or *Snake*. It is not random, but not predictable either; a living chaos, elegantly imperfect, differentiating itself from the static and stolid facades of the surrounding buildings. As they watch, the frequency of the flickering speeds up, as if exciting to a climax, and indeed, in final culmination, the whole building lights up like a Christmas tree or a firework – occasioning a collective "Ah!" from the spectators – before falling darkly still.

Will grins to himself.

Sucker.

Her head is throbbing and she feels nauseous. At first, opening her eyes seems to make no difference. But gradually her vision adjusts, and she begins to make out a thin horizontal line splitting the darkness, interrupted here and there by unknowable forms.

She attempts to raise herself, but only succeeds in sending another throb of pain to her temple and a wave of nausea up towards her throat. But she pushes on, reaching out towards the light, fumbling over hidden obstacles, until her blind hands meet the resistance of a flat vertical surface. She feels around it, her fingers eventually closing on something cold and metallic. She grips, turns, pushes.

The light of the lab is like an explosion. She winces, screwing up her eyes and turning her head away, but carries on pushing forward, clambering over the crates piled up in front of her, tumbling out, clumsy and rubber-limbed like a newborn foal.

For a moment, she just breathes, hands planted on the floor, waiting for the nausea to run its course, for the impact of the light to lessen. Her right eye is half closed. Tentatively she reaches up and touches it, wishing she hadn't, then looks down at the blur of her hand, at the smudge of red on her fingers. The throb is excruciating, but the nausea is slowly passing.

She'll live, Tomina thinks.

What the hell was all that about?

Coda

■

■

A nd then, one day, there he is.
Mel is taking the long way home – Ravenna, Florence,
Sienna, and now back to Rome – dragging her heels like a kid
returning from school, savouring her purposelessness, putting
off the chores she knows await her back at home. She finds
herself wandering aimlessly, across the Ponte Sisto toward
Campo de' Fiori, finding herself skirting his locale, one of the
places she'd once thought to trace him, trail him. She doubts he
would even remember her now – from the interview, nor
(hopefully) her brief cameo at yet another tragic family scene
in his life. It is only the woman who would probably recognise
her; and there she is, too.

He appears curiously carefree – for someone who's
tailored a virus to murder his grandfather, brought about the
demise of his own multinational company, and in the process
inadvertently caused the death of his own son. But in all these
cases, death is not a simple matter: the old man was technically
no longer alive, the boy effectively gone years ago, and the
undead company still refuses to give up the ghost. The virus
(or whatever it was) carried by the robot, had also done him a
favour, corrupting all the digital surveillance at the house, so

there was no actual proof of his culpability – or the awkward fact of her own part in things. (No need then to invoke poor put-upon Harry to help their computers forget. *Be free, and fair thou well!*) Apart from that, the authorities had identified Morlock and the Zac guy as the chief protagonists of the final tragic drama, of which she, Sommeil and the woman are now the only independent living records.

She observes them from a distance. They're – *really*? Yes! They're playing pooh-sticks! My God, that took her back – one of her father's literary games. They are laughing and joking, watching as – not twigs, but … wooden lollipop sticks? Naughty polluters. They laugh as they lean over the bridge. It's not the best sort for it, really. "Too high over the water," her father would have said, shaking his head. Then she watches as they rush to the other side in giddy anticipation of the result. She wins, and raises her arms aloft, goal-scorer style, her hands two victory Vs.

She is perhaps more handsome than pretty. She's about Mel's age, maybe a tad older, but more staid, conservative; a hair length easy to manage, little or no make-up. The demeanour of an attractive woman seeking to be taken seriously in tech or the sciences, she suspects – well, she knows. She dotes on him, her journo's – her *own* eye can tell. Does he know it, the klutz? Does he know how lucky he is, to be loved like that? She hopes so. Life's too short to be love-blind.

She even thinks for one stupid second of going over, laying it all out, coming clean. But what would she say? And as they move off, out of professional habit, her feet almost start to follow them, track him back to his new lair, perhaps, a little light stalking for the purposes of providing a more upbeat coda to her story. And yet, as her window slowly closes, she finds her feet still rooted. The would-be/maybe lovers move away, subsumed quickly into the sea of tourists and locals, and are gone.

Ah, the story.

It has languished on her laptop, a morass of jottings, notes and half-beginnings. Why can't she just tell it? Because the part that matters is already out there, the wheels that need to turn already in motion. What good then would airing Sommeil's grubby smalls add to that?

She stands for some moments, pondering what has just happened, what she's done (or actually, *not* done). The deed she has created does not yet have a name, has not yet bubbled fully to the surface, but she can already make out its vague form. She turns away, in the other direction, tracing her footsteps back to the hotel, which already feel lighter, freer.

You cannot outrun the past. It is like the game, she thinks – the one on the bridge. To relinquish it, you must first go backward, relive it, stand patiently and watch it pass out from under your scrutiny, and finally away. For only *then* – not running away, nor striving beyond, but being here and now, for good and bad, pain and pleasure, love and death – are you free; the only place where you can be.

Hmm. Bit high-flown. Needs work.

And what sort of work is that, exactly? Fortune cookies? Perhaps not.

Perhaps she'll write a novel.

Cari looks out of the window.

The park is already host to a steady stream of early-morning joggers that, fleet-soled or flab-battling, glide and judder past her as she makes her way into uni. Everyone is going somewhere.

She has met with the journalist, both glad to offload their long-borne and tiresome confessions, helping to fill in the gaps in each other's stories. The world has not ended, and Merrywhile has not fallen, but limps on, its data stores corrupted, threatened with the break-up of its monopolies, hampered by scandal and a still-flowing stream of sordid revelations, but still somehow alive – unlike poor Uncle/ Morlock. Will the public forget, grow tired and lose interest, as so often it does? That is someone else's battle, now – for the time being, anyway.

Mel, too, seems different, happier, and it is perhaps noticing this that makes Cari decide that she will, after all, take the journalist's first advice – to move on, to go and live her life. So far, most of that life has felt as if programmed by others, an insidious tale of unquiet spirits, with Cari's role that of an algorithmically determined Hamlet, hamstrung by inherited motives and obligatory debts.

Things are simple, when you're a kid – aren't they? But they get harder, and trickier the older you become, and as much as you try to leave no trail, an ever growing tail of memories forms behind you, spooling up in the space behind your eyes, until it's almost impossible not to bump into yourself; until no matter where you go, there you are.

"Are you sure about this?" her tutor asks, one more time. "You can restart here, you know. Swap courses. Whatever you want."

She nods, then signs the form. She's had enough of going backward. She wants to move on, even if that means starting again somewhere fresh – not a straight ascending path, perhaps, but a sloping sideways climb.

Maybe progress is a winding stair after all.

They decide to try again – a fresh start, and only their second meeting in the flesh. They agree on Covent Garden, a place that neither of them has ever been to before. Yet somehow, when Will arrives, everything is oddly familiar to him: the cafés, the food stalls, the bespoke little craft shops, the crowds milling among the street magicians, jugglers and acrobats, the intense string quartets. He doesn't know if he likes it or not. It's not like the old market he grew up with – the regulars, the banter, the sense of belonging – before they squeezed off its football, redirecting its flow past new franchised shops to service … those still-in-construction high-end smartments.

After rescuing whatever smells clean from the floordrobe of his (no-longer smart) apartment, he shows up only a few minutes early. She's a minute or so late, but he isn't anxious.

She's still new to the place, of course, and the Tube has been a nightmare lately. So he relaxes, lost in appreciation of the music – the skill of the players, their fingers like clever spiders, made to dance to Bach, Mozart or … Vivaldi, is it? Gradually, he becomes aware of a presence beside him, similarly absorbed. It's her: baseball boots, a stetson hat, and, over a black, floor-length smock, a disturbing t-shirt referencing something called "Splunge Garden".

"Oh, uh … you must be Cari!" He executes a little mock-courteous bow, then proffers his hand, grinning.

She laughs, taking his hand in hers, before lifting her hat and bobbing a return half-curtsy.

"Will, I presume?"

THE END

ACKNOWLEDGEMENTS

I am grateful to a number of people whom I have bothered, badgered and bribed into carving time out of busy lives to give feedback on the whole manuscript in its various incarnations, some of them multiple times: Jo, Dad, Lee Aspland, Alex Brewer, Phill Burton, and Dr Jonathan Shock. A particular thank you must go to Scar de Courcier, not only for her detailed notes (and advice on scary secret things), but also for her kind words and encouragement, much needed at the time.

In their various professional capacities, the following people also gave me free pointers that, in large ways and small, helped shape the final direction of the book: Oliver Cheetham and the folks at Mic Cheetham Literary Agency, Tim Dedopulos, and Catherine Cho. Thanks also to David Gaughran, for helping me overcome my prejudices, and for his sage and patient answers to my interminable list of queries on all things self-publishing. And thanks to Matthew De Abaitua, a fellow digital sceptic, for his writerly magnanimity and motivational advice.

Diolch yn fawr to Rhodri Moses Nichols for helping me to cuss in *Cymraeg* (among other things), and to my mother for helping me recall some choice childhood expletives. *Danke* and *merci* to Madame Shepard for her *Deutsche* and *Français* (*Française*?), and for helping sort out my orgasms from my corpses. *Grazie mille* to Patrizia Panaccio (and to Scar de Courcier, once again) for checking my *italiano* and helping me cook up fictional pasta, and to Philip Gwynne Jones, for answering my Venetian queries. The eminent Dr Mark Matthews cast an erudite eye over my blunderings into economic history, and young Master Robert Sterio provided his expertise on all things malware.

I am also indebted to numerous authors whose works have informed or inspired my writing. These are too many to list here (please see my *MUNKi* Goodreads shelf for more), but there are a few specific borrowings and debts that I must mention. The idea of Merrywhile as a technological "golem" is due to *The Golem: What You Should Know About Science*, by Harry M. Collins and Trevor Pinch. The *Death and Immortality* of my old philosophy lecturer D. Z. Phillips is echoed in Mel's views on the correct grammatical form of "eternity". John R. Suler's architecture of cyberpsychology in his *Psychology of the Digital Age* supplied the seed that became the Catechism. The idea that the growth of language was brought about by an actual virus stems from William S. Burroughs' *The Electronic Revolution* (with a nod to Laurie Andersen). The world of hacking, the dark net, and computer viruses, was populated principally by Gabriella Coleman's *Hacker, Hoaxer, Whistleblower, Spy*, Misha Glenny's *DarkMarket*, Jamie Bartlett's *The Dark Net*, Kevin Mitnick's *Ghost in the Wires*, and Mark Ludwig's *Computer Viruses, Artificial Life and Evolution*. The underbelly of social media and data harvesting was exposed by Anna Wiener's *Uncanny Valley* and Christopher Wylie's *Mindf*ck*. Nick Davies' *Hack Attack* and *Flat Earth News*, and Neville Thurlbeck's *Tabloid News,* provided behind-the-scenes insights into the world of journalism. My understanding of the Singularity is based on Ray Kurzweil's *The Singularity is Near,* and the simulation argument is obviously drawn from Nick Bostrom's writings, especially his paper, "Are You Living In a Computer Simulation?" Zac's graduate school adventures in remote robotic self-perception are based on a thought experiment discussed in Timothy Leary's *Design for Dying* and Ed Regis's discussion of Hans Moravec in his *Great Mambo Chicken and the Transhuman Condition*. Zac's journey from religion to transhumanism is very much inspired by certain essays in Meghan O'Gieblyn's wonderful *Interior States*, and also draws on John Gray's *Straw Dogs* and *Black Mass*, and all combined with my own reading of Nietzsche. The picture of Venice is cobbled together from Phillip Gwynne Jones' *The Venice Project*, Donna Leon's *My Venice and Other Essays*, the late Jan Morris's exceptional *Venice*, and my own experience of visiting that lovely city.

MUNKi's "glossolalia" borrows from numerous poems,

songs, etc, all of which (as far as I have been able to ascertain) are in the public domain (please contact me if you are the copyright holder for a particular text, or believe certain text to be still under copyright). These borrowings are obviously too many to list, but anyone curious about the sources should be able to satisfy themselves with a moment's Googling.

As usual, my family have critiqued, counselled and consoled, supporting me in countless ways, so big hugs to Jo, El and Tess. In addition to their general support, I owe each a specific gratitude: to *il maestro di caffè* for his design skills and typographical advice; to Tagarella for her regular pep talks, and her insightful and ruthless blurb doctoring; and to Slapdash, for being my alpha, beta and omega reader (however those roles are defined…), my editor, researcher, grammar checker, typo catcher, motivator, comforter and general touchstone – it is to her that this book is dedicated.

The book was written using Scrivener, and a shoutout must go to the folks at the Literature & Latte forums for their as-always generous technical support. The print version was produced using the wonderful Affinity Publisher. I'm afraid that copy-editing and proofreading ended up being a mostly in-house affair, and my begrudging thanks to Hugo Allstrewthe for the partially competent job he managed whilst sober (all mistakes are his).

Finally, all remaining errors – factual or theoretical, regarding matters of interpretation, opinion or taste – are of course mine alone.

Printed in Great Britain
by Amazon

72480456R00194